MW00615475

PRAISE FOR WINNING THE QUEEN'S HEART

After her life was turned upside down when her parents and brother were killed in a car accident, being kept under close watch by an uncle who didn't really show love, Queen Christiana has had a difficult time trusting and building relationships. Her uncle is arrested for suspected treason. She turns to a mysterious man and believes they're in love only to find out he was going to poison her after their wedding, (only days away).

— MF LITERARY WORKS

Queen Christiana has been hurt by someone who was very close to her and now it seems as if everything is falling apart. Alexander Bayfield, one of her staff who is very close to her, steps in with a proposed solution to this problem. Can she trust him? Or will he turn on her, too? I loved every single minute of this book. Not one down moment. Not one.

— SUSAN S

Winning the Queen's Heart

Carol Moncado

USA Today Bestselling Author

CANDID
Publications

Copyright © 2015 Carol Moncado

All rights reserved. No part of this publication may be reproduced, stored in a retrieval system, or transmitted in any form or by any means — for example, electronic, photocopy, recording, for personal or commercial purposes — without written permission of the author(s). The only exception is for brief quotations in printed or electronic reviews.

This is a work of fiction set in a fictionalized southwest Missouri and a redrawn, fictionalized Europe. Any resemblance to real events or to actual persons, living or dead, is coincidental. Any reference to historical figures, places, or events, whether fictional or actual, is a fictional representation.

Scripture taken from the Holy Bible, King James Version.

Cover photos: Copyright: ryzhov/depositphotos.com
    Author photo: Captivating by Keli, 2010
    First edition, CANDID Publications, 2015

"**A**rrest him and throw him in the dungeon." Queen Christiana Elizabeth Marissa Abigail the First stared as seven slightly different versions of herself in a cloud of white satin and tulle stared back from the multifaceted mirror. The satin hugged her curves in a way that made her uncomfortable. But it was the dress *he* had picked for her. And she wanted to make *him* happy.

The man behind her nodded. "I will give the order, Your Majesty." He bowed slightly at the waist and turned to walk out, but she called after him.

"Alexander?"

He stopped and turned, meeting her eyes in the mirrors. "Yes, ma'am?"

"You are certain?"

Alexander Bayfield nodded. "The assassination would be carried out on your honeymoon allowing your fiancé to claim his 'rightful' place as King of Ravenzario. The drugs were found in his possession."

"That's not how the Commonwealth works." Without an heir,

Ravenzario would be broken up and absorbed into Mevendia and Montevaro.

"I know. I doubt he does. Many people do not."

Christiana allowed nothing of her feelings to show as she dismissed him with a curt nod. Alexander held the door for the seamstress to return.

"I would like to change out of this." The implications of her fiancé's betrayal were beginning to fly through her mind. Not only would there be a trial and the man whose name she refused to think would be paraded in front of the people, but so would her personal life. And her judgment would once again be called into question. This time, however, there would be truth to the allegations.

Now there was a wedding to call off.

As the gown slipped over her shoulders and she stepped out of it, Christiana merely nodded, the seamstress's words floating in one ear and out the other as the consequences to her country began to assail her. A year after ousting her uncle who had been usurping her throne and authority, she wouldn't be getting married as planned. Foreign dignitaries would have to be told. The crowds expecting to see the royal couple would be disappointed.

And her family's good name would once more be dragged through the mud.

The seamstress carried the dress out, leaving Christiana alone. As she slid into her linen pants and retied the cobalt wraparound silk blouse, for the first time in her adult life, Christiana wished to merely be a normal person. To have the weight and pressures of ruling her country fall away. Where the only concern would be how much of a refund she would get from the vendors, not if her countrymen would lose their already fragile trust in her.

Her heels clicked along the stone floor in the hallway as she retreated to her personal apartments. Here no one entered without explicit permission. It gave her the privacy she craved -

and the solitude she detested. For nearly an hour, she sat in an arm chair, staring out the window and over the storm tossed waves of the Mediterranean. The gray sky and torrential downpour matched the turmoil inside until the buzz of the intercom interrupted her reverie.

"Yes?"

"Alexander to see you, ma'am." The disembodied voice of her assistant, Diana, crackled through the air.

"Send him in."

She did not move as the door to her sitting room opened and closed. "Your Majesty?"

One hand waved toward the armchair across from her. "Have a seat, Alexander." As he sat, she shifted to look at him. "You have a report?""

"He is in the dungeon, ma'am, per your orders. Bail has already been denied due to the eminent threat to your person. The judge and security teams believe he would try something else, though they are certain you will call off the wedding. No official statement has been made, of course, but that is the presumption among those in the know."

"The wedding will be called off," she answered softly. "I have not given the orders yet, but it is only a matter of time. My only saving grace at the moment is his anonymity. His subterfuge gives a valid reason for his insistence on utter secrecy surrounding his identity as my intended."

"It does," Alexander confirmed. "Since he had not been associated with you, he was able to get what he needed from otherwise unsavory characters who would never betray the crown so directly."

"The press will have a field day." Christiana turned back to the window, standing and moving toward it until she could feel the chill rolling through to reach her. "My country is like the weather. We were stable for so long. Following the death of my parents and brother, there was a brief time of turmoil, but my uncle ruled on my behalf, giving continuity and gravitas to the government. The turmoil of his arrest has not been settled very long, if truly at all. The wedding and tour of the country was to have been the occasion to restore the trust and let my countrymen lay to rest their concerns."

She drew in a deep breath and blew it out slowly. "I fear what will happen when this becomes public. Not for myself. I would be lying if I said I did not enjoy the trappings of royalty most of the time, but a revolution or civil war will result only in needless deaths and chaos for my people, and I must do whatever is in my power to stop it from happening." She turned to look at Alexander. "If only there was a solution."

Alexander's stomach churned much like the weather outside the queen's windows. So many things in her statement he had a response to, but so many he felt the need to bide his time on. If she knew everything he did, Queen Christiana would likely suffer an emotional collapse. He would need to dole the information out slowly, as she needed to know.

But first and foremost, she was correct about the wedding. Calling it off could have a disastrous effect on the people, but what other option was there?

"You have several days before you need to make the announcement, ma'am." He'd known Christiana for a number of years before he'd known she was queen of the country where his parents owned property and operated a wedding venue. The venue where every royal wedding for the last several centuries had been held. Where her wedding was to have been. "The only people who know are ones with complete loyalty, not only to the crown but to you personally. The judge has sealed all of the information for the time being. There will be no leaks."

She turned, looking as vulnerable as he'd ever seen her. Even when her uncle's deceit had been uncovered, she hadn't looked like this. "Thank you, Alexander. I know I can count on you."

He had no background in security or police work, but had lucked into the information leading to her uncle's arrest. In doing so, he'd truly earned his way into her inner circle. At the same time he missed the casual acquaintance with the young woman he'd known and talked with on occasion. Her laughter was a distant memory, one he cherished.

"What is the next step?" she asked.

"The barrister will finalize the case against him. He will be given the opportunity to plead guilty and avoid a trial and the death penalty. If he accepts the deal, he will live the rest of his life in solitary confinement in the dungeon or another place of your choosing. I would recommend either the dungeon or Pirate's Island."

"I cannot bear the thought of him being in my home, even if he is far away, and I will never see him." She gave a delicate shudder. "Pirate's Island would be better."

Alexander nodded. "I agree, Your Majesty."

She sighed. "In private there is no need for such formality, Alexander. Please call me Christiana."

He nodded his acquiescence but knew he would go no less formal than "ma'am" for the time being.

"If he chooses not to accept the deal?"

"He will be assigned an attorney. There will be a very short list of approved names for him to choose from. While every letter of every law will be followed to the utmost, he will not be given the chance to drag you through the press with unfounded allegations of all sorts by giving him an attorney with no scruples."

Her brow furrowed, deep in thought. "I have no desire to be sneaky and underhanded, but see if you can find some leverage to convince him that pleading guilty is in his best interest, and in return we will do something for him. Something to help persuade him to go quietly."

"I believe we can find a way."

The uncertainty returned to her face. "You are certain, Alexander? There is no mistaking what he planned to do?"

He felt his heart break for her. "No, ma'am. There is no question."

"Very well. See it is done."

"Of course." Alexander stood and decided to take a chance before he could change his mind. "Christiana." He used her name for the first time. "I know you believe you love him, that he loved you. Somewhere out there, there is a man who will love *you*. Not the queen and the trappings of power that come with the royal family, but the girl who laughed at her favorite sitcoms with her best friend." Something he knew all too much about, even if she didn't know that. "The girl who only eats M&Ms in even numbers and saves the green ones for last, unless she's in public. Who never, ever walks around without shoes on, even in here. The one who orders unicorns of all kinds online then scatters a few throughout her apartment and the rest in the cottage where others rarely go. The one who collects those unicorns because they are beautiful and strong, like she wishes she could be. That man is out there, and someday soon, he's going to find you."

She turned a sad smile his way. "I do not meet a lot of men, Alexander. How am I going to meet a man who loves me for me and not my position, especially after the debacle that is about to descend on my life?"

He took several steps until he stood less than a foot in front of her. "Marry *me*."

C hristiana blinked. Alexander stood close enough she could see the flecks of gold in his hazel eyes and smell the mint of his toothpaste. "Pardon?"

"You heard me, Your Majesty. You're right. The cancellation and assassination plot is more than your country can bear. Even if the assassination never comes to light, and we're planning to keep it under tight wraps, the cancellation of the wedding will cause potentially irreparable harm to your reputation. You said it yourself. Your saving grace is the secret of your fiancé's identity. You could walk down the aisle with anyone, and few people would know the difference. Those who do are loyal and would keep your secret."

She felt drawn to him in a way she could not explain. "You are an American. You would be willing to denounce your citizenship, give up the women I know make themselves available to you on a regular basis, and volunteer for a loveless marriage that can never end in divorce without throwing the country into a revolutionary uproar, while being required to produce heirs with a woman you do not love?"

He did not answer her question. Instead, he took a step closer until his fingertips slid down her arms to link with her own. A gentle tug pulled her close enough for her body to come in contact with his. Before she knew what was happening, he lowered his face. His lips on hers sent a thrill down her spine as she leaned on her toes, following him as he pulled slightly away, saddened when he was too far to reach.

"I may not love you, Christiana. You may not love me. But I will always be faithful to you. I will never leave you. Divorce isn't an option for me, no matter the royal status or legal statutes surrounding my wife. And I have a feeling, even if we don't love each other right away, we'll find a way to make the 'producing an heir' part not awful."

Alexander took a step back. "Think about it, Your Majesty. If you agree, I will take care of everything short of getting you to the chapel. Most of it is already done, but between my parents and my knowledge of the wedding industry in Ravenzario, we can finish the arrangements. This country has been my adopted home for many years. I love the people. I love the culture. I love the land." He ran his forefinger down the side of her face. "I adore the royal family. I have since before I knew you were royal." After a swift movement, pressing his lips hard against hers, he moved away.

Christiana watched the door close behind Alexander, still somewhat slack-jawed. She knew it was unbecoming a queen, but could not help it. Not only had he proposed to her, Alexander had kissed her.

Really kissed her.

Her first kiss.

He had said he planned to keep their first kiss for their wedding. To make it special.

She had not pushed him on it, though deep inside she had been supremely disappointed when he refused to kiss her even after she accepted his proposal.

Alexander had sent her stomach reeling and her mind spinning in directions she never ventured before. Could she be considering his proposition? Would she marry him?

No one but a select few would know the difference. Her entire courtship had been carried out in private, and now she knew why.

The rest of her afternoon and a number of meetings stretched before her. In some ways, it was an easy day. In others, not so much.

Twenty minutes later, Christiana emerged from her apartments and went to the reception room where she would spend the next several hours. First, a troop of Royal Scouts arrived. Their scores in the countrywide competition netted them first place, and a chance to meet the queen. With her smile fixed in place, she greeted the young men, ages nine to twelve. Around the room, they had set up several exhibits of the types of things they did in the competition.

The door opened, and everyone turned. Alexander walked in, catching her eye and smiling. A slight bow of his head showed his deference to her position, but that wasn't what caught her attention. He'd changed out of his collared shirt and navy pants. Instead, he wore a very expensive, well-tailored suit and looked very...she barely dared think it. Royal.

She turned to him. "Gentlemen, this is an associate and friend of mine, Alexander." She left off his last name. The Scouts greeted him before she started to visit the different displays while Alexander talked with one of the other boys about some of them. She made sure to talk with each of the young men. All of them had a parent or grandparent with them, though the grown-ups mostly hung back, allowing the young men to have the spotlight.

Christiana stopped at one of the displays and picked up one of the pieces of wood that looked something like a small bow. "And what is this for?"

One of the younger members of the troop took it from her. "You use it like this-" He demonstrated. "-to build a fire."

"Who is the best in your troop?"

The boy looked both proud and a bit bashful. "I am." He pointed to an older man standing in the background. "Poppo taught me."

Christiana felt her smile become more real. "Perhaps you can show me sometime." She looked at his name tag. "David. Your poppo must be a wonderful teacher, and I imagine you will be as well." Prince Richard of Montevaro had tried to teach her once. It had not gone well.

David waved his grandfather over. "Poppo will help you."

The older man bent at the waist. "I would be happy to, Your Majesty."

David's face lit up. "We're having a parade in our town for your wedding trip. Mom said you'll be spending the night a couple blocks from us."

Her stomach fell into the pit. "I would love for you to show me more when I come to your town." She would make sure to schedule a visit within the next year. David and so many others would be disappointed when the announcement was made.

As the group moved on, Poppo stayed behind. "Your Majesty, I know it has been many years, but I have never had the privilege of speaking with you before, and I would like to say something."

Christiana stood with him while Alexander talked with the boys about camping. "Do go on." She took his arm as they slowly walked after the group.

"The death of your parents and brother caught everyone by surprise." He shook his head. "Such a tragedy. All of us went through gut-wrenching pain. It hit your nanny's family hard as well, but I cannot imagine what it must have been like for you, losing your family and becoming queen at such a young age. My family and I have been praying for yours for as long as I can remember. But I'll never forget the pictures of you that day." He squeezed her hand inside his elbow. "I've prayed for you every day since."

The biggest problem was that she had few memories of her

own. Many of them came from the news stories and videos she had found, most of them online while out of the country, rather than personal times. "Thank you, sir, for your kind words. It *has* been many years, but your sympathy is very appreciated." Poppo's words were the first time anyone had mentioned her family to her in such a way in many years, and they brought tears to her eyes.

Poppo stopped and looked at her, concern in his gentle brown eyes. "I did not mean to upset you, Your Majesty."

One tear leaked down her cheek, but Christiana smiled. "Oh, no. It is nice to hear that people still think about my family, and that people out there are praying for me."

"Your mother was one of the classiest women I ever saw. David's father was at a meeting like this one many years ago, and I accompanied him as well." He smiled softly. "You are much like her." They started walking again, slowly to accommodate his gait. "I remember how beautiful she looked on her wedding day. I imagine you will eclipse her." Poppo nodded toward Alexander. "That is a lucky young man."

Christiana stopped, her eyes wide.

Poppo chuckled. "Oh, I know the identity of your fiancé is a state secret, but anyone who watched closely could see the glance the two of you exchanged when he walked in."

Panic settled in her stomach. What did Poppo see that she did not? "Poppo?"

His eyes showed his shock.

"Do you mind?"

Poppo shook his head. "Of course not, ma'am."

In that moment, Christiana knew her decision had been made. "Poppo, would you, David, and your family be my guests at the wedding?"

This time tears filled the eyes of the older gentleman. "You would like us to be there?"

"Very much so." They stopped at the back of the crowd of Scouts. "If you would speak to my assistant on your way out, she will make certain the paperwork is taken care of and the invitation sent as quickly as possible." Security would be tight. Background checks would be more intense than they would have been otherwise, but it had to be that way.

Poppo smiled at her. "We would be honored to come. Thank you." He bowed slightly at the waist. "I will be praying for both of you."

As they left, Alexander shook hands with all of the Scouts, promising to stop in at one of their meetings if he was ever in the area. Christiana made sure to introduce Poppo to her assistant, out of Alexander's earshot, and told Diana to make the necessary arrangements. Diana gave Christiana an odd look but left with the Scouts. Before she did, Diana told her a girls' football team would arrive in ten minutes.

She turned to see Alexander leaning against the wall, arms casually crossed in front of him. The smile on his face reminded her of something, but she could not quite put her finger on it. He pushed off of the wall, walking toward her until he could take her hand. "Have you thought any more about what we talked about?"

"It has been an hour," Christiana pointed out, sliding her hand out of his. "I have not had time to think much about it." Truth was she had thought about little else. "Is that why you changed and came in here looking dapper?"

His grin widened. "You think I look dapper?"

With his dark hair falling over his forehead and his twinkling eyes, he always looked dapper. She felt color flood into her face as she nodded. "You look quite handsome."

The twinkle dimmed somewhat. "Handsome enough to marry?"

"I will not marry someone because he is handsome." *He* was handsome. Pretty faces could not always be trusted.

"I know."

David and Poppo flitted through her mind. How crestfallen the boy would be when she did not visit on her wedding trip.

How Poppo remembered her parents' wedding. How they were a microcosm of the rest of her country.

Though she knew what she would do, Christiana needed time before telling him, before making it official. "When must the decision be made?" His family ran the venue. He would know these things.

"You're the queen. You get a lot more leeway on cancellations and changes than most people."

She glared at him. "I am serious, Alexander."

Before he could answer, their conversation was interrupted by the door opening. He stayed with her for the next three hours, firmly cementing himself at her side. When she accepted his proposal, word would get out that he had been seen with her several times.

Normally, she enjoyed days like this. Meeting with young people reinvigorated her in a way few other things did, but still, she found herself being very glad for Alexander's supportive presence. By the time the last person in the final group left the room, she knew it was time.

So many had mentioned how much they were looking forward to her wedding. The older visitors, those thirty and older or so, told her how much it meant to them that she was recovering from the gilded cage her uncle kept her in while lining his own coffers rather than caring for her country. Several besides Poppo had mentioned her parents' wedding, and one even mentioned the wedding of her grandparents.

Christiana sank into one of the wingback chairs in the sitting room, looking out over the Mediterranean. So many windows in the palace had a similar view, and she loved it more than anything.

"Are you all right?" Alexander asked quietly.

"My answer is yes."

Alexander nodded, not ready to let his feelings show. "What changed your mind?"

Christiana sat with her back straight, staring ahead, though he doubted she actually saw much of anything. "David and Poppo. They put a face to the people who will be most affected by this if I do not marry in a couple weeks."

He sat in the chair next to her. "No, Your Majesty. You are the one whom will be affected the most. You, your life, your legacy, all of it hinges on this decision. Even your children are affected by who you choose to marry and when. It *will* affect your people. People like David and Poppo and others. But *you* are the one who will be affected most by it."

"I understand your point, but part of being queen means I put my people's needs above my own. You are a good man, Alexander. I would not make this decision if I did not trust that you would make a good prince consort who would never try to take my throne."

He knew she'd had enough of that to last a lifetime. "Never."

"And I believe we are well suited for one another. I do not know about falling in love, but I believe there could be far, far worse people to spend my life with."

How flattering.

"But very few better choices, if any at all."

That's better. "I agree, or I never would have offered." Where did one buy an engagement ring for a monarch? He could afford just about any ring for any other girl, but a queen? If her father were still here, he'd ask for an heirloom of some sort. Did any of it still remain in the royal collection or had her uncle disposed of it all, somehow? The next week and a half would be spent finding the perfect ring.

The next two weeks would be spent convincing his family this wasn't the craziest idea he'd ever had.

Groom Revealed?

People from several groups who visited the palace today mentioned a man joined the queen in greeting guests, but the identity of the mystery man remains just that - a mystery. Those in attendance said there was a definite spark between the two, even though the queen introduced the man as a friend and not as her fiancé. With the wedding now less than two weeks away, the groom's identity remains the biggest mystery, except, of course, what the bride's dress will look like and who, if anyone, will walk her down the aisle.

"There is water damage throughout the chapel?" Christiana's head began to throb.

Her fiancé, a word that still didn't seem to apply to Alexander, sat in the chair on the opposite side of her desk. He looked completely at ease in her office though she could see worry lines between his brows. "Not only water damage but damage to the roof as well. It won't be repaired in time for the wedding even if we work around the clock."

Roll with the punches. "Maybe this is a sign we ought to cancel the wedding."

"We do have an alternative. There's another facility on the property that we regularly use for wedding ceremonies."

She could tell he did not want to tell her.

"But it's the barn."

Her incredulity could not be measured. "The barn?"

"It's not a working barn. It's been completely redone to serve as a wedding venue."

"I have been there," she reminded him. "Many times."

"Never for a wedding," he pointed out. "It has proper air

conditioning, heating, insulation, and even bathrooms. We often have two weddings a day, one in the barn and one in the chapel, but because it's your wedding the other venue wasn't available to anyone else."

"What will the people and the press say? The queen getting married in a barn?" Personally, she thought it sounded a bit charming, but it was not about her.

"I think the people care more about the queen being happy than where her wedding is, especially due to circumstances beyond her control."

Perhaps he had a point.

"Your people adore you, Your Majesty. They care about *you*."

"Every monarch for the last several hundred years has been married in the chapel." She twirled a pen in her fingers. "I will be the first to be married somewhere else since the chapel was built."

A buzz announced her next appointment had arrived. "Please put together some alternative plans? Both at the same location and others within a reasonable distance. I do not, however, want to push anyone out of a wedding venue."

"I doubt there are many other weddings scheduled. The reception can go on as planned, but if there are other weddings that day, from what I've heard through the grapevine, they're scheduled for the evening. Some will want to share your day with you, but they won't want to have their ceremony at the same time."

Christiana nodded. She stood as the door opened. "Thank you for your assistance, Alexander." They smiled at each other as her next appointment walked in. No need for anyone to know who he was to her just yet. Not until the wedding in a few days.

"I know you've always had a bit of a crush on the queen,

Alexander, but are you sure this is a good idea?" Christopher leaned back in his office chair half a world away.

It had been more than a bit of a crush, but even his twin brother didn't know the extent of Alexander's feelings for Queen Christiana. They'd texted and e-mailed a number of times since he'd told his family he was the one who would be marrying the queen, but this was the first video chat they'd found time for. "Just promise me you'll be my best man."

"Of course. Just because I think you're making a mistake doesn't mean I don't want to be around to watch you do it." The teasing tone of his voice only masked the sincerity of his words.

"You'll be on the plane tomorrow?"

"Tonight, actually. At least tonight in Serenity Landing. Mom and I will take off as soon as we can, but Dad's flying commercial tomorrow afternoon. He has a meeting he can't miss or telecommute to."

"If we need the royal jet, the queen has given me permission to use it. I don't think it could get there in time to pick up you and Mom, but it could for Dad."

Christopher shook his head. "Not necessary. Have it on standby in case there's a plane malfunction or something, but commercial won't kill him. He'll still be there in plenty of time."

Alexander switched subjects. "Are you bringing a date? The wedding planner is asking."

"Nope. No girl is tying me down. Not for a long time."

They'd both been hurt by women in the past, some when they were really too young to be in even a semi-serious relationship, but fame would do that to a guy.

"I have a surprise for you though." Christopher grinned at him through the webcam. "Don't bother asking, but if you can get married at the last minute, just be glad I managed to scrounge something up."

Great. Who knew what it would be. Anything from a mud pie

to one of those women the queen had mentioned the day he proposed.

And he still didn't have a ring for her.

Who could he talk to about that?

"What is it?"

Of course Christopher could see the wheels turning. Sitting back, Alexander sighed. "I don't have a ring for her. I don't know where to get one. I've been thinking about it for days and a wedding band, sure. That's simple. But an engagement ring to go with it is proving a bit more difficult. The longer I wait the harder it gets."

"And they won't buy that she just wanted something simple to forgo expensive jewelry?"

"People who know Queen Christiana well enough wouldn't be surprised, but she's very interested in making sure she gives the people what they want out of this. And the people, especially the women, have been wondering about her lack of engagement ring since the wedding was announced."

"She's a queen. You need something fabulous."

"Tell me something I don't know." Alexander ran his hand through his hair. "I got nothin'. Any other girl I could buy anything, but just buying a ring isn't gonna cut it for Queen Christiana."

"Dude, are you seriously calling her that all the time? She's your fiancée. Don't you have some sort of nickname for her? Or at least drop the 'queen' bit?"

Except for the one time, he'd never called her anything but "Your Majesty", "Queen Christiana", or "ma'am", but he supposed his brother was right. After he moved in, lounging around their apartment, chilling at the end of the day, those titles might feel a bit off. Or maybe he'd just worry about it after the wedding.

So he stuck with the subject at hand. "It's too late to have something commissioned. I'm afraid at least some of her family heirlooms are gone because of her uncle's treason. But even if there was a family ring she wanted, how would I get my hands on it without asking her for it and that takes some of the romance out of it?" He amended his statement. "No. That takes *all* the romance out of it."

"Is there *any* family member or staff who could help you? What about someone from her mother's side of the family?"

Who could get him into the family vault? What about the ring her mother had worn? Could he get it? Would Christiana want it?

How well did he really know his fiancée?

Not well enough, but he already knew that.

A beeping sound startled him out of his thoughts. Alexander looked up in time to see Christopher looking at his phone.

"I gotta go, but I'll see you tomorrow." Christopher reached for the keyboard just before Alexander's screen went black.

Even if they weren't completely certain he was doing the right thing, his family was being supportive. Queen Christiana had never really had a family. He knew enough about her history to know she'd spent many of her growing up years at boarding school in nearby Montevaro. Her holidays were often spent with the Montevarian royal family, but she hadn't had a good old fashioned family Christmas since she was four, if ever.

Leaning forward, he pulled up the itinerary she'd sent him for their wedding trip. Two nights at the exclusive honeymoon cabin on the Baicampo property, a week on the royal yacht visiting the more populated islands, then eight weeks traveling the country. He gave a slight shake of his head. You could drive around both main islands in less time than it took to drive from his childhood home in southwest Missouri to Los Angeles, California where he spent most of his teen years. The next page had the schedule broken down further. Two or three stops a day in different towns, spending the night at local establishments.

A good will tour. It wasn't so much a honeymoon as it was a tour of the country trying to foster her relationship with her people. Though most of them were sympathetic to her plight, some were talking about using her weakened status to get rid of the monarchy all together. As much as he admired and respected the queen, Alexander wasn't opposed to a non-monarchy government, in theory, but the most vocal members of the movement advocated a weird cross between anarchy and communism. He couldn't advocate that.

A quick shake of his head brought him back to the question at hand. When would they return to the palace? With a flip of his finger, he scrolled through the detailed, dated itinerary. The day before Christmas, they were scheduled to return to the capital city.

In the meantime, he still had to figure out what to do for an engagement ring for a queen.

Christiana's heels clicked on the rustic wood floors of the barn, the staccato rhythm keeping time with her tripping heart. She looked around at the high ceilings, rustic chandeliers, and white chairs in rows.

Alexander walked next to her. "What do you think?"

What was the right way to say it?

"It's better than you feared based on the other events you've been to here?"

Christiana turned to see the grin on his face. She blushed as she nodded. "Yes. I am afraid I did fear the worst."

He leaned closer to her, until he could whisper in her ear. "We know what we're doing here, Your Majesty." The warmth of his breath on her skin sent chills down her spine.

But would he ever call her something else?

Just once, she wanted someone to be comfortable enough with her to let their guard down, to lose the veil of formality, and be themselves with her. *He* never had, unless he was being snippy and rude. Would Alexander?

"It is lovely, Alexander." Not what she had pictured in her mind, but it was more than acceptable. "How will this work? The reception is to be held here as well, yes?"

"It is. Unfortunately, the wedding coincided with some renovations to the main hall. They were already underway when it was scheduled. Try as we might, we are unable to have them completed by Saturday."

"How will that work?" She gestured to the room. "The entire room is taken up with seating. What will people do for the reception?"

He reached for her hand and tucked it into his elbow as he escorted her around the perimeter of the room. "Only about half of those invited to the ceremony are invited to the reception, mostly friends and those considered more important. Like other heads of state, certain members of Parliament, ranking members in other parts of the government, people like that. Once the ceremony is over, we'll be taken to the mainland for the parade around the city and the presentation on the balcony of the palace. Those invited to the reception will stay here. There will be several alternatives for them to choose from, but most will likely head over to the small ballroom for mingling and appetizers. By the time we return, this will have been transformed into a fairytale ball wonderland, and the guests will be waiting."

She nodded. "Very good."

"The reception will last until about seven-thirty. Dancing will be followed by dinner, toasts, and the cake, then more dancing. At that time, a carriage will be waiting to take us to the cottage on the east coast of the island."

Right.

The cottage.

Christiana had been looking forward to that night. Excitement and trepidation warred for control of her emotions whenever she thought about being a *wife*. Now, she did not know what to think.

From under her lashes, she glanced up at the man walking beside her. What would he expect? What would she be able to give?

The minister and several other people walked into the room, drawing her attention away from her questions. For the next half hour, they walked through the wedding ceremony. Melancholy swept over Christiana. Her parents were not here. Her father would not walk her down the aisle.

She was queen of her country, but she had no one.

No family.

Only her people.

In eighteen hours, she would become a part of Alexander's family, but that still did not give her anyone on her side specifically. Her first meeting with his parents and brother over an early dinner had gone well. Stiff and formal, but well. Given several decades, perhaps they would warm toward her. Her fiancé's slightly younger brother's eyes twinkled when they met. Christopher was greatly amused by the whole situation.

Once the rehearsal was over, she returned to the palace. Alexander and his family would stay at their home on the property, but he accompanied her. Rather than escorting her to her quarters, he asked if she would like to go for a walk.

Her feet hurt in the heels she had worn for far too many consecutive hours, but she sensed he had something he wanted to say. The garden was cool, and Alexander shrugged out of his suit coat.

"Here." He wrapped it around her shoulders, its warmth enveloping her.

"Thank you."

When they reached a concrete bench, he gestured for her to sit down. "There's something I want to talk to you about."

Wedding Venue Changed

The venue for the royal wedding has changed. Due to damage done by the recent storm, the chapel on the Bianisola Island property is unavailable. Every monarch for hundreds of years has been married there, but Queen Christiana and her still-unnamed groom will be forced to hold the ceremony in the property's other venue - a barn. Pictures of wedding ceremonies in the barn are quite lovely, but it is believed she will be the first member of any of Europe's ruling families to be married in one in centuries, if ever.

With just days to go before the big event, everything seems to be in place - except the groom's closely held identity and who will represent the queen's family. All local channels plan to cover the wedding for several hours. Several American news networks also plan to show the wedding, though it is not yet clear why. The Baicampo Property on the island is owned by an American family but it is not believed to be enough of a reason for them to do so. This has led to speculation that the new prince consort may be an American.

4

She was marrying him in just over eighteen hours.

He could do this.

Queen Christiana sat primly on the bench, her back straight and legs tucked to the side as her hands clutched his coat around her. She looked up at him, expectant.

Taking a deep breath, he reached into his pants' pocket and dropped to one knee. "Queen Christiana, will you marry me?"

Alexander popped the box open, showing her the ring nestled there.

He could tell the moment she recognized the diamond and emerald ring. "Is that my mother's?" she whispered.

Removing it from the slot in the box, he nodded. "I talked to Diana to see if I could get it. She helped me." He looked up, suddenly unsure. "I hope that's okay."

She nodded, a tear slipping down one cheek. "It's perfect."

He reached for her hand. "I just hope it fits. I haven't had time to get it sized." Sliding the ring on, he felt his heart constrict when it fit perfectly. Kissing the back of her hand just above where it nestled, he closed his eyes and breathed a prayer for her peace of mind.

"The size is just right." He let her pull her fingers from his hand. She used both to wipe her cheeks, causing the suit coat to fall to the bench behind her.

Alexander stood and held out his hands. Queen Christiana took them and let him pull her to her feet. He wrapped the coat back around her and tugged her closer to him. Looking down into her soft blue eyes, he wanted nothing more than to kiss her, but something held him back. He wanted their second kiss to be perfect. It wouldn't be with the thoughts running through his head: what the Prime Minister had told him earlier in the day, and how Christiana would react when he told her.

Instead of kissing her, he pulled her close, wrapping his arms around her as she rested her head on his chest.

"Thank you for thinking of my mother's ring, Alexander." She moved back and looked up at him again.

The trust in her eyes almost made him want to tell her everything.

A throat clearing from the other side of the hedgerow caused Alexander to take a step back.

"Your Majesty, there is a phone call for you." Diana stepped around the corner. "I am sorry, but it cannot wait."

Christiana nodded, but looked up at him. She looked like she regretted moving away.

"I will see you in the morning." Her soft voice drew him in. Tomorrow, she would be his wife.

And this time tomorrow night, they would be in the cabin on the Mediterranean coastline of his family's property. Where they would be expected to begin attempting to conceive an heir.

As she walked away, one thought kept running through his mind. *How am I going to tell her we're expected to make love tomorrow night, though neither one of us is ready?*

Christiana peered in the mirrors. Her reflection stared back. The multipaned mirrors showed her in a gown very different from the one just two weeks earlier. She would need to find a way to thank the seamstress who spent every waking hour - and many when she should have been sleeping - designing and crafting an entirely new dress, this one full and with royal blue accents in the color of the Rensselaer family's crest. In light of *his* betrayal, she could not bear to wear the original one he'd chosen. Or the crown he'd preferred. She hadn't liked them anyway. Instead, she wore a simple tiara that had also belonged to her mother, given by her grandmother on her parents' wedding day.

She even took some comfort from marrying Alexander in a different venue, though it was still a barn.

"Your Majesty?"

Christiana turned around to see Diana standing there. "Yes?"

"David and his family are here to see you."

"Show them in."

She stepped off the riser and maneuvered her way toward the door where they entered, Poppo leading his family. Immediately, his eyes filled with tears as he bowed.

"You look lovely, Your Majesty." As he straightened, she reached her hands toward him. He took them and she smiled.

"Poppo, I have a favor to ask of you and your family."

"Anything, ma'am."

Christiana turned to the rest of the group. "As you all know, I have no family left. My only family is the people of my country. I would be honored if you would stand in for them."

Puzzled looks greeted her. "How would we do that, ma'am?" Poppo asked.

She turned to his wife. "Mrs. Engel, would you stand in for the mother of the bride?" Then to his daughter and daughter-in-law.

"Mrs. Sanderford, Mrs. Engel, would you do me the honor of being my bridesmaids, acting as sisters of the bride would?" They all nodded, dumbfounded. "Mr. Sanderford, if you would escort your mother-in-law, I would appreciate it."

He inclined his head her way. "It would be my honor."

She turned to Poppo's son. "Mr. Engel, my groom's brother will be his best man. Would you stand up with him as well?"

Mr. Engel blinked twice, then nodded. "Of course."

Christiana rested her hands on her knees and bent over a bit. "David and Annie, would you be my ring bearer and flower girl? See? Your dress and your mama and aunt's dresses match mine." Her wedding party had been gutted with the change in the groom, though she had no idea who he had planned to stand with him. He'd even asked a friend of his to be her maid of honor. Earlier, she had forced herself not to think too much about it. Now, it struck her as odd.

With the change in groom came an entirely new wedding party. Alexander did not have anyone close to him to fill any role but the best man. When she heard from Diana the make-up of David and Poppo's family, the idea sprouted. Her assistant made sure they were all appropriately attired in the same blue from the family crest.

Childish squeals filled the room, and Christiana laughed. "That is a 'yes' then?"

She turned to Poppo. "Poppo, I would be honored if you would walk me down the aisle and give me away on behalf of my people?"

The tears streaked down his cheeks as he bowed deeply. "It would be my honor, Your Majesty."

Diana came forward. "Thank you all for agreeing to be a part of Queen Christiana's special day. If you would follow me, there are a few forms I need you to sign. Mainly agreeing not to profit off of your involvement."

Poppo looked indignant. "We would never do such a thing."

"I am sure you would not, sir." She led them out of the room. "However, everyone involved with the wedding has to sign the agreements. It is for the queen's protection."

Once again alone, Christiana settled carefully into a chair near the window. With the heavy tint, she could see out but no one could see in. Employees scurried about with last minute preparations. Poppo and his family had been asked to arrive extra early so she could request their participation. Soon, the rest of the guests would arrive. Somewhere nearby, Alexander was getting ready.

A knock sounded at the door.

"Come in," she called.

"Good morning, Christiana."

She turned to see her closest friend in the world walk in. Queen Adeline of Montevaro had been like a sister at times, her family the closest thing to her own family Christiana ever had. If not for her position as monarch of Montevaro, Christiana would gladly have asked her to be in the wedding.

Addie sat in the chair next to Christiana. "How are you, my friend?"

Christiana smiled. "Nervous."

"I would imagine so, what with the change in groom at such a late date."

The queen felt her smile falter. "I should have contacted you."

"I heard through the grapevine. I must say I am glad you are marrying Alexander rather than…"

Christiana held up a hand. "Do not use his name. How did you find out about Alexander?" She did not think anyone outside of a select few had that knowledge.

"I know it has not been announced, but I managed to get my hands on one of the programs and saw Alexander's name."

Addie was one of the few who knew of Christiana's relationship with her former fiancé. At his insistence, their relationship had been kept quiet. The press hounded her public affairs office until she promised all of the major news organizations individual interviews once the tour of the country began in a few days.

"Would you like to tell me what happened?" Addie asked softly.

"Not today. Perhaps some other time. Suffice it to say, there was plenty of reason to call off the wedding."

"Why not just cancel it? Why marry Alexander instead? Do you love him the way we always talked about? The way I love Charlie, and he loves me?"

A sad Christiana looked over at her friend. Though not much older, Addie's life had been much different than Christiana's. "No. I do not love him like we discussed. I respect him. He is a good man, a kind man. But love? No."

"So why change grooms and not just call it off?"

"I pray nothing similar ever happens to you, my friend, but when your country has just gone through the turmoil mine has and needs such an event to help the healing process, you would do the same thing. To cancel the wedding would have been a blow the monarchy may not have survived, and the alternatives being bandied about by fringe groups? I have no desire to see my people in such a place. If it means sacrificing the love we've always talked about, so be it."

Addie nodded. "I suppose I can understand that, but I am glad I was never faced with the choice." She grimaced. "Parliament had to approve of Charlie, you know. It's not just my father who had to decide if he was 'good enough for a princess.'" She mimicked her father's voice poorly enough to make Christiana smile. "Besides," Addie went on. "Malachi and Jessabelle seem happy enough. I saw her the other day. She definitely looks pregnant."

Christiana knew someone was missing. She must be distracted not to have noticed sooner. "Where is your sweet baby boy?"

"At home. We only came for the day and will return to Montevaro after the reception. He and Lindsey are with the nanny."

Of course. At just a few months old, Stephen Jedidiah Charlemagne Nicklaus would not do well at the wedding. Christiana did not let herself dwell on the small baby's big name. Too much bitter and not enough sweet knowing he was named for her brother. "Are your parents here?"

"No. Father is not feeling well. They wanted to be here, though. It is only the six of us here. Charlie, Rick, Ellie, Ana, and Jonah are here somewhere. You are very dear to all of us." Addie stood. "What can I do to help you?"

Christiana shook her head as the first guests walked along the sidewalk in front of the hay field. She did not recognize them, but it was a sign. Almost time.

Diana walked in and nodded toward Addie. "Ma'am, the photographer is back and would like some more pictures."

"Of course." Tedious as it was, Christiana knew she would appreciate them someday. Even if she did not, the people and posterity would. Diana handed her the long gloves. One loop went around a finger, and they extended past her elbow. She snagged the loop on one of the ridiculously long fingernails her stylist insisted on. Once they were in place, the photographer came in.

After a few shots with Addie, the next forty-five minutes were spent in various locations around the property, careful to avoid the spots with Alexander and his family taking pictures of their own.

Poppo, David, and the rest of the family joined her for many of the pictures, as did a number of her staff. No members of the government did, except the Prime Minister and Minority Leader. Though, the photos were generally tedious, before she knew it, the coordinator had moved her to the waiting room in the main building. From there, she and Poppo would walk to the barn. Everyone else was led to the other building where they would wait for her to arrive then precede her in.

An assistant to the wedding coordinator nodded at them.

Poppo looked down at her, a tender expression on his face. One she could imagine from her own father or grandfather.

It was time.

***

Wedding Updates

An examination of the program reveals several interesting tidbits:

In order of their appearance in the program:

Queen Christiana's family will be represented by several of her subjects, said to be standing in as representatives of "the people of Ravenzario."

The groom is Alexander Bayfield, son of the owners of the wedding facility. Though he has lived in Ravenzario for the last several years, he was raised in both Serenity Landing, Missouri and Los Angeles, California in the United States. Speculation is running rampant as to how the queen and Mr. Bayfield met. His twin brother, Christopher, will stand up with him, along with another representative of the people of Ravenzario.

5

Alexander walked in from the side door to the front of the barn-turned-wedding venue, near the center. He would meet Queen Christiana at the bottom of the stairs, and they would walk up them together. In moments, he would be a married man and the prince consort of his adopted country.

Taking on either role would be enough to make most men think twice, and he had, but ultimately, he knew this was the right decision. He believed he loved the queen already, but knew would easily grow to love her even more. Hopefully, she would grow to love him as well. Christopher stood behind him as the music started to play. Alexander had asked questions about the ring bearer or her maid of honor, but Christiana hadn't given him any answers. There was no sense of stress, but a feeling that she trusted it would all work out. He wanted to believe the prayers he'd said for a stress-free transition to a new groom had something to do with it.

An older woman Alexander didn't recognize was escorted by a man in his mid-thirties, and they sat in the front row. They were followed by another couple he didn't know, then a woman walking by herself. The last man came to stand on the other side of his brother while both women stood opposite them. Okay. So she found a bridal party. A flower girl and ring bearer walked sedately down the aisle. Alexander's grin widened as he recognized David from the Royal Scouts. Perfect. The music changed and everyone in the room stood to their feet. He'd had no trouble seeing the other end of the aisle up to that point. Now, everyone's heads blocked his view. The coordinator had told him where to stand, *precisely* where to stand, but he couldn't help it. He took a step forward until he had a clear view.

The doors at the other end opened.

First, he saw Poppo and smiled. What a perfect choice to walk her down the aisle.

Then Alexander felt his breath stolen right out of him. Queen Christiana walked toward him. He knew he would never remember what she wore, but he'd always remember the way tears filled his eyes and blurred his vision. As a rule, he didn't cry often, but this time a couple tears found their way down his cheeks.

Alexander couldn't contain his smile as she came closer. He wanted to walk toward her, to reach for her, but his brother's steadying touch on his shoulder kept him in place. She and Poppo stopped a foot from him.

"Who gives this woman in marriage to this man?" The voice boomed over the loudspeakers.

Poppo stood a bit taller. "On behalf of her country and her beloved people, I do."

Alexander saw a tear drop as Poppo bent over to whisper something in her ear then kiss her cheek. As she let go of Poppo's arm, Christiana reached for Alexander.

He took her right hand in his and his left hand came to rest on the small of her back as they ascended the ten stairs to the stage.

Did she need the support? Probably not.

Did he feel better giving it? Making sure she didn't trip? Absolutely.

The ceremony passed in a blur. Queen Christiana's trusting blue eyes stared into his as they both repeated the time honored words. Alexander promised to love, honor, and cherish her. To be faithful to her.

For as long as they both shall live.

And she did the same.

This wedding would differ from most, and Alexander faced disappointment when the preacher reached the part of the ceremony where he would usually tell Alexander he could kiss his bride.

Instead, they heard the words, "I now pronounce you husband and wife. What God has joined together in this place and in the presence of these witnesses, let no man put asunder. Ladies and gentlemen, I give you Her Majesty, Queen Christiana and Alexander, Prince Consort and Duke of Testudines."

The title surprised him, but that emotion got lost in the overwhelming urge to kiss his wife. He might not be able to, not really, but that didn't stop him from wanting to. Instead, Alexander framed her face with his hands, the pads of his thumbs running along her cheekbones. Wariness filled her eyes, but when he pressed his lips to her forehead he could feel her relief.

Tradition dictated the royal family did not have the first kiss during the ceremony. Much like several other countries, including both Great Britain and Montevaro, that he knew of, that kiss would come in full view of the public while on the balcony of the palace. Alexander rested his forehead against hers, his eyes closed as he tried to soak in the enormity of it all.

The applause from the crowd told him what he needed to know. While their first kiss would likely grace the front page of newspapers and websites, the tender moment he now shared with his bride would be the one plastered everywhere for all eternity.

God, help us make this work. We can't do any of it without your help. Help me to love her selflessly and for Christiana to learn to trust me with her heart.

A softly-cleared throat behind him brought Alexander back to the present.

He turned, took Queen Christiana's hand, much as he had on the way up the stairs and, this time with his right hand, supported her on the way down. Once they reached the floor, he tucked her arm in his elbow, a feeling of protectiveness spreading over him.

Those in the audience continued to applaud as Alexander escorted his bride up the aisle. When they exited, a horse-drawn carriage awaited. They were settled in the padded seat before he spoke directly to his wife.

"Are you comfortable, Queen Christiana?"

Now, out of the view of most of the cameras and other prying eyes, but not completely alone, she let her guard down a bit. "I am fine, Alexander. This ride will be short."

Right. They were only going down to the dock where they would board the royal transport speedboat and go to the mainland. Another carriage awaited them on that side. The parade route led the mile or so through the city streets to the front gate of the palace.

The speed boat ride was both windy and loud. The queen sat in the front, protected as much as possible from the wind by the Plexiglass barrier. Alexander sat behind her, buffering her as much as he could.

He leaned forward and spoke in her ear. "Are you all right? I know this wasn't what you'd planned for today." What he meant was that he wasn't who she'd planned it with.

She turned to face him as best she could. "I am very happy I married you today, Alexander."

Alexander barely heard her and moved closer so she could hear him. "I hope it's okay that I can't wait to kiss you. I understand why, but we can't get to that balcony soon enough for my taste."

The conversation with the Prime Minister came flooding back to him, but he ignored it.

There would be time enough once they reached the honey-moon cabin to deal with it. Until then, he wanted to relish every moment of his wedding day.

Christiana took a deep breath. Alexander's hand was wrapped around hers, warm and reassuring, as they prepared to step out onto the balcony. In just a moment, he would kiss her. She would kiss him back. The whole world would be watching.

And if they were not, they would see the replays of it on the news for the next few days, especially once word got out she had married an American.

What was she thinking?

The doors in front of them opened and the others in the wedding party preceded them onto the balcony. Several hundred feet away throngs of people yelled and screamed as they walked out. She did not understand the fascination, but did her best to give her people what they wanted. What they deserved.

Were those words a chant to kiss?

Alexander's arm came around her waist, pulling her to his side. The moment, earlier, when he cradled her face in his hands and kissed her forehead would forever be implanted in her memory as one of her favorite moments of all time. As queen, she bore so much responsibility, but it was like he had made a pledge to take care of her, to give her someone always on her side, to help shoulder the load. It meant the world to her.

Now, she faced Alexander as he lowered his face to hers. The warmth spread from the zing in her lips all the way down to the tingle in her toes. As kisses go, it was "less" in many ways than the one two weeks earlier, but at the same time, it was "more."

They waved to the crowd for several minutes. Poppo stood on her other side, a proud father or grandfather for the day. His mere presence did wonders to still the butterflies rampant in her stomach. She would have to make sure to keep in touch with the Engel family.

After about five minutes, they returned inside to take a number of pictures on the property, including a number in the throne room and the garden. As they left the palace, they took a longer parade route until they reached the dock to head to Alexander's family's property again.

More pictures took another hour or longer, though this time Christiana did not mind. Alexander was so solicitous, making sure she had a bite to eat, that she would not get hurt or be uncomfortable while shooting pictures in odd locations - like the top of a hay bale. Only fitting, she supposed, since the wedding had taken place in the barn.

No longer were there any restrictions on when Alexander could kiss her. Only the first kiss was reserved for a specific place. He seemed to take great pleasure in following the instructions of the photographer when instructed to "lay one on her." Alexander's words. The photographer looked scandalized.

Eventually, they returned to the barn, now transformed into a banquet hall. Only a few more hours until she would be out of the limelight and behind the privacy of closed doors.

Then it hit her.

She would never truly have that privacy again.

For in a few hours, her husband would join her behind those closed doors.

Apprehension filled her as she tried not to think about what the night could bring.

Husband was such a wonderful word.

Unless one really did not want to be married to him in the first place.

Wedding Updates

The new prince consort, Alexander, Duke of Testudines, appeared to wish he could buck tradition at the end of his wedding to Queen Christiana. The Duke instead pressed a kiss to his bride's forehead, reserving the official first kiss for the balcony at the palace where the couple appeared after the parade through the streets of the capitol city of Pagosa. They have since returned to the Bianisola venue where the reception will take place, lasting well into the evening. The royal couple will spend two nights in the cottage on the Baicampo property before spending a week at sea on the royal yacht. They will embark on a two month tour of Ravenzario where they will spend most of their time with Ravenzarians.

6

Princess Yvette of Mevendia looked around the barn and wondered if her non-wedding reception would be held here as well.

An arm landed around her shoulders, and she looked up to see one of her older brother standings there. "What's up, kid?"

She glared at him. "Don't call me that. I'm practically a married woman."

Malachi laughed. "You're still in secondary school. I don't think 'practically married woman' is the right term."

"When's my wedding?"

He winced. "June."

"How far away is that?"

"Seven months."

"So guess what I'm going to be doing while I'm trying to finish my last year?"

"Planning a wedding." She could hear the sympathy in his voice. He loved her, even if he did poke fun at her sometimes. "Sorry, kid."

Yvette leaned her head against him. "He's dead. Why is Papa making me do this?"

"It's in the contract he signed. The engagement isn't officially over unless Nicklaus still hasn't shown up a week after the wedding date, even if he hasn't been heard from in years or is dead and buried."

"But why? I was maybe six months old when he signed the contract. Why would he do that to me?"

"The contracts aren't always bad, even if they aren't what we think we want," he reminded her gently.

She looked up at him again, but this time he was looking across the room. At his wife. Jessabelle sat with the Montevarians - Queen Adeline along with her younger sister, Anastasia, and her sister-in-law, Ellie. "She looks comfortable."

"She is." She could hear the pride in his voice. Jessabelle had been awkward and definitely unsuited for royal life at the wedding and for the first few months afterward. It took some time, and patience, on the part of Malachi, but she came around, slowly. Learning the truth about her parentage had thrown all of them for a loop, but in the six months since, they'd all grown closer. Now, she had just a couple months left before bringing the first Van Rensselaer grandchild into the world.

"How's she feeling?" Jessabelle had dealt with some morning sickness early in her pregnancy, but not too much. More recently, though, Yvette had noticed she seemed off.

"She's tired. Much more so than she has been. In fact, Father suggested she back off on some of her engagements. She agreed readily."

Yvette felt her eyebrows rise. "Father suggested it?"

Malachi chuckled. "Yes. I was more shocked than you."

"Have you come up with a name for my new niece yet?" No one outside the family knew the gender of the baby.

"Catherine Alicia Yvette. But we haven't told Mother or Nana yet."

"So you're not naming her after me?" She faked the shock in her voice.

"Sorry, but no. Nana Yvette."

"As well it should be."

They stood there for a couple more minutes, not saying anything when Yvette decided to go back to the original topic. Not because she wanted to, but because she knew she couldn't avoid it forever.

"I don't know anything about planning a wedding, Kai." Her family had long called him Mal, but when she overheard him tell Jessabelle how much he hated that, she made a concerted effort to change.

"Like I do? My wedding was planned in less than two weeks. Jessabelle didn't even know what dress she was going to wear until that morning."

"She told me." Yvette had asked her for help already.

"Ask Lizbeth. She loves planning stuff."

Yvette nodded slowly. She didn't know her brother's friend well, but it did seem like something she'd enjoy. "Do you think she would?"

"All you can do is ask. She's been acting odd for the last few months, though. She won't tell me or Jessabelle what's going on, though."

"I'll call her tomorrow." Maybe. "My wedding is supposed to be in the chapel. So was Christiana's. I wonder if I can have a beach party reception here." The only way she would get through this would be to make light of it.

"I don't think Father will go for that, even with the lack of groom."

"Probably not."

It was worth a shot, though.

And after the wedding didn't happen, maybe then she could get around to her first date.

The wedding ball passed as though in a dream. Alexander never strayed far from Queen Christiana's side. Unless she was dancing with Poppo or one of the other men who claimed her time, he remained close. He danced with her several times, but always formal, as though she knew people were watching and didn't want to be seen as weak? Emotional? Connected? Dependent?

He didn't think her people would see it that way, but he did his best to respect her wishes and remained fairly formal, at least until the tapping of silverware against glasses urged him to kiss her. Alexander relished each tender moment.

After dinner, dancing, toasts, and mingling with guests, the time came for them to be whisked away. Alexander, with Queen Christiana's hand in his, ran through the hail of bubbles back to the waiting carriage. Those gathered cheered as the horse began to trot off. He and his *wife* waved, smiling and laughing as they did.

"Did you have a good time?" he asked her as they settled back, his arm around her shoulders to ward against the evening chill. The ride wouldn't be long, but he didn't want an awkward silence to set in.

Queen Christiana relaxed against him. "It was lovely. Thank you for helping with the arrangements."

"My pleasure." He kissed the side of her head. The carriage turned to head down the hill as the cabin came into view. Rustic, like something out of the American West, but with all the modern conveniences. Built just a decade earlier, it held the position as the newest building on the property. The photographer hovered off to one side as they drew to a halt. Once the door shut behind them, they'd be alone, but until then, it would be recorded for posterity.

Alexander stepped out of the carriage and turned, taking the queen's hand in his to help her to the ground. When they reached the porch, Alexander turned. "Are you ready?"

She nodded.

He swept her into his arms and kicked open the door, left slightly ajar by whoever had prepared the cabin. The soft clicking of the camera stopped as his heel tapped the door closed behind them. Lowering her to the floor, Alexander left his hands resting on her hips.

"Alone at last." He kept his tone light.

The queen gave him a tremulous smile. "I suppose we are."

This wasn't Alexander's first time in the cabin, but he'd never really paid much attention, at least from the stand point of a guest. Stepping back, he led her to the nearby couch, motioning for her to sit down.

Situating himself far enough away from her that they weren't touching, he leaned forward until he could rest his forearms on his knees. "There is something we need to talk about, ma'am."

Christiana stood in front of the mirror in the large bathroom. Not nearly as ornate as the one in the palace, the slate tile flooring and large Jacuzzi tub were very nice. The subtle lighting meant her reflection looked good. She *felt* like she looked good. But her stomach remained unsettled about what was about to happen.

But when she closed her eyes, all she could see was Alexander telling her what the Prime Minister had said...

"Three hundred years ago, the custom of making certain the king and his new queen attempted to produce an heir as quickly as possible was codified into law. It hasn't been thought of in well over a century as all kings were married long before they took the throne and there was no reason to believe they wouldn't consummate the marriage on their wedding night." Alexander had refused to look at her but stared into the distance.

Christiana blinked a few times. "Why would they do such a thing?"

"Apparently, in the 1600s, the king died with no male heirs. He had a daughter who everyone believed should inherit the throne but a law from a hundred years before required any queen to be married before she could take the throne. Her uncle ruled as a conservator until a marriage could be arranged." She winced as he hurried on. "Unlike your uncle, he only had the best intentions and planned to turn power over to the queen upon her marriage. She and one of the dukes decided to marry but as a political alliance only. When the rest of the aristocracy got word of this, they demanded proof the marriage was consummated. What kind of proof wasn't mentioned, and the last time the law was invoked a sworn statement was required of the prime minister at the time."

"And this law is still on the books?"

"Yes, ma'am."

The title made her uncomfortable. Alexander was her husband, not a subject. Even as a friend she had asked him to drop the formality, but he never had. Just the one time before he proposed.

"How long have you known?" How long had he been keeping it from her?

"Since yesterday morning. I didn't want to stress you out. You had enough on your plate without worrying about tonight."

"I already worried about tonight," she admitted, shocking even herself.

He turned to look at her. "Given our circumstances, my thoughts were that we should wait until we were both comfortable to take that next step. The prime minister said the law allows him to choose the kind of confirmation. He told me he will take our silence on the matter as confirmation that attempts to conceive an heir began as soon as reasonably possible. His words, not mine. The statement is so ambiguous as to mean just about anything."

Of course. Prime Minister Caruso was one of the few people who knew the sordid details of the last few weeks. He was doing his best to give them a way out while still upholding the letter of the law.

"He's been researching it. For centuries, the newly married king or Crown Prince and his bride would enter the bridal chamber while the party continued. The king or prince would emerge some time later to great cheering as the royal line had now been guaranteed for another generation. Or so they believed."

"This is before the law?"

"Yes. And part of the reason why the law was written. When it became known this daughter and her duke would enter the bridal chamber, and the new prince consort would emerge sometime later without consummation taking place, they felt the need to make it official."

"I see." The sound of her thudding heart filled Christiana's ears. "What do you propose we do then, Alexander?"

She watched him take a deep breath in and exhale slowly. "I will leave it up to you. There is no reason for anyone to ask us about it. The prime minister believes he's the only one even aware of the law. Everyone will assume they know what happens here tonight."

"It would be dishonest to let Prime Minister Caruso believe something that is not true, correct?"

A quick nod. "It absolutely could be interpreted that way. However, 'as soon as reasonably possible' could be anytime between now and the time either one of us dies. I believe he fully expects us to wait until we're ready."

"But he did not actually say that?"

"No, ma'am."

Thoughts and emotions swirled into a vortex inside. "Very well." She stood, her wedding dress feeling more constricting than before.

Alexander stood with her. "Whatever you choose, Queen Christiana..." His voice trailed off.

"Thank you, Alexander."

Now she stared in the mirror, still uncertain as to what her decision would be. It felt dishonest to allow the prime minister to believe something that was not true, no matter how he worded it to Alexander.

But to be intimate with him? Was she ready for that? Was he? Would the champagne from the toasts cloud her judgment? It could not be *wrong* in the same sense it would be if they were not married, but would she make the same decision if she were not a bit tipsy?

Christiana looked herself over. Comfortable pajamas. Flannel pants. Long sleeved t-shirt. Not exactly romantic or sexy, but she knew the cabin contained only one bed. She would not ask Alexander to sleep on the couch. Except for their time on the yacht, they would be expected to share a bed until they returned to the palace in nine weeks' time. She had packed accordingly.

When she decided she had stalled long enough, Christiana emerged from the bathroom to find Alexander sitting on the back deck, overlooking the Mediterranean. Long tan legs emerged from his cargo shorts as he stretched out on one of the Adirondack chairs. If he was disappointed by her attire, it did not show.

Christiana sat in the chair next to him. "It is a lovely evening."

"It is."

"Could we just talk for a while and see what happens?"

"Of course." He turned and gave her what had to be his best smile. "Let's talk."

Alexander leaned his forearms against the railing and stared out at the surf. Sipping from his mug of coffee, the ring on his left hand caught his eye. His first full day as a married man. They would spend another night at the cabin then board the yacht for a week at sea visiting the islands of the country. He did have a meeting finally scheduled with Yvette about the wedding scheduled for June. He hated to do it on their honeymoon, but there was enough of a break the day they returned to Bianisola that he could work it in then.

He hoped Queen Christiana would sleep most of the morning. With her expertly applied make-up removed, he could see the dark circles under her eyes. She desperately needed the rest.

After finishing his coffee, he sat on the porch swing with his Bible and a devotional book for husbands. Of course, none of the devotions said anything about marrying a queen, but surely the concepts would be applicable. Alexander spent over an hour on the porch, pulling out his Kindle once his quiet time was finished.

It was a few minutes after noon, when he heard stirring inside. The shower turned on a moment later, and he went back to his book. Another hour passed, and he started thinking about lunch when Queen Christiana emerged from the cabin. Her slender legs were encased in blue denim tucked into cowgirl boots. A button-down shirt completed the American West look.

A chuckle escaped when she clapped a cowgirl hat on her head. "Very nice."

She shrugged. "We did get married in a barn. I thought it appropriate. Did I get the look right?"

"You did." He stood and went into the kitchen. "Do you want breakfast or lunch?"

"Whatever is easiest." She perched on a barstool to watch him. "Do you cook?"

"Oh yes. Mom made sure we both knew how even though it wasn't something we had to do often." He pulled an egg carton and some milk out of the fridge. "How about French toast, scrambled eggs, and bacon?"

"Sounds lovely."

They made small talk as he expertly moved around the kitchen and while they ate. "What do you want to do for the rest of the day?" he asked as he cleaned up.

"I brought some work with me. It is not my first choice, but I do have a few things I need to get done before we arrive at our first stop tomorrow evening." He could hear the regret in her voice, though he imagined she didn't really want to spend all day with him. Things could easily get awkward.

"I don't mind," he told her, putting the last of the dishes in the drainer. "I have several books downloaded onto my Kindle that I've been looking forward to."

The rest of the day passed quietly. At some point, the queen turned on some soft jazz music as she worked at the counter in the kitchen. Around six, he made a simple dinner of spaghetti and a tossed salad. By midnight, he'd finished two books, and she was asleep on what was now her side of the bed. Turning off the lights, Alexander slid under the covers, rolling to stare at the moonlight glinting off the sea. Whispering a prayer over his wife, their marriage, and his adopted country, he closed his eyes and went to sleep.

"Are you feeling okay?"

Lizbeth kept her arms wrapped around her stomach as she stared over the bright blue ocean beyond the balcony.

"I guess."

Robe clad arms slid around her waist, pulling her back into his strong chest. "Don't lie to me, sweetheart."

Lizbeth sighed and turned, winding her arms around Robert's waist. "I wish we didn't have to hide. I'm glad no one knows, but I still wish..."

He kissed the top of her head. "I'm ready to tell everyone when you are, but I understand the reasons to stay quiet."

Like her father and the threats he'd made after being kicked out of the king's birthday party. She was pretty sure he knew what happened with the house guest in Ravenzario, but just as certain he didn't know the consequences of that night - including her secret wedding to Robert Padovano.

She let go and turned back around. "I'm here helping Yvette plan her wedding. It makes me sad that we didn't have a real one."

His hands rested on her shoulders. "We had the only kind of wedding that counts. A legal one. All that matters is you're protected from your father and anything he might want to try to make you do or do to you."

"And if he catches us here together?"

"We're not at your family's property. We're checked into a very exclusive hotel run by friends of mine. He won't know we're here and there are no memories for you."

They'd tried to stay at her family's house once, but her anxiety ramped up before they even got there, and he'd insisted they go somewhere else.

"I do have to leave soon, though." Robert pulled her back to him again. "I love you, Lizbeth Padovano."

"I know. I love you, too." She hadn't understood what love was until the night she told Robert everything, the things no one else knew, including things her father never suspected.

"Don't forget, we have a dinner Friday night."

She turned and smiled as he walked into the bathroom to brush his teeth. "I know. I can't wait." Everyone knew they dated occasionally. A fundraising dinner gave them a chance to be together in public.

As he reemerged, Robert adjusted his suit coat. "Don't let the wedding planning get to you, love." His hands came to rest on her hips. "If you want a ceremony when we're ready to go public, we'll have one. As big or as small as you want."

Lizbeth rested her hands on his chest. "I know, and I appreciate that." She gave him a wicked grin. "I'm just glad Queen Christiana's honeymoon trip to Bianisola coincided with a time Yvette could come, and you happened to be here for that Commonwealth meeting yesterday." The queen and her new husband would be on the island, nearly a week after the wedding, visiting with the locals like they would be in so many other places. Prince Alexander would be able to talk with them at least for a little while about the early planning and give them all of the paperwork for planning Yvette's non-wedding to the late Prince Nicklaus.

"Me, too." He pressed a gentle kiss to her forehead. "Call me tonight?"

"Of course."

One more kiss, and he left. Lizbeth went back to staring out the window. She had an hour before she needed to leave to make it to Bianisola on time. The royal plane would land on the airstrip there. She and Yvette wouldn't need to go back to the main islands to head home after the meeting.

Turning off my phone. Love you. TTYL.

Lizbeth smiled, but wouldn't text back for a few minutes. That way Robert would see it when he turned his phone back on. He could work on a flight, pay for the in-air Wi-Fi, but the trips were short enough he liked to just relax.

Ninety minutes later, she sat in the office with the newest prince consort in the Commonwealth. "Thank you for meeting with us, Your Royal Highness." Yvette sat next to her, but looked like she had no desire to get involved.

Alexander chuckled. "We've met before, Lizbeth. Several times."

She shifted. "I know, but you're married to the queen now. You're a duke."

"I'm still just Alexander." He pulled a binder out of his drawer and turned it around so it faced them. "This is your planning binder." He looked at Yvette. "I'm sure the protocol people at the palace will have their own version of plans."

Yvette shrugged. "I guess. I don't really care."

"You have to care." Lizbeth tried to be gentle. "I know why you don't, but you have to give this at least lip service. Think about it." She tried to appeal to Yvette's fashionable side. "You can pick everything without anyone else caring. That might not happen next time." Lizbeth glanced at Alexander in time to see the odd look on his face quickly replaced by an impassive one. "The dress you want. The flowers you want. The music you want."

Yvette seemed to be thinking that over. "Fine. Whatever." She reached for the binder. "Let's get started."

<hr />

First Couple of Ravenzario to give First Interview

Today, Matt Markinson of TCBC will sit down with Queen Christiana and Alexander, Duke of Testudines, for their first interview since their wedding Saturday. Portions of the interview will air during this evening's five, six, and ten o'clock news.

Since the wedding, the people have been learning about the new prince consort. Speculation as to the reasons to keep his identity a secret continue to run rampant, but those who attended the wedding and the reception, as well as those who have seen them on their stops in the days since, report that the two are very much in love.

The one hour special will premiere Friday evening at seven p.m.

8

Christiana lay stretched out on the top deck of the royal yacht. The sun beat down, though it was not warm enough for swim suits. The last few days had been both slow and hectic. The travel from island to island was pure enjoyment. She loved being on the water, but when they arrived in port, she and Alexander had to put on their happy faces and act as though they deeply loved each other. He held her hand or offered his elbow to escort her, but there was no kissing or even the linking of their fingers together. In some ways, she was glad those public displays of affection were taboo for herself, as the monarch, and Alexander, as the prince consort. Deep inside, though, she longed for that more intimate connection that came with that kind of affection.

He had not kissed her since their wedding day, or rather, their wedding night.

Alexander sat in the lounge chair next to her. "Today is our first interview."

She looked over to see him with his eyes closed, soaking in the sun. When she noticed the interview on the schedule this morning, she cringed. The lead royal reporter for the largest network in Ravenzario would be sitting down with them for an hour long interview then following them throughout their time in Whisper Cove.

"Do we need to get our story straight?" Alexander asked.

"What story is there to keep straight? We met a number of years ago. You proposed one night in the garden using my mother's engagement ring. We decided to keep your identity a secret for the time being for personal reasons. Now we are married, and you continue to call me 'Queen Christiana' and 'ma'am' even in private." It irked her more than a little. It kept her heart protected, not letting anyone close enough to get beyond the formal barrier. But Alexander was her husband now. Surely, he could drop the formality, at least in private.

A glance over the railing showed the next island stop in the distance. Christiana stood up and Alexander stood with her. "I need to get ready." She guessed they had a little over an hour before they would arrive. A quick shower, hair, make-up, and figure out what she would wear for her first interview as a married woman. She did not give interviews very often and never with someone by her side. Alexander seemed comfortable around all sorts of people, and she had seen him give statements to the press after the arrest of her uncle. He would be much more at ease than she would be.

They started down the stairs toward the lower deck. "Why did we decide not to release my identity?"

"Because of your involvement in the take-down of my uncle." She reached the bottom of the narrow staircase. "We did not want anyone asking those awkward questions. Now, it's been a year, the statements have been given, and we make it clear those questions are off the table." It had come to her in the last few minutes. A plausible explanation while not allowing too many questions.

Just over an hour later, she slid her feet into soft leather knee boots, tugging them up over her jeans and zipping the side. A bright purple pea coat went over her sweater and a wispy purple and pink scarf around her neck. Checking her appearance in the mirror, she left the master suite of the yacht. The one she had planned to share with *him*. Part of her wished she shared it with Alexander. The rest of her was glad he had not pushed.

As she walked down the hall, he emerged from his suite. Tan slacks, and a button down, open collared shirt. He wore boots of his own, though she could only see the lower portion. A brown leather jacket hung open around his broad shoulders.

Christiana had to admit he looked wonderful. Hot, she believed was the vernacular. He did not belong with her. He belonged with a supermodel who would help raise money for starving children in Africa and with his other charities. One of the women who had accompanied him to more than one ball. She did not want to think about what may have happened after they left palace grounds.

"You look lovely." Alexander reached out and touched her cheek with the back of his index finger.

Why did he say such things where no one would overhear? "Thank you. You look very nice yourself." Did he have an ulterior motive?

The yacht had docked a few minutes earlier, and she knew the plank would be down and waiting for them. Alexander stayed a step behind as they walked down the gangway. When she reached the bottom, the mayor of Whisper Cove, who she had met twice before, waited. He bowed slightly at the waist.

"Good morning, Your Majesty."

Christiana inclined her head his way. "Good morning, Mayor Giusseppe." She gestured to Alexander. "Have you met my husband, Alexander, Duke of Testudines?"

The mayor held out a hand, and Alexander took it. "It is a pleasure to meet you, Your Royal Highness."

"Likewise." Alexander moved to her side and rested a hand on the small of her back.

The mayor led the way off the dock. "We have a car waiting for you and a bit of a parade route through Whisper Cove." Most of the towns had. "Our first stop today is an orphanage the royal family has supported for many years, then the city hall where you'll meet with the reporter from TCBC, and we'll finish up with a ribbon cutting at our newest bed and breakfast."

"Wonderful." He stopped to let her get in the car first. She and Alexander sat forward facing while the mayor rode backwards. The route took them about two miles through town.

Christiana's heart swelled as the crowds cheered and waved. More than once she saw someone in the crowd holding up a picture of her and Alexander from their wedding. The most common was the one of him kissing her forehead at the end of the ceremony. She needed to get a closer look at it. There seemed to be two versions - a full color one that most people held - and a backlit shadow one a few people did. Though reliable Internet access was available on the yacht, she had avoided anything to do with the wedding. Perhaps it was time.

The car pulled to a stop in front of a nondescript building with a welcome sign hanging over the door. With a deep breath, Christiana emerged from the car.

Time to get her happy on.

Alexander found himself twitterpated.

The word from the childhood movie was the only way to describe how he felt. Queen Christiana sat on the floor of the orphanage, a little girl sitting on her lap and a little boy at her side, as they listened intently to the story the twelve-year-old was reading.

He watched as she turned her head just enough to brush a kiss against the hair of the little girl. A glance to the other side told him the official photographer, the one that traveled on the yacht with them but rarely spent any time with them while on board, was immortalizing the moment. So was the cameraman flanked by the reporter they'd meet with later.

Alexander had figured out why their first interview was scheduled for today.

By this time, the queen was to have been dead.

As the newly appointed king, *he* would have been able to address the nation with a sympathetic view of himself caring for others even during his time of deepest sorrow.

Even if *he* had no such emotions.

Alexander's stomach tightened at the thought of his beautiful wife lying cold and dead on a slab somewhere. *He* would have made sure the autopsy was delayed long enough for the toxins to disappear.

It wouldn't have happened like that, of course. Princess Yvette of Mevendia would have become queen with her father as regent until she came of age, but obviously *he* hadn't known that.

Though Alexander stood in the background, leaning against the wall with one ankle crossed over the other, he was aware of everything going on. The children were enthralled with the queen. It didn't have as much to do with her royal status as everything to do with *her*. She was fabulous with them.

For a moment, everything else faded away. *He saw her, sitting in a rocking chair at the palace, holding his child as she sang softly. Moonlight spilling in through one of the windows gave a soft glow around his toddler's blond hair. She looked up at him, and everything he longed to see shone back at him in her eyes. Love. Trust. Then he looked down in his own arms.*

Someone said something to him, interrupting his daydream.

After spending more than an hour with the kids, Christiana spoke for a few moments with the directors, asking for more information on a couple of their programs and thanking them for all of their hard work. Most of them also made small talk with him, but he was not the source of fascination like she was.

Not even like the Duchess of Cambridge had been when she married the heir to the throne of Great Britain. He supposed it was because so many girls wanted to be her and, in his experience, they were the primary consumers of that sort of information. The fascination surrounding her late mother-in-law didn't hurt. He'd met both the Duke and Duchess of Cambridge after the wedding. They had been Britain's official representatives and joined the young royals crowd. Sweden, Lichtenstein, Japan, Luxembourg, Norway, and several others had sent younger members of the families.

Regardless, they didn't treat him quite the same way they treated either the Duchess or Queen Christiana.

Before long, they had retreated to the city hall. The route was much less crowded this time, though the few spectators represented the most ardent of the bunch. Once at the city hall, they found themselves situated in a sitting room, already set up with lights and cameras. Queen Christiana shook hands with the reporter. Alexander followed suit. The reporter gave him an odd look, one Alexander couldn't quite figure out. Was he on to them? Had he discovered Alexander's past? It wasn't a secret per se, just not something he chose to discuss often, and he certainly didn't want to overshadow Christiana's first real interview as queen.

Alexander kept his arm stretched across the back of the couch behind her. There were sure to be at least a few difficult questions, and he wanted to be able to lend his support immediately when it happened.

"Your Majesty, Queen Christiana, thank you for agreeing to do this interview."

"It is my pleasure, Matthew. Thank you for being willing to meet us here."

"Most of Ravenzario isn't familiar with your husband, the

newly-titled Prince Consort Alexander, Duke of Testudines. Can you tell us how you met?"

She nodded. "We met a number of years ago when I attended a function at Baicampo, the property on Bianisola long owned by his family. We saw each other from time to time at official gatherings, balls, and so on. However, it wasn't until about eighteen months ago that we began to see each other regularly and realize there could be something more between us."

"Eighteen months ago? The public wasn't aware of what was going on until several months later, but wasn't that about the time the case began to build against your uncle?"

"Yes. Alexander was instrumental in bringing my uncle and the rest of those involved to justice." Alexander could sense her tension.

"The accusations and swift conviction rocked the nation to its core. How did they affect you, personally?" Matthew's head tilted in that way reporters' heads often did.

Alexander moved his hand slightly until he could rub the back of her shoulder with his thumb. He hated the questions but knew they would dog her until she answered them.

"You cannot begin to imagine it. My uncle is my sole surviving family member. I was raised at least partially overseas, in nearby Montevaro with a short time in Mevendia, but my formative years were not here. I wish they had been. My uncle did everything in his power to manipulate a young girl who had lost her beloved parents and brother at a young age. He took the opportunity to install his own people throughout most of the palace. When I returned, he hid me away, practically a prisoner in my quarters. He claimed it was due to a threat on my life. My every move was watched. I was led to believe many things that were not true. I know better now, and I pray that does not make the people think less of me, but when you are told one thing from the time you are five years old, it is not easy to change your thinking."

"What are you doing to ensure there is no further threat to your person or to the country as a whole?"

The queen rested a delicate hand on Alexander's knee. "Alexander has worked closely with the members of security my uncle could not fire, namely my head of security. They worked tirelessly behind the scenes and continue to seek out any information leading to sleepers involved in the plots but not yet brought to justice."

The line of questioning continued for several more minutes before Matthew turned to him. "Alexander, tell us a bit about yourself. Most citizens of Ravenzario have no idea who you are."

Alexander chuckled. "There's not much to tell, I'm afraid. I'm just a guy who fell in love with an amazing woman who happens to be a queen."

"What was life like growing up in the States? You are from the Midwest, correct?"

"Yes. My twin brother and I were born and raised in Serenity Landing, Missouri, a town near Springfield. We spent most of our teen years in Los Angeles, then returned to Serenity Landing at twenty. We both attended Serenity Landing University and have our MBAs. I moved here to run the property on Bianisola, where the queen and I were married the other day. My brother stayed in Missouri to run a family business there."

"In recent days, your family has been compared to the Kennedys. Do you find that comparison accurate?"

Alexander couldn't begin to understand the comparison. No one in his family had ever been in politics. Even he wasn't. "Not really. We don't live in Camelot, for instance, and aren't involved in politics. The men in my family are well known for their fidelity to their wives, going back generations, and even prior to marriage. We were raised, as were my father and grandfather, to believe that there was one special woman out there for each of us, and our fidelity began long before we ever met."

Despite all the opportunities he'd had, Alexander had been a virgin on his wedding night. Something he was not ashamed of in the slightest.

"Why Ravenzario? Why didn't you stay in Serenity Landing instead of your brother? Or with your brother?"

Alexander shrugged. "I've always loved this part of the world. I'll even admit the presence of the queen was a draw. We'd only met a couple of times before I moved here permanently but I was already smitten." She looked up, and he gave her a tender grin. "In fact, you could say I've been twitterpated for quite some time."

9

Twitterpated? What on earth was he talking about?

After Matthew spent several minutes talking with Alexander, he returned to Christiana, asking a number of questions about legislation and other official business. Then he asked about the response to the wedding.

"I have not seen any of it," she told him with a shake of her head. "I seldom pay attention to the press. Given life as a celebrity for any reason, you learn to take everything in the media with a grain of salt. Most do a good job of reporting the news fairly, but I would never have time to trawl around online looking for stories about myself. I have no desire to do so. My assistant will let me know when she's come across something of interest, but I rarely seek them out."

Matthew pulled out his tablet. "Do you mind if we looked at a few?"

Christiana shook her head. "Of course not, though we do reserve the right to request you not ask certain questions."

With a nod, he opened the first photo. "This is the two of you immediately following the pronunciation of man and wife. What was going on here?"

Alexander's voice rumbled through her. "I wanted to kiss my bride, but tradition dictates the first kiss comes on the balcony. Instead, I chose to kiss her forehead, which is apparently acceptable." She looked up to see his grin offsetting the words. "Gotta say, I'm kind of glad that's the only time there's a rule about when I can kiss my wife."

Matthew chuckled. "Prince Alexander, what do you expect your primary duties will be?"

"For the next two months, I will accompany the queen on her tour of Ravenzario. After that, I may continue to help my parents with the properties until they have someone to take my spot. I plan to spend most of my time assisting the queen in whatever capacity she needs me to."

"Do you have any charities you'd like to support?"

"I already support a number of charities, both here and abroad."

"In the States?"

"A few. Some are based in the States, but their focus is elsewhere. Convoy of Hope, for instance, is based near my hometown, but they do great work around the world, particularly in the aftermath of natural disasters. I plan to find some new ones, of course. Those announcements will be made when the time is right."

He remained so comfortable. Would she ever learn how to do that? She could fake it, but he wore his skin much more comfortably than she did.

"What about a family?" Matthew looked back and forth between the two of them. It took everything in Christiana not to squirm. Queens did not squirm. She learned that lesson well from Queen Alexandra of Montevaro.

Fortunately, her husband answered for both of them. "We both want a family, when the time is right. However, that is something for us to decide together, and we will let the people of Ravenzario know when the time comes."

"Sooner rather than later?" Matthew pressed.

Christiana decided it was her turn. "Matthew, how would you feel if your mother-in-law asked you those questions, much less someone you do not really know, regardless of the potential news value?"

"Touché, Your Majesty." He gave a deferential nod. "Now, a question about another family. At the wedding, you were walked down the aisle by a man identified only as Poppo. Other members of the wedding party are identified only by their first names. Can you tell us who they are, and what your relationship is with them?"

"Poppo and David, his grandson who was the ring bearer, came to see us at the palace a few weeks ago as part of a Royal Scout troop." Christiana felt a real smile cross her face. "Poppo and I had a few minutes to talk, and I realized something. I had long lamented the fact I had no one to walk me down the aisle. The now-former King Jedidiah is the closest thing I have ever had to a real father in many years, but that did not seem right. Then I realized, I do have family. Not necessarily in the traditional sense, but the people of Ravenzario are my family. I asked Poppo if he would walk me down the aisle." A tear streaked down her cheek. "He told me he remembered my parents' wedding and that I reminded him of my mother. I have few memories of my parents that are actually *mine* and not culled from news pieces or magazine pictures." She wiped away another tear with one, now shorter, manicured nail. "I know there are many, many people who remember my parents far better than I do, and I was honored to have one of them stand in for my father."

"Will you be seeing Poppo and his family on your tour?"

"I am not certain if we will or not. We plan to keep in touch with them, but the schedule for the tour was set quite some time ago." Christiana looked up to see Diana walk in and make a "wrap it up" motion with her finger. "I am being told that our time is up, Matthew. Thank you for taking the time to sit down with us."

He nodded to her. "Thank you, Your Majesty." Then Alexander. "Your Royal Highness."

They stood, Alexander with his left arm around her as he shook Matthew's hand. Together, they were projecting a much more united and comfortable front than the reality behind closed doors. The reality was Christiana had seldom seen her husband while on board the yacht. Was he avoiding her? Giving her time to adjust and respecting her space?

Or was there more to it?

Christiana pushed those thoughts out of her head. He had given her no reason to think that. In fact, she had done her research. There had never been any serious allegations of infidelity against any of the men in his family. A moment of small talk, and they moved on. Lunch would be served with students from the local schools joining them.

As they walked around the campus with the high school students, Christiana noted how good Alexander was with the young men. When they reached the gymnasium, her husband played basketball with several of them. He was a good shot.

"He's cute, Your Majesty."

Christiana turned to the young woman standing next to her. "He is, is he not?"

"Don't you ever use contractions?" The blonde girl sat on the bottom of the bleachers.

"Pardon?"

"Contractions. Don't. Can't. Won't. Isn't. I don't think I've ever heard you use one."

Christiana tilted her head. "I have never thought about it. I spent many of my school years in Montevaro. Their royal family was my closest friends. Queen Mother Alexandra has very strict ideas about what is proper for a member of any royal family.

Contractions do not exist in her household. I would imagine I picked up on that."

"You should loosen up a bit. Be a bit more casual. I think people would like you more."

Something about the words cut Christiana to the core. "People do not like me?"

The girl shrugged. "I don't think they *dis*like you, but like you said. You didn't grow up here. We all know it was your uncle being manipulative. Now we do anyway, but I remember my parents saying they wished you were here because how would you know how to be queen if you'd never lived here."

"Sadly, that sentiment does not surprise me. I do hope I can change some of that thinking while I am on this tour."

"I hope so." The girl spoke frankly. "I like you. I hope everyone else does, too." She nodded toward Alexander who held his hands above his head in victory as his shot went cleanly through the hoop. "Plus, you married a really cute guy."

"I did not marry him because he is cute." Her husband started toward them with the young men at his side.

The girl flashed a grin. "I'm sure you didn't, but it is a nice bonus."

Alexander held out a hand to help her up. Did she imagine the tingle that ran up her arm as his fingers curled around hers? She squeezed his hand.

He really was pretty cute, wasn't he?

Alexander followed Queen Christiana up the gangplank back onto the yacht. Overall, it had been a good day. He'd enjoyed his time with his wife. He always did, but seeing her first with the young children and then with the teens, he caught a glimpse of their future. What he hoped their future would be.

"Your Majesty?" He stopped her before she went into her suite.

She sighed. "We are alone, Alexander. You are my husband."

"Would you do me the honor of joining me for dinner?"

She hesitated.

"Please?" She wanted him to call her something less formal, but wasn't sure about joining him for dinner?

"Of course." She gave him a tentative smile and closed the door behind her.

Alexander went to the galley to see what he could find. The cook, Paul, was in there working on dinner for the crew.

"Can I help you, sir?" Paul looked up from carrots he chopped on a cutting board.

"I'd like to have a romantic dinner with the queen tonight. Candles on deck, good china, the whole nine yards."

Paul's face lit up. "Of course. What do you have in mind?"

Alexander shrugged. "I'm open to suggestions. I know it's too late for you to shop. What do you have?" They spent ten minutes going over dinner options before they settled on an entrée, side dishes, and dessert that could be prepared in the next hour. Alexander offered to help, but Paul sent him away. A steward would take care of the table setting.

Instead, Alexander knocked on Christiana's door.

"Yes?"

"May I come in?"

The door opened. She had changed into something much more comfortable than she'd worn earlier in the day. Yoga pants with a rugby shirt from one of the country's universities and the Rensselaer family name on the back. "Is it time for dinner?"

Alexander shook his head. "No. Not yet. We have about an hour before it's ready. I did want to see if you wanted to dress up for dinner or dress down?"

He could see her turning it over in her head. "Would you mind if we dressed down? I am quite comfortable and would prefer not to get dressed up again."

"That's fine with me." With one finger, he touched the side of her face. "You always look beautiful."

A blush spread across her cheeks as she ducked her head. "Thank you. The girl I spoke with at the gymnasium told me she believed you were very cute."

He could feel the twinkle in his eyes as he leaned closer. "And you, Queen Christiana? Do you think I'm cute?"

Her face reddened further. "Yes."

"I'm glad." He turned, whistling as he walked away. "I'll see you in an hour." Despite her desire to dress down, he would wear one of several tuxedos he had with him. He wanted to woo her. He wanted to go all out and sweep her off her feet.

Nearly an hour later, he tweaked his bowtie as he waited for her to join him on the upper deck of the yacht. When her head came into view, he heard her gasp. The white twinkling lights provided the sole lighting, save the moon and two flickering candles on the table.

"Has the ship stopped?" she asked as she turned.

"Not completely, but we have slowed down so we could enjoy our meal by candlelight while not worrying about the candles blowing out."

"What did Paul make us for dinner?"

Alexander grinned. "That, my dear, is a surprise." He bowed to her with one hand outstretched. "May I have this dance?"

"There is no music."

As though on cue, soft jazz filled the air. "May I?"

Christiana put her hand in his. "Of course."

He pulled her to him, far closer than the other night. There was no one watching. No one but the two of them.

"I did not think we were going to dress up." The white lights behind him reflected in her eyes.

"I wanted you to be comfortable." He shrugged. "But I wanted to have a romantic, very nice, candlelit dinner with my wife. To me that means tux."

He pulled her a bit closer, loving the feel of her close to him.

They moved slowly around the deck. "Were you okay with the interview today? I'm sure you weren't ready for some of those questions."

"No. I was not. But I knew they would be coming sooner or later. I avoided planning my answers and hoped they would not, but they always do."

"I know I told you the other day, but I am so glad you asked Poppo and the others to participate." After the interview, thoughts that had been trying to coalesce in his mind since the wedding came closer to taking shape. The question became, could he pull off the idea without her knowing about it? And in the next eight weeks. Before the anniversary of her parents' death.

"I think I know why the interview was scheduled for today." She moved even closer to him, resting her cheek on his chest.

"Why is that?" He tucked her hand close and hoped her answer wasn't the same one he'd come up with.

"I was to be dead by now. It would have been his first interview as the bereaved king. A few days after my death but quickly enough it would help him establish legitimacy. It just furthers the idea that he did not know the specifics of Nicklaus's marriage contract or the Commonwealth's pact."

Alexander didn't know what to say so he just kept dancing.

"You had come to the same conclusion, had you not?"

"Yes, ma'am, we had. Or I had. I never discussed it with anyone else."

He sensed she wanted to say something about his continued formality in the way he addressed her, but she didn't. It made no sense to him why he kept on being formal with her, not coming up with a nickname or pet name for her. It seemed wrong somehow. Not when they weren't yet growing closer as people in a relationship for life. With his cheek against her hair, they danced for several more minutes. "Are you ready to eat?"

She nodded. He had every intention of dancing with her again before the end of the night. Alexander held her chair, before lifting the silver dome off the platters and setting them to the side.

"Do you mind if I pray over the meal?" They hadn't eaten together much. Most of the crew of the yacht didn't know much about either the situation or what life was like for them on board. She and Alexander were left alone.

"Please go ahead."

He held her hand as they bowed their heads. A few brief words of thanks, and they began to eat.

10

"Tell me your favorite part of today?" Alexander asked her as she took a bite.

Christiana thought about that as she chewed then took a sip of her wine. "Talking with the girls at the school, I think. Or playing with the children at the orphanage. They have lost so much but are still so happy. I love that. What was your favorite?"

"Seeing you with those kids," he answered without hesitation. "You were a natural."

Her eyes widened. "Me? A natural with children? I have not been around them much. Not even when I was one."

"Then you are a natural because they adored you, and it was clear you adored them." He appeared to be considering something else to say. "In fact, based on what I saw today, I believe you will be a wonderful mother."

She could not contain her incredulity. "You do? Me?"

Alexander nodded. "Do you want to know what I saw while I watched you with them?" Taking her rapid blinking as assent, he went on. "I saw us, in your apartment at the palace. You were rocking a toddler as you both looked out over the sea. I looked down and saw, in my arms, an infant. Two children, conceived together, borne of our commitment to each other. The continuation of your family line. A family of your own, something you've never had."

His image blurred. "You saw me? As a mother?"

He covered her hand with his. "Yes."

"You see us with children?" She knew, on some level, it was required of them. They were required by law, after all, to begin trying to conceive as soon as possible. But the actuality of it was quite foreign to her. She never imagined herself as a mother, holding a child.

He gave her a tender smile. "Yes. I do. Someday." Alexander picked up her hand and gently kissed the back. "When the time is right, you're going to be a wonderful mother."

She did not say anything, but began to eat again.

The rest of the meal passed in near silence until Alexander asked her to dance again. Christiana shook her head. "No. I am quite tired. I believe I will turn in for the evening." He stood and held her chair for her. He really did look quite dashing in his tuxedo. "Thank you for a lovely meal." Before he could say or do anything, she turned and walked away. She waited until she was out of his site to pick up the pace and nearly run to her suite. The suite she should be sharing with the man she had just left. The man who was invoking feelings in her she did not know how to deal with. As they danced, she had wanted him to tip her chin up, to kiss her, to hold her even closer.

But at the same time, she was not ready to open herself up for the hurt that could come from allowing someone into her life.

She wanted it while at the same time actively repelling the very connection she longed for.

The restless night that followed was the last they would spend at sea. For the next three weeks they would tour Corsisnos followed by five weeks on Ichnusia. And those nights, she would be expected to sleep in the same room with her husband. Eight weeks until she could escape to separate quarters.

How could she handle being in the same room with the man so often, much less sharing the same bed, without her fragile heart being severely compromised?

The answer was she could not, but she would have no choice.

All too soon, their time on the yacht ended and they entered the first of many hotel rooms.

"Queen Christiana?"

She looked up from where she sat at the desk in the hotel room. For over an hour she had looked through information on charities and approved them followed by signing checks drawn up based on the approvals she had made last month. Alexander stood there, but not dressed as she had last seen him.

No.

He wore a pair of pajama bottoms emblazoned with the emblem of a sports team from the States. She was not familiar enough with them to venture a guess as to which sport, much less which team.

Her husband wore no shirt.

After three swallows, she attempted to speak. "Yes?"

"I am ready to turn in. We haven't talked about the sleeping arrangements now that we're staying at hotels, but I don't see how we could get a separate room without drawing undo attention to ourselves and our relationship. However, I don't want to make you uncomfortable. Our options are for both of us to sleep in the fairly large bed, or I can sleep on the couch."

Christiana glanced at the couch to her right. She had sat down on it when they first arrived. She would not wish for anyone to be forced to sleep on it. Ever.

"We are both adults. We can share." She turned back to the work at hand, not wanting to give the conversation more time to turn awkward. "Besides, we are married. It is hardly inappropriate."

"Hardly so, but are you truly all right with that?"

"Given the comfort one is likely to find on that couch, I have little alternative but to be all right with it. I fully expected this to be the situation. If you are ready to retire for the evening, do not wait up for me. I have a bit more work to do before I can turn in." The goodwill tour was going well, very well if the press coverage was to be believed. Spending most of her days in parades in each of the towns they visited or ribbon cuttings at grocery stores or spending time with children at a hospital meant she had little time for the rest of her work until after retiring to the yacht or now the hotel for the evening.

"Very well. Please don't stay up too late, ma'am. You need your rest and you have not been sleeping well."

How could he presume to know that? He would surely figure it out now that they shared a bed, but up until now?

"You look tired." He answered her unspoken questions. "I doubt anyone else notices, but I do."

Of course he did.

She heard his footsteps travel into the bedroom and then came the sound of sheets rustling as he settled in. As quickly as she could, because he did have a point, Christiana finished signing the checks. Already wearing her pajamas, she went into the bedroom, not surprised to find him asleep. Tiptoeing to the other side of the bed, she slid under the covers taking great care not to disturb him. She breathed a sigh of relief as she appeared to be successful. She would do her best to sleep well.

But the sound of Alexander's even breathing, so close and yet so far away, did more to keep her awake than even the largest cup of coffee would have.

When would she feel comfortable enough to let her guard down?

And if never, what would that mean for her future?

Feeling very lonely, despite not being alone, Christiana closed her eyes and prayed for sleep.

Alexander didn't move a muscle when the other side of the bed dipped slightly under the queen's slight frame. He could tell she had a difficult time getting comfortable, and over half an hour passed before he could sense her relax and finally fall asleep. With that, he rolled onto his back to stare at the ceiling.

Having her so close, and still so far, was a cruel kind of torture. He thought he'd felt something shift for the better when they danced, but something changed over dinner. Perhaps his comments about having a family caused her to draw away. Until a few minutes earlier, he had not seen her in private since. She met him at the gangplank. They went about their day. Happy, smiling faces put on for the crowds. They returned to the yacht and she went straight to her room, having a tray delivered for dinner.

This day had started out the same as every day the week before, but instead of returning to the yacht, they stayed at the premiere hotel in the capital city of Pagosa. Though the palace was less than two miles away, this represented the first part of the land based portion of the tour. As such, the decision had been made - long before it was known he would be her companion - to stay at a hotel.

Perhaps it was because *he* had planned to be renovating the monarch's apartments in the palace after her death?

Alexander didn't like to think about the woman lying beside him succumbing to the evil plot of the man she was to have married. Instead, he decided to focus on praying for her. Repeatedly in the Bible, husbands were instructed to love their wives, to care for them, to pray for them. He couldn't love her like he wanted to, and he didn't think she'd let him take care of her. Besides, she had "people" for that. She didn't need him.

But he could pray.

No one would pray for her like he could.

With his eyes closed, he decided it was time to boldly approach the throne of grace, to ask the Creator for favor, for Him to work in both of their hearts and lives until they were the people God intended for them to be.

By the time he awoke, he could hear the shower running in the attached bathroom. Alexander yawned and stretched before swinging his legs over the side of the bed. The water stopped as he headed for the sitting area.

"Good morning, sir." Justin shot a half-grin at him. "Sleep well?"

His assistant knew he hadn't been sleeping in the same room as his wife. "Fine. Why are you here?" At least when they returned to the palace they could lock people out of the apartment instead of having assorted assistants waiting when they woke up.

"I wanted to give you an update on the project." Justin held out a tablet.

Alexander swiped the screen with his finger, looking over the details for several minutes. "It looks good. Think we can pull it off?"

"I think so."

"Good." He handed the tablet back over. "We have an hour before breakfast?"

"Yes, sir."

"Thanks for your help." Knowing they were done for the moment, Justin turned and left. The door to the bedroom opened and the queen walked into the sitting area. Her hair hung around her shoulders, still damp, though she wore a nice shirt and slacks.

One of these days he'd get her to wear a pair of ratty jeans and an old t-shirt. Maybe one of his, and a baseball hat with her pony-tail tugged through it.

Somehow he doubted it'd ever happen.

But a guy could dream.

"Why are we here again?" Yvette had a whine to her voice.

Lizbeth stifled a sigh. "We're here because Princess Anastasia is sick, no one else from their family can be here, but they wanted a contingent from Belles Montagnes. Then we're going to Bianisola to work on wedding plans."

The orphanage in Ravenz-by-the-Sea had been rebuilt along with most of the rest of the town after the flooding during a medicane the year before. Now, they were having a celebration. As bad as it was, it could have been so much worse. Dr. Jonah Fontaine, now a duke with his marriage to Princess Anastasia, was there along with their adopted daughter, Stacy, who had survived the medicane with them the year before.

Officially, they were gathering supplies to take to an orphanage in Africa, one Dr. Jonah had been to many times. In reality, Lizbeth was glad for the excuse to spend the previous night with Robert. At the moment, she had no idea when her next chance to spend that much time alone with him would be.

They spent two hours working with Dr. Jonah and others before returning to the hotel to get ready for the trip to Bianisola.

Alexander was waiting for them in his office when they arrived.

"Thank you for taking time to see us, sir." Lizbeth shook his hand before they all sat down.

"Of course. Today is basically an off day for us. One stop this morning at breakfast, one at dinner, and nothing in between. I'm happy to stop by and go over what you've decided. We can talk more about the timeline and what decisions need to be made by when. I know you've known the date of the wedding for a long time, but, Princess Yvette, you've just started wrapping your mind around the idea that you actually have to plan this thing. So why don't we start with what you've done since I saw you a few weeks ago?"

Yvette just sort of sat there while Lizbeth went over the few things they had already decided. Not much. Lizbeth had vetoed several of the choices with just a glare. She was *not* going to let Yvette even pretend to plan for a black wedding dress and veil. The decisions that had been - things like time of day, preliminary VIP guest list, songs to be played during the wedding - had been done with the help of the palace protocol officer. All of those were dictated by tradition. As much as Yvette wanted to break some of the royal molds, she wouldn't be able to. Not with this anyway.

Alexander nodded as Lizbeth finished. "Good." He gave Yvette what could only be described as a "dad look." The prince did it well. "You need to find a dress. Soon. Despite your status, it's not something that can be whipped out at the last minute. Queen Christiana had a last minute change in her dress, and it added years to the lives of everyone involved, even though we all knew the decision was for the best."

Yvette had perked up at that. "What? That wasn't the dress she planned to wear all along? It was gorgeous."

He shook his head but refused to elaborate, instead he went over the next few steps they would need to complete by the end of the year for the June wedding date.

"I don't even have a ring," Yvette groused. "If I'm engaged shouldn't I at least have a ring?"

"The queen didn't have one until the wedding," Lizbeth pointed out. "There are lots of good reasons why people don't sometimes."

"Most of them don't have a dead fiancé," she muttered. Then louder, "Why didn't you give Christiana one sooner?"

The prince consort hesitated for a split second before answering. "I wanted to use her mother's ring, and I couldn't get a hold of it until right before the wedding."

Made sense. Half an hour later, they all stood at the door, ready to leave. They started to walk out, but Yvette turned. "I love what you're doing for her, Alexander. I'm a lot younger than Christiana, but I remember when she'd stay with us sometimes, and how sad she'd be at Christmas and stuff. She'll love it."

Alexander shifted, clearly uncomfortable. "Please don't say anything to her. It's a surprise, and so far we've managed to keep it from her."

Yvette nodded then shocked both of them by throwing herself at the prince consort. He caught her in a hug. "Take good care of her," Yvette whispered. "This wedding thing is going to be harder for her than me. I'm glad she has you."

As quickly as she'd started the hug, Yvette let go and nearly ran out toward the tarmac nearby. Lizbeth smiled as she watched the girl. That was the Yvette she was getting to know. The one who cared more about others than herself. The one who would get her heart broken when the wedding didn't happen, even if she'd never admit it. The romance of the long lost prince returning just in time for the wedding couldn't be denied.

"This is going to be tough for both of them," he said.

Lizbeth looked up to see Alexander watching Yvette's retreat as well. "Then we'll have to make sure they're not alone during it."

Alexander nodded, and Lizbeth moved to leave, but his hand on her arm stopped her. "She has to take this seriously, Lizbeth. Don't let her blow it off or be half-heartedly involved. She'll regret it, and so will everyone else."

She nodded, but before she said anything a throat cleared on the other side of the room. Alexander released her. "Let me know if I can help in anyway. Have a safe trip home." He turned to leave.

Lizbeth watched him go. Something more was going on here. But what?

Seventeenth Anniversary

Today is a day that needs no reminder. It is the day King Richard, Queen Marissa, Prince Nicklaus, and their nanny died in a tragic car accident, making five-year-old Princess Christiana the youngest monarch in Ravenzario's history. For the next fifteen years, the country was run in her stead by the brother of Queen Marissa. Approximately eighteen months ago, Henry Eit's plot to overthrow the queen came to light. Though the specter of her uncle no longer surrounds Queen Christiana, the seventeenth anniversary is likely to be a difficult one for the monarch.

The queen and duke are scheduled to lay flowers at the marker where the car disappeared over the edge of a cliff. Tonight is the reception discussed online for the last several weeks. For more information, please see the news story from November 1. 2016.

It would be a difficult day no matter what was planned. She purposely avoided looking at her plans for December 23. Someone, she still did not know who, had juggled the schedule a bit so that the visit to Ariston would be the last one before returning to Pagosa and the palace on Christmas Eve. It was supposed to have been a few days earlier. The country was not so big that trading two towns would cause much disruption in travel plans.

After breakfast in the town where they had spent the night, they waved to the few people who gathered to see them off. But instead of getting into the back of the limo where they usually

CAROL MONCADO

traveled, Alexander took her hand and led her to a little black roadster.

He held open the passenger side door, kissing her cheek as she slid into the seat. A minute later, they waved again to the few members of the press as they pulled out of the parking lot.

"Where did this come from?" she asked once they were out of town.

"I had someone bring it from my place." He smoothly upshifted into the next gear. "I thought it would be fun to drive together, just the two of us."

Did he know what day it was? How difficult it would be? Much less driving along the same stretch of road?

Part of her wished for the top down and the wind whipping through her hair but the late December day was too cold for that. The miles and curves flew past as they wound their way through the countryside. A car stayed in front of them at all times, another stayed behind. Security. Probably Tony. He would not leave her security to anyone else. Not this day. Likely there was at least two other cars somewhere with assorted other personnel.

"What is on our agenda today?" She should have checked despite her reservations, but instead she had spent extra time in the shower, letting the water cover the sound of her tears.

"We have a stop to make, then we'll meet with Poppo and the rest of the family for lunch. They're finishing a Christmas present drive. We're going to help them wrap presents and make sure all of them are labeled properly to be delivered tomorrow. After a late snack with the workers there, we're scheduled to help serve dinner at a local soup kitchen. Our own dinner will be a banquet this evening. Not a big one, but about a hundred people or so. Poppo put it together."

Big enough. All she really wanted to do was skip spending the night in Ariston and go back to the palace. There, she could sneak a carton of ice cream out of the freezer, soak in the Jacuzzi tub, and wallow until the day ended. Not very befitting a queen but what she wanted to do.

Instead, she would put on her happy face once more.

Christiana did not know for certain where the section in the road was and she was not sure she wanted to know. The spot where her parents' car, driven by her father much like Alexander did now, hit a patch of ice and slid off the side of the road and down the cliff into the river below.

Alexander slowed the car down considerably as they came to a turn. He pulled off onto a small parking lot on the side of the road. Next to the small gravel lot was a concrete marker with a bronze plaque on top.

This was it.

The spot.

Where her whole life changed.

She stared across the valley at the trees on the other side, willing the tears to stay in place. Alexander opened the door for her, taking her hand when she finally felt ready.

"Have you ever been here?" he asked quietly, keeping his hand around hers.

Christiana had to clear her throat twice before she could speak. "No. I may have driven past when I was too young to realize where I was, but to my knowledge, I never have been."

He led her to the plaque. She reached out and ran her fingers over the inscription.

In Loving Memory
King Richard George Louis V and Queen Consort Marissa
Christiana
Their son, Crown Prince Nicklaus David Richard Antonio,
and Michaela Engel, beloved nanny
December 23, 1999
May their Maker receive them into His loving arms
We are poorer for having lost them so young

We are richer for having them as long as we did
Commissioned on behalf of their beloved daughter
Queen Christiana Elizabeth Marissa Abigail I

"Who had this put here?" *Not my uncle. Please not my uncle.*

"I believe the Prime Minister at the time had it commissioned on your behalf."

She felt a breath of relief leave her body.

"I thought you might like to lay some flowers?"

"We do not have any."

Alexander squeezed her hand and turned, motioning to someone. She looked to see Diana bringing over the bouquet Christiana made the day before with some children. She'd thought they were for a Christmas pageant.

Christiana took it from her, not bothering to stop the tears streaming down her cheeks.

"Usually, the Prime Minister comes for a flower laying ceremony, but I thought you might want to today." He wrapped an arm around her shoulder, pulling her tight to his side and kissing the side of her head.

"You were right." She had never thought about it, never even knew there was a marker here. Alexander helped her fit the flowers in the vase put there for just such a purpose. After a minute of fussing with them, trying to get them "just so", she moved to the side of the marker. Her hands rested on the railing as she stared across the valley. It took everything in her not to look down, to see the actual spot where it all came to a screeching halt.

Alexander moved behind her, his arms wrapping around her waist. His chest solid against her back. Here, in the place where her parents and brother died, she felt safe and protected. Something she rarely felt, even before the plots came to light. When she was still oblivious.

Did she have to leave his arms?

She did not want to, but she could not stay in this place any longer.

"I am ready to go." Christiana moved away from Alexander and headed for the car.

When they had made their way another mile down the road, he spoke. "Was it too much?"

With a shake of her head, she replied. "No. It was good. I just could not take it any longer."

"I understand." Another mile passed in silence. "We will stop at the hotel room first and freshen up. Poppo and the family will meet us for lunch in the private dining room."

"Thank you, Alexander. I appreciate all you have done for me."

He took her hand in his and brought it to his lips, kissing her knuckles above her wedding ring. "My pleasure, Your Majesty. As your husband, it's my job to do those things for you. I am glad to."

HER HUSBAND. The man who had slept in the same bed with her for two months, rarely coming in contact with her. But today, he hoped to ease some of the pain buried deep inside. The pain she let no one see, but he knew existed.

A few minutes later, he pulled to the rear of the hotel. They had purposely shared misinformation with the public and the press. He knew she wouldn't want anyone to see her after a crying jag. From there, they went into a nearly empty corridor to an elevator and then to the plush royal suite they would call home for the night.

His wife disappeared to the bedroom and into the bathroom beyond without saying anything else to him.

"Is she okay?" Diana walked in, satchel in one hand, coffee in the other.

"She will be."

"Thank you, sir. If the people knew how much pain the death of her parents still caused her, it would rip their hearts to shreds." She glanced through the open door to make sure the queen was still gone. "That's why tonight will be such a success."

"Thank you again for all your help with the arrangements."

"My pleasure, sir." She headed for the bedroom. "I'm going to help her get ready for the luncheon."

Diana took good care of the queen. Somehow, despite the machinations of her uncle, people who cared deeply for Queen Christiana surrounded her. The next hour flew by and before he knew it, her hand was tucked in the crook of his arm as they walked into the private dining room. The first person he saw, the first person he knew she saw, was Poppo.

Poppo held open his arms and the queen gladly ran into them. Alexander had no problem releasing his wife into the other man's embrace. Turning, he shook hands with the rest of the family members, giving Mrs. Engel a kiss on each cheek.

Five-year-old Annie tugged on his shirtsleeve. "Are you a king now?"

He knelt on the ground next to her. "Nope. Even though I married the queen, she's the one in charge, not me, so I don't get to be king, and I'm just fine with that."

"Are you a prince then?"

Alexander nodded. "I am. And I'm a duke, too." He still didn't quite understand the reasoning behind that title, but it officially belonged to him.

"I'm glad you married Queen Christiana. She's nice. You're nice, too."

"Thank you, Annie." He kissed her cheek. "You're super nice. I like you."

Whoever did the seating arrangements set it up so he was

nowhere near Christiana. He wished to be seated next to her, but there were reasons for it. Even though he knew that, he couldn't keep from watching her closely.

There was a new sadness around her eyes, but there seemed to be a bit of hope in them as well. She laughed with Poppo and Nanny. He wished he could be the one to illicit that kind of response from her more often. One day he would.

He enjoyed talking with Poppo's daughter and son-in-law. The lunch wasn't one where they would linger. The whole family would accompany him and the queen to a local rec center where they would wrap presents for several hours. The knots in his stomach tightened every time he thought about the plans for the gathering later in the evening. Alexander hoped it wouldn't be too much and overwhelm her.

They did ride together to the rec center, though Poppo and his wife accompanied them. The parade through town was similar to so many others before it. He was proud of his wife, putting on her smiley face and waving, doing her best to make eye contact with each of those lining their route. He would do his best to keep her busy to keep her mind off the significance of the date.

It was also the anniversary of the day she became queen. Seventeen years since she became the monarch of Ravenzario. Had they ever celebrated that? Had she ever had a real coronation?

These were things he needed to look into. To see what he could do without making her uncomfortable or the people feel either one of them was being pretentious. They pulled up in front of the rec center. He and the queen both spent several minutes shaking hands with and talking to the children gathered in the foyer. Several of them gave her flowers that she gushed over. Alexander was getting to know her well enough to know she was genuinely thankful for them.

The later it got, the more his stomach tied in knots. Tonight needed to go perfectly. It would be difficult enough for his wife anyway. He wanted to make it better, not worse. It was too late to change the plans, though. So he prayed for grace, and for it to go well.

So the queen could finally remember the things she'd never been able to before.

11

Christiana wished she knew Alexander well enough to have him find a way to get out of the dinner reception. Really, she wished he knew her well enough to get her out of it without needing to ask. Instead, she slid a deep blue silk wraparound dress on, tying it on the side before slipping into heels.

Last year, she had spent this day wallowing like she never had before. Finally out from under her uncle's thumb.

She was asked to put flowers at their gravesites, but refused. She wished this year could be the same. When she walked out into the living room, Alexander sat in one of the chairs with a tablet, scrolling through something.

"Anything interesting?" She settled into a chair across from him.

"You know there have been a few official pictures released every day, right?" When she nodded, he went on. "Hundreds of others haven't been released. We've been approached about putting together a coffee table photo book telling our love story through Christmas this year." She started to protest, but he held up a hand. "I just found out about it. Diana and Justin said they wanted details before passing it on to us to decide. The proceeds would go to a charity or charities we designate. The photographer gave me access to all of the shots he's taken since the Royal Scouts meeting."

Christiana did not know what to think so she asked his opinion.

"I think we should consider it. Skip the love story part, mostly. Perhaps include a few pictures from our earlier lives and start the day we agreed to get married. There are some great shots."

"When do we need to decide?"

"Soon, I think. They'd like to release it as a commemorative edition for our first anniversary but these things take time. I can ask Justin when they need to know for sure." He set the tablet on the side table and stood up. "Are you ready?"

"Do we have to?" Christiana knew she sounded like a whiny child.

Alexander held out his hands. She took them and allowed herself to be pulled to her feet and into his arms. Resting her head against his chest, with his arms around her, she felt safe. She never wanted to leave.

"We have to go." She felt him press a kiss to the top of her head. "I promise it'll be worth your time."

A discreet knock at the door ended the moment. She moved back and turned, needing to put some distance between them. A minute later, they rode down the elevator and walked into the hotel ballroom. Just before they entered, Alexander slid his hand around hers, the warmth lending calm to her frazzled nerves.

The voice over the loudspeakers introduced them. The doors in front of them opened. Rather than the applause and line of people she expected, the room was nearly silent. Everyone stood next to their chairs, but they just watched as she and Alexander moved through the room. Some smiled, some bowed their heads, but all remained quiet. It was more than a bit disconcerting.

They reached the front of the room, where the head table sat on a dais. Poppo's family stood there along with a few others. In front was a stand of flowers, the kind you'd see at a funeral, with a ribbon across it. *In Loving Memory.* She glanced up at Alexander who let go of her hand and rested his on her back, using pressure to turn her toward a microphone set up on the side.

Poppo walked to the podium. "Your Majesty, tonight we have come together, here and around the country, as this is shown on a live television special, to remember some very special people. You told me once that you had few personal memories of your parents. Almost everything you remember about them comes from news programs or articles you found online. Tonight, we can't give you new personal memories, but we can share ours. Through the stories we tell this evening, we hope to give you a greater sense of why your parents were so beloved by the people of Ravenzario." Poppo moved to the side as Alexander guided her to their seats on the dais.

A slide show began to play on the screen behind the podium. Pictures of her parents popped up, one after the other. Starting as newborns and continuing through their childhoods and teenage years.

They met her mother's freshman year in college. From then on, most of the pictures were of the two of them together. Dating. Engaged. Several from their wedding. Christiana barely noticed the tears streaking down her cheeks until Alexander slipped her a handkerchief.

She wiped under one eye as a picture of her mother, looking radiant and very pregnant, came on the screen. It was followed by several others. Her parents were obviously very much in love. Next, a picture of her father holding her minutes after her birth. The rest of the slide show contained pictures of the two of them as well as some with her. Then her brother. Little Nicky who died far, far too young. Nicky who should have been king.

The last picture was of the four of them. She was five, and they were decorating the official Christmas tree. Her father had hoisted her up to put the star on top. Her mother, holding Nicklaus, watched as all four of them laughed.

The picture faded to a black screen with their names and dates of birth and death on it.

Christiana had mostly tuned out those in the crowd as she watched the pictures, but she had noticed some laughter and a few "aw" noises. Now the applause started. A minute later, it reached a crescendo as everyone stood. Alexander stood and moved past her toward the podium. Christiana stopped him with a hand on his arm. He held her chair as she stood. The applause died down as she took a spot behind the microphone.

"Ladies and gentlemen, thank you very much for being here tonight." She gripped both sides of the podium to steady herself. "As Poppo, Mr. Engel, said a few moments ago, I have few memories of my parents. Many of these pictures I had never seen before, and I thank you for bringing them to me. I hope you enjoy your meal and thank you again, from the bottom of my heart."

Polite applause followed her back to her seat. The first part of her meal was waiting for her when she returned. She spoke with both Alexander and the mayor seated on the other side of her. Dinner ended, and she thought they would leave, but instead, Poppo returned to the microphone.

"Your Majesty, two months ago, I had the honor and the privilege of walking you down the aisle at your wedding. I told you how much you reminded me of your mother. You both have such elegant grace and care for the people of Ravenzario in a way no one else does." He went on to tell about meeting her mother one time at the palace. "Tonight, several others are going to share their memories of your parents with you, Your Majesty. We know it will not replace memories of your own, but we hope to help make them a bit more real for you."

One after another about twenty people came to the podium and shared memories of her parents from all parts of their lives.

One of her mother's best friends from elementary school shared a funny story about throwing water balloons at their principal without anyone ever finding out their secret.

Her father had not attended a school but had a series of tutors over the years. One was not much older than he was. The tutor shared a story about how, instead of studying French, they snuck out, disguised themselves, and went to the pier for lunch. A couple even told stories of her little brother and their nanny.

Poppo returned to the podium when the last person finished. "Your Majesty, we know how overwhelming this must be and that you'll never remember all of these stories. Tonight's dinner has been recorded and will be available for you to watch, but..." Annie and David wound their way through the tables and up to her side. "All of these stories and many more are found in these books." She took a scrapbook from Annie and flipped it open to find page after page of stories. Some printed off from email, some on fine stationary with flowers around the borders, some childlike drawings. "There are many such books waiting for you when you return to the palace. If you look in the front of each one..." She did. "...there is a DVD with people telling their stories. Some are ones we arranged, others were sent in by those who loved your parents, by those who love *you*. Never doubt that, Your Majesty. Your father was a great monarch whose time was cut tragically short. You walk in his footsteps, and beyond and we, the people of Ravenzario, thank you."

Christiana gave Annie and David both a hug. Alexander stood and held her chair for her. He whispered in her ear. "We can stay and talk to people if you'd like, but everyone will understand if this has been too much, and you'd like to return to our room."

She nodded and made her way to the podium. "I said thank you earlier not knowing just how inadequate those words would be. From the very bottom of my heart, I thank all of you - those of you who could be here and those of you who joined us from afar. I look forward to spending many hours looking through the scrapbooks and watching the videos." She took a deep breath. "I do hope you understand when I say that I am completely over-whelmed and will bow out of any further activities this evening. I would like to invite all of you here tonight to a reception at the palace or another location sometime in the near future, when I will be able to more fully convey my gratitude. To all the people of Ravenzario, thank you."

She stepped back to find Alexander waiting for her. His arm wrapped securely around her waist as they exited out a rear door and into a cleared corridor. The walk to the elevator and then to their suite was silent, but as soon as the door closed behind them, Christiana flung herself into his arms.

One of Alexander's arms wrapped tightly around his wife while the other clicked the chain into place. For now, the rest of the world was locked out and it was just the two of them. Her tears soaked into his shirt as she sobbed. He lifted her easily into his arms and carried her to the sitting area. Once there, he set her on her feet, sat down, and then pulled her onto his lap. He held her until she moved away.

"Feel better?"

She nodded. "You arranged all of this?"

"I did. I hope it..."

Alexander's words were cut off by her kiss. Her lips on his, warm, soft, supple, expressive, as her hands framed his face. Try as he might, he couldn't help but kiss her back, pull her closer, and intensify the kiss as a soft moan fell from the back of her throat.

Logic told him he needed to slow things down. Desire told him this was where he wanted to spend the rest of his life

Reason said he should stop. Longing told him she was his wife, and if she wanted to kiss him, so be it.

Love told him he needed to be sure. He needed *her* to be sure.

"Christiana," he whispered as he moved away, dropping tiny kisses on the corner of her lips and trailing a line toward her ear. "Are you sure?"

"I want you to love me, Alexander. I want to love you the way my parents loved each other." She brushed his hair back off his face. "What you did for me tonight was incredible. I cannot begin to tell you how much I appreciate all you have done for me. I cannot begin to tell you what you..."

She kissed him again, but he pulled away. "If you want this, okay." His fingers tangled in her hair. "But if this is just something borne out of sorrow or gratitude or..."

Once again she stopped his words with her lips. The kiss grew even more intense as she shifted closer to him. When she moved away, they were both breathless, but she looked him straight in the eye. "I want to be your wife tonight, Alexander. I'm sure."

This time when she kissed him, he didn't try to stop her, didn't pull away, didn't fight the torrent of feelings unleashed inside him. With a mighty groan, he stood with her in his arms. He carried her to the bedroom, kicking the door closed behind him despite the chain on the front door. He set her on her feet next to the bed. Moonlight filtered in around the closed curtains. "Tonight, Christiana, tonight I want to be your husband."

The drive to the palace in the roadster was as quiet as the ride the day before. Despite everything they had shared once the doors to their suite closed behind them, Christiana did not know what to say to him in the light of day. It seemed Alexander struggled with the same thing as he said barely six words to her during the course of the trip. He seemed to be deep in thought about something, though she had no idea what.

As they approached the capital city, she could see the palace rising in the distance. She needed to say something.

"Thank you for last night, Alexander." She felt her cheeks color as it hit her what he could think she meant. "The dinner, the scrapbooks, all of it was incredible."

"I am glad you liked it, ma'am."

The title cut like a knife. She thought they were past all of that. After she kissed him, he called her "Christiana" twice before things went any further than kissing. When he kissed her hair as she fell asleep, he called her "sweetheart" but now the formality had returned. Would she ever feel loved for herself? Feel she could just *be* around him?

As they neared the palace gates, another crowd had gathered. She plastered on a smile and waved as they slowly drove through the people lining the street. Alexander parked the car under a portico leading into the administrative side of the building. Her main office was there as was Alexander's new one.

So much for thinking he would want to take her to their new home and, maybe, just maybe tell her he loved her. Then show her he did.

Instead, she went into her office to begin playing catch up with the correspondence that had piled up. Much of the important matters, she tended to in between functions or at night, but some had been put off.

"Your Majesty?"

Christiana waved Diana in. "Yes?"

Diana sat in one of the wingback chairs across the desk. "There are just a few things to cover. We do need an answer on the photo book by the end of the year. There is an official thank you letter we have to send to all of those who contributed to the books for last night. Would you like to sign them all personally or sign one and have it copied?"

"I would like to sign them all." Her hand would feel like it was about to fall off, but she could not let them have some copied or automatic signature. No. Those people had poured their hearts out for her. The least they deserved was an actual pen to paper signature. "Please be certain it says that I wish I could write each of them a personal note, and I hope to be able to do so in the future, but at the moment it is just not possible."

"It does."

"Thank you. I think I would like to start on them as soon as I can. I will not be able to do all of them in one sitting, of course, but perhaps we can have them ready to mail by the first of the year? I think I would like to send them as one bunch rather than several smaller bunches. We do not want anyone to feel slighted because they did not receive theirs in the first batch."

"I agree, ma'am."

They went over a few things before Diana left. Christiana decided she was done hiding completely from what the press had to say and opened one of the news sites on her tablet.

Queen Christiana Surprised by Memorial Dinner

Last night's memorial dinner for the late King Richard, Queen Marissa, Crown Prince Nicklaus, and his nanny, came as complete surprise to the reigning monarch, Queen Christiana. For the last eight weeks, the country, in conjunction with her new husband, Alexander, Duke of Testudines, conspired to keep a secret from the queen who seldom visits news sites unless directed to them for one reason or another. The stunt was pulled off in spectacular fashion. The event was shown live on our sister television network TCBC with roughly one-third of the homes in the country tuning in to see the events in the reception hall as well as the special that aired while those in attendance ate their meal. The queen released a statement earlier this morning thanking everyone for making a normally difficult day a bit easier and that she looks forward to reading through and watching all of the stories sent in.

The night was the last one on the road for the newlyweds who will return to the palace later today. They are expected to host the annual Christmas Eve ball later tonight and will spend Christmas together with the duke's family at his family's property on Bianisola where the two were married. They are not expected to stay the night.

THE ARTICLE WENT on to mention a bit more about Alexander's family, but Christiana just skimmed it.

She had forgotten about the Christmas Eve ball but she would need to get ready. Opening her appointment calendar, she noticed her stylist would be arriving in less than an hour. Forcing herself to focus, she rushed through the things she could, setting aside a number of others for a later time.

By the time she finished showering, her stylist waited. Mary had worked for her long enough Christiana knew she was a bit annoyed by the not-quite-dripping-wet hair. When on the road, Diana often helped her get ready when needed, but they were home now. Christiana closed her eyes and let the other woman work her magic. When Mary finished, Christiana checked her reflection in the mirror.

"Very nice, Mary. Thank you."

"You will be the belle of the ball tonight, ma'am."

Christiana stood and tightened her robe around her. "Thank you." She walked into the sitting room of her apartment to find Alexander walking in from the other bedroom. He wore a tuxedo, though not the coat or tie as yet. His face softened when he looked at her and he smiled. "You look beautiful from the neck up, Your Majesty. I look forward to seeing how beautiful you are in your gown."

There was a light, teasing tone to his voice, but something about it irked her. She gave him a tight smile and a nod before going into the other room where her ball gown waited. The shimmering pink was just right to set off her blond locks. The off-the-shoulder sleeves and short train would lend an air of elegance while not being so long as to be terribly cumbersome.

Mary had followed her and now assisted in sliding the dress on. The fabric clung to her like a second skin in all the right places. Though not an overly full skirt, it had plenty of room for her to walk and even dance easily.

Would Alexander ask her to dance again? Would it be more like the dances at their wedding? Or like the one on the top deck of the yacht? Or something else entirely, just as awkward as the rest of their encounters had been on this, the day after she truly became his wife? Because she wanted to not because of some ancient law that said she had to.

Would they continue to share a bed? Twenty-four hours earlier, she would have relished the chance to sleep apart once more, but now? Now she wanted to fall asleep in his arms and wake to the sound of his quiet snore. To his good morning kiss, something she had missed that morning when she woke to an empty and cold other side of the bed.

Had she committed a grievous error in trusting herself to Alexander? She doubted he would ever hurt her intentionally, but unintentionally, he held more power than she was comfortable trusting one person with.

She would have to find a way to fix that.

ALEXANDER FOUND himself aware of the queen in a way he never had been before, not even after their change in relationship status at their wedding.

The very brush of her skin against his as he used his left hand to help her settle hers in the crook of his right arm to escort her into the ball sent his senses reeling. How could he continue to keep up the happy couple façade when it tore him apart inside to know she had cried in her sleep the night before?

They were seated at the same place they always were, the center of the head table. Tonight, they were surrounded by leading members of government rather than local dignitaries. At other tables around the room, he spotted his family, and Poppo and his family. They were quickly becoming part of the queen's inner circle. For that, Alexander was grateful. She needed more people she could count on.

He was told the dance would normally begin with he and the queen dancing, but just a few minutes before it was to begin, she excused herself saying she would be back in a minute and not to wait for her.

What did that mean? Should he dance with someone else and if so, who? Or just allow the dance to start without the traditional first dance?

When she hadn't returned ten minutes later, the social secretary started to look antsy. Alexander motioned with his head for the woman to come over. He explained the situation as he understood it, but it didn't alleviate her concerns.

"No. The first dance has to be the queen's." She spoke into the ear piece she wore. "Someone find the queen, and let her know it's time for the dance. We need her in here."

For a moment, Alexander felt a bit sorry for Queen Christiana. The woman couldn't even use the restroom in peace. Before the thoughts could take hold, the queen entered through a side door he hadn't noticed. He stood and walked to her side as the orchestra started playing a traditional Christmas Carol.

"I believe they're playing our song." He held out a hand and tried to put a playful grin behind the words.

With her hand nestled in his, he walked out onto the dance floor. She didn't move as close as she had on the yacht, but she wasn't as far away as on their wedding day.

"Are you looking forward to tomorrow?" he asked, just to strike up a conversation.

"I do wish we were spending it here instead of at your family's place, but that is only because I would really like a day of rest. I am looking forward to seeing them."

They had been on the go for quite some time. Had she truly had a day off since the wedding? He thought back. No. And neither had he. Granted, most of what they did on Sundays was pretty low key. A service at the local church and a meal with local dignitaries, perhaps a visit with children in some form. But never a day off.

He would have to check the calendar for the day after Christmas, and see if he could arrange it. Turn off all alarms, pull the curtains more tightly shut than normal and let her sleep until she naturally awakened. If it couldn't be pulled off then, he'd have to find a day that would work. He'd put Justin and Diana on it.

When the music came to an end, he bent down and brushed a kiss against her cheek. "Merry Christmas Eve, Your Majesty."

She bowed her head in acknowledgment as Prime Minister Caruso came forward to claim the next dance.

As Alexander expected, his dance card was full. One dance after another with women of all ages. From the youngest in Annie to an octogenarian who told him what a wonderful thing he'd done to help the queen remember her parents. The great-grandmother three times over told him several stories about the queen's grandparents, who died many years earlier. In between, there were dances with women of all ages - and all manners of decorum. Most were wonderful. A few he was certain managed to slip their number into the pocket of his tuxedo jacket. He'd need to make sure to remove those and give them to Justin. Justin would have them checked out to make sure none of the women were an actual threat to him or the queen.

Alexander would also have Justin do his best to make sure they were never invited to another official function. No sense in being in the presence of those who would try to make him forget his wedding vows.

The last dance was also reserved for the queen. Though it wouldn't be only them on the dance floor this time, they would leave before the song ended, officially signaling the end of the ball.

And so, he found himself walking through the corridors of the palace with his wife. Her shoes dangled from his fingers after she'd slipped them off as soon as they reached a section of the palace where there would be no outsiders.

"Did you enjoy yourself?"

She nodded, and he noticed how weary she seemed. "I did. Thank you."

That was when he knew. Alexander had gone back and forth all day about whether he planned to sleep in the same bed with his wife, finally deciding to follow her lead. Tonight, she needed sleep without worrying about him and his expectations, even if he didn't have any.

They entered the apartment they now shared. He walked her to the door of her bedroom and dropped a chaste kiss on her forehead. "Sleep well." He glanced at the clock. After midnight. "Merry Christmas."

She looked up at him, studying his eyes for long seconds. "Thank you, Alexander. Sleep well." Turning, she walked into the room and shut the door behind her.

Alexander sighed and headed for one of the other bedrooms. He'd made his bed. Now it was time to lie in it.

13

Yvette sat curled up in a big chair in one of the less formal sitting rooms in the Mevendian palace. Presents had been opened that morning. The orphanage had been visited, just like every year.

Heavily pregnant, Jessabelle came to sit in the chair next to Yvette's.

"How are you feeling?" Her poor sister-in-law looked miserable.

"I'm ready for this baby to arrive," Jessabelle admitted. "I'm kind of over being pregnant."

"Are you ready to be a mom?" The mere thought petrified Yvette.

Jessabelle rested a hand on her belly. "I don't think anyone's ever ready, not really. But I think we're as ready as we can be." She smiled down as the bump in her stomach shifted. "Malachi is definitely ready. He's more excited than anyone I've ever seen."

Yvette nodded. Her older brother, the one she'd always looked to for protection and who cared about her more than anyone else, had shifted his allegiances. Rightly so, of course. His first priority should be his wife and now his child.

He hadn't been able to be there for her when Yvette needed him most the last year. Her world had been rocked with the news just like everyone else's. Her father was also Jessabelle's father. Her brother was really her half-brother and the result of a staff member - long in love with her father's mistress - exacting his revenge on their mother and getting her pregnant.

The whole situation had been used for good, Yvette supposed. Her mother had been considering leaving her father over the long-running affair. When the incident that led to Malachi's birth came to light, her father ended the affair, never knowing his mistress was pregnant. The child, Jessabelle, with help from Nana Yvette, was adopted by an old friend of the king's. Nana Yvette had also helped orchestrate the marriage between the two, bringing Jessabelle into the family fold despite her scandalous birth.

But there was no one for Yvette to turn to except maybe William, but he'd been absorbed in his own drama of some kind. She'd never figured out what it was.

Now, months later, they'd mostly settled into the new normal. Yvette rarely thought about it, except times like now.

Jessabelle's eyes closed as she rubbed her hand along her belly.

"You all right?"

Subtle strain lines appeared around her half-sister's eyes. "I think so. I'm not sure if it's indigestion or contractions or what, but it's annoying."

Yvette's attention was drawn elsewhere when the door opened and several other guests walked in, including Lizbeth and her boyfriend, Robert Padovano. With her history with Malachi, it kind of surprised Yvette she'd shown up, but given the looks exchanged between Lizbeth and Robert, they were closer than everyone realized. Lizbeth's father? Yvette hadn't seen him since her father kicked him out of the country house last April. She still didn't understand what happened there.

Yvette noticed Lizbeth staring at Jessabelle. Not for long. Just long enough for Yvette to notice a look of sadness and regret cross her face. The moment was broken when Robert slipped an arm around Lizbeth's waist and pulled her into his side. He whispered something as her eyes closed. If Yvette had to guess, she'd say Lizbeth was struggling to hold back tears. That didn't make any sense, though. Did it?

Regardless, the gentleness with which Robert treated her made Yvette wish for something that couldn't be.

That, in just a few months, she'd walk down the aisle to find, miraculously, Prince Nicklaus waiting at the other end and that, when times got tough, she'd be able to find comfort in his arms.

Tears now threatened her own eyes.

She'd long ago learned not to wish for things she couldn't have, like open affection from her father. He'd gotten better in the last six months, she could admit that, but it made her wish for more. It made wishes sneak up on her unexpectedly.

Like the wish that the prince from her past would somehow wind up in her future.

Lizbeth stood in front of a window in the palace, staring out over the capital city of Erres below.

"Feeling better?"

She didn't turn, seeing Robert walk toward her in the window instead. When she'd complained of not feeling well, the queen had insisted she go lay down in a guest room. Robert had stayed at the Christmas gathering.

Until now.

"I know it's hard, love." His arms slipped around her waist, holding her tightly to him.

"I haven't seen her in a while," Lizbeth whispered. "I knew she was pregnant, but to see her *so close* to her due date..." She took a deep, shuddering breath. "I didn't think it would be so hard."

His hands came to rest on her flat stomach. "You were expecting to be in the same place, love. Of course it's hard."

She nodded, the night she'd told him ran through her mind. He had shown up while she was still in tears.

"What is it, Lizbeth?"

She barely knew him. Could she tell him what she'd so recently discovered? Finally, she couldn't hold it in any longer. "I'm pregnant."

Robert's eyes went wide and remained open for what seemed to be an eternity until he finally blinked the shock away. "Okay." If his mind was running a million miles an hour, it would never catch up to hers.

"I didn't mean to sleep with him," she whispered, tears falling. "I'd never slept with anyone before, but we both got drunk at my family's house in Ravenzario, and..." She couldn't continue for a minute. "I'd never gotten drunk before either."

She wiped the tears from her cheeks. "I'm sorry I'm not up for going out tonight after all, Robert. And I'm sorry I got involved with you when I knew I'd had this one night thing with this other guy."

"We still haven't defined our relationship, Lizbeth. You shouldn't feel guilty about that."

His arms wrapped around her, and she buried her head in his shoulder. "I don't know what I'm going to do," she whispered. "Abortion is out, but if I have this baby, whether I keep it or give it up for adoption, my father will disown me. I'll lose everything I've ever known. I'll be pregnant and out on the streets."

Robert tipped her chin up with one finger. "Marry me, Lizbeth."

Before she could answer, he kissed her. A long, sweet kiss meant to convey feelings, but not passion. The passion was kept under tight control.

"I mean it," he whispered when the kiss ended. "Marry me, and let me take care of you and the baby. No one has to know it's not my baby unless you want them to."

The thought rolled round and round in her head. "I don't know."

"You don't know if you want to marry me, or you don't know about the logistics and telling your father?"

"The second." She rested the side of her head on his chest again. "My father scares me."

"Then we won't get married here. I have a trip to Denmark next week. We can get married there quickly and quietly. It's legal and everything, but the officials here won't know unless we file paperwork."

Lizbeth looked up at him through tear-filled eyes. "How do you know that?"

"I have a friend who eloped last year." He kissed her again, softly. "Think about it. And tonight, instead of going out, why don't we watch a movie and order pizza?"

She'd given him a weak smile and a week later, they'd eloped in Denmark, spending two nights there before returning home separately. Two months later, she'd learned the tragic truth. Her pregnancy had never advanced beyond the initial stages.

There would be no baby.

Here, now, she should be just days away from giving birth less than a week after Princess Jessabelle's due date.

"When the time's right," Robert reminded her, kissing her shoulder. "I know it's hard."

He'd been looking forward to being a father. He'd bought pregnancy books and even a baby bedtime book or two. All online, of course. No sense inviting scandal by purchasing them publicly.

"Yvette's going to need you this spring. As much as I wish the baby would be arriving any day, I'm glad you won't be splitting your attentions."

"I wouldn't have agreed to work with Yvette if the baby was still coming."

"I know. I also know she's going to need you." He kissed the side of her head. "I wish I could stay with you, but I have a flight leaving in a couple of hours. I promised my parents I'd come after Christmas." He hesitated, and she knew why. Robert wanted to tell his parents. She'd always said no, but maybe there was truth to what he was saying. Maybe it was time to have another shoulder to lean on.

She met his eyes in the mirror of the window. "Is it too late to get me a ticket?"

Two weeks into the new year and life had yet to slow down for Christiana. She hoped, once they were back at the palace, things would settle into a routine, and they had. Of sorts. One where she rarely saw her husband. Where she tossed and turned. Where an upset stomach was the norm.

Diana sank into the chair across the desk from Christiana. "The doctor will be here later this afternoon, ma'am."

Christiana looked up from the papers she was reading through. "The doctor? Why?"

"You haven't been eating well in a month. I know you've thrown up at least five or six times in the last couple of weeks. It's time to make sure nothing is wrong."

Christiana did not think anything was *wrong*, per se, though she started to suspect something was not quite *right* either.

"Very well." She continued working, straight through lunch, until Diana ushered the family doctor in. This man had been her parents' doctor until her uncle had found someone else for her. Though the other doctor had been cleared of any wrong doing, Christiana felt it time to repay this man's kindness and discretion. Besides being at the top of his field, he was someone her parents had trusted.

"Good afternoon, Your Majesty." Doctor Chambers bowed his head her direction and took a seat in the same spot Diana had been. "I understand you're feeling a bit under the weather?"

Christiana nodded. "Yes, though I believe I know why."

Dr. Chambers raised a brow. "You do?"

She twisted her pen between her fingers. Such a huge statement to make, and the doctor should not be the first one she said it to. Too late now. "I believe I am with child, Doctor."

The man blinked twice. Then a third time. "Congratulations, ma'am. I do believe that is the best news I've heard in some time."

Christiana raised a hand. "I am not certain, but I do suspect." She tapped her pen on the desk. "Everything I tell you is in the strictest confidence, yes?"

Dr. Chambers leaned forward until his forearms rested on her desk. "Your secrets go to the grave with me. I will share one, only because it will prove my point, and because it does no harm to be shared now. Not with you. Your mother miscarried several babies. One before you were born and three after, that we know of. Then Prince Nicklaus was born. There was at least one more after him. There are medical records for all of them. They were not turned over to the new doctor after your uncle had me removed as royal physician. Have you ever heard anything about them?"

Christiana shook her head. "No. I believe you. And I trusted you before, but I needed to ask."

"Shall we go to the medical wing so I can do a couple of tests? How far along do you believe you are?"

She stared at the pen. "I can tell you the date of conception, if I am, in fact, pregnant."

More blinking was the only sign of his surprise. "All right."

"I was not engaged to Alexander the whole time," she confessed. "Another man had captured my heart, or so I thought. It turned out, he had been plotting to kill me and take over as a distant relation and as my husband. In cahoots with my uncle, we suspect, though last I heard it had not yet been proven. Two weeks before the wedding, his duplicity was discovered. Alexander asked me to marry him. Ravenzario could not take another scandal of those proportions and a canceled wedding, plus the doubt it would instill about my judgment."

Dr. Chambers thought for a minute. "I disagree what it says about your judgment, but I can see how it would be a concern."

"Alexander is a good man. His family and mine have been acquaintances for many years, but he was instrumental in bringing down my uncle. I trust him implicitly." Just not with her heart. "Ours is not a typical marriage, though I believe we both hold out hope that someday it will be." A lone tear streaked down her cheek. "I know of the ancient law that says we must begin trying to conceive an heir as soon as possible. I also know the Prime Minister knows all of this and was not going to do anything about his part of the law with the confirmation of such activity." She sighed. "The anniversary of my parents death, the dinner reception, the memories of my parents, all arranged by Alexander. It was overwhelming, and later that night..." She let him draw his own conclusions.

"So conception would have been about a month ago?"

Christiana nodded.

"If that is the case, you are about six weeks along. We could do a urine test to confirm and then an ultrasound to make sure everything looks good. With your mother's history, I'd like to keep an even closer eye on you than usual. It may mean we decide to bring in a specialist, but I don't think it's necessary at this point."

Christiana pushed back from her desk. "Shall we get this over with?"

14

Something was going on with his wife, and Alexander had no clue what it could be.

She had visits from a doctor, though the man was always smiling when he left, so it couldn't be too serious. The queen didn't eat much but rather picked at their shared meals. He didn't know if it was his presence or something else that induced her lack of appetite, but it was enough to concern him. It had been almost two months since that night. And it was Valentine's Day. They'd been invited to a luncheon put on by the Romance Readers and 'Riters of Ravenzario. He didn't know who'd decided they would attend, but raising money for babies and children with heart problems was a worthy cause.

Alexander hadn't seen his wife in a couple of days, except in passing. It ate at him. The distance and separation from his wife. He didn't know how to fix it. In fact, they would arrive separately at the event. She had something going on that morning. If he could, he'd meet her after whatever it was, and they could go together.

Alexander pressed the intercom button on his desk phone. "Justin?"

"Yes, sir?"

"Do you know where the queen is this morning? Her schedule is blocked off, but it doesn't say where she is."

"I can try to find out. Any particular reason?"

"I'd like to meet her and go to the R-cubed luncheon together."

He could almost see the wheels turning in Justin's head. "I'll see what I can do, sir. Can you be ready to leave shortly if you need to?"

Rather than answer, he walked out of his office into the outer reception area where Justin sat. "I'm going to go to the apartment now and change into something a bit more Valentine's-y." He had a heart tie, didn't he? "Are the flowers taken care of?"

Justin confirmed, "I got a call from the florist a few minutes ago that they'd been delivered. Are you sure you don't want to meet her there with them instead?"

Alexander considered that. "No. I'd rather go together and slip away for a few minutes to get them."

He went to the apartment and found his black suit laid out for him, along with a red shirt and a black tie covered in shiny red hearts. Good. Just what he'd hoped for. As he straightened the tie, a knock sounded on his door. "Come in," he called.

"Sir?" His valet, Martin, entered. "Do you require any other assistance?"

"No, I've got it from here. Thank you." He flipped the tie up. "Did I already have this, or did you get it for me?"

"I found it at my brother's clothing shop. You did have a tie with hearts on it, but I thought you'd like that one better."

"You thought right. Is your brother's shop here in town?"

"Yes, sir. It's in the plaza just down the street."

"I'd like to stop by there sometime soon. I need a few new suits, and I'd love to give him the business if he carries or can get what I need."

"I'm sure he can, sir. The queen's father did most of his shopping there. As a child, the queen loved to hide among the tie-racks. It would be an honor to serve another member of the royal family."

Alexander grinned at him. "I'll tell him you sent me."

A minute later, a call came from Justin. His car was waiting to take him to meet the queen at the hospital.

Alexander couldn't keep his mind from spinning a million directions as the car drove through the streets. Did she simply have an appearance at the hospital, or did it have to do with her recent appetite or something else?

They appeared to have timed things just right. As they pulled up to the portico, the queen and several others, including the royal doctor, walked out. Alexander exited the car and walked to her side.

Did her eyes light up? Or did she put on a front for the cameras clicking away in the distance? "Good morning." He leaned over and brushed her cheek with a kiss before shaking hands with the good doctor. "Did you have a productive visit?"

Queen Christiana nodded. "I was able to spend time with the children who must stay here and had a productive discussion with Dr. Chambers about a few other health related issues I needed some advice on."

Maybe the doctor was advising her. That was good.

Alexander extended his elbow. "It would be my honor to escort you to the R-cubed luncheon, Your Majesty."

She slid her hand inside. "I would love that."

Seated in the back of the day limo, Christiana fidgeted. She had not spent much time alone with Alexander since she discovered she did, indeed, carry his child. She wanted to tell him, truly she did, but the connection she felt with him that night, beginning with the stop at the memorial plaque, disappeared when she awoke alone.

She would put on a happy face, something she had always been good at faking, for the public. Enter on his arm, speak adoringly of him during her comments after lunch, perhaps even a kiss or two, but her heart remained shuttered.

Soon, she was seated in the place of honor, with Alexander at her side. The meal looked lovely, but she only managed a bite or two. As it neared its end, Christiana enjoyed her conversation with the president of the Romance Readers and 'Riters Club seated to her left. It was time for her to speak, but as she walked to the podium, a wave of dizziness nearly overwhelmed her.

She gave her prepared speech, something about love and hearts for the young children who need them, and the love of Christ, but if asked later she doubted she would be able to repeat any of it. Not more than three words in, Alexander slunk away from the table. The butterflies in her stomach amped up their activity.

When she finished and turned, she saw Alexander standing there, off to the side, an enormous bouquet of blush colored roses in his arms. She took a tentative step his direction. He strode purposefully her way. Another step to meet him as he neared. Another wave of dizziness.

A tilting world.

A spinning bouquet.

Blessed darkness.

C rushed flowers lay everywhere as Alexander knelt next to the queen. He'd dropped them as he reached out to break her fall. Her dark eyelashes lay against pale cheeks. He looked around, frantic.

"A doctor?" he called. "Is there a doctor...?"

Doctor Chambers raced onto the dais before Alexander could finish his sentence. "Can you carry her?"

Alexander scooped her into his arms. The president of the club led them to an ante room off to the side where he laid her on a couch.

"I was afraid of this," Dr. Chambers muttered, as he pulled a stethoscope out of his bag.

"Afraid of what?" Alexander clutched her limp hand in both of his.

The doctor hesitated.

Alexander gave a jerk of his head telling the other people in the room to get out. The second the door closed, "I'm her husband, Dr. Chambers. You have to tell me." No one else would know he had no clue what was going on.

"It's not my place to say, sir." He shook his head. "We need to get her back to the palace. I can get her some IV fluids, and I think she'll be just fine, but I answer to the queen, not you. Unless it becomes vital, I keep her health information private from everyone."

Alexander cursed under his breath. "Then let's get her home."

"An ambulance is on the way."

"I'm riding with her."

Dr. Chambers shook his head. "I'm sorry, sir. There's only room for one extra, and that's me."

Another muttered curse. "You can't be serious?"

"I am completely." Compassion spilled out of the other man's eyes. "I'm sorry, sir. I can't imagine how you must be feeling, but we have to do what's best for the queen, and that's for me to ride with her."

Reluctantly, Alexander agreed as sirens blared outside. In minutes, the ambulance pulled away. Alexander watched for a moment, running a hand through his hair and cursing again, internally this time. No sense in some long distance mike picking it up. His car pulled in front of him, and he waved off the chauffeur, letting himself into the back seat. The car peeled out the second the door closed, a police escort helped them keep up with the ambulance.

He didn't think the sirens were necessary, but they remained on as they flew through the streets. The normally fifteen minute drive took five. Nearly an hour later, he still hadn't seen his wife except for a moment as she was wheeled inside, still unconscious.

Dr. Chambers walked into the waiting room. He looked haggard but not distraught. Alexander took that as a good sign. "You can go in, sir. She wants to see you."

Alexander took a deep breath. "Thank you." He went in, surprised by how frail the queen looked. "How are you feeling?" he asked, keeping his distance while wanting to move closer.

"Better." She held up the arm with the IV running into it. "Fluids are helping as is the anti-nausea medicine in it."

"Nausea? Is that why you haven't been eating?" He pulled a chair next to her bed. "What is it, Christiana? Are you ill?"

She didn't look at him but fiddled with the nubby blanket. "Do you know you rarely call me Christiana? You always use Queen Christiana, Your Majesty, ma'am. But rarely my name. Never a pet name or nickname. Except twice."

Did he? He never felt comfortable enough to be informal with her, but had he really never used her first name?

"Once before you proposed the first time," she went on. "And that night. When we kissed, when you asked me if I was sure and told me you wanted to be my husband, you called me Christiana. Later, I was almost asleep, but I remember you calling me sweetheart and kissing my head."

He remembered the moment vividly. She couldn't be too ill if she was waxing on about nicknames, could she? "What is it?"

She still didn't look at him. "I am with child."

It took a minute for the words to sink in. "You're pregnant?"

The queen nodded. "Nearly ten weeks."

He stood and paced around the room, running a hand through his hair. "Why didn't you tell me?"

"When have I seen you in a setting where it would be appropriate for me to tell you?"

She had a point. "You couldn't make time? Knock on my door at night? Leave me a message you wanted to talk?"

"You were gone the next morning." The quiet accusation in her voice cut to his core.

"There was a phone call from my mother. Justin sent me a text telling me. I had to take it. My grandmother had a heart attack. She was fine, overall, but Mom needed to talk it out with someone not quite so close to the situation. By the time I got back, you were in the shower with the bathroom door *locked*. I checked."

He'd wanted to talk to her, to make sure she was okay after the emotions of the night before, but she'd, literally, locked him out.

"I see."

"How are you? The baby?"

Christiana heaved a sigh. "My mother apparently had a number of miscarriages both before and after my birth, plus one after my brother was born. Dr. Chambers has been extra careful with my care and what he's allowed me to do. Everything seems to be fine except for the nausea."

"And that's why you haven't been eating?"

"Yes."

"And why you passed out?"

"Yes. The flowers were beautiful. I did notice them." For the first time, she looked around. "Could you have them brought to my room? Dr. Chambers says he will let me recuperate there."

My room. She still had no intention of sharing with him. His stiff formality returned. "I would, ma'am, but they were dropped when I caught you. Last I saw, they were scattered all over the dais."

"I see."

He bowed slightly at the waist. "If you'd be so kind as to let me know when you have doctor's appointments, particularly ultrasounds, I would appreciate being allowed to attend. If you need anything from someone to hold your hair or to get you pickles and ice cream at midnight, please be sure to call me."

Heart wrenching, he turned and walked out.

PHOTO: Prince Alexander watches as an unconscious Queen Christiana is loaded into an ambulance

Queen Christiana and her husband, Alexander, Duke of

Testudines, attended the Fifteenth Annual Have a Heart Fundraiser of the Romance Readers and 'Riters Club. After giving her speech, the queen turned to see her husband approaching with a large bouquet of blush colored roses. The queen took a step or two toward him before collapsing. The Duke dropped the flowers and caught her before she hit the ground. After being taken to a side room with the royal doctor in attendance, the unconscious queen was loaded into an ambulance for transport to the palace. Her frantic husband followed in his own car, with both vehicles surrounded by a police escort.

The palace has remained silent, except to say the queen is resting comfortably. Speculation, however, is rampant among those in attendance at the luncheon. "The royal couple seemed a bit awkward with each other," one attendee stated. "After nearly four months of marriage, you'd expect them to be a bit more comfortable." Another mentioned the queen had eaten very little of the meal, chosen because it is normally one of her favorites.

PHOTO: Prince Alexander walks toward his wife with a bouquet seconds before her collapse

PHOTO: The Duke holding his wife as she lay on the ground.

The most common speculation has the queen in a rather delicate condition. "I think we'll have a new heir to the throne sooner rather than later," Lady Gweneivere of Carrington, the eldest member of the club, added sagely.

The palace public affairs office responded to all further questions with a simple "no comment."

He left. Again. Christiana suspected she would be crying if not for the dehydration that plagued her. Dr. Chambers returned, saying nothing as he checked the bag of fluids and the assorted machines she was hooked to.

As Dr. Chambers moved to leave, he stopped. "He cares a great deal for you, Your Majesty. I know you're accustomed to being hurt by those you trust, but I would ask you to try letting him in. At least let him help take care of you and the baby. Let him be a part of this pregnancy. Don't keep him from seeing his child even from this early stage."

He hesitated. "I've seen fathers who take a great interest from the time the test comes back positive and those who don't take an interest until much later. I've seen mothers who allow and encourage their husbands to be an active part of the pregnancy. I've seen mothers who refuse to allow their husbands to be involved at all. I've not pushed you either way until now, Your Majesty, because I didn't feel it was my place, especially until he knew, but he wants to be involved. He wants this baby, and he wants to love you. The prince wants you to love him. I know how hard that is for you to believe, but at the least, don't keep him from his child, from watching the baby grow and develop. From watching the changes in *your* body as you give that child a safe place to grow."

Christiana could only nod. The tears still did not come, but the lump in her throat had grown as the doctor spoke.

"Someone will help you move in a few minutes. Please don't try to get up on your own. They'll take you to your room." And he left.

She rolled until she could stare out the window. The only thing she could see was the rock wall on the other side of the courtyard. Clouds had settled in at some point since they arrived at the luncheon. The gray skies matched her mood.

Dr. Chambers said her hormones were completely out of the norm and that, combined with the nausea and lack of food intake, caused her to be more emotional than was her norm.

She wanted to trust Alexander, to allow him the place in her life he should have. To be his wife in more than just name. To be his friend, his confidant, his encourager, and yes, his lover. And for him to fill those same roles for her.

Her reverie was interrupted by Diana and two men she did not know entering the room with a wheel chair. In minutes, she was being pushed through the hallways toward her apartment. Her lethargy followed her into her room where Diana helped her into bed. One of the men had been pushing a metal stand from which hung a bag of fluids. Diana helped arrange the pillows so she was reclining rather than flat.

Christiana stopped her assistant before she left. "Would you ask Alexander to come in?"

Diana hesitated. "I believe he left, ma'am. Something about needing to see his family."

Of course. "When he returns would you tell him I would like to speak with him?"

"Yes. I will let Justin know as well."

"Thank you."

Christiana closed her eyes. The medicine made her sleepy. She drifted off, wishing her husband was there to keep her company.

Alexander piloted the speedboat across the open channel toward his family's property. He couldn't begin to define, much less explain, the emotions roiling around inside.

His wife was pregnant.

And he hadn't known until she was forced to tell him. How much longer would she have kept it a secret if she hadn't fainted? And how could he not have noticed just how bad things had become? Part of him, the part that always turned to his brother when he needed his best friend, wanted to call Topher. The rest of him wasn't sure his brother could help this time.

His brother had no experience with such a situation. The only time his brother had been in a real relationship had been in their teen years with the costar of *2 Cool 4 School*. The Saturday morning teen sit-com had been wildly popular in the mid-00s, giving both Christopher and Alexander a level of fame and notoriety they'd never been comfortable with. At the end of the series, both had gone back to using their given surname - rather than their mother's maiden name used to avoid confusion with other actors and similar names - and their more natural dark hair color. The changes gave them a chance to attend college and enter the professional world without their acting background affecting others' perceptions of them.

A result of the show had been Topher's only real relationship. Ironically, it had been Alexander's character that was her character's love interest on-screen. The three-year, very public courtship with Margie McCoy had ended on the rocky hill of charges of infidelity against his brother.

Alexander had known the truth all along, but even when the girl in question admitted to setting Topher up, the tabloids hadn't let it go. The show was coming to an end anyway. Margie used the "jilted lover" angle to propel herself into a successful movie career. Alexander suspected she may have even had a hand in the scandal, especially since they weren't sleeping together in the first place.

Regardless, his brother hadn't dated since. He wouldn't be able to give Alexander advice about what to do when his wife was sleeping in another room but pregnant and not telling him about it.

Did he dare confide in his parents? They'd proven themselves honest and trustworthy over the years, taking only a modest salary as the managers of his and his brother's careers. Most of the money still sat in the bank, untouched except for college, as the two of them made their own way as adults. The salt air cleared his mind.

Husbands, love your wives, even as Christ loved the church, and gave himself for it.

Right. Sacrificial love. Laying down his life.

One who has unreliable friends soon comes to ruin, but there is a friend that sticks closer than a brother...Greater love has no man than this: to lay down one's life for one's friends...In this same way, husbands ought to love their wives as their own bodies. He who loves his wife loves himself.

Turning the wheel of the boat, he made a wide arc and caught the glare of the security team that had followed in his wake.

Right. Something he still wasn't used to when he wasn't with his wife.

He started back toward the royal dock. He didn't need his brother. He had needed some time to clear his head, to listen to the still, small voice telling him what he already knew. No matter what else, it fell to him to take care of his wife as he would take care of himself. Better than he would take care of himself.

When he arrived at the dock, he slowed and let the man standing there tie the boat off as he hopped out. Trotting to the car, it was time to try to make things right with his wife.

16

"You wanted to see me?"

Christiana turned from staring out the window at the sea to find her husband leaning against the door frame, hands shoved deep in his pockets. A short-sleeved, casual collared shirt in dark green offset his eyes - and his muscular arms. With one leg crossed over the other, he looked maddeningly casual and incredibly handsome. The serious look on his face, though, gave some indication of what was to come.

"Thank you for coming." She fluffed the blankets around her then smoothed them again.

"We need to talk, Christiana. You and me. No holds barred." The muscles in his arms shifted under his shirt as he lifted one of the wingback chairs and moved it to where he could sit and face her at the same time. The shirt strained across his shoulders as he leaned forward. What would it be like to be held by him whenever she wanted instead of the occasional dance, crying jag, or after throwing herself at him on an emotional night?

"You are right, Xander. We do."

He cocked an eyebrow her direction. "Xander?"

"I complain you never call me anything familiar, but I do not call you anything but Alexander. I thought your family must call you Alex, and I wanted something else."

He chuckled and the sound settled over her, warming her like the blankets had been unable to. "Nope. Some of my friends did, still do, but my family calls me Ander or just A. Not quite the same, but close. Christopher is Chris to his friends but Topher or C to the family."

She gave a petulant pout, but she did not care. "The only other one I came up with was An or Ex or Der and, well, no thank you."

Another chuckle brought a small smile out of her. "No, those don't work either, Tia." She felt her brows knit together. "A nickname for Christiana."

She sobered again. "I would like to apologize, Alexander. I should not have kept this from you for so long." Christiana reached for the scrapbook sitting at her side and handed it to him.

"What's this?" She didn't answer as he flipped it open. He stared at the first page, then at her. "Ultrasound pictures?"

"Yes. Because of my mother's history and the all-day sickness, Dr. Chambers has done a scan every week. I do not know that it could have stopped something bad from happening if he detected anything, but it certainly has calmed my fears."

He ran his fingers over the plastic protecting the photos, one from each ultrasound. "So small," he whispered. "A peanut."

"More like the size of a kumquat now, at least according to the website I've been looking at." She picked at the quilt on her bed. "I owe you an apology for not making sure you were there to see your child the first time."

He set the book on the bed and reached for her hand, his long fingers gently brushing the back. "Let me take care of you. I know you're the queen, and it's your job to be everything that comes with that, but I'm your husband. Our children won't have my last name, and I'm good with that, really. But you're my wife. My job is to love you like Christ loved the church. To take care of you better than I would myself.

"I know you don't love me, and I get why you don't trust me completely. You've been hurt and betrayed so often. It will take time to convince you I won't, but please let me take care of you in the meantime. Your *first* priority has to be the health of yourself and the baby. Let me take care of everything else."

His earnest plea made her nod. "I know. And I thank you."

Alexander stood, leaned over and pressed a sound kiss to her forehead. "I need to go check out the publicity sure to be surrounding today. I'll make sure no one releases the information about the baby until you're ready to do so."

"Only Dr. Chambers and Diana know." She squeezed his hand. "She suspected before I did."

"How long have you known?"

"A few weeks. I think we should wait until after the first trimester ends to make the announcement. Dr. Chambers agrees." She did not want him to focus on how long she had known without telling him, but rather on how much longer they had to go through together. "The baby is due in September."

"We'll be parents before our first anniversary," he mused. Another kiss to her forehead, and he moved away. "Get some rest. I'll be back in a bit with a press release for you to look over."

He walked to the door but stopped when she spoke.

"Thank you."

One of his drop dead gorgeous smiles crossed his face. "My pleasure."

For the first time, she truly believed he meant it.

PHOTO: Prince Alexander storms out of the palace in his roadster

Less than two hours after an unconscious Queen Christiana was taken to the palace, a stormy Prince Alexander took off in his roadster. His drive only took him to the royal dock at the marina where he hopped in a speedboat and took off before his security could catch up. He headed for Bianisola, perhaps to speak with his family about matters better discussed in person. The speedboat never arrived at the royal dock on Bianisola, but Baicampo, the property his family owns, does have a private one. He returned much more quickly than expected. If he did visit the island, it was a short visit, likely less than fifteen minutes.

A more relaxed, but still intense-looking prince drove back to the palace. A short time ago, he and the queen released this statement:

Queen Christiana has been under the weather for some time but has put her obligations first, refusing to take time off to recuperate as she has needed to do. Today, this led to the incident at the Have a Heart Fundraiser. On the advice of her doctors and at the urging of Prince Alexander, Her Majesty will be canceling appearances for the near future. His Royal Highness or another representative will attend in her place whenever possible, but for now, the queen and duke insist her health must come first.

The queen's hiatus will fuel further speculation that she is expecting the couple's first child, likely before their first anniversary.

"How is she feeling, Diana?" Alexander strode into the apartment around ten the next morning.

Diana sat at a desk situated outside the queen's bedroom, moved there to allow her proximity to the queen while allowing the queen to rest. "Better, sir. The medicine and fluids seem to be having the desired effect." She tilted her head toward the bedroom. "I think she'd like to see you."

He winked at Diana. "I hope so. Thank you for helping me get these."

She grinned. "The florist was happy to help."

Alexander tucked the flowers behind his back, knowing it wouldn't hide them completely. "Good morning," he repeated softly as he walked into her bedroom.

The queen ducked her head, seeming a bit shy. "Good morning."

"I brought something for you." He swept the flowers from behind his back.

Her hands flew to her face as she gasped. "How did you get those the day after Valentine's Day? They're gorgeous!"

Alexander chuckled. "It helps that they're for the queen and her people happen to adore her." He pulled the vase out of the spot where Diana had hid it for him earlier, setting the roses in it and putting them on her side table. He kissed her forehead before walking around to the other side of the bed and settling on top of the covers.

"Speculation is rampant?"

He took her hand in his. "I think the entire country believes you are pregnant. Half the States probably do, too. Your spell yesterday made the news there, asa well, since I'm American and all."

"What about your parents? Your brother? Will they be here anytime soon so we can confirm to them in person?"

"They were planning on a visit this weekend anyway."

"Good." She changed the subject. "What is on the agenda today?"

"Not much. A few guests visiting." He brought her hand up and kissed the back of it. "I've got it covered."

"Who?"

"Another group of students. I think today it's the country's top group of senior drama students. The National curling team is supposed to be by later, but Diana offered to let them reschedule since she knows they'd really like to meet you specifically."

Christiana shook her head. "No. Dr. Chambers said he would remove the IV this morning. I will do my best to convince him I can sit in the reception room. I will not walk around, but will let them come to me. Take a few pictures, but this event has been rescheduled at least twice already."

Alexander looked at her and decided she really did look better. "If Dr. Chambers agrees, okay."

"I would prefer to be in there and seated before the team arrives rather than walk in appearing frail."

They talked for a few more minutes, and he left to get some other things done before the first meeting.

Alexander helped her out of the wheelchair Dr. Chambers insisted on. Christiana, feeling weaker than she ever had both physically and in how she was viewed, relished his strength as he helped her into the seat brought in for this very reason. The large, well-cushioned chair had an almost throne-like feel to it, she realized as she settled in.

The wheelchair was whisked away. "Are you ready?" Alexander asked, squatting down at her side.

Christiana took a deep breath and nodded. Her long sleeves covered the cotton ball and bandage on the inside of her elbow. Alexander motioned to one of the doormen. How she wished she could remember the names of everyone who worked for her! But she had not been blessed with an eidetic memory for names and faces like some she knew. Former King Jedidiah, father of her dear friend Queen Adeline of Montevaro, was one such person.

He knew the names of everyone he came in contact with on even a semi-regular basis.

The Ravenzario National Curling Team was more subdued than she expected. Only about twenty people entered, surprising her with their small numbers. The furniture had been arranged in a semi-circle facing her. "Won't you have a seat?" she gestured toward the couches and chairs. "I do apologize for not standing to greet all of you. I am certain you have been informed that I am under the weather, as they say, but you have all been so gracious in rescheduling this meeting that I could not in good conscience ask you to again."

One of them walked straight up to her and handed her a bouquet. "It is our pleasure, Your Majesty." He took a step back and bowed. "We would be happy to reschedule again if you need to."

She held one of the blooms up to smell it. "Lovely. No, it is not necessary. I am to remain seated and rest, under strict orders from my doctor and..." She looked up under lowered lashes. "...enforced by my husband."

They all took seats, though several looked rather uncomfortable. She turned to the one closest to her who had given her the flowers. "And what is your name?"

"Antonin, ma'am."

"Antonin, can you introduce me to everyone else? I am afraid I do not know much about curling. Could you each explain to me what your role is?"

Antonin went around the room, introducing her to each one and letting each of them explain their role on the teams. After about an hour of answering her questions and explaining patiently, Antonin and the captain of the women's team both stood.

"We do have something for both of you," he said, nodding to Alexander. The women's captain brought out a box. Antonin opened it and lifted out two jerseys. On the back of Alexander's was his last name and a number two. On hers was Rensselaer, the Ravenzarian version of the common dynasty name shared with the other countries in the Commonwealth and a number one.

Taking care, she stood and took it from him. "How wonderful!" It was not the first jersey she had received and would not be the last, but every time, it overwhelmed her. Carefully, she slid her arms in. Alexander had already put his on. She sat back down, exclaiming over the jersey.

"May we get a picture, ma'am?" Antonin asked.

"Of course!" They all gathered around the chair. Alexander knelt on one knee at her side, with Antonin on the other. The official photographer took several pictures with his own camera then several more with the cameras or phones of the guests.

By the time they left a few minutes later, Christiana had to admit she was worn out. "I think I would like to go rest now, Alexander." Originally, she had tried to convince him to let her stay for the next meeting, now but knew he had been right to veto the idea.

He accompanied her back to her room, helping to pull the covers up over her legs after Diana helped her change into something more comfortable than her pants' suit.

"Rest well," he whispered, squeezing her hand. "I'll see you later."

17

C hristopher lifted Alexander off his feet in a giant hug when he walked into the palace apartment. "I hear you're gonna be a dad, brother."

Alexander groaned. "Don't believe everything you read in the tabloids. You of all people should know that. Weren't you supposed to be having a baby with that girl? Or one of a dozen others?" How many times had the tabloids linked one or both of them to a girl who was supposedly pregnant? Not just the one that ended Christopher's relationship with Margie McCoy.

"True. But neither of us were sleeping with anyone at the time, so it was easy to know there was no truth to the allegations. Now, brother dear, you're married. And your wife is quite the hottie of the royalty world."

Alexander glared. "Don't talk about her like that."

"What?" Christopher shrugged. "The queen is hot."

"Thank you for your assessment, Christopher." Both brothers turned to see Queen Christiana walking into the room.

Alexander grabbed his brother's arm and leaned close. "My wife is beautiful. Gorgeous. And *hot*. All of those adjectives. But she deserves your respect because she is the queen of the country where your family does a lot of business. She deserves it because she is my wife. Some women would not take offense at your statements, and if she were one of them, I wouldn't have a problem with it, but I'm warning you..."

Christopher looked taken aback. "Chill, big brother."

"We'll talk later." He turned and walked quickly to Christiana's side, wrapping an arm around her waist. "Are you sure you're up to this?"

"Leave your brother alone." She settled into the chair he'd learned was her favorite, a large one his mother had always called a "grandma chair" because it was big enough for a grandma to sit with a grandchild and read a book. If he and Christiana were more conventional, and she weren't the queen, he would share it with her. Instead, he took a seat on the end of the couch closest to her. His parents and brother were seated around the living area a moment later.

"We do have some news to share," he told them without preamble. "This time, the papers are correct." He took her hand. "Christiana is about ten weeks pregnant. She's had a difficult time, and there is a history of miscarriage in her family so we don't plan to announce it for several more weeks."

Christopher whooped, both arms lifted in victory. "I knew it!"

Mom looked like she was about to cry. "Oh! You two! I didn't believe a word I read, but I'm so glad!" Dad just grinned and let the others do the talking. "When are you due?" Mom went on, not letting Christiana answer. "If you're ten weeks, that's around Christmas, so September?"

Christiana could only nod.

"Oh, good. We planned to spend most of the fall here already." She clapped her hands like a giddy schoolgirl. "Our first grandchild!"

Christopher rolled his eyes. "At least the tabloids were wrong all the other times. Otherwise, you'd have a dozen already, starting when you were forty. You would have hated that."

"The tabloids?" Christiana looked puzzled. "Why would the tabloids follow either one of you?"

Alexander rubbed the back of his neck. "Ah, we haven't really talked about one part of my life. You know I spent several years in LA, right?"

"Yes."

"Christopher and I starred in a teen sit-com but under Mom's maiden name. There was already a Christopher Mayfield in the Screen Actors Guild, so we used the last name Slate."

Christiana gasped. "You're Alexander and Christopher Slate? From *2 Cool 4 School?*"

Was his royal wife a fangirl? Alexander glanced at Christopher who raised a brow.

"I had one of your posters in my dorm room. Addie gave it to me. She *loved* the show. I loved the freedom Alex and Chris enjoyed. I never had that."

"Addie?"

"Queen Adeline of Montevaro. But that's not important. How could you not tell me?"

Alexander shrugged. "It didn't seem necessary. It ended nearly ten years ago. I've been out of the industry ever since. I felt, we both did, that continuing would only lead to us being asked to compromise our morals. If you watched the show, you know Alex and Chris kissed a girl or two but nothing more was even hinted at until the wedding episode at the end. And then not until *after* the wedding. The writers and producers wanted to take things further more than once. There was even talk of Alex's girlfriend being the teen pregnancy, but Mom and Dad put their foot down."

Christiana still seemed to be in shock.

"We both returned to Serenity Landing for college, and the rest is just like I told you. With the change in last names and letting our hair go back to its natural color rather than the light blond it was on the show, we don't get recognized very often. We've turned down all of the 'where are they now' shows and offers to do a reunion, though that has more to do with how C's relationship with Margie McCoy ended than the show itself, I think. All the offers come through the agent we still retain. I don't think our real names are public knowledge at all, though I'm a bit surprised someone didn't put two and two together after the wedding."

"Your faces were all over the news in the States." Christopher laced his fingers behind his head. "There are a few people who know enough to put it together, but if they did they kept their mouths shut."

That made Alexander frown. "Blackmail?"

"Why? What would they gain? If it did come out that the star of *2 Cool 4 School* married the queen of Ravenzario, what does it change? A bit more interest from twenty-somethings who fancied themselves in love with you in high school? There's no gain."

"Believe me, we thought it through." Dad joined the conversation. "We talked about it with Tony and the palace security team as soon as you told us about the engagement. There doesn't seem to be any reason to worry. They'll keep an eye on any fan mail that may come for Alexander Slate, but it's unlikely for two reasons. First, someone has to put it all together. Second, someone would have to get close enough to one of you two, or now the baby, to be a threat. We believe the worst that could happen would be accusations of an affair. All of us know they would be completely groundless. Hold yourself above reproach with other women, and there's no concern." Dad raised an eyebrow of his own. "And I know you know to do that, so I don't see a problem, except that your wife had no idea."

Alexander gently squeezed Christiana's hand. "We'll talk more later, okay?"

She nodded.

"I'm more interested in baby names." Mom clapped her hands

again. "Have you picked any out yet?"

"No. We haven't had a chance to discuss them in depth yet." He didn't tell them he'd only known for a few days, and he felt Christiana relax a bit when he didn't mention it. "I think both of us are waiting to breathe a sigh of relief when this first trimester and the worst of the danger is over."

Mom and Dad exchanged a glance. "I think that's wise," Mom said. "We debated whether to tell you this, but we, too, had a couple of miscarriages. We'd only ever planned on two children and when twins came along, we thought we were done. God had different ideas, though neither pregnancy lasted much past the positive test."

Alexander felt sucker punched.

"But for whatever reason, God chose to give us those babies for a short period of time. We praised him at the time. So often with babies that are miscarried that early, it is because of something outside of the mother's control. Perhaps a genetic disorder or any number of other reasons. It has given me great empathy for women who miscarry. I've worked with the pregnancy center in Serenity Landing for many years and counseled more women than I can count in the process."

Dad cut in. "I've talked with the dads. He's not the one whose body carries the baby or changes through pregnancy, but those dads feel a deep sense of loss as well."

Alexander interrupted. "I'd rather not talk about miscarriages. Both of us are concerned enough as it is, without dwelling on the possibility. Now, dinner is ready whenever we are. Who else wants to eat?"

Christopher jumped up. "Me!"

Everyone laughed, though Alexander noted Christiana's laugh was subdued. She remained so throughout the meal. His family left to stay in another part of the palace rather than take a boat ride over to the property.

Once they'd both changed into their pajamas, Alexander went

to check on her. "Are you all right?"

Already settled in the bed, she gave a slight shake of her head. "I know your parents meant well, but..." One tear after another slid down her cheeks. "Thank you for changing the subject."

He sat on the edge of the bed and scooted over until he sat next to her. Wrapping an arm around her shoulder, he pulled her close to him, feeling hot tears land on his bare chest. He whispered a prayer for peace over her.

"I am supposed to be strong," she whispered. "I am the queen. I should not rely on anyone to be strong for me. It is my job."

"Sh," he breathed into her hair. "'*My grace is sufficient for thee: for my strength is made perfect in weakness.*' It's not your job to be strong, love. It's your job to rest in the One strong enough for all of us."

"Stay with me?" she whispered. "Please? I do not want to be alone."

"Of course." Somehow, he managed to keep an arm around her and slide under the covers at the same time. With his wife's head heavy on his chest and her tears weighing down his heart, he prayed for peace for them both.

PHOTO: Prince Alexander's family arrives at the palace

Lending fuel to the pregnancy speculation, Prince Alexander's family visited the palace last night. Reportedly, the trip has been planned for some time, but the palace would neither confirm nor deny anything. The family did stay overnight rather than moving to their own property on nearby Bianisola.

Neither Queen Christiana not Prince Alexander has anything scheduled with the public today.

18

"**Y**ou're not Alexander."

The man who looked a lot like the prince consort chuckled. "Nope. I'm his twin brother, Christopher." He held out a hand to shake Lizbeth's. "He's home with the queen today and, since I'm in town, he asked me to cover for him today." He held up a file folder. "Everything I need to know is in here. Let's go over a few things, then we'll walk over to the chapel. There are a few vendors here with options set up."

It didn't surprise Lizbeth. The queen had passed out in the last few days. Valentine's Day had always been lonely, but this year, she'd managed to sneak in a few hours with Robert. Since meeting his parents and telling them the truth at Christmas, it had been a bit easier for her, knowing they were praying about it. They'd seen the news together and spent several minutes praying for the queen. She wanted to ask for more information but something held her back. Instead, Lizbeth pulled out her own binder. Yvette remained quiet. She'd been more involved, but there still seemed to be something a bit off about it. The meeting with the seamstress had gone much better than Lizbeth could have hoped and the sketches would be ready in the next week.

After a few minutes of going over some details, the three of them crossed the property, riding in something Christopher called a Gator. Lizbeth had never heard the term before, but, on a cold, gray day, it was much nicer than walking.

"All right." Christopher looked in his binder. "We have three florists, four bakers, and five photographers. I know it sounds overwhelming, but we need to get moving on all of this. All of them have been approved by the security teams and both royal photographers. We talked about having the royal photographers do the wedding photos, but, it was decided to use a wedding photographer. When you head over to the palace after this, the head chef will discuss the reception dinner with you."

Overwhelming was one word for it. Each of the florists was set up in a different corner of the chapel with their vision for the princess to look at. They also had portfolios with other work they'd done, just in case. The photographers had their photos staged all around, including in some of the pews. The bakers were still setting up in the entry. They'd get to them last.

Lizbeth trailed behind, taking all of it in as Yvette took her time studying the different flower arrangements and looking through the portfolios. She asked few questions, but the ones she did ask were good ones. Several times, the vendors looked like they wanted to say more, to give a more thorough pitch, but the look on the princess's face didn't invite the comments. Instead, the work had to speak for itself.

After looking at all the floral arrangements, she turned to the photographs lining the chapel. All of them had worked on the property before, including the one who had done Christiana and Alexander's wedding. She walked up and down the pews, not the ones with the pictures leaning on them, but the row in front. At one series of pictures, she stopped, put a knee up on the pew in front of her and studied all of them for a long time. Finally, she nodded and started back up the aisle.

Lizbeth wasn't sure what she'd seen in that particular series. All of the photographers were very, very good.

Back in the entry, Yvette did much the same. Quietly tasted every cake offered. Looked carefully at the portraits set up of their work. Flipped through the portfolios. Made notes on her phone. That part was new. Probably because she needed to decide not only *who*, but *what*. And multiples. There would be cake in multiple flavors, after all.

Finally, she turned to Christopher. "I'm ready to go back to the office."

Once seated again, she told him exactly what she wanted. She'd liked florist A, but not what was set up, one of the things in the portfolio. She'd picked photographer C, the one who took the pictures she'd stood in front of for so long. Baker D and three different cake types. She also mentioned a groom's cake to be designed by the groom - should he happen to arrive at least a week before the wedding.

He wouldn't.

But it was an interesting way to keep people guessing.

Lizbeth's stomach grumbled, and Yvette smiled for the first time in a while. "Why don't we go back to the palace and get some food?"

Christopher laughed. "I think that sounds like a great plan."

PHOTO: Queen Christiana and Prince Alexander on their wedding day

After three weeks of speculation and very few sightings of the queen, the palace made the official announcement.

Queen Christiana and Alexander, Duke of Testudines are pleased to announce their first child will arrive later this year. Due to hyperemesis gravidarum, or extreme morning sickness, the queen has been working a much lighter schedule than the norm. This will continue for the foreseeable future.

Experts guess the new prince or princess will arrive sometime in late summer or early fall, perhaps as late as the royal couple's first anniversary, but likely earlier.

The sudden, searing pain doubled Christiana's body onto the floor. She cried out in pain, but before she could actually call for anyone Alexander was at her side.

"Call Dr. Chambers!" he yelled toward the door of her bedroom. "What is it?"

"I hurt," she whimpered.

He lifted her into his arms and carried her back to the bed. "I thought you were resting." His voice held no accusation.

"I needed to use the restroom." Fear flowed through her heart. "I should have asked Diana to help me."

"Don't start second guessing yourself, Tia." He sat next to her, holding her close as though to give her some of his strength. The cramp had dissipated, but she could not shake the feeling that something was horribly wrong. Could it just be her imagination running wild?

Oh! She prayed it was so.

Her ears tuned into her husband's voice. He too prayed for peace and for the health of the baby, but, he prayed, most importantly for her health and for the strength to deal with anything that came their way together.

No! her heart cried. The life of their child was just as important as hers, though intellectually she could admit without her, there would be no child either. They stayed there until Dr. Chambers arrived, his nurse in his wake along with the ultrasound technician and equipment in tow.

Though she had been tired, the nausea had started to abate, and he had seen no reason to do another ultrasound in the last couple of weeks. This would be Alexander's first chance to see their child. She prayed it would not also be the last. When directed by Dr. Chambers, Alexander moved away from her, though he reappeared a moment later on the other side, lacing his fingers through hers while she told the doctor what happened.

"First, we're going to do an ultrasound. Then likely an exam. I've called a friend of mine who is a perinatologist. As long as things remained fairly calm, I was comfortable managing your care, but I'd like an expert at least for today."

"Of course. Tell Diana..."

"I got her on the list weeks ago." Dr. Chambers looked straight in her eyes. "I would never, *ever* endanger you or your child, Your Majesty. I would not have invited her if I did not trust her implicitly. A background check has already been done, but you have nothing to fear, either for your health or for her to discuss things she shouldn't."

Christiana nodded, tears still leaking into her ears. Not very queenly. "Thank you, Dr. Chambers."

She managed to stifle her gasp as the goo hit her stomach. Her eyes squeezed shut as the wand came to rest on the exposed skin. Alexander's grip on her hand tightened.

"Is that him?" her husband whispered, awe coloring his voice.

"Right here," Dr. Chambers confirmed. Likely he was pointing. She could not bring herself to watch. "And there's the heartbeat. It's a bit faster than I'd like but not so much that I'm extremely concerned." A bit more pressure and movement on her stomach as the doctor muttered to himself and had the nurse or technician make notes she did not understand.

"Okay. I'm done for now."

She opened her eyes.

"I do want to do an exam, but I think I'd rather wait until Dr. McCall gets here. She likely will want to do one herself, and there's no sense in two if we don't need to." He asked her more questions about the last few days until Dr. McCall arrived.

Time would tell.

Alexander couldn't begin to give voice to his thoughts. They weren't coherent enough to mutter aloud. Thank God, He understood the inane ramblings of Alexander's heart of hearts.

Seeing the baby was just about as close to an other-worldly moment as he'd ever experienced. Hearing the heartbeat and seeing the flutter on the screen was a moment he'd never forget.

Now another doctor was asking questions. Christiana answered them, though Alexander couldn't focus on the words.

"Alexander!" Dr. Chambers's voice had a bit of a bite.

He shook off his stupor. "Yes?"

"Dr. McCall would like you to step outside, just for a moment. Can you send Diana in?"

Alexander's gut churned, and he wanted to protest, but a glance at Christiana's face sent him to the door. She was stressed enough without him arguing with the doctor she trusted. Besides, though he'd been sleeping with her again for a while, she would be more comfortable with Diana if they needed her to change clothes.

Instead, he paced in front of the floor to ceiling picture windows, staring out over the crashing waves as they met the rocks below. He prayed as he'd never prayed before though he still wasn't sure they were coherent. A glance at his watch told him it had been over ten minutes. Then twenty.

"Your Royal Highness?"

Alexander turned to see a tired looking Dr. Chambers standing there, and he felt sucker punched. "Is she...?"

"She's fine, for now." There was a wariness in his voice and his eyes. "She's bleeding, worse than spotting, but not enough that we feel miscarriage is imminent. For now, she's on complete bed rest. We'll both check in on her often and reevaluate as necessary."

"Thank you." A sigh of partial relief escaped.

"I don't think this would be a concern, given how much you care for her and her condition, but she's also on complete pelvic rest." The slight lift of the other man's eyebrow told Alexander what that meant. No...marital activities. "I just needed to tell you. I don't think you'd..." Dr. Chambers shook his head. "Never mind. She's on both bed rest and pelvic rest. Whatever food she can keep down, let her have. Even if it's pickles and barbecue sauce over sauerkraut at three in the morning."

Alexander's stomach turned at the thought. "Really?"

Dr. Chambers shared his grimace. "I hope not, but yes."

"Okay. I can do that."

"Would you like to see her?"

Before Dr. Chambers finished his question, Alexander was in the bedroom. He sat in the chair still pulled to her bedside. "How are you?" She looked pale and the streaks from her dried tears begged him to wipe them away.

"Tired."

"We've given her some medicine." Dr. McCall made a note on her tablet. "It can make her sleepy. She needs to rest."

"Absolutely. If I'm not here to help her, someone will be. Twenty-four, seven. She won't ever be alone."

After a few more minutes of instructions, everyone left, leaving the two of them alone, though Diana was just outside. He moved to the other side of the bed and stretched out next to her, though on top of the covers. One hand protectively rested on her lower abdomen, something he hadn't done before. "Promise me you'll be careful?"

"I promise. Dr. Chambers said it likely would have happened when I stood up, even if someone helped me, but I will not attempt to do anything more than roll to the side without assistance from now on."

"Thank you, love." He kissed the side of her head. "Why don't I let you get some rest?"

"I do not want to be alone, Xander." Big, trusting, eyes looked up at him. "Will you stay?"

"Of course." He pulled his pillow over and bunched it under his head. "Do you want to rest or talk?"

"Will you talk while I close my eyes?"

"Name the topic."

"Life on the set of *2 Cool 4 School*. Was Derrick DiMarco as cute as everyone said?"

Alexander chuckled. "I never thought of Rick as cute, though the girls seemed to think so. The tabloid stories Christopher and I mentioned? A lot of them could truly be attributed to him, though he never got the press we did, even though we didn't do those things. I think he resented us for that."

"Do you keep in touch with any of them?" She sounded as though she was starting to drift.

"Not really." Her head slid slightly to the side, and he knew she was asleep. He rolled until he could stare at the ceiling. Prayers tossed around and around in his head until he dozed off for an afternoon nap himself.

"How on earth do you work this thing?" Christiana lay nearly flat and held a remote the size of her tablet.

Alexander lay on his side next to her and held out his hand. "I'll show you." He pressed one of the buttons that looked like a movie screen. A slight whirring sound and then a screen lowered out of the ceiling. A monstrous screen.

"Why do we need a screen this big?" The installation had gotten her out of the room for a bit, but just to the couch and not for all that long.

"Because you can work from here with a big enough screen." He brushed her hair back. "Look." Rolling to the other side of the bed, he picked something up and handed it to her. "Wireless keyboard and mouse. Your computer is hooked up to the projector, too." On the remote, he pointed to another button. "Just click here."

She pressed it and the screen suddenly switched to her login screen. A picture of Alexander kissing her on the forehead at their wedding hovered behind the password box. This was the other picture though. Not the full color one, but the backlit shadow version. She felt her face color as he grinned.

"You like that picture?"

It was her favorite. It showed a loving, tender side of Alexander. Her eyes were closed with an almost wistful look on her face, but she didn't answer.

"Well, I love it." He kissed the side of her head. "So that button brings up your computer. This one takes you to movies and TV shows." It looked like a DVD disc. "Every movie ever created pretty much is on here." She raised her eyebrows, and he shrugged. "What? I have an extensive collection."

She scrolled through the movie choices with the swipe of her finger. "Impressive, I'll give you that."

"There's also a bunch of TV shows. Most of them are American, but there are a few others, like *Dr. Who*."

A thought occurred to her and she scrolled quickly to the numbers. "Every season of *2 Cool 4 School*? Really?"

"Topher gave them to me as a wedding present." He pointed to another button. "You can use this part here to make playlists so it'll show one program or movie after another. You can just put a whole season of a show in there or your favorite episodes." Alexander pressed the TV button. "This is the television and remote."

A news story popped up as he changed the input to television. The visual of herself being wheeled into the ambulance brought her up short. "Turn it up?"

"Reports from the palace seem to indicate the queen is doing well and the baby is doing fine. However, the queen's schedule remains clear for the rest of the week. All of her appointments for next week have been warned they may need to reschedule.

"Prince Alexander has been seen filling in for the queen on several occasions in the last few days. When asked about the queen, he said a few words."

Alexander's face filled the screen, exceptionally larger than life.

"Ouch," he whispered next to her. "Maybe I didn't think this through."

"Queen Christiana is resting comfortably. She and the baby are doing fine. The doctors are acting out of an abundance of caution, so she will remain on bed rest for at least the next few days. After that, we'll leave it up to the experts to decide. She does miss being at events like this and thanks the good people of Ravenzario for understanding. The queen is slowly working her way through all of the cards and letters that have been sent. She hopes to get to the emails, too, but those are a bit trickier on bed rest." He winked at the camera. "I've got a plan to help her with that, too, though. She sends her deep, heartfelt thanks to all of you for your thoughts and prayers the last few weeks."

The Alexander sitting on the bed next to her turned the television off. "If you have any questions about how it works and I'm not around, ask Diana." He kissed the side of her head again and rolled off the bed. "I have a meeting in a few minutes. Do you need anything before I go?"

She shook her head. "No. I think I have everything I need, but could you ask Diana to come in?"

"Sure. I'll be back later."

Christiana watched him walk out admiring the cut of his shirt across his shoulders and his pants...She shook herself out of it then grinned. *2 Cool 4 School* marathon, coming right up.

19

Yvette sat on the front pew of the chapel and tapped her foot impatiently. She wanted to get this over with and get back to Mevendia. To home and homework. Was it really "palace work" when one lived in a palace? At least she wasn't off at boarding school like Christiana had been.

Her father had talked about it, with her being the only girl and it being more important to have her in a secure facility at all times or something, but her mother had put her foot down and refused to send her baby away.

Thank goodness.

She had a few friends she was pretty sure she could trust completely, but she was never certain. Yvette had never had that "I can tell this person anything" friend. Too many risks. She knew she would be pressured to name her maid of honor in this meeting, and she didn't want to. Not even a little bit. Christiana had used representatives of her people. Ana and Addie had stood up for each other. Yvette had been Jessabelle's the year before but that had been a weird fluke, and she wasn't sure she wanted to ask her half-sister/sister-in-law to stand up with her anyway.

As long as she wasn't asked to pick the best man.

"There you are, darling." Her mother's heels clicked up the aisle. Other voices could be identified as the rest of her little entourage waited. "I wondered where you ran off to."

"I didn't run anywhere." She'd walked. Away from the discussion of pictures and cakes and everything else that pointed to this being a real wedding.

"We could not find you," her mother reproved gently.

"Sorry." *Not really*. The closer the wedding came, the more her heart ached. The more she wanted to find Nicklaus at the other end of the aisle. Or her idealized version of Nicklaus anyway. If he were alive, he would have been king since he was three. He could be an ogre and egomaniac. Or maybe he'd be the sweet, kind man Yvette had always imagined herself with.

Alexander took a seat about halfway up the stairs leading to the platform. "All right. Nearly everything is in place. You have another fitting this week right, Yvette?"

Yvette nodded. She loved her dress and hated she likely wouldn't get to wear it for her actual wedding. What man would want her to wear the same dress she wore to a non-wedding with a dead man?

She only half listened as he went through the rest of the vendors and discussed the guest list. She'd worked on it for days, though she didn't know most of the people invited. The invitations would need to be mailed out in the next week. Calligraphers had already done most of them.

"One more thing we need to know, Yvette." Alexander gave her a kind smile. "Who is going to stand up with you?"

"I haven't asked anyone yet," she told him, hoping to buy some more time.

"You need to." Her father's voice came from behind her.

"I know." She didn't want to.

And then it hit her. Like a bolt of lightning. Who she wanted to stand with her.

"You need to pick someone, sweetheart." Her mother.

Yvette could feel her eyes light up. "I know who I want it to be." One person who had never let her down. Ever.

"Well, who?" her mother demanded.

"Nana Yvette. I want Nana to be my matron of honor." It was fitting in so many ways. If only they would let her.

But her announcement was met with several long seconds of silence. Then...

Her father's voice, thick with emotion. "I think she would love that, Yvette."

Good.

Everything was set.

Except the groom.

Alexander waved to the gathered crowd as he walked out of the hospital. It wasn't the biggest crowd of his still-brief career as prince consort, not even close, but he wanted to make sure to greet some of them. Shake some hands. He walked over to the rope line, smiling. The first person he reached was a little girl. He squatted down next to her. "Good afternoon. How are you?"

She bit her lip. "Good." She held out a card and a flower. "This is for the queen."

He took them from her. "Well, thank you. I will be sure to give them to her as soon as I see her. What's your name?"

She ducked her head shyly. "Lily."

"Thank you so much, Lily. I know the queen will appreciate it."

"I hope she feels better. We pray for her before bed."

"She does feel much better already." He stood and shook hands with the woman who must be Lily's mother. "Thank you."

She rested her hands on Lily's shoulders. "We are all so happy for both of you."

Lily tugged on his pants. "Is it a boy or a girl?"

"We don't know yet, sweetie, but I promise, if your mom will give me your phone number, I will make sure you are one of the first ones to know."

Lily's eyes went wide. "Really?"

He nodded. "Yep. It might not be until after the baby is born, but you, Lily, will be one of the first to know."

A hand tapped his shoulder, and he looked over at one of his security guys. "I think that means it's time for me to go. It was a pleasure meeting you, Lily."

As they walked to the car, he asked what was going on. "Sorry to interrupt, sir, but your brother called and asked to move your teleconference up an hour. He's expecting you in about fifteen minutes."

Ten minutes later, Alexander settled into his office chair and fiddled with his computer until the camera and settings were just right. A minute later, the computer buzzed, and he clicked the button. Time to focus on the family business for a while then go check on his wife.

Christiana typed her name and title to another email and clicked send. She needed to have Diana set up a signature on the bottom so she would not have to sign them - and she did not know how to set it up herself. The giant screen made it a lot easier to try to get work done. She had sent out emails to many of the groups she had canceled meetings with as well as responded to the well-wishes on the palace website with an official statement now found on the main page.

She looked up at the light rap on the door. Her husband stood there, a beautiful calla lily twirling between his fingers. "This is for you, Your Majesty." The smile on his face took a bit of sting out of his formality.

"It is lovely, Alexander."

The grin expanded as he pulled up a chair next to the bed. "I wish I could take credit for it, but a little girl gave it to me for you. Her name is Lily. I promised she would be among the first to know if this is a boy or a girl when the time comes to make the announcement." He handed her an envelope. "Also from Lily who told me her family prays for you and the baby every night before bed."

Christiana sniffled. "That has to be one of the sweetest things I have ever heard."

"Christopher said the same thing." Alexander propped his stockinged feet up on the bed, his gold toe socks wiggling with his toes. "He sends his love. So do Mom and Dad. Do you mind if I change this?" He nodded toward the screen still filled with the palace website.

"No."

Alexander pushed a button only to see a giant picture of himself and his brother pop up. Christiana did not know if she should be embarrassed for herself or for her husband.

He tilted his head to look at the title screen from his show. "What's that all about?"

"I decided to watch some *2 Cool 4 School*, if you must know. It has been a long time since I had the chance, and knowing you as I do now, it makes me see things a bit differently."

Now he watched her. "How so?"

"When your character kisses his girlfriend, for instance. I know she was really dating your brother."

"You're only in season one if this is the episode you watched. I don't think they kissed until season three or four."

She shrugged. "I skipped around some. I watched the last episode already."

Alexander clutched at his heart. "Say it ain't so! You don't watch a series out of order until you know it so well you can quote large chunks and place in the top ten in the annual trivia tournament."

Christiana found that hard to believe. "Annual trivia tournament? Really?"

"Yep. Every year a group of fans get together in LA. They have costume and trivia contests and tours of the old sets that are in use as part of other shows. They try to get some of the actors and actresses to show up, and we get an invitation every year, but we've never gone. Usually it's one or two of the recurring characters. They also have awards for the best fanfic stories written that year."

She blinked rapidly. "Pardon? What is fanfic?"

"People take the characters from the show and write their own stories about them. There's a bunch of websites online for all different shows and such, but the 2C4S.com site is where almost all of these are posted. It's run by a lady in the Eastern U.S. who uses the initials AC. She says it has nothing to do with me and Christopher. The other gal is in the British Isles, and goes by the name *Labby*."

"Really?"

He nodded.

"I had no idea."

"You'd be surprised at how obsessed some fans are. It's part of the reason why Topher and I work so hard to separate ourselves from the show. I'm sure it'll come out eventually, but until it does, we keep it under our hats."

"Do you ever plan to attend?"

Alexander shuddered a bit. "No. Maybe in a few years, after the furor over the show died down some more. I might have considered it, but not with being married to the queen of Ravenzario." He took her hand and kissed her knuckles. "I'd much rather be here with you than in LA with a bunch of fangirls."

A wicked grin crossed her face. "Perhaps, once it becomes

common knowledge the prince consort of Ravenzario is really Alex Slate, they will move their annual convention here. Think of what a boost it would be to the tourism sector."

He groaned. "Oh, I hope not. I mean, I know it would be, but let them keep it in LA."

She turned serious. "If it ever does come out, would you meet with them if a group came here?"

Alexander laced their fingers together. "I don't know. Maybe."

A knock sounded on the closed door, interrupting the conversation.

"Come in."

Diana walked in, a tablet in her hand. "Ma'am, Dr. McCall has just pulled through the gates. She'll be here in a few minutes."

Christiana closed her eyes. Another visit. Possibly another intrusive exam. Definitely another scan. Seeing the baby was always a good thing. "Thank you, Diana."

Her assistant turned, but stopped when she saw the screen. "Oh. My. That's a big picture of you, sir."

Alexander grumbled and turned the projector off as Diana walked out. "What do you need to do to get ready?"

"Nothing." For the moment. "She mentioned only planning to do a scan today."

His grin could light up a dark night. "It's pretty cool, isn't it? Seeing the baby."

She reached for his hand, holding it with her right hand while her left fingers played with his wedding band. "I am sorry for not letting you experience the first ones, Xander."

He squeezed her hand. "It's done. It's in the past. I've seen the pictures, and I'm here from now on."

Fifteen minutes later, they were looking at the heart fluttering on the screen. Dr. McCall smiled as she moved the wand around. "Everything looks wonderful, Your Majesty. I see no evidence of the subchorionic hemorrhage. Have you been spotting at all?"

She shook her head. "Not in a couple of days."

The doctor wiped the goo off her stomach. "If it was anyone else, I'd give you the green light to get off bed rest and return to light activity. Still resting and reclining as much as possible, but allowing you to meet with groups who come to visit as long as you remain seated most of the time, things like that, for the next couple of weeks. If there was still no bleeding or spotting, I'd let you resume normal activities but with restrictions on lifting and so on as is normal for pregnancy."

Christiana held her breath.

"However, given who you are, I'd like to act with an abundance of caution and keep you to that restricted level of activity for a few more days. I'll come back on..." She looked at her calendar. "...Friday afternoon, and we'll reevaluate then."

They both thanked her, and she left.

"Are you okay with a few more days?" Alexander asked her.

She was not, not really. If truly necessary for the baby, she would be, no question, but being treated differently because of who she was and being told to severely curtail her activities longer than truly needed? That did not sit well with her.

"Do I have a choice?" Christiana answered honestly. "I will do what it takes to keep the baby healthy."

He squeezed her hand again. "I have another meeting, but I'll be back to talk to you later. We'll have dinner in bed."

She would have dinner in bed. He would lounge on top of the covers or sit in the chair next to her. The doctor's words came back to her. She would do what was necessary, but not recommended "out of an abundance of caution." A plan began to form. Necessary? Those recommendations she would take with a grain of salt.

And make her own plans.

Alexander sat in one of the board rooms across from a screen. On the screen were two faces - the CEO of the largest wine distributor in Mevendia and their Crown Prince William. Alexander had met the young royal several times, but didn't know him well and only remembered that he was quite tall.

"Gentlemen," he said as he leaned forward. "Subject to approval of the queen and Parliament, we have a deal." Though he was authorized to negotiate on Christiana's behalf, she still needed to approve the details. "I would imagine the approval will be forthcoming in the next few weeks. Mevendian wine will fill up the shelves here in Ravenzario again before Thanksgiving."

The two men exchanged a glance. "Thanksgiving?" William asked. "That is an American holiday, is it not?"

Alexander chuckled. "I suppose it is." He looked up as Justin walked in the side door. The near frantic look on his face told Alexander all he needed to know. "Gentlemen, I'm being called away on a matter of some urgency. We'll contact you if we need anything else and, please, be sure to do the same."

"Of course," William replied. "Please give our best to the queen."

With a nod, Alexander had the connection terminated. "What is it?" he asked Justin.

"The queen is missing." No preamble, just straight to the heart of the matter.

Alexander's stomach clenched then dropped to the floor. "How long?"

"Ten, maybe fifteen, minutes."

"So she can't have left the palace."

"Possible, but unlikely."

Alexander trotted through the halls of the palace to the apartment. Diana paced in front of the windows, wringing her hands. "I'm sorry, sir. I don't know where she went. She asked if I would get her something to drink, and when I got back she was gone."

"She can't have gone far." He ran a hand through his hair and wished he knew her better.

"Why...?" Tears snuck down her cheeks. "She's on bed rest."

That's when it hit him. "Dr. McCall said she was being extra careful and with anyone else she would have lifted the restrictions already. The queen wouldn't do anything to hurt the baby, but if she thought Dr. McCall was being unreasonable, she might have been willing to go do something. Nothing big but..."

An idea came to him. He had to check. "Keep looking." Alexander ran as fast as he dared with staff members darting out of his way as he pounded through the palace. He burst through the door into the garden and skipped as many stairs as he safely could before bolting through the maze.

Alexander skidded to a stop as he rounded the hedge into the center. There she sat, on the bench where he'd proposed to her.

"Tia!" He dropped to a knee beside her. "What are you doing?"

She looked up at him, her face pale. "I needed some air. Dr. McCall said with anyone else she would give clearance to stop bed rest."

He pulled his phone out of his pocket and called Justin. He didn't take time for pleasantries. "I found her. She's fine. I'll bring her back in a few minutes. You can stay put." He slid his phone back into his pocket. "You scared us, Tia."

Moving to sit next to her, he wrapped an arm around her shoulders. Pulling her close, Alexander let relief wash over him. "Are you all right?"

"I am. I just got tired more quickly than I expected." She rested her head against his shoulder. "I thought I would sit for a few minutes and then go back. I did not intend to worry anyone."

His heart had nearly resumed its normal rhythm. "I know."

"How did the meeting with Mevendia go?"

For the time being, he let the subject be changed, and he told her about the meeting.

"Thank you for taking care of that. It is likely a better deal than I would have negotiated."

They sat there for several minutes, soaking in the sun and watching the waves in the distance. "Are you ready to go in?" he finally asked.

"Yes."

Alexander stood before she had the chance to and helped to her feet. Not giving her a choice in the matter, he swept her into his arms.

"Xander!" Christiana squealed and grabbed his shoulders. "I can walk."

"No, Queen Christiana. You are not going to walk." Walking much more slowly than before, he retraced his steps to the apartment, setting her back on the bed. "Promise me you'll stay here?"

Her eyes fluttered shut as she nodded. "I think I will take a nap. I promise."

Alexander covered her with a blanket and left the room. Once out of her line of sight, he sagged against the wall and let out a huge breath. Stress bled off of him in waves as he whispered prayers thanking God for her safety.

The curtains were tightly closed when Christiana awoke. A glance at the clock told her she had slept for nearly two hours. Who knew a walk to the garden could take so much out of a girl?

Reaching for the remote control, she lowered the screen and turned on the projector. Before she could change the input to the *2 Cool 4 School* shows, a face appeared. One that haunted her dreams from time to time, though she had been told his transfer to Pirate's Island took place while she was at sea with Alexander.

Curious, she turned up the sound.

"...a prominent businessman in Vashta was to make an appearance at the local orphanage today. For the last week, organizers have been trying to get a hold of him only to be told he would be unable to attend. Given his appearance at the fundraiser for the last several years, one of the organizers took it upon himself to find out why."

Another man appeared on the screen with a microphone held in front of him. "I can't explain why I felt something was off, but I did. I contacted his family, even his wife clammed up when I asked about him. I went to the police. No one was interested in talking to me. But a couple days ago, I talked with a guy who said he'd been arrested by the palace security team. There's no record in the public database, but he's not anywhere to be found."

The picture returned to the reporter. "We reached out to the palace earlier today, but there seemed to be some sort of incident taking place and none of our calls were answered or messages returned. We hope that the palace security team will tell us what they know or that anyone with information on..."

Christiana clicked off the sound before the reporter spoke his name.

And then it sank in.

Even his wife clammed up when I asked about him.

She bolted for the bathroom but knew she would never make

it. Grabbing the rubbish bin next to her desk, what little she had eaten for lunch came out.

Over and over, she heaved. Even after her stomach emptied, it continued. Muscles in her abdomen began to cramp as tears flowed down her cheeks.

Where was Alexander when she needed him?

Behind her the door opened, slowly at first then faster.

"Christiana?" He knelt beside her, his hand on her back as she finally managed to get the heaves under control. "What is it, sweetheart?"

She pushed the trash can away from her, and sank against him, sobs shaking her body. He held her, cradled her, and rocked her until the storm subsided.

"What is it, sweetheart?" he repeated.

"He was married," she whispered. "The whole time he courted me, insisted we keep everything a secret, proposed to me, he was already married."

Alexander's voice echoed her own disbelief. "It's not possible. We've checked out everything about him. Nothing points to him having a wife, or even a girlfriend or sister someone might mistake for a wife."

Christiana told him about the news story. He shifted slightly, and she knew he wanted to go check it out for himself. "Help me back to bed?" she asked. "I am all right, and I would appreciate it if you would look into it for me."

He helped her stand, then held her close. She loved the feeling of his arms around her, supporting her, comforting her. Loving her. After a minute, he brushed his lips against the top of her head and lifted her into those arms. She loved his strength. There would have been no way *he* could have made her feel the same, though she once thought he did. What she felt then was a mere shadow of what she felt for this man.

"I'll send Diana in to sit with you," he told her as he helped her get comfortable. "I don't want you to be alone. When I know something, I'll tell you, okay?"

She nodded. Her stomach muscles were sore from the "work out," and she was worn out again already. "I think I will try to sleep." The television had moved onto other stories. "Would you turn that to a different input then turn it off?"

He changed it to a black screen with her favorite classical music playing softly in the background.

"Thank you." Alexander took such good care of her. Why had she not fallen in love with him first?

The thought startled her, though she could not muster up the energy to even open her eyes.

When had she fallen in love with him?

And did he feel the same about her?

PHOTO: Mystery man enters side gate onto palace grounds

Speculation is running rampant about the connection of this man to the palace. Several pictures have surfaced of him entering the palace grounds over a year ago so he must have been known to them. What remains to be seen is what exactly his relationship with the palace was.

Speaking on condition of anonymity, a source tells us he was arrested a few weeks before the wedding and put in the dungeon. No longer a dungeon in the medieval sense, the prison housed in the basement of the palace is seldom used for anything more than the occasional tour or on the rare occasion a guest needs to be detained for some reason.

The source did not know why the arrest was made, only that now-prince consort Alexander was a part of the process. The prisoner was later moved to Pirate's Island.

Some of the speculation includes an attempt on the life of either the queen or the, at the time, soon-to-be Prince Consort. Other rumors suggest espionage or spying on behalf of a corporation.

The palace has responded to every request for information with a "no comment at this time" reply.

21

"What do we do?" Alexander forced himself to remain seated. He wanted to walk. To pace. To find the dude and deck him.

"For now we continue with the 'no comment at this time' responses to the stories." PR Director Charlyn Turani looked as tired and stressed as he felt. At least he'd known what happened. She'd had no clue about most of it.

"That's not going to last. The press won't let up until they find out what the truth is."

"I know. We don't have much time, either. The story is going to come out one way or another, and it's up to us to spin it the best way we can."

"There is no need for spin."

Everyone turned to see Queen Christiana standing at the door to the conference room. Alexander jumped to his feet and helped her to a seat.

"We will tell the truth. Nothing more. Nothing less. The truth is, I was taken in by a very smooth operator who planned to kill me after our wedding - a wedding that would not have been valid

165

in the first place as he already belonged to another." That bit of information had been confirmed in the last twenty-four hours. The marriage had taken place in Australia, and the couple never filed any paper work in Ravenzario to indicate what their relationship was. "Even before he was arrested, I had begun having doubts and questioned my feelings both for him and for Alexander. When the arrest took place, Alexander and I discussed our feelings for each other and saw no reason why the wedding needed to be called off."

Everything she said was true. They had discussed their feelings, or lack there-of, prior to agreeing to go ahead with the wedding. He would talk to her later about whether or not that was the best way to handle it. Or should they be honest with the public? Given the recent past in Ravenzario, they both believed calling off the wedding and the story being publicized would shake the very foundations of their government. In the interests of her people, she decided to marry a man she didn't love but knew she could trust and respect. If done right, she would earn the sympathy and respect of the people. If handled poorly, things could end up much worse than they already were.

"We will have the press conference tomorrow." Christiana's tone brooked no argument. "I am not feeling able today, and we need the time to prepare the official statement. Tomorrow morning, we will meet with the press in the garden. I will make a statement. I may or may not take questions depending on the state of my health at the time. Set up a time and get the announcement out as soon as possible."

She pushed back from the table. "I am going to rest and do some work from the apartment. If you need anything else, please call."

Everyone stood, though Alexander was the only one who followed her out. Holding her elbow to keep her close to him, he asked her those questions.

Christiana considered his words. "Have them prepare two

statements to send me. One with the official, not lying but not quite the whole truth either, version and one with everything as you said it. I will look them over from the apartment, make notes, and send them back."

One of the aides he didn't know appeared with a wheelchair. That made Alexander feel better. She likely had them bring her close enough to the room to walk in on her own and now was being assisted back.

Alexander turned and went back into the meeting room. "Okay. So, what do we say and when?" By the time the meeting adjourned an hour later, two drafts of a speech had been written for the queen. He had given them his tentative approval since much of it revolved around him as well. A press release was sent out calling for reporters to meet for a statement and possibly a few questions at ten the next morning.

When he made it to their room in the apartment, Christiana sat cross-legged on the bed, staring intently at the screen and the documents visible.

"Wow. I never knew Times New Roman 12 point font could be quite so big."

"It is the size of the screen, not the font." A number of red notations showed on both versions.

"Working them side by side?" The question was more to make conversation.

"The opening paragraphs are identical so I made identical changes to both." She scrolled down on one and made a few more notes.

"Have you decided which one you're leaning toward?"

"No." Her brow furrowed as she continued to scroll and make tweaks.

Okay. When his wife was "in the zone", she didn't like to be bothered. Good to know. He pulled out his tablet and opened one of the books his brother had gifted to him. Not his normal genre, he still found himself enjoying the outer space saga written by an actual physicist named Randy Ingermanson and a biochemist named John Olson. Reclining against the headboard it seemed like a good way to get his mind off of everything for a bit.

Alexander was so engrossed in *Oxygen* that he jumped when she spoke again.

"Here." She held out the wireless keyboard. "I emailed them to you. Would you go through and make any more notes or changes while I take a shower?"

He watched her walk carefully to the bathroom before picking up the wireless keyboard and reading through both versions. The changes she'd made were good ones, and he only noted a few others. After emailing them back, he pulled his tablet back out and immersed himself in the space adventure once more.

Christiana smoothed down the front of her black wool coat. Why had she insisted this press conference be held outside again? Right. The sunshine. The temperatures were warmer than they had been but not as warm as summer would be. Her gloves would remain on until just before she walked out to the podium.

And she still had not decided which speech to give.

"How're you holding up?" Alexander slid his arm around her waist.

"I will be fine." Another deep breath.

He moved closer and around until they faced each other. Their fingers laced together as he rested his forehead on hers. "Father, we come before You and ask that You give Christiana strength and wisdom. Let her words come from You. Keep her strong. Keep the baby safe. Let Your peace surround us both. Go before us into the garden and behind us as we leave. We thank you for your everlasting goodness and mercy." His words stopped but the moment continued until Charlyn cleared her throat, and then he stepped away.

One more pass with her hand over the baby bump just beginning to show and Christiana nodded.

Charlyn led the way, with Christiana following. Alexander walked a half step behind with his hand resting on the small of her back, comforting and supporting her. After adjusting the microphone, Charlyn made a short statement.

"Ladies and gentlemen, thank you for attending on short notice. The queen will make a statement. As you are aware, the queen has been placed on restricted activity at this point in her pregnancy. If she feels able, she may take a few questions. However, it is possible she will decide the statement is all she is up to for the day. A copy of her prepared remarks will be available after the press conference ends." Because Christiana still had not decided which speech to give. Both versions waited for her on the podium.

A hand raised and Charlyn nodded toward Matt Markinson. "Will Prince Alexander answer any questions?"

Charlyn leaned back in toward the microphone. "Perhaps." She turned and Christiana nodded. "Ladies and gentlemen, Her Majesty, Queen Christiana."

Christiana took a deep breath. "Thank you for coming today. I am going to address some of the rumors that have been spreading regarding a man from Vashta and my wedding to Alexander, Duke of Testudines."

She slid the green folder into place. Time to tell the truth. "I have known Alexander's family for a number of years. We met several times, and I would have defined our relationship as 'acquaintances' until about two years ago. At that time, he was instrumental in removing my uncle from power. We grew to be friends throughout the process of prosecuting my uncle, though I was being courted by another man. Beginning about eighteen months ago, this other man and I grew serious though he insisted his identity remain a secret for a number of reasons I will not go into today. I agreed, and my public relations office reached an agreement with the press corp. Privacy then in exchange for more access and interviews during our nine week honeymoon."

"So you weren't dating Prince Alexander?" someone called.

She ignored the woman. "A few weeks before the wedding, I was already having doubts. I considered calling the whole thing off, but told myself it was just cold feet. As you all know, I led a sheltered life, with no family and very few friends I could turn to. This is not exactly something you discuss with the Prime Minister, after all." She glanced up to see a few reporters give half smiles. "On October 7, Alexander came to me with some information about this man. Proof had been found that he planned to drug me while on our honeymoon at sea that first week. He would use our marriage as well as his 'newly discovered' distant relation to my family as justification to be crowned King of Ravenzario. We believe this was to take place within thirty-six hours of the first scheduled interview with Matt Markinson. This would have allowed him to play the grieving widower while establishing his position as the 'rightful' king."

Her stomach churned, and she gave serious thought to losing what little breakfast she had kept down, but managed to maintain her composure. "The Commonwealth Agreement with Montevaro and Mevendia means it would not have happened as he would have wished. At best, Princess Yvette of Mevendia, as the fiancé of my brother with a marriage contract still in force, would have been crowned queen with her father as regent. At worst, the country would have been divided between Montevaro and Mevendia. Ravenzario, as we know it, would have ceased to exist."

There were a few murmurs from the reporters. Many likely either didn't know or had forgotten the codicils of the agreement.

"Alexander and the palace security team arrested him. Though I was not involved in the day to day events, I have seen the reports. He was given a secret trial under the Treason to the

Crown Act of 1862 and sentenced to life on Pirate's Island. The news of his wife, that he was already married, did not come to light until a few days ago. Copies of the declassified sections of the files will be made available, and you can see for yourselves the lengths he went to in order to hide that relationship.

"As I mentioned a moment ago, I was already having second thoughts. Alexander came to me later that day and asked what my plans were. I truly believed it was in Ravenzario's best interest to go ahead with the wedding, because canceling it and the information about the assassination plot had the potential to rock the government to its very core. Coming so soon on the heels of my uncle's lifetime of betrayal, I wanted nothing more than to spare the people the additional trauma."

Here went nothing. "Alexander is a good man who has proven himself time and again in service to the crown, despite his lack of citizenship prior to the wedding. I have long admired and respected both his family and Alexander himself. Even prior to this, Alexander had proven himself a valuable and loyal friend. Given my belief calling off the wedding would harm more than the economy, when Alexander proposed, I accepted. We believed as virtually all of the kings and queens who came before me, that a relationship based on trust, respect, friendship, and admiration would withstand the test of time. We believed that, perhaps, one day we would grow to love each other with that fairy tale love read about in books. Until then, commitment, respect, and following the Biblical commands to honor one another, we could turn our friendship into a marriage based on those same qualities."

Almost done. One more deep breath. "Many of you have reported on the qualities I find most dear in my husband. He is a good man who takes care of me and now our child with everything in him. Alexander loves this country with a love many natives would be hard pressed to match. He has a passion for people, helping those who cannot help themselves, both here and abroad. If given the ability to create the man best suited for his job, Alexander is better than any man I could have created. I thank God he was brought into my life at just the right time. To stop both my uncle and this other man, to be my Prince Charming, and my knight in shining armor."

She closed her eyes as everything started to sway. "I thank you for your time and for listening to our side of the story. I am unable to take any questions at the moment, but the public affairs office will do their best to make sure every question is answered in the next few days. If you would submit your questions to Charlyn, I will..." The world spun. Before she could make a conscious decision, Alexander was there. His arm tight around her waist as he walked her back into the palace until she was seated in the wheelchair waiting just out of sight.

He pressed a kiss to her forehead. "You did great. Get some rest, and I will be there soon." He squeezed her hand, let go, and walked back out to face the reporters.

Before he even reached the doors, he could hear the shouted questions. "What does Alexander think?"

Charlyn's calm voice answered. "Despite the recent revelations, he is the prince consort. As such, he is addressed: Prince Alexander; Alexander, Duke of Testudines; Your Royal Highness; or sir. I will thank you to remember this."

Alexander moved to her side. "Thank you, ladies and gentlemen for staying while I helped my wife inside. Queen Christiana is under doctor's orders to rest as much as she is able and currently tires easily. Though she is able to keep up with most of her duties, the queen has curtailed her official schedule with regards to personal visits or meeting those who visit the palace. We thank everyone for their patience and understanding when the group before or after you was able to meet with her, but your group was not, or when she attends one event a day, but it's not the one you're attending." He didn't speak to the reporters but to the people beyond. The ones who were streaming this live and watching in their living rooms or offices, those who would catch it later online.

"Your outpouring of love and support has been beyond anything I could have imagined. Queen Christiana looks forward to taking some time every day to read the cards, letters, and emails, and listen to the voice mails left. I often find her sneaking a few minutes of reading them in between phone calls.

"As for the circumstances surrounding our wedding, I have long admired and respected the queen. Nearly two years ago, I happened upon information that led to the arrest of Henry Eit. Over the next eighteen months, I got to know her well. Would I say I had fallen in love with her before the wedding? No. Did I love her then? Yes. Do I love her now? Even more. I have loved every moment of getting to know her better, to learn her nuances, her pet peeves, her little idiosyncrasies. I also loved getting to know my adopted country better during our nine week honeymoon and tour. Though I have lived here for a number of years, I have never traveled so extensively, and I thank all of you for making me feel so welcome." He wanted to go find his wife, make sure she was okay, but he knew what he needed to do.

A deep breath, in then out.

"I will take a few questions." Alexander nodded toward Matt Markinson.

"Prince Alexander, how did you find out about Queen Christiana's uncle and former fiancé?"

"I did business with her uncle in his official capacity on behalf of my family's properties here in Ravenzario. A few things he said just didn't quite add up. One day, I happened to overhear him on the phone, and everything clicked into place. The plot to remove Queen Christiana for reasons of insanity came to light with a few well-placed questions to associates. I went to the head of palace security. I felt I knew him well enough to know his loyalty to the queen was unquestioned.

"The queen's former fiancé attempted to get certain drugs from drug dealers who, for whatever other faults they may have, are also loyal to the crown. They heard things that didn't quite add up and reported the information anonymously to the authorities. I was informed by the head of security and took it upon myself to inform the queen. Her immediate instructions were to throw him in the dungeon - which isn't quite what it sounds like - and follow the investigation to wherever it led."

More than a dozen hands filled his field of vision as questions were shouted his way. Alexander pointed to a young lady who interviewed them on their honeymoon. "Queen Christiana talked about why she didn't want to cancel the wedding. I don't think any of us believe you are a gold digger who would only marry her because of the title. So why did you propose? What made you willing to marry a woman you didn't love?"

Alexander straightened the binder on the podium. "When I told Christiana about the plot on her life, I could see her heart and her trust shatter before my eyes. I knew I would do anything it took to give that back to her. As I said earlier, I've liked and admired her for some time, but in that moment, I knew I wanted to protect and take care of her. I knew I would never break her heart. I didn't want her to take the risk of having it broken again by someone else. All of us have someone in our lives we'd do anything for. For me, that's my parents, my twin brother, a few close friends, and the queen."

She asked a follow-up question. "If you'd do anything for the queen, give up anything for her, did you also feel you were giving up your chance at true love?"

"No." His answer was emphatic. "Absolutely not. I knew I didn't love Christiana the way I always thought I would love my bride when I got married. I also knew, without a doubt, I would love her that way sooner rather than later. I didn't give up a thing. In fact, if she hadn't been queen, I would still have married her. Her status had nothing to do with it."

Charlyn touched his elbow and whispered in his ear. Alexander nodded. "Ladies and gentlemen, thank you for your time. I have just been informed of some pressing business I must take care of. The queen and I ask for and covet your prayers. Thank you."

He turned and walked to the door, shouted questions following him.

One stood out above the others, and he nearly turned back to answer it.

"Do you love Queen Christiana now?"

Alexander kept walking and a few minutes later, he walked into the darkened bedroom to find Christiana lying on her left side and curled around her pillow. He'd discovered some time ago it was her favorite way to sleep, and the way the doctors recommended.

He turned to leave, but her voice stopped him. "I am not asleep." She didn't move but asked a question. "How did it go? Do you think the people will abandon us?"

Alexander stretched out on the bed next to her, propping his head on his hand as he reached out to cover her baby bump. "I think it went okay. Releasing the information about the assassination attempt helps engender sympathy, as does the difficult pregnancy. I'm not saying we exploit those, making them out to be worse than it is though it's bad enough already, but it helps." His hand shifted from her belly to brush the hair off her face. "I think it also helps everyone can see how much we care for each other even if we didn't quite have the best beginning in that regard."

The question called after him as he left continued to haunt him.

Did he love her?

When had she become such a news junkie? For the third day in a row, Christiana found herself watching the news on the giant screen in their room.

"Reaction from around the country has been mixed, but overall positive. Ravenzarians recognize the difficult position the queen was in and believe she made the best decision possible under the circumstances. They believe the queen and Prince Alexander do care deeply for each other and are working together for the good of the country. Many stated the hand-signed thank you notes sent out by the thousands after the memorial for the queen's late parents had something to do with the overwhelming good will amassed."

Her hand hurt for days after she signed those, but she knew at the time it was the right thing to do. That they would engender sympathy never crossed her mind. She had no idea they would need the sympathy.

"Those who have spent time with the queen and Prince Alexander have said they appear to be very comfortable around each other and never would have guessed they weren't in love on their wedding day." The picture of Alexander kissing her forehead appeared. *"Those watching on television, online, or in person certainly remember this moment. Tender and captivating, it seems there was more to the relationship than either of them realized at the time. That, too, goes a long way in convincing the people the best decision was made."*

Diana knocked on the door. "How are you feeling this morning, ma'am?"

Christiana gave her a weak smile and turned off the television. "Much better, though I am still concerned about how all of this will shake out."

"You do have a guest, ma'am. I think it would do you a lot of good." The secretive smile piqued Christiana's curiosity.

"Very well. Give me about fifteen minutes." Diana shut the door behind her, and Christiana twisted until her feet landed on the floor. In ten minutes, she dressed, brushed her teeth, and walked into the living area.

She felt her face light up when she saw who sat there. "Poppo!"

"Hello, Your Majesty." He bowed his head, but she reached to give him a hug instead.

"I am so glad to see you," she whispered.

"I'm glad to see you. To see for myself how you're doing."

She closed her eyes and breathed in the essence of the man she had adopted for a grandfather. "I am always glad to see you, Poppo, but what brings you here?"

They sat on the couch. "I needed to talk you and to see for myself." He took her hand in his. "I also wanted to let you know that we're here for you. Everyone I've talked with supports you and Alexander."

"I am sorry to have misled you before the wedding, Poppo." It had eaten at her, that she had let the man believe she and Alexander were in love and planned to get married all along.

Poppo chuckled. "Oh, sweet girl. I knew the truth from the beginning. Not everything, mind you, but that you and Alexander had no idea what you were in for. I didn't know the circumstances, but I did know everything wasn't as it seemed. I also knew you would be fine. God made the two of you for each other, and He will make it work."

"Thank you for your support, Poppo." She squeezed his hand. "I thank God He brought you and David into my life the same day the arrest happened."

Poppo raised a brow. "The same day? It doesn't surprise me, I suppose. God's timing is perfect."

"Yes, it is." She stood when Poppo did, giving the older gentleman a hug. "Thank you for coming to check on me."

"I wish I could stay longer, but I promised Annie I would read a book to her class this afternoon."

"Then thank you for coming when you knew you could only stay a few minutes." He gave her the kind of hug she had longed for as a child. The protective arms of a beloved grandparent. The only thing better would have been the loving arms of her parents.

And now her husband.

Being in Alexander's arms gave her a feeling she had never known anywhere. The feeling of being home.

Poppo kept his arm around her shoulder and she left hers around his waist as they walked to the door of the apartment. As they neared, the door opened. In walked Alexander. His face lit up, much as Christiana imagined hers had.

"Poppo! Good to see you!"

"I needed to check on our girl here. On both of you, really." Poppo left his arm around her shoulders as he talked with Alexander for a moment. With another squeeze and promise to be praying for both of them, Poppo left.

"Are you feeling up to spending time with some visitors today?" Alexander wrapped his arm around her shoulders as they returned to the living area.

"Perhaps. What group?" She looked up to see his eyes twinkling.

"That, my dear, is a surprise, but one I promise you'll enjoy."

Christiana sank into her favorite chair. "Very well. When do I need to be in the reception room?"

"You don't. Meet me in the main kitchen at noon." Alexander rested his hand on the top of her head. "I promise you'll love it." She heard the phone buzz in his pocket. He pulled it out and looked at it. "My next appointment is here. I'll see you in a bit."

Diana emerged from somewhere as soon as he left. They spent nearly an hour going over Christiana's plans for charitable donations for the next few weeks.

"Do you know who we are meeting with?" she asked Diana as she slid her shoes back on.

Her assistant grinned. "Nope. Not telling."

Time to find out.

23

Alexander hung a dark blue apron around his neck and tied the strings behind his back. "All right, we're going to get started."

"Where's the queen?" A precocious five-year-old with bouncy brown curls sat on one of the barstools, her chin propped on her hands as her elbows rested on the counter.

"She should be here in a few minutes." He set several loaves of bread out on the counter, followed by several platters of "fixin's" and then set a plate in front of each child. "We are going to have a picnic. Everyone brought their coats, right?"

Everyone nodded. It was cool enough they'd need them.

"And for a picnic we need sandwiches."

"A picnic?"

All of them looked up to see Queen Christiana standing there.

"How lovely. I cannot remember the last time I went on a picnic."

Every one of the children jumped down from their barstools, each of them bobbing a curtsy or bowing. "Good morning, Your

Majesty." They weren't quite in unison, but close. They must have practiced.

"Well, good morning." She stopped at Alexander's side, slipping her hand through his arm. "A picnic sounds lovely. I believe even I can make sandwiches." She leaned toward the children and whispered, "I have never been much good at cooking."

More likely she'd never had much of an opportunity. He loved to cook, but even he'd only had the chance a few times since the wedding and never yet for his wife. He'd have to fix that soon.

Alexander handed her an apron. "Okay. Let's get started." They spent the next twenty minutes making sandwiches. Helping children spread mayo or mustard, then using cookie cutters to make them into designs. Each child had a lunch box and thermos. The thermoses were filled with hot chocolate, made by Alexander and one of the seven-year-old boys. It was cool enough outside for it to be welcome.

All of them took off their aprons and put on their coats. Justin chose that moment to walk in. "I'm afraid there's going to be a change of plans. It has started to drizzle."

His mind raced a mile a minute. Where else could they have a picnic? Then it hit him. "How about in the Reception Room? It's cool enough that a fire would be nice. We could make s'mores." He grinned like a little kid at the thought.

"What are s'mores?" His wife looked at him, curiosity winning over amusement.

"You'll see."

Laughing, the small group followed him through the halls until they reached the Reception Room. Someone was there lighting a fire in the massive stone fireplace. Christiana thanked the aide as Justin showed up with some blankets and together they spread them out in front of the fire. Christiana sat with her legs tucked to one side. Alexander took a seat across the blanket from her, where he could see her but the kids could be spread out and closer to one of them than if they sat next to each other. He understood how important that was to a five-year-old. In fact, a certain little girl had plopped down right next to the queen.

The next twenty minutes flew by as they both talked with the kids. They cleaned up their messes, and Alexander hopped up to get the tray of supplies Justin had brought while they ate.

He set it down in front of the fire. "Okay, has anyone ever heard of s'mores?"

All of them shook their heads.

"All right then. Who likes chocolate?" Eleven hands, including Christiana's went up. "Marshmallows?" Eleven again. "What about graham crackers?" Another eleven. "You know I grew up in the United States, right?"

The five-year-old, whose name he discovered was Elana, piped up. "Yes! You're an American!"

"Well, I am, but I'm also a Ravenzarian now. Growing up, my twin brother and I would have these whenever our parents would let us. When we had a fire, or went camping, or for our birthday." He picked up a metal skewer. "First, you have to roast the marshmallows. Elana, how about you help me first?"

Before he finished, the little girl was at his side. He showed her, and the other kids, how to hold the marshmallow over the fire until it was toasty brown.

"Now, some people like them burnt, but I like them just like this." Alexander picked up half a cracker with part of a Hershey's bar on it and another cracker half. "Set it right here." He nodded to the chocolate and, when she did, used the other cracker to help slide the marshmallow off the skewer.

He helped Elana hold it as she took a bite. Her eyes went wide as she chewed. "Yum," she mumbled around the mouthful. "It's good."

Laughing, he turned to help the other kids get started. Elana was the youngest by about two years. Each of these kids had won a drawing to be here. The actual age for the drawing was seven, but somehow the form Elana's mother filled out was misprinted so they allowed her to win, though she wasn't technically eligible. The other kids were old enough to need less supervision, so once he got them started, Alexander motioned Christiana over.

"Let me help you make one." He showed her how to put the marshmallow on and how to hold it.

"Mr. Alexander?"

As Christiana tentatively reached for the fire, Alexander turned his attention to one of the boys whose marshmallow was done.

He spent fifteen minutes helping the kids make their s'mores. Christiana had put her skewer down and helped hold the crackers and chocolate for others.

She did things like that often, he'd noticed. Put others ahead of herself. Always giving. The last few weeks where she'd had to take it easy and let others put her first went against the grain for his wife.

Two hours after meeting in the kitchen, the kids were all picked up by their parents. Laughing and full of stories, they each introduced their parents to him and Christiana. He was able to tell each parent what a good kid they'd raised. It took another half hour to send the kids off right, after three extra hugs from little Elana.

"I am going back to get some work done." Christiana started for the door, but Alexander stopped her with a hand on her arm.

"Nope. You haven't had a s'more yet. Come on. Have a seat."

She sat in front of the fire, legs tucked to one side again. Alexander sat right behind her, so the fabric from his shirt brushed against her back. Reaching both arms around her, he put another marshmallow on the skewer. "Like this."

Christiana shifted back until she leaned against him, letting Alexander roast the marshmallow for her.

He glanced down and swallowed hard. The line of her neck beckoned him. He couldn't help it and pressed his lips to the curve where her neck and shoulder met.

"I'm so glad you said 'yes', love," he murmured, pressing another kiss closer to her ear. "I can't imagine my life without you in it."

Christiana shuddered a bit as his words literally reverberated through her. "I am glad I said 'yes', too, Xander."

He kissed his way up her neck. Her eyes fluttered closed, and her head leaned back against him, giving him better access. Deep inside, things began to stir. She found herself wishing for things that could not be until the doctors released her from restrictions.

"Xander," she whispered. "I need you to stop."

Christiana felt him pull away, both physically and, though she could not see him, emotionally. Before she could correct his misimpression, her phone buzzed. Her eyes closed again, for a different reason this time. She looked at the screen. "This cannot wait, Alexander. I am sorry."

"Of course." His tone was distant.

"Xander..."

Before she could at least attempt to straighten things out, Justin walked in. Alexander moved away from her and stood up. While talking to Justin, Alexander helped her stand. He gave her an absent-minded kiss on the cheek before walking off, looking at the tablet his assistant handed him.

With a sigh, she headed for her office. Today was the first day she would work out of it for at least a short time. A video conference meant she needed to be somewhere besides the apartment. She settled into her office chair and turned her attention to the paperwork resting on her desk.

After two hours of work, she was more than ready to go back to her room and rest. Would Alexander be waiting for her? When had he started worming his way into her heart? Why had she let him, so quickly?

Did making love with him have anything to do with it? If that never happened, or if she had never gotten pregnant, would she still feel these same things for him? Was it just the hormone shifts that came with pregnancy?

No matter. Entering the bedroom he had shared with her since the concern for the baby grew, and she was confined to bed for a time, she shed her clothes and went straight for the shower. The hot water washed over her as tears slid down her cheeks.

A sob caught in her throat.

On the heels of her uncle's betrayal, she swore to herself she would never rely on another man. Her first fiancé was safe. She felt comfortable. Felt attraction. But she never felt anything like what she did for Alexander.

She had checked his schedule before leaving the office. He would not be back to the apartment until after her usual bedtime.

Perfect.

After a light dinner she forced herself to eat, Christiana watched one episode of *2 Cool 4 School* - her favorite one - and read until she was ready for sleep. As she drifted, she wished she could let herself truly believe in love. In her love for Alexander and in the love she believed he had for her.

Alexander knelt next to Christiana's side of the bed. He wanted to kiss her awake, but after she pulled away from him earlier, he didn't dare. Especially not when he was telling her he had to leave.

Instead, he ran a hand over her arm. "Christiana?" He shook her arm lightly.

Her eyes blinked open. "Xander?"

"I'm so sorry to wake you, but I have to fly to the States. My grandma had another heart attack, and this one's worse than the last one. We won't know for a few days, but I have to go, just in case."

She pushed up on her elbow, the sheet sliding down to reveal a nightgown he'd never seen. Pale lavender. Spaghetti straps. Dipping lower than anything he'd ever seen her wear. He forced his eyes to her face.

"You're leaving?" she croaked with morning voice.

"I have to see my grandmother."

She nodded. "Okay." One hand pulled the sheet back over her shoulder as she settled into her pillow. "Be safe. Give your family my love."

"I will." He leaned over and pressed a kiss to her temple. "Sleep well." It wasn't what he wanted to say, but he'd rather make his first real declaration of love when she was awake.

Half an hour later, he settled on board One Royal Air. His family's plane was ferrying family members from around the States.

Hours later, he deplaned, the chill of the Canadian air mass settling into southwest Missouri dropping the temperatures considerably. The wind cut through his wool overcoat and made him wish he'd brought his warmest gloves.

Alexander trotted down the steps of the plane to the waiting car. A glance up showed a couple of photographers in the distance with lenses as long as his arm. Though he didn't have near the following of his wife, even when in his home country, the spouse of royalty was always a photograph waiting to happen. Word must have gotten out the Ravenzarian plane would be landing. He opened his own door and slid into the warmth of the back seat.

Christopher waited for him.

"How is she?" The car pulled away from the plane.

His brother finished a text and slid his phone into the inside pocket of his suit coat. "Better. Mom's with her. The media did get wind that you're headed this way so we could expect some of them to show up. There's not a big paparazzi contingent here right now, but the local stations may run stories. Depending on how busy the news day is, it might get picked up by the national networks."

Alexander shrugged. "I don't care. The hospital won't let them in and security should already be over there." A friend of the family owned a security company. Before leaving Ravenzario, he'd called in a favor to get someone up there ASAP. He'd met Jonathan Langley-Cranston a few times, and the man knew how to get security.

"About an hour after you called, Jonathan had someone over there."

Even without an escort the drive took about twenty minutes. Alexander directed the driver to one of the buildings across the street when he saw a television truck in front of the hospital. There were at least four entrances besides the main one. They couldn't all be covered.

The walk was a little further, but it was worth it. Alexander had looked up the floor plans on his tablet and directed his brother up one elevator, across the bridge above National Avenue, and onto the first floor of the main hospital building. One of the lesser used staircases took them down one story to the ground floor and the CardioVascular ICU.

The stark hallways, with their white linoleum tile and occasional landscape or happy medical photograph, were broken by doors to go through to the next section of the hospital. The beeps and intercom pages broke his concentration on counting the tiles to pass the time. They reached the CVICU and waited for the staffer to finish a phone call before inquiring about their grandmother.

The staffer clicked buttons on the computer. "It looks like the doctor is with her right now and her family and friends are in the waiting room." She pointed to door behind her. "Right through there." She eyed them. "Do I know you?"

He smiled politely. "I don't believe so, but thank you for your help." The last thing he wanted at the moment was for some hospital employee to accidentally let it slip where in the building he was hanging out.

With a deep breath, he followed his brother into the waiting room to find his family.

24

Christiana rolled over and groaned. Her entire body ached as she tried to resist the urge to throw up again.

Diana laid the cool washcloth on Christiana's forehead. "Dr. McCall is on her way, ma'am."

"Why not Dr. Chambers?"

"He's out of town today. He'll be back tomorrow, but I didn't want to wait."

As much as she wanted to protest, Christiana simply nodded. Had she ever been so sick?

"Elana's mother called the office. Apparently, she took sick about two hours after she left here. I didn't tell her you were ill. She felt badly enough without knowing that."

Christiana's eyes closed, and she willed herself to sleep. Sleeping, she knew, was the best thing for a stomach bug. Let the abdomen rest. Her mind drifted. She had not heard from Alexander since he left. It had not been very long, but she would have liked a phone call when he arrived. Or at least a text. She would have heard if anything had gone wrong, but would it have been too much to ask for her to hear from him herself?

Her thoughts were interrupted by another round of gut-wrenching into the trash can. By the time she finished, Dr. McCall was in the room with her.

The good doctor helped her lay back down. "How long as this been going on?"

Christiana closed her eyes and put the washcloth back on her forehead. "About eight hours. I have thrown up at least nine times."

Dr. McCall removed the washcloth. "I want to get your temperature," she explained. "We'll give it a few minutes. Diana said you were in contact with a sick little girl?"

"Apparently."

She spent a few minutes taking Christiana's vitals and then her temperature. "No fever, but I am a bit concerned. I don't think the anti-nausea meds are the way to go this time. We'll let it run its course and give you IV fluids for support. The duke is out of town?"

"Yes. Diana offered to stay as long as I need her since she has already been exposed."

Dr. McCall's nurse chose that moment to walk in, and they put the IV into her hand.

"I am seriously considering a pallet in the bathroom." Christiana attempted a joke, though she only smiled weakly at best.

"I hope it doesn't come to that." Dr. McCall squeezed her hand. "Hopefully, you're on the down slope of this now."

"From your lips to God's ears." After a few more minutes, Dr. McCall and her nurse left, and Christiana tried to get some sleep. When she couldn't, she picked up the massive remote and turned on the projector as the screen lowered.

Before she could flip over to the movie screen, the news came back from commercial. Had Alexander been the last one to watch? American News Network International was not usually her first choice.

"And in international royal news, Prince Alexander is back in

Serenity Landing for a few days. Sources tell us his grandmother suffered a heart attack two days ago."

The picture on the screen changed to a shot of her husband trotting down the stairs of Royal Air One and getting into a waiting car.

"The prince and his twin brother were seen walking through the halls of Cox South hospital in Springfield, Missouri, but the family has made no comment to the press at this time. His departure so quickly on the heels of the truth of his engagement and wedding to the queen has led to speculation that all is not well in Revenzarian palace. The queen, who has been on bed rest and restricted activity for much of her pregnancy, did not accompany him."

They moved on to some other story as Christiana changed the input to movies. At least he was there. He was safe. He had security with him, and she knew he had friends who ran a security firm who would be there as well. Why did the thought of something happening to him bother her so? There were no known threats. Perhaps because all of the threats were against her.

Her stomach roiled. With just enough time to get to the bathroom, she hurried that way.

"Next up, Margie McCoy of 2 Cool 4 School *talking with us about the possibility of a reunion."*

Julia's ears perked up. A reunion? Alex and Chris Slate hadn't been seen since the show ended, and they disappeared back to whatever Midwestern town they'd emerged from a year before the show started.

She hurried through her morning routine and urged her own Alex to move a bit faster. The bus would be here before she knew it. By the time they came back for the bottom of the hour news break, she was brushing her teeth.

"And in international news, Prince Alexander of Ravenzario is in Springfield, Missouri visiting his grandmother after a heart attack." The picture shifted to show Alexander with his twin brother. *"The American is making his first visit to his homeland after marrying Queen Christiana in the fall. The royal couple is expecting their first child later this year. Back to Abby and Tod in New York."*

This time the picture showed the two co-hosts sitting with Margie McCoy on tall barstools.

The actress had a look on her face that Julia couldn't quite identify, but it was quickly replaced by a pasted-on smile.

After exchanging pleasantries, Margie leaned forward.

"I think I may have just solved one of the biggest entertainment mysteries of our time. I think I know what happened to Alex and Chris Slate."

Abby's eyes went wide. "You haven't kept in touch with them? We know they dropped out of the limelight, but they haven't kept in touch with their costars?"

"Not that I'm aware of. Chris and I had a very public relationship for several years, but even I never knew for sure where they came from."

"But you think you've solved the mystery?" Tod asked.

Margie looked off-screen. "Can you put that picture of Prince Alexander back up and put it next to one of the promo shots with the Slate brothers?"

Julia gasped as the two pictures appeared side-by-side.

Margie went on. "I don't know for sure, obviously, since it only just occurred to me, but the names can't be a coincidence, can they? Everyone knew Slate was a stage name, and if I'm right, it's probably because of Christopher Mayfield from the movies in the sixties, seventies, and eighties. The names were too close." The picture returned to the two hosts and the actress. *"I'm saying that perhaps the new prince should clear it up if it's not true. Or Alex and Chris should."*

"Well, the rumors about a reunion have been around for a long time. With all the other reunions going on, like Girl Meets World *and* Fuller House, *it seems the time could be right." Tod shifted in his seat. "It's been*

assumed it would go on without the Slate brothers. If this supposition is correct, and looking at the pictures, it certainly could be, it doesn't seem likely Prince Alexander would be involved anyway."

Margie shrugged. "Who knows? Even though our characters were the main couple on the show, I never knew Alex very well. He was intensely private about most things, even more so than Chris."

"Isn't it odd that no one ever knew where they were from? Never visited their hometown with them?" Abby leaned forward in her chair. "I've been to Tod's house many times. His wife makes a great brisket."

"Oh, we did get together, but always in LA." She waved a hand in the air. "Regardless of what Chris and Alex decide to do, there's always been a huge call for a reunion. I've been talking with several of the others, including creator Dusty Ring, and we'd like to do this thing sometime in the next year or so. With the fifteen-year anniversary coming up, the timing seems right."

Julia clicked the off button on the remote and grabbed her coat, rushing Alex outside ahead of her. Her boss's brother was currently in the CVICU at Cox South. It gave her a reason to visit and see if Alexander remembered her.

Or the night he took her home.

"Did you see the news this morning?"

Alexander looked up as Christopher walked in the room. The grim look on his brother's face told him he should have.

"No. Why?"

"Margie was on some morning show, saw a story about you being stateside, and put two and two together on the air."

Alexander grimaced. "Did they buy the theory?"

"Lock, stock, and barrel. I talked to Mady half an hour ago. The calls are coming in fast and furious. Everything from the reunion show to *BoyzGoneWild* magazine. Again."

"We've turned down every public appearance for a decade, and they think we'll start now?" Alexander shook his head. "I'm married to the queen of Ravenzario, and they think I'll do a photo shoot like that?"

"No, but nothing ventured, nothing gained. Guess they're hoping one of use would do it."

Running a hand through his hair, Alexander stood up. "Guess we should go face the assembled masses. How many reporters are in front of the hospital?"

"About half as many as there will be in a couple hours. Is there someone we want to give the story to rather than just a press conference?"

Alexander thought about that. "Not right now. I'll make a statement. You can if you want to, but I think we leave it at that for the time being. No questions." He started for the door.

"Don't you think you should call your wife first?"

Right. His wife. Had he talked to Christiana since arriving in Missouri? He didn't think so. The timing hadn't worked out. When he had a minute, she would have been sleeping or in a meeting. He didn't want to wake her up or interrupt if he didn't have to.

His brother had a point, though, so Alexander pulled his phone out and waited for the call to go through. But instead of Christiana, her assistant answered.

"Good morning, Diana."

"It's afternoon here, sir." He could almost see the smile on the woman's face. "How can I help you?"

"I need to speak with the queen."

Alexander sensed hesitation on her part. "I'm afraid you can't right now, sir. She's asleep."

Another pass of his fingers through his hair. "Okay. Will you tell her to call me as soon as she wakes up? I have to give a press conference. I wanted to talk to her first, but I really don't want to put it off any longer."

"About the news program this morning? She's already seen the replays."

How had she known about it before he did? And asleep? "Is she feeling all right? Or just tired?"

"Um, she didn't sleep well." There was the hesitation again. What wasn't she telling him? "She's feeling much better though. Dr. McCall checked on her earlier."

He knew there had been no appointment scheduled. Why had the doctor stopped by? He started to ask, when something on the television caught his eye. Christopher had changed it to the news network, and they were replaying the spot. "Have her call me, would you?"

"Certainly, sir."

He didn't say good-bye but hung up, crossing his arms across his chest as his brother turned up the sound. "Nothing earth-shattering," he said as it cut back to new anchors speculating away. "Except for the revelation of our identities, but we knew that would happen someday."

The camera switched to the outside of the hospital. "I guess we need to find the hospital PR people and figure out where we can have a short press conference. If they'd rather us just walk out and do it there, that's fine with me, but I'd rather work with them than irritate them."

"I agree."

Mom walked into the small waiting room, the weight of the world resting on her shoulders and visible on her face. "I heard the news. Dad and Gramps are with Mom. What's the plan?"

They talked for a few more minutes before heading out to find the hospital PR people.

Christiana was finally feeling a bit better. She no longer felt like her insides were going to explode or that the smallest sip of Sprite would send her running to the nearest trash can. Her entire body still ached, sore from using muscles rarely exercised. The hot, but not too hot, bath had helped, but not nearly enough. Maybe she should have Diana arrange for a massage.

The thought brought to mind Alexander's shoulder massage several weeks earlier. The man knew what he was doing as he'd expertly kneaded her stress away. What she wouldn't give to have him lying next to her, rubbing her lower back, maybe even holding her as he slept.

He did that every once in a while. She did not think he realized he did it. The first time she woke up with his arm around her, she barely dared to breath. The warm cocoon had lulled her back to sleep in record time. It had not happened every night, or even all that often, but often enough she missed it when it did not.

Diana walked quietly into the room. Christiana needed to make sure the woman got a nice bonus. She had been going above and beyond for some time but with the pregnancy, she rarely went home, choosing instead to live in the staff apartments.

"I am awake." Christiana pushed herself into a sitting position. "Have you heard from the prince?"

"He called a bit ago, ma'am. He had just found out about the revelations on television this morning and wanted to speak with you."

Right. Everyone now knew she was married to teen heartthrob Alex Slate.

"The press conference will be starting in a minute." Diana picked up the remote and lowered the screen, pulling up the live feed of one of the news networks as they waited.

Alexander had not consulted her? Had he spoken with Charlyn?

The exterior of the hospital showed behind a local reporter who was being picked up by the network. Likely she hoped it would be her chance to break into the big time. It was not a huge story like 9/11 had been or covering a natural disaster would be, but nonetheless a chance to get some limelight.

The sound stayed turned down but Christiana's eyes narrowed as she looked through the glass doors. Was that Alexander? Or Christopher? Whichever one it was, he was hugging a woman. A long hug. Perhaps an old family friend? *Please, God, let that be an old family friend.*

Whichever brother it was finally released the woman and turned. When he did, Christiana's fears were confirmed. Alexander walked out of the doors first with Christopher hot on his heels. Alexander stepped up to the microphones with his brother just behind and to his right. Diana turned up the sound in time to hear the shouted questions quiet down.

"Thank you for coming on such short notice." Alexander shuffled the papers in front of him then looked directly into the camera. *"This morning, Margie McCoy made a supposition that my brother and I are also Chris and Alex Slate from the show* 2 Cool 4 School. *In that moment,*

she uncovered something we worked very hard to keep from the public. After the show ended, Christopher and I both just wanted to begin our 'grown-up' lives. College, careers, families, without the celebrity specter hanging over us all the time. We always knew this day would come, but we were able to have private lives successfully."

He gave a wry grin. *"Until, of course, I married a queen. That was something none of us could have anticipated. I don't regret it for a moment and never will. We do ask that you continue to respect our privacy, especially that of our family and friends. The press organizations that cooperate will be given the chance to be among the first we do interviews with. On a personal note, our family asks that you keep our grandmother in your prayers as she recovers from her heart attack. I also ask for your prayers as Queen Christiana continues to struggle,"* Christiana winced. *"with a difficult pregnancy. Thank you for your time."*

"Except for making me sound like an invalid, it is about what I anticipated." She did border on being an invalid, but the world being told that irked her. Christiana dragged her attention back to the screen as Christopher took Alexander's spot.

"I don't have much to add, except to thank all of you for the continued support of 2 Cool 4 School. *Neither of us anticipates being involved in an official reunion special at this point in time."* He started to back away then returned. *"And for the record, all requests from* Boyz-GoneWild *and similar magazines or websites will be met with the same resounding 'no' they always have been."*

He turned and walked away, ignoring the shouted questions. Christiana took the remote and turned it off.

"Shall I contact the Office of Tourism? I would imagine the number of tourists will jump in the next few weeks."

Christiana turned the thought over in her head. "Yes. We need to begin to anticipate the additional tourists, doing our best to encourage the highlighting of our culture and lands while discouraging the exploitation of Alexander personally."

"Agreed." Diana picked up the phone and placed the call. After speaking with the Minister of Tourism for a moment, she hung up. "The prince already called them. Or rather Justin did at his request."

"Good." Something about the whole thing left her unsettled. Perhaps once she spoke with Alexander, it would help.

Diana answered an incoming call. Christiana saw the smile cross her face. "Yes, sir. She's right here." She held out the phone. "It's your husband, ma'am."

"Hello?" She did not know quite how to address him.

"Diana told me you heard?" No greeting. Straight to business.

"Yes. I saw your press conference. Have you really had offers from *BoyzGoneWild?*" Whatever possessed her to ask such a thing?

"Just this morning," he confirmed. She could almost see the grim set of his mouth. "Don't worry. Neither of us would ever agree to it, much less together."

"I did not doubt that. I just did not know you received such offers."

"Many times. Starting about six months before we turned eighteen. We've turned them all down." She heard him blow out a breath. "I'm heading back in a few minutes. As soon as the plane can be ready. There's not much I can do here except draw unnecessary attention to the hospital and interrupt already stressful times for lots of other people. My family will keep me updated."

"Very well. I will make sure everyone necessary is notified on this end."

"I already did."

"Oh." Christiana deflated back against the pillows. "I suppose I will see you later tonight."

"It'll be late when I get in." He sounded distracted. "I'll probably just sleep in my room so I don't bother you." Before she could respond, he went on. "I gotta run. I'll see you in the morning."

Christiana stared at the buzzing phone. "Good-bye."

"You're fired."

The words rang over and over in Julia's head as she drove home twenty minutes after she arrived at work. She'd tried to explain to her boss that she'd gone to the hospital to visit his brother, a former classmate of hers. It was the absolute truth. She'd also hoped to get a chance to talk with Alexander, even for just a minute. Just because.

She wouldn't have stalked him. Just if she happened to run into him while she was there. Checking up on her old friend really was something she'd been meaning to do anyway. Running into Alexander had been a bonus.

And she had talked to Alexander for just a minute. He seemed to recognize her though she couldn't be sure. Unfortunately, she'd forgotten about the meeting she was supposed to set up for. Normally, it didn't matter too much what time she got to work as long as she got her work done, but today she was to have gotten the conference room ready. Julia had even left a message for her boss telling him she'd be late. Their normal procedure. But with the conference room not ready for the meeting it was too much.

By the time she reached home, her headache had reached epic proportions, and her tears had long since left her dehydrated. Once inside the apartment, she sat on the couch, staring into space.

Julia had no idea, how long she sat there before her phone buzzed, but the text from her mom about her trip sent her into a fresh round of tears.

Her Alex had picked the place for their spring break trip. And because he wanted to visit the country where the nice man his mama knew lived, she'd booked the trip to Revenzario. A splurge. One she shouldn't have made. She knew she shouldn't have even when clicking the buttons. Sales helped. And the islands were gorgeous. They had a wonderful week and a half planned. They had no idea what Prince Alexander's schedule was, but she'd planned to look it up when they arrived and hope there might be a good time for them to at least see him in person.

The tickets were paid for. The rental car was paid for, as was the ferry crossing and the deposits on some of the hotel rooms had already been put on her credit card, with money set aside to cover it. None of it was refundable.

Alex would be devastated if they didn't take the trip. With her help, he'd researched all the cool places to go and painstakingly mapped it all out. He helped pick the hotels and planned to tell all of his friends about it when they returned.

Julia texted her mom back. It was only a few days away, and she'd do her best to keep her job loss a secret until after they returned. No reason to stress anyone else out over her downturn in income.

And maybe, just maybe, Steve would cool down. She'd screwed up. Big time. She knew that, but she'd also been an invaluable asset to the company for some time. Maybe he'd give her another chance.

If not...well, she'd cross that bridge when she got to it.

Alexander reached for the other side of the bed, not quite awake as he wondered where the warmth he usually found spooned behind his wife had disappeared to. Was Christiana sick?

He opened one eye and looked to see the other side of the bed hadn't been slept in. Sitting up he realized why. When he got back to the palace in the wee hours of the morning, he'd changed into pajama pants and collapsed into the bed in the room he'd used when they first returned to the palace.

But...he leaned back against the headboard. The bedding was the same as Christiana's room. Had it been when he'd lived in here before? He swung his feet over the edge, grabbed a t-shirt, and walked out into the living area. Diana was at her desk, talking with someone, though he couldn't figure out whom. She held up a hand to keep him from going into Christiana's bedroom.

A minute later, she hung up. "It's good to have you back, sir. How's your grandmother?"

Alexander shrugged. "Last I heard, she was recovering as well as could be expected, and her doctors anticipate a mostly full recovery though it may take some time." A thought crossed his mind. "Have you heard something else since I got in?"

She shook her head. "No, sir."

"Is the queen in?"

"No, sir. She'll be back in a little bit."

Did Diana look uncomfortable? "Where is she?"

"Out for a walk. Not a long one, but she wanted to get outside for a few minutes. Dr. McCall's nurse went with her."

"Why was the nurse here?"

Definitely shifting uncomfortably. "Dr. McCall was here earlier checking on the queen."

"Do you know where she is?" Oh, for a normal house. He'd have to change at least into jeans and a collared shirt before he could go find her. Even the baseball hat and sneakers he'd toss on would get him questionable looks.

"No, sir."

Great. He was ready to walk out in three minutes flat. Morning breath didn't bother him. No one would be close enough, but he felt the need to find his wife. Alexander trotted through the hallways until he reached the main door out to the garden where he'd proposed and where he'd found her the first day she needed to get out again. One thing he didn't like about living at the palace was the large staff, many of whom he'd never met personally. He needed to fix that and at least try to get to know them by sight.

Then maybe they wouldn't look at him like he was nuts when he passed.

He had to stop to open the heavy door, but as soon as he did he saw the person he was looking for.

Christiana walked slowly up the steps with the nurse at her side, but not holding onto her. Alexander gave a nod of dismissal to the nurse. "I got it from here."

The two women exchanged a glance he couldn't interpret but didn't fight him. He wrapped his arm around Christiana's waist as she went up the last few steps. "How're you feeling?"

"Fine." She didn't elaborate and the walk back to the apartment was quiet. "I think I am going to lay down for a bit. I am sure you have plenty of other things to do." Something sounded a bit off, and it seemed to Alexander like she was trying to get him to stay out. He ignored her and walked into the room they'd shared for the last couple of months.

The first thing he noticed was that the bedding had been changed to something he didn't recognize.

The second thing was the IV stand with a bag still hanging from it next to the big recliner.

His hand dropped from her waist. "Is there something I need to know?"

Christiana didn't look at him. "Diana received a call from Elana's mother that she came down with the stomach flu. It appears I did as well."

Everything in him wanted to explode, but Alexander forced himself to take a deep breath and blow it out slowly. "And you didn't think I should know about this? I would have come straight back. Or did you know before I left?"

"The first round hit about two hours after you left. I would have told you if you had called to speak with me."

"I did call."

"Not until you had been gone over a full day. And I was finally sleeping when you did. Diana was right not to wake me." His wife refused to look at him until she sat carefully in the chair. The nurse moved to her side and helped her take her sweater off.

Alexander waited until she'd hooked the tubing back up into his wife's arm then jerked his head. The nurse rolled her eyes but left the room.

"And you didn't think I should know that you were sick? Like need fluids sick. After everything else that's happened over the last couple months?"

"You were taking care of your family, just as you should have been. Your parents, your brother, and your grandmother needed you."

"*You* are my family now, Christiana! You and the baby. I thought we agreed you wouldn't keep things about the baby from me anymore!" Red was starting to tinge his vision. What if something had happened, and he'd been halfway around the world? Could he have made it home in time? What if she had...miscarried without him here with her? "I have to go." He turned on his heel and walked out of the room, not waiting to see if she called him back. Not sure if he was glad she didn't.

If only he could just go for a run to burn off some steam. Not around here. There was no place for him to do so on palace grounds. Time to head for the island and the Biacampo property where he could pound the pavement until he had a better grip on his emotions.

Christiana closed her eyes and struggled to keep the tears at bay. He had slept in the other room. Even when he burst out into the garden, he seemed annoyed, not happy to see her and had not known she had been sick at that point.

This marriage stuff was not as easy as she thought it might be.

It would be easier if her heart never got involved.

Diana walked in, a tablet in her hand. "Ma'am, there's something I think you need to see."

"Is it bad?" Christiana asked, unable to keep the weariness out of her voice.

"It's not good."

She took the tablet from her assistant. The picture was one from a different angle than what she had seen with her own eyes through the television camera. Alexander hugging the woman at the hospital. Christiana skimmed the article. *Prince Alexander...hugging an unknown woman...not his wife...seemingly long, full-bodied hug...potential extra-curricular activities overseas?*

With one hand she squeezed her thumb and forefinger at the corner of her eyes and with the other she handed the tablet back.

"I'm sorry, ma'am."

"Alexander has not cheated on me." She did not believe it. She could not. He always made such a big deal out of his family's commitment to fidelity, out of the fiction the tabloids had made up for him and his brother all those years earlier.

"Something you need to consider, though, ma'am, and we need to discuss with the PR Office is the fact that there will likely be at least one woman, if not more, coming forward claiming to have given birth to his child. Those claims are an unfortunate reality of his former celebrity status and the revelations of that status in the last day."

"I am aware of the tabloids. I also believe him when he says there is no chance at all that he has any children out in the world. He would not have abandoned them if he did, but I do not believe he did in the first place."

"I will contact the PR Office. I'm sure they've already thought of this and are working on his response."

His response. Not hers. Did it matter what she thought about the possibility of her husband fathering a child with another woman who would now try to get what was "due" the supposed step-child of the queen? It happened with Addie's step-daughter the year before.

"I am going to take a nap." One good thing about her cleared schedule. She could send everyone away, tell them she was tired, and wallow to her heart's content. Now that she felt better, maybe she could even sneak some of the ice cream out of the small freezer in her closet. "Please see I am not disturbed by *any*one."

Diana opened her mouth as though to protest but snapped it shut when Christiana glared at her. "Yes, ma'am."

The rest of the day passed slowly. Christiana stayed in her chair, staring out at the Mediterranean beyond the walls of the palace. The walls that both protected and isolated.

Her hand rubbed across her belly. She did not let herself think, much less think too deeply. Perhaps she should find a book to read. But getting up to find one took more energy than she had at the moment. As darkness descended, she still heard nothing through the door of her room, nothing but Diana taking care of business. Dr. McCall's nurse came back and removed the IV. After answering the call of nature, Christiana settled into a different recliner with her laptop and mouse.

Time to get to work.

Christiana awoke the next morning feeling a sense of loss she could not explain. Her first movement went to her belly where flutters quickly assured her everything was just fine. She opened her eyes and immediately realized why she felt that loss.

The other side of the bed was empty again. It had not slept in at all.

Her husband, the one who had been hugging a woman halfway around the world just thirty-six hours earlier, had not slept with her.

She closed her eyes again and evaluated her physical state. Her stomach seemed growly, but in a hungry way not upset. Good. After checking the time, a luxurious shower helped the day improve just a bit. Breakfast at the small table in the kitchen consisted of a scrambled egg and a couple pieces of toast. The orange juice proved to be a bit much, and she only took a couple sips of it.

Justin walked in as she took her last swallow of milk. "Good morning, Your Majesty."

"Good morning, Justin." She wiped her mouth on her napkin and thanked Paul for his assistance. "What does my husband have on his schedule today?"

Justin frowned. "Nothing. We cleared it when he left for the States, but I haven't seen him yet." He shifted from one foot to the other. "The Duke left right after you, uh, talked yesterday. He went to his family's property for a proper run. He texted that he planned to return yesterday evening, but I never heard from him. I didn't want to intrude into your private quarters any more than we already have given your working situation."

Christiana fixed her face into a stoic mask. "I have no idea if he has returned. You might check the room he lived in when we first returned to the palace. He may be in there, but I did not see him before retiring last night or since I woke this morning." She knew she was being snippy with Justin, and it was not be his fault, but everything in her wanted to make a much more vigorous attack than she had. She should be commended for keeping her cool as much as she did.

Something flitted across Justin's face, and she noted he stood up a bit straighter, sounded a bit more formal. The ache in her chest grew. She and Alexander had a wonderful working relationship with both Diana and Justin. A bit more informal perhaps than with others on staff, but when working so closely with someone so often, it was hard not to. The veneer of formality had now returned with Justin.

He smiled at her, though she noted the smile did not quite reach his eyes the same way it would have a few days earlier. "Very well. I will see if I can find him. Have a wonderful day, ma'am."

"Thank you."

She started to pick up her dishes and carry them to the sink, something Alexander always did, but Paul waved her off. "Diana said you have a meeting coming up, ma'am. I'll see to it."

"Thank you," she murmured, searching her brain for who the meeting was with and drawing a blank.

Her assistant waited for her as she walked out of the kitchen. "Who am I meeting with?"

"Prime Minister Caruso asked for a few moments of your time. When he heard the Duke had returned, he asked that your husband be included as well." Diana trailed a half-step behind as Christiana walked to the door leading out of the apartment. What waited for her stopped her in her tracks. "I know you would prefer to walk, ma'am, but the Council Meeting Chamber is quite a distance."

With a nod and weariness sinking onto her shoulders, Christiana sat in the wheelchair. Diana kept up a running commentary about what else the day would hold - not much of anything strenuous. Christiana would spend some time in the office, had two phone and one video conference, and a web conference about the dinner she still needed to hold for those who were present the last night of their honeymoon.

The wheelchair came to a stop two turns from the meeting room. Diana helped her stand and she walked the rest of the way, glad she chose to dress in one of her new pantsuits for the day. Perhaps this was why Diana left it laying out for her. Unsurprisingly, she was the last to arrive.

Six men and three women all stood as she walked in. She never knew how they knew it would be her coming. Maybe someone made an announcement beforehand? Christiana stood in front of the large chair at the head of the table. "Please be seated." Her husband, she noted, sat to her right but had barely looked her direction when she walked in. Instead, he looked somewhere over the top of her head. She turned to the prime minister. "How can I help you today, Mr. Caruso?"

A myriad of emotions flitted across his face before his shoulders slumped, and he pinched the bridge of his nose. "Your Majesty, I wish there was an easy way to tell you this, but there's not." He slid a form her way.

She skimmed the top. "Annual Good Friday Pardon?" The tradition dated back to the fourteenth century, but had been codified, as had so many other things, in the 1700s. "What about it?"

"Four people are allowed to request pardons. The monarch, the consort when there is one as there now is, the prime minister, and the leader of the minority coalition. All of these pardons are sent before the Pardon Board as all other pardon requests are, but in the last two centuries we can find no instances where they have not been upheld."

Christiana nodded. "I filled out the paperwork several weeks ago. A man I believe to have been wrongly convicted. The only witnesses against him have recanted under oath. There was never any physical evidence tying him to the crime. We have taken enough of his life."

"Correct. You also know the names are never, ever made public until the Pardon Board Meeting the end of the month prior to Easter. This year, with an April Easter, that meeting takes place first thing Monday. Generally, those being pardoned are released by the end of the business day. The only thing that cannot be pardoned with the Good Friday Pardon is treason. Those are limited to a one time monarch's special exemption."

Her stomach started to churn. Though she had filed the paperwork based on the information given to her for the last several years, she never paid much attention to the process or the restrictions. The first few years, her uncle had recommended people she now knew were his henchmen. The last two years she had one of the royal attorneys find a suitable candidate. "Who is it?" Only two names would cause this much discomfort.

The prime minister glanced around the room. "I have not shared this with anyone else, yet, ma'am." Everyone else looked just as nervous as she imagined she did. "The Minority Leader turned in his paperwork to me this morning."

"Who is it?" she asked again.

His face looked grim as he reached over and flipped up the first page of the documents in front of her.

All of the blood drained out of her body when she saw the name listed there.

Her uncle.

"How much longer, Mom?" Julia rolled her head to the side to see Alex curled up in the seat next to her.

"We're almost there." She looked at her watch. "A couple more hours. Get some sleep."

Her first time traveling internationally, and all she wanted to do was sleep. It was to be expected. They left for St. Louis Thursday evening, spent the night with a friend, and flew out just before noon on Friday. After a short layover at JFK in New York, they flew an exhausting who-knew-how-many hours to Rome, arriving at seven the next morning. They'd both slept some on that flight and, after picking up the tiny rental car, drove to a tour company and took a quick look around the city. There wouldn't be time on the way home.

After a full day in Rome, they boarded the ferry about ten at night. Julia debated for a long time about whether to splurge for a cabin or to get the first class seats. She had initially reserved the cabin, but was able to change it to the chairs when they arrived. It didn't save much money, but at this point, every penny counted.

The chairs were comfortable, and the ship was only about half full so they had plenty of room. They would arrive in Ravenzario at six after traveling for nearly three full days. Alex seemed to have slept well enough, but Julia's mind continued non-stop. She came up with every idea she could to save money while not cluing Alex in to what she was doing.

Their first stop would be the port city where the ship would dock. Acron offered a museum and an old Roman church they'd tour. By nightfall, they'd be in the capital city of Pagosa for the first time. Because she knew Alex was fascinated with the prince he shared a name with, she'd decided to keep the room with the palace view. Just this once. The rest of the trip, the views would be whatever was cheapest. In fact, she was contemplating canceling one or more of their reservations and renting camping gear at one of the national campgrounds.

But she wasn't sure yet if her frugality would stretch quite that far.

Camping meant bugs, and Julia didn't do bugs.

She dozed fitfully before finally pulling out her tablet and logging into the ferry's Wi-Fi. She'd bookmarked the local weather page and checked it first, followed by the country's main newspaper. What she saw there made her blanch.

Prince Alexander's Extra-Curricular Activities Overseas?

PHOTO: A couple is seen hugging through tinted glass

THIS PHOTO, **taken in the States during the prince's recent visit, is making the rounds of the tabloid papers and television shows. With the revelation that Prince Alexander and his brother were the teen heartthrob stars of 2 Cool 4 School, rumors of women in his past have come out of the woodwork. No woman has actually come forward with stories or proof of her relationship with the duke. This snap of what observers**

said was too long to be just a friendly hug from an old acquaintance, could be the first bit of evidence of such a relationship.

The woman remains unidentified.

JULIA STIFLED a groan and closed her eyes. So she was Alexander's other woman. Not that there was any truth to that accusation. How on earth was she going to live this down? What if someone else identified her?

An announcement over the ferry's loud-speakers drew her attention back to the present. They would be disembarking in half an hour. Time to wake Alex up and get ready.

It was nearly ninety minutes later before they actually moved off the ferry. Breakfast was the first order of business. Then find their first stop, the museum. As she turned, she realized what was taking so long. Some sort of check point had been set up, and they were checking everyone.

Before they even reached her, she had her passport and driver's license out and ready. Hopefully they wouldn't need anything else. With the window down, she smiled at the guard. "Good morning."

The sunrise was gorgeous. If only they'd be able to find a place to enjoy it one of these mornings.

"May I see your ID, please?" The man replied in accented English. Though she knew Ravenzarian English was the official language, it still surprised her to hear it after the Italian of the last day.

"Of course." She handed over her documents then decided to grab Alex's and pass it over as well.

He looked at both passports for a long time before calling another man over. A glance in her rearview mirror told Julia the people behind her were growing impatient. "Is there a problem, sir?"

A third man joined them, glanced at both passports then gave an order she couldn't hear.

The second man came to the car. "Ma'am, I'm going to need you to follow the black car there. We have a few questions for you."

She nodded, unable to force herself to ask for her passport back. For the moment, she was at their mercy. The black car in front of her didn't go far, but pulled into a parking lot less than half a mile away. Alex clung to her hand before wrapping his other arm around hers. She squeezed his hand and did her best to put on a brave front for him. The reality of her fear was one she didn't want him to see.

They seemed to be at a police substation of some kind. The third man seemed to be in charge and led them to a conference room. Her fears subsided a smidge. Not an interrogation room.

"Please, have a seat." He gestured to the far side of the table.

She sat in one chair with Alex scooting as close as he could. "What's going on?"

The man sat across from her and leaned forward on the table, his fingers interlaced. "Ma'am, we need to know what your relationship with the prince consort is."

She felt the blood drain from her face. These were questions she did not want to discuss, especially with her son right there. Julia knew she had no choice, though. She would have to give answers.

Time to face the music.

Alexander hadn't sworn so much in his entire life. Combined. He paced his office, yelling at no one in particular. He picked up the stress ball and threw it against the windows overlooking the sea. It bounced back to him. He threw it again. Over and over.

What he really wanted to do was break things. Smash them to smithereens. Or blow them up.

Where was TNT when you needed it?

With one more curse flung toward no one, he collapsed into his desk chair.

"Are you quite done?"

Alexander looked up to see his brother standing in the doorway, looking as serious as he ever had. "What do you want?" he growled.

"That little voice that tells you things you know you should listen to but rarely do?"

Alexander nodded.

"It told me to head this way a few hours after you left. I didn't listen. Until I woke up from a dream in a cold sweat." Christopher sat down across from him and propped his feet up on Alexander's desk. "You had been assassinated."

Alexander barked laughter. "Me? If anyone would be assassinated, it's my pregnant wife, not me."

Christopher shook his head. "You know I don't believe everyone who says they can see the future or whatever, but there are documented cases, in the Bible no less, of men and women having dreams that served as warnings. I've never felt like this before, and I hope I never feel like it again. You, Christiana, the baby. There's some danger lurking out there. I don't know if it's really an assassination attempt or not, but something big is about to come down the pike, and I felt the need to be here to help you with it."

Picking up his phone, he called Justin and asked him to send in Tony, the head of security. For ten minutes, Christopher filled him in on the goings-on at home. Granny was doing fine and expected to head home in a few days. Idle chitchat filled a couple more minutes. Silence descended while Alexander pulled his email up on his computer to see if anything needed his immediate attention. Nothing that kept his focus until a discrete knock preceded the door opening, and Tony walked in.

After introducing him to Christopher, the three sat at the conference table on the other side of the office as Justin joined them.

"How may I be of assistance, sir?" Tony asked.

"Have you heard the pardon news yet?"

"Yes, sir."

"That is obviously a huge concern, but my brother, and myself, if I'm being honest, have a nagging fear that there's something else coming, and we need to make some plans to figure out how to deal with it." He leaned back in his chair doing his best to project a confident air and not one of fear. "My brother and I both had our Conceal and Carry licenses in the States. We'd had enough crazies after us over the years that neither one of us wanted to be unprotected should the need ever arise, though it never has."

"I still have mine," Christopher pointed out. "I just requalified at the gun range a couple months ago."

"Technically, I guess I still have mine, too, though I have never carried in Ravenzario, except on our property on Bianisola when we had some problems with wild boar."

Tony nodded, thoughtful. "We'll go to the range so I can see for myself. I don't have a problem with either one of you carrying a weapon on your person for the time being. Sir, you'll need to make certain you're with security at all times. No more running off like yesterday."

Alexander felt properly chastised. He knew better. "Of course."

"The queen is practically in seclusion anyway," Tony reminded them. "No one is going to get anywhere near her without us knowing about it."

"Are there any active threats you haven't already told us about?" Alexander's daily briefing had been postponed because of the meeting with the prime minister.

"No, sir." He hesitated. "None of any consequence. No more than the usual nut jobs with conspiracy theories."

"What about the hoopla over the TV show?" Christopher answered his own question. "I finally had to turn my phone off. Too many calls from old 'friends' and girls who wanted to be girlfriends. I talked to Mady, and she's gotten some interesting calls and emails, including some threatening Alexander's 'girlfriend.'"

Alexander leaned forward. "I don't have a girlfriend. I *might* remember who that girl was, but I'm not even sure about that. I think we had a couple college classes together. I don't even know her name."

"Chill. No one else knows who she is either. The picture's too blurry and the lobby was pretty cleared out. Apparently, the threats against her are more because of your wife than in addition to your wife."

"What's that supposed to mean?"

"People who seem to think the queen needs their help ousting her 'competition.'" He held up his hands. "I'm not saying I agree. I'm saying that's the word on the street."

"Great." He sighed. "So what now?"

"The two of you come with me to the shooting range and prove to me you know what you're doing with a handgun. Not that you, sir," He nodded at Alexander, "would ever really be charged with anything short of treason, but I'll get you both permits."

"So how is this..." - he stopped short of comparing his uncle-in-law to the back side of a donkey, - "...person able to get a pardon? What he did was treason, right?"

Tony shook his head. "No. Well, yes," he corrected quickly before Alexander exploded. "It was. But he pled guilty to conspiracy to a bunch of stuff and agreed to life in solitary. Otherwise, he was going to insist on a very public trial. Henry knew enough about the law to get around most of the ones protecting against a public trial in that situation."

Alexander stood and began his pacing again. "I never saw that paperwork, not like I did later since Christiana was already my wife during the last trials. I had no idea." He stopped and turned. "But last fall, that was treason, wasn't it?"

"High treason," Tony confirmed. "But we could never be sure we could prove her uncle was trying to kill her."

"Wouldn't trying to undermine the lawfully established line of succession count?" Wasn't that what he'd read when all of this went down the first time?

"Yes. But he was the one tasked by the government to run things on the queen's behalf until she came of age. Until two years ago, no one knew for sure he was still manipulating her. Some of us suspected, but it was the phone call you overheard, sir, that was able to give us the direction we needed to arrest him six months later."

Tony seemed to want to say something else, but didn't until Alexander pressed him.

"I am not questioning your fidelity, sir, but there is one other point. If a woman comes forward claiming to have had an affair with you, most of them won't realize they can also be charged with high treason." He looked Alexander straight in the eye. "As can you."

This time Alexander did swear, though he kept it under his breath. "I have never cheated on my wife, and I have no intention of starting now. There will never be any validity to any of the claims." His voice rose to a roar. "I. Have. Not. And. Will. Not. Cheat. On. My. Wife. *Period.*"

"That is good to know."

Alexander turned on his heel to see his wife standing there, hands resting protectively over her baby bump.

"What can we do for you, Your Majesty?"

Her face hardened at the title. "I was informed of a meeting between my husband, my brother-in-law, and my head of security. I thought, perhaps, I should be included." With a grace he could never hope to imitate, she crossed the room and sat in his chair at the head of the table. "So, gentlemen, what is the plan? I am finally recovered from my morning sickness and my bout with the stomach flu. I refuse to remain cooped up here for the rest of my life or even the rest of the day. So I suggest we come up with a protection plan because I am about to resume my full schedule."

Alexander stared at her, slack-jawed. "You're going to what?" Was she crazy?

Her demure smile did nothing to reassure him.

Just as she expected, her husband balked at the idea of her leaving the palace. He would have, no matter the problem of her uncle's likely impending release.

She took charge of the meeting. "Gentlemen, it appears we are going to have an increase in security concerns on Monday. Is there any way for my uncle to gain entrance to the palace grounds?"

Tony answered her. "Not that we're aware of. All of his security codes have been overridden. Passwords, code words, everything changed." He sighed. "But given the extent of his schemes and the length of time he had unrestricted access to the palace, there's a very real possibility of something we don't know about. Something by sea, perhaps, or a tunnel we're unaware of. Even though I was head of security before his arrest, I was not privy to his knowledge."

"Which is the only reason you were able to retain your job," she pointed out. "Despite your efforts on my behalf, if it became known you were one of his inner circle, you would have been relieved of your duties."

"Yes, ma'am. I am aware of the dichotomy."

"Is there anyone else we can interrogate?"

Alexander snorted. "I draw the line at interrogating. No way *we* are doing that. Tony, possibly me, but not you."

She waved a hand at him. "I had no intention of actually being involved. Now, is there anyone we can interrogate?"

Tony leaned back in his chair and crossed his arms over his chest. "Maybe. I'll look into it. In the meantime, your protection detail will be doubled." He glared at Alexander. "Both of you, despite the other thing we discussed."

Alexander gave a single nod. He stayed standing, his arms crossed, looking formidable. Without his suit coat, his dress shirt did little to hide the strength in his upper body. Though she tried to push it away, the memory of being held in those arms surfaced and would not let her go. The feeling of safety, of comfort. How she missed that! Being held in his arms as she cried on the anniversary of her parents' death, even before she kissed him, would always be one of her most cherished memories.

"I am leaving the palace this evening," she decided suddenly. "I have not been to church in months and tonight, I feel the need to do so before the threat increases again." She pushed back from the table and stood. Staring her husband in the eyes, she told them all, "Any of you who would like to join me are welcome."

Christiana turned and left the room. They would let her know what she needed to know when she needed to know it. When she needed more information, she would insist on it. Until then, she needed to be back out among people besides Alexander and Diana.

They'd missed their tour of the cathedral. As soon as they emerged from the police station, Julia called and canceled their reservations for the evening in Pagosa. The officer had handed her a keycard and told her they had given her a room for her trouble. She followed the directions to the hotel and discovered it was much nicer than anything she'd booked even before losing her job.

"Wow!" Alex's exclamation as they drove along the coastal road toward the hotel made her smile. She wasn't sure if the police officers believed her story, but they'd let her go. She even had their passports, though she'd been warned not to leave the country until they gave her permission. He seemed to think it wouldn't be a problem for them to head home as originally planned. He'd even given her some money for her troubles. To reimburse her for the missed tour and a little something extra. Probably enough to cover a cheap meal for dinner.

Half an hour later, Alex hung out on the balcony as she finally opened the envelope. She pulled the bills out and stared at them. Sure there were quite a few, but she expected maybe fifty bucks worth of small bills. They were Euros so she had to do some math, but it came out to around two thousand dollars and tickets for a hiking excursion and zip line tour the next day. She gaped. She'd looked at that when planning the trip. It was way out of her price range.

But whatever. She wasn't going to look a gift horse in the mouth. "You ready for dinner, kiddo?"

He bounced back in and onto his bed. "Can we order room service and eat on the deck? Please, Mom?"

Even with the sudden influx of cash, she wasn't going to do that. "How about we take some of our snacks down to the beach and have a picnic?"

Alex jumped down off the bed and ran to the door. "Let's go!"

Julia laughed and followed him to the elevator. They grabbed a blanket out of their car and the lunch basket they already had packed for the trip. They followed the sidewalk down until they reached the beach. It was nearly deserted, though Julia had no idea why. The day was a bit cool, and they were facing east so the setting sun behind them did little to offer additional warmth.

The meal passed quickly, and they didn't talk about much. Alex said he didn't want to talk about the police station. They had been separated for about half an hour, and she wanted to make sure he was okay, but all he'd say is they let him play games on the computer.

As darkness fell, they followed the lighted path back to the hotel. She tucked her son into bed and pulled out her tablet. Time to work on their new plan some more.

Alexander didn't want to be at church. In fact, he'd rather be just about anywhere else. Since Christiana hadn't been up to going, he'd stayed home with her, choosing to watch a service online. But when she insisted on going to the Saturday evening service, he knew he would go with her. Not for appearances' sake, or not only for them, but because she wouldn't go anywhere without him except maybe the bathroom until they figured out what to do about her uncle.

As the service was about to start, they pulled up to a side entrance. Someone he didn't recognize opened the car door. He slid out and turned, holding a hand out to help his wife. She emerged, looking as elegant as always. When they entered, the pastor was there to greet him. Alexander helped her with her coat while they exchanged pleasantries. With both of their overcoats over his arm, he rested his other hand on the small of Christiana's back, following her into the door near the front of the sanctuary. Given the three empty buffer rows, someone had planned ahead for them. He knew she wouldn't like being so "isolated", but security was right. For now, it needed to be that way.

He heard the hushed whispers in the seconds before the music started playing. Christiana wasn't the head of a church the way the Queen of England was, but if a church knew she was coming, they waited for her arrival to signal the beginning of the service. Out of the corner of his eye, he saw the pointing, especially from the women. He knew why, and, despite recent revelations, he was pretty sure it had nothing to do with him.

Instead, it was likely due to the baby bump his wife was sporting. She'd been showing a little bit for a while, but it was like someone had thrown a switch and suddenly she went from "maybe she could possibly be pregnant and not just too many donuts" to "definitely having a baby." Not that he'd ever thought she looked like she'd eaten a few too many donuts. He thought she still looked a bit gaunt. Giving a small smile to the people three rows behind them, he turned and did his best to pay attention to the service.

The pastor spoke on God ordaining the path of kings. It seemed to be a continuation of the previous week's lesson so not specifically tailored for his wife, but in the lessons about how God ordained the footsteps of David to lead him to such a place where he could be the king Israel needed when Israel needed him.

Back in the apartment, Alexander stared out the window, always looking for some danger.

"Do you suppose God has a hand in all of this?"

Christiana's quiet voice made him turn. "Pardon?"

"What on earth could God use everything in my past for? My parents and brother dying so young. My uncle's plots and betrayal and now potential release. My fiancé, the one man I *should* have been able to trust beyond a shadow of a doubt, planning my murder and to take my crown."

He turned back to his window. "Marrying a man you barely know and don't love? Carrying his child?"

"All of that. What possible plan could God have in it?"

"I don't know. Maybe it's not you God has a plan for. I mean He does, of course, but maybe it's one of our descendants who will do great things. The story of Rahab is a good one, and she certainly did her share of helping God's people, but it was her son who was Boaz, Ruth's second husband. Both were ancestors of David and, eventually, Christ. Ruth and Boaz had a son named Obed." He'd read about this recently, or he never would have remembered. "Obed was Jesse's father and David's grandfather. Does the Bible ever mention Obed's wife? Jesse's mom? Not that I recall. But without her, there would be no David. No Christ. At least not through the same lineage."

He fiddled with a button on his coat. "So were the parents and grandparents and great-grandparents of Mrs. Obed any less important to Jesse's birth? I doubt it. The sequence of events had to happen to get to David. So maybe it's not you, or me, or even the baby that this set of events influences. Maybe it's our grand-child who will grow up to be a force to stop another Hitler or Stalin. Or, given our geography, a Mussolini or Napoleon, even. That doesn't mean what happened to you in the past doesn't have meaning, just that it led you to where you are today. To *this* child who would be that child's grandparent." He turned to her. "Does that make sense?"

She nodded but didn't look at him. "I suppose, but I wish there were some meaning, in the here and now." Christiana laced her fingers together. "Do you think we'd be married now if my parents had lived?"

There was a loaded question if he'd ever heard one. "For starters, your brother would be helping plan Yvette's wedding with her. But I don't know. I think it's probably unlikely. They probably would have married you off to some duke or something. Or you wouldn't be married yet. Playing the field." He tried to add a teasing note but it fell flat.

She didn't respond.

"Sorry. Even if your parents had lived, you wouldn't be like that."

"I know there is a plan. Sometimes I just wish I knew what it was."

That made two of them.

Christiana did not sleep a wink. If Alexander had been there perhaps they could have talked, he could have alleviated her fears, or faced them together. Instead, as he had since his return, he slept in the other bedroom.

By the time dawn broke, she was showered, dressed, and eating breakfast. She was nearly finished when Alexander walked in. He wore a suit, complete with silk tie and jacket already on.

"Are you going to the hearing?" she asked, not looking at him.

"Yes. As the one who obtained the first key piece of information, they asked me to be there." Paul handed him a plate of bacon and eggs. His favorite. "Will you be?"

"No." She had no inclination to be there and was not required to be. Despite being the focus of his crimes, her presence had not been requested.

He sat next to her and covered her hand with his own. "I know they usually rubber stamp these pardons, but there's a chance it'll go the other way."

She slid her hand from underneath his and used her cloth napkin to wipe her mouth. "It will not. As much as we would like to believe they will do the right thing and leave him in prison, this has been part of his grand back-up plan all along. I do not know what his next move is, but I guarantee you there is one. He will try something to remove me and take the throne himself. He'll try to find a way, even though the agreement with the Commonwealth countries has been in the news lately."

"Won't the baby be the next in line for the throne?"

She shook her head. "If he succeeds in removing me, any child born after my ouster is not in line for the crown. The throne would either go to Yvette or the country split in two."

"I see."

"If he does not succeed in killing me and the baby, he only has a few months to make his move. I would imagine his preference would have been to take his time. But since his plot to take me out on my honeymoon failed, this was his plan B. He never expected for me to get married anyway, much less for me to get pregnant."

Alexander took a bit of his eggs and thought on that. "You're right. If we hadn't married, and especially if you weren't pregnant, he'd have unlimited time to carry out whatever the next step of plan B is. At least until he gets rearrested."

Christiana sat up straighter. "Is that the answer?"

"What?"

"Tony said he was never charged with high treason though we know he was committing it, correct?"

"Yes, but that's because the evidence wasn't there. Believe me, if he could have been charged with it, he would have been. But this seemed like the most expedient way to get what everyone wanted. Your uncle behind bars for life. Quietly. None of us dreamed he'd be able to do something like this."

"Can he not be arrested on suspicion of something else as soon as he is released?"

"I'll talk to Tony about it. Someone will be watching him 24/7. If he so much as jaywalks, he'll be in cuffs so fast his head will spin."

"That is a small comfort."

He took the last bite of his breakfast. How did he eat so fast? "I know." It surprised her when he leaned over and kissed her head, right along her hairline. "We'll figure something out. If I'm going to talk to Tony, I've got to go."

Maybe she would be able to watch on closed circuit television. Sometimes she could.

But then Alexander pointed a finger at her and told her not to do that. "It will just stress you and the baby out. It won't change anything. I know you'll be stressed anyway, but seeing him, seeing the proceedings will make it worse."

He had a point, though she did not want to tell him that. Squeezing her shoulder, he went on. "I'll call you as soon as it's over."

"Thank you."

An hour later, she was in her office arguing with Diana. "I do not want to watch the whole thing. Tony said his case will be last. I want to see the other three."

"And I don't think it's a good idea," Diana argued back, putting her foot down for the first time, really, in ever. "The Duke told me as much before he left. No television feed for you."

The proceedings were closed to the public. The names would not be released until after the hearing ended, though there seemed to be some sort of word leaking out. A few minutes earlier, she had heard Diana telling Charlyn there would be no comment until at least this evening.

Doing her best to put it out of her mind, she tried to get down to work. It had been scheduled to be a check-signing day anyway. Something that required just enough of her attention but not so much she would not be able to focus. Ninety minutes after the hearing was to have started, Diana buzzed and told her the first three cases had been heard and pardons given. They were taking a mid-morning break before anything else was done. Her stomach tied in knots when, after another two hours, there had been no word. She walked back to the apartment, a security guard flanking her. He would be either with her or right outside her office/bedroom door at all times.

No one had asked her about it.

When she finally reached the apartment, Christiana wanted nothing more than to lie down for an hour. Lunch held no appeal, though she knew she needed to eat. As she walked into the living area, she sensed more than saw another presence in the room. She stopped short until the man with his back to her stood and turned around.

Christiana nearly collapsed onto the floor in relief. "Poppo," she whispered as he came toward her. He held her in his arms as the tears began to fall. "Poppo, I'm so scared."

He rested his hand on her head as he tightened his hold. "I know, sweet girl. I know."

Alexander hadn't bitten his tongue so much in a very long time.

The appeals board had recessed to discuss their decision and would be back shortly. They *could* decide to deliberate overnight, but he didn't think they would. Not starting this early in the afternoon.

He spent the deliberations with Tony in a conference room. All of the top secret files were pulled up on his laptop. He'd put them on an external hard drive which would be erased and destroyed before he left. No changes would be made and only cryptic hand-written notes would leave the room. Only the two of them knew what Tony had on that drive. The decision to bring it all had been made less than twenty minutes before departuring for the hearing.

"Is there anything in there?" Alexander ran a frustrated hand through his hair.

Tony leaned back in his chair, with his fingers laced behind his head and his eyes closed. "There's something here. Something I can't quite put my finger on. Like when you wake up and try to remember what your dream was but it's just out of reach." He sat forward and started scrolling again. "It's not clear enough to even give me a direction." A few clicks. "I don't know where to look. Suspects. Witnesses. Evidence. Interviews. Photographs. It's there *somewhere*."

Alexander paced around the table. "How do we find it?"

"I don't know. Can we prove a connection between the two men? No one ever saw them together." He looked up. The look in his eyes stopped Alexander in his tracks. "There's one person we've never talked to."

Alexander read Tony's mind. "No. Absolutely not."

"We never had to talk to her before," Tony pointed out. "There was enough evidence of the death plot last fall without needing to. Even with talking to her it was unlikely we'd get the evidence needed to keep this all out of the press with her uncle. We took the plea. There was no way he'd ever get parole. Or a pardon."

"Except this way."

"Right. And no one had any idea he'd have a man on his side who would rise to such a place and pardon him."

Something else occurred to Alexander. "What if he doesn't?"

Tony leaned back again. "Go on."

"What if this guy really believes this is all it is? What if he doesn't know about the unprovable high treason? Face it. For the charges he actually confessed to, life in solitary is a bit extreme. Given the other circumstances, not at all, but for someone who doesn't know other facts..." Alexander sat next to Tony. "Can he pull the pardon petition? Postpone it somehow? I've met the man. He seems like a genuinely good guy, and he wasn't in office to get the briefings when this all went down."

"As long as he does it before the decision. It's worth a shot." He called to one of his officers outside, and they waited. Twenty minutes passed before the minority leader walked in.

"I'm not changing my mind, gentlemen." He didn't say hello or anything. Just cut to the chase. "The penalties for accessory to a bunch of charges shouldn't be so much worse than for those who actually committed the crimes."

"Which crimes?" Alexander crossed his arms over his chest and tried to look intimidating.

The man didn't back down. "Conspiracy to defraud the crown was the worst one, wasn't it?" He glanced at Tony then back at Alexander. "Look. The guy's slimy. Even I can admit there's something not quite right, but life in prison when the worst sentence anyone else got was twenty years? I don't like it."

Tony spread a file folder out on the table. "This is only some of the documents. There's more safely stored at the palace. It wasn't conspiracy to defraud, Mr. Michaels. It was attempting to kill the queen. And he was the ringleader."

Michaels's face turned white as the implications settled over him. "What?"

Christiana knew the hearing was over, but after six o'clock, she still had not heard the verdict. Poppo sat on the next couch over. His wife was not feeling well and could not make the trip with him, but when Alexander called and told him Christiana needed him, he had come anyway.

The door to the apartment opened. Christiana looked up to see a disheveled Alexander walk in.

"Well?" Had he found a way to stop it? Why had he not called?

"We tried everything we could." He sank into the chair across from her. "We even got Michaels to agree to withdraw the petition, but it was too late. The decision had already been sealed." Alexander leaned forward and rested his elbows on his knees, clasping his hands together in front of him. "They read it in the chamber today but everyone is under a gag order until morning. He won't be released until noon."

She slumped into her chair like a rag doll. "Is there no way to keep him in prison? Nothing else he can be charged with?"

Alexander told her about Tony's feeling that something existed just beyond his reach that would prove the high treason, but neither one of them had come up with anything.

A knock on the door interrupted their conversation. One of the maids, one Christiana did not know well and she suspected truly worked for Tony, answered it. She stepped to the side and allowed Prime Minister Caruso and Minority Leader Michaels to enter.

The last man she wanted to see.

Both men bowed from the waist but she did not have the energy to stand in greeting. "Good evening, gentlemen. How may I help you?" The polite words forced their way out.

Michaels spoke first. "Your Majesty, I cannot begin to tell you how sorry I am. I had no idea."

Alexander did not let her ask her question. "Why did you do it in the first place?"

"I wanted to right a wrong with this pardon. I spent my career in law defending those who had the odds stacked against them. It might be the only one I get, you know, so I asked my staff to find instances where the sentences didn't fit the crimes. There were a number of others brought to my attention. Long sentences for a first offense when most second or third offenders got less. Things like that. But, on the surface, this was by far the most egregious. I couldn't see more than ten years, maybe fifteen, for the crimes he pled guilty to. If I knew I'd get more chances, I would have waited. Let him serve some of the time. But we all know I lucked into this job and it may not stick the next time around." He bowed again. "If I had any idea of the real crimes that couldn't be proved, you have my word, Your Majesty, I never would have considered it."

"Why didn't you ask someone about it?" Alexander nodded to the Prime Minister. "Caruso knew everything. If it seemed so outrageous, wouldn't you think maybe there was more to the story, and you should find out?"

"Perhaps." He clasped his hands behind his back. "I knew the Prime Minister and anyone else I talked to would try to talk me out of it. I thought it was just sour grapes. The two of them never got along and everyone knew it. In retrospect..." He sighed. "Everything is 20/20 in hindsight. I don't know what I can do to make it right, but if there's anything, I will be happy to. I'm sorry, ma'am. I don't know what else to say."

Christiana nodded her head once to accept his apology. "I have no idea what you might be able to do to help fix things, Mr. Michaels, but I would appreciate your cooperation with the head of palace security and my husband. Perhaps, somewhere in the paperwork you received with this information or somewhere else is some tidbit that will help prove high treason. There is no statute of limitations, of course, on such a crime, but I fear if we do not find something quickly, he will act again, and this time he will be much more careful."

"We're much more careful, too, Christiana." The grim set of Alexander's mouth and the clenched jaw told her exactly how he felt. "The only ones allowed around you are the ones personally vetted by myself and Tony."

"No one can absolutely guarantee my safety." Weariness overwhelmed her.

"True," Alexander acknowledged. "But we're going to do everything in our power to make it so."

Minority Leader Michaels shifted from one foot to the other. "I will have all of the paperwork sent over first thing in the morning."

Alexander shook his head. "No. Tony will go with you tonight and collect it, including all of the other cases you looked at. There may be a clue in one of them somewhere."

A clue to what? She did not ask, but what sort of clue would be in files that did not pertain to her uncle?

The men moved to the door where Alexander shook their hands. Without waiting for him to return, she went straight through her bedroom and into the luxurious bathroom that did not offer nearly enough sanctuary. A long, hot shower was just what she needed at least for the time being. When she emerged, back into the living room and clad in her favorite pajamas, she just thanked God they still fit. The only person left was Alexander. He did not look up from the manila folder he held.

"Feeling better?"

"Yes." Physically she felt better. Emotionally? Not close. Anger. Fear. Anxiety. Nausea. All of those things and more flitted through her mind.

He glanced up. "Is there anything else you need from me?"

"No." Yes! Her mind screamed the answer. She needed his strength. His arms around her. Comforting her. Reassuring her. Promising her without words that it would all work out. Protecting her.

She continued on, through to the kitchen. A glass of milk, brushing her teeth, and bed. It was all she could handle.

Alexander stared at the papers in front of him as Christiana closed the door to her bedroom. He knew he should follow her in there, make sure she really was okay. He didn't believe her words when she said she was. But what could he do?

Just be there for her.

How could he do that? He needed to do *something*. Find a way to keep Henry from being released. To have him rearrested immediately. Something. His time would be more productively spent stopping this... He stopped his thoughts before they went there. He'd found himself cursing entirely too much lately, even if most of it was internal, under his breath, or arguably justified. But still...

A soft knock on the apartment door caught his attention. Tossing the folder onto the table, he stood and walked to answer it. Before it was completely open, his brother pushed past.

"I ran into your security guy on my way in. He'll be here in a minute." Christopher went straight to the kitchen and emerged a minute later with a Dr Pepper. "I put the coffee on. We'll keep looking for something as soon as he gets here." He sat down and propped his feet up on the coffee table. "How's Christiana taking it?"

Alexander went back to his seat on the sofa and picked the folder up. "She says she's doing okay, but I think she's lying."

"Is she getting any sleep? Is she still sick?"

"She's over the bug, but I'm not sure how well she's been sleeping." His absent-minded answer wouldn't appease his brother, but right now the folder held his interest. Tony was right. The answer was here. Somewhere.

"You don't know if she hasn't been sleeping well? Don't you sleep like twelve inches away from her?"

"Sleeping in the same bed as someone doesn't automatically mean you know if she's sleeping well or not." He set the folder down in one stack and picked the next one up from the other.

Christopher didn't say anything, but Alexander could sense his disapproval. He leaned over and picked up one of the discarded folders. "So, what exactly are we looking for?"

Five hours later, they still hadn't found it. Whatever *it* was. Tony went into the kitchen and poured himself another cup of coffee. Christopher stretched his back then dropped to the floor to do a few push-ups, followed by a couple of one-handed pushups, then one-handed push-ups with one foot in the air. Then he switched. Alexander rolled his eyes, though he knew his brother was doing it to get his blood pumping and not to show off his mad push-up skills.

Tony walked back in, but before they could get back to work, a cry came from the other room. Alexander shot off the couch toward the bedroom. He threw open the door and was halfway across the room before he realized what he was doing. Christiana sat up in bed, blanket clutched to her chest, gasping for air.

Alexander sat next to her and wrapped his arm around her shoulder, pulling her into his chest. "I'm right here. I've got you. It was only a dream." Over and over, he reassured her, even as Christopher shut the door leaving the two of them alone, until her trembling stopped, and she relaxed in his arms.

She hiccupped as she moved away. "Thank you for your quick response, Alexander. I am fine now." His wife moved around him and stood up, one hand on her belly as she walked to the bathroom. He heard water running. When she emerged a few minutes later, the spots of water on her shirt told him she'd splashed water on her face. "Why are you still dressed?"

He'd changed into jeans and a polo shirt earlier in the evening, when comfort became his top clothing priority. "Christopher and Tony are here looking through the files with me."

She gave a single nod and climbed back into bed, pulling the covers over her as she rolled away from him. "Thank you."

Alexander rested his hand on her shoulder. "Want to talk about it?"

He could sense her hesitancy. "Only a dream."

"A very real one that left you shaking." Would she open up to him? Had he given her reason to?

"He was coming after me." He felt more than saw her shrug. "Really an unsurprising dream given his release tomorrow."

"Would you like me to stay?" His eyes struggled to stay open. A long day and now a longer night. But the answer was out there somewhere. They just had to find it.

"No. Finding a way to stop him is more important."

"Are you sure?"

"Yes."

He leaned over and placed a lingering kiss on the side of her head and left the room.

Christopher looked up from his tablet. "Everything okay?"

Alexander told them about the dream as he picked up his laptop. "Have you found anything else?" He already knew the answer. They'd been through all of it before.

Tony closed his laptop. "No, and I don't think we will. We're all too tired. I'm going to crash on the couch in my office and catch a couple hours of sleep. I'll get up early and get back to it before heading over to the courthouse." He picked up a few files. "Let me know if anything happens." He pointed a finger at Alexander. "Anything."

Alexander nodded. "I will."

Christopher stood as Tony walked out and walked toward the room Alexander usually occupied. "I'm gonna crash in here, brother. Nothing we can do tonight. I'll borrow some clothes in the morning." Without waiting for a response, he shut the door behind him.

That gave Alexander a couple of options. Stay up. But he knew he was too tired to concentrate. Catch a few winks on the couch. But he knew he wouldn't sleep well. Sleep in one of the million other bedrooms in this place. But he'd be too far away to hear Christiana if something happened.

That left only one.

With a deep breath, he went to sleep with his wife.

Christiana felt the bed dip and the covers shift when Alexander came to bed. He did not roll toward her, did not whisper to see if she was awake, did nothing but get situated far on the other side of the bed.

So why had he come at all? She opened her eyes just enough to see the clock. Four in the morning. Eight hours until the release. She needed sleep. All she could do was close her eyes. And eventually drift off.

When she awoke, even before she opened her eyes, she knew he no longer lay next to her. What had happened to change things between them? While things weren't where they should have been, they were nothing like they'd been in the first days of their marriage. She needed to decide what her official response to Henry's release would be. As she finished getting ready for the day, Diana walked through the open door.

"What did I originally have scheduled for today?" Christiana asked before her assistant could say anything.

Diana tapped on her tablet. "A visit to the children's wing of the hospital, a grand opening of a nursery school, and a meeting about the rescheduled banquet from December."

Christiana nodded. "Very well. I'll leave as soon as breakfast is over."

Diana's eyes went wide. "Are you sure, ma'am? What will the duke and Tony say?"

"I do not particularly care what the duke says. I told him and Tony the other day that I would no longer be curtailing my schedule any more than necessary. Were the plans canceled?"

She looked at her tablet again. "Not in so many words. They were told it was unlikely you would make it, but the decision had not been made yet."

"Good." Christiana walked purposefully into the kitchen. "Good morning, Paul."

He smiled at her. "Good morning, ma'am. What can I make for you?"

After a quick, simple breakfast, she headed for the car pool and the squad of security sure to surround her. Five cars headed to the hospital rather than the usual two. She had still not seen Alexander. Nonetheless, she did not want to think about him or what else was going on, possibly right at this minute. She did not know when the announcement would be made, but she planned to be very busy elsewhere. Her security team would keep her safe. And, if they failed in some way, God would protect her.

Dr. Jonah Fontaine, husband of Princess Anastasia, was visiting from nearby Montevaro, and showed her around the new state-of-the-art children's floor in the Women's and Children's wing of Pagosa General. He'd already spent a week at his favorite orphanage in Ravenz-by-the-Sea, working with the children there. She spent some time in the community room, talking and coloring with different children. Their parents took pictures of her with them, and she answered questions about the baby. She could tell when the announcement was made. The demeanor of the parents changed. They became more sympathetic. Though no one mentioned it, she could see it in their faces and hear it in their voices.

At least she had some time before his release. Not much but some. After nearly ninety minutes with the children, she and Dr. Fontaine, flanked by royal security and them by hospital security, retreated to his temporary office in a conference room.

"How are you?" he asked gently as they sat down.

Christiana shook her head. "It is not about me, Dr. Fontaine. Right now, it is about the children. Tell me what else you need and how we can help."

By the time she left the building, her stomach let her know it was time for lunch. When she realized it was only a few minutes after eleven, she directed her driver to take her to the nearby bistro she often frequented rather than make the longer drive back to the palace.

Her instructions were met with protests, but she overrode them. Grumbling, arrangements were quickly made and a plan carried out. She would find a random family and have lunch with them. She had not done that in over a year, but did often before then.

Suddenly, the idea held great appeal.

Julia groaned in frustration and kicked at the tire. Flat. Just what she needed. And Alex wasn't with her. He'd stayed at the program for kids while she made a quick - *yeah, right* - run to the store. Though their first night's hotel stay had greatly exceeded her expectations, the rest had been stepped down a bit, despite the money burning a hole in her pocket.

But now, she sat on the side of a Ravenzarian road with no clue who to call for roadside assistance and no jack in the car. Digging through the paperwork from the car rental company, she finally found someone to call. She knew how to change a tire. She just didn't have the proper equipment. The company agreed to send someone out to help her, though they seemed to think she should have everything she needed.

With her flashers on, she pulled out her tablet, glad she'd decided to get the data plan for the month. Her first stop was the main Ravenzarian paper.

Uncle Released from Prison While Queen Dines with Subject

The obviously pregnant queen didn't let the release of her uncle affect her plans for the day. After spending nearly three hours at Pagosa General and talking with hospitalized children and their families, she headed straight for Pagosa Bistro for a bit of lunch. As is her practice most times she goes, she found a family in line, waited together, paid for their meal, and spent an hour or longer talking with them. The family, like so many before them, refused to discuss the conversation in any detail.

After the announcement by the Pardon Board regarding The Royal Uncle, as he was known, at the Good Friday Request of Minority Leader Michaels, the boat from Pirate's Island contained one of the country's most notorious criminals. Though he pled guilty to relatively minor charges of conspiracy to defraud the royal family, among others, his life sentence in solitary confinement led many to believe there was more going on behind the scenes. The official response from the palace is an unsurprising "no comment."

WHAT WAS the story with the uncle? Had she ever heard it? Julia didn't think the queen had really been on her royal radar until the wedding neared. She'd missed all the uncle stuff, and she hadn't set up an email alert for news stories until she discovered Alexander was the groom. She thought about Googling the uncle, but she didn't know his name and the article hadn't been much help on that level.

Movement in her rear view mirror caught her eye. Black cars. Several of them. A motorcade? Her breath caught in her throat as the first one whizzed by too close for comfort. It slowed down as did the others and pulled off to the side a ways up the road. A man in a dark suit and sunglasses climbed out of the passenger side of the last vehicle and made his way back to her.

She rolled the window down an inch. "I'm sorry. I have a flat and no way to fix it. There's a truck on its way."

"I'm sure it is, ma'am, but this is a fairly treacherous road. Can we be of assistance?"

"I don't have a jack to change the tire."

He pressed a finger to his ear and turned away. A second later, he turned back. "Ma'am, we'd be happy to fix it for you. If you'd go to the second car back, we'll transport you somewhere a bit safer than the side of the road and bring your car to you."

Her eyes narrowed. "Can I see some ID?"

The man gave her a half-smile. "Of course." He held up his badge and ID card to the window. She had no clue if it looked real or not, but his willingness reassured her a bit. She handed over her ID when he asked. Probably because there had to be someone important in one of those cars.

Julia nodded and grabbed her purse, looking down the road before getting out of the car. Another man waited on the tree-lined side of the second car, a limo, and opened the door as she neared.

He nodded as she gave him a tentative smile. "Ma'am."

"This really isn't necessary." Who could be in the back seat? Wasn't this how people ended up buried in the woods and on one of those Saturday night news programs?

"Our pleasure, ma'am."

She slid into the seat then turned to see who sat next to the other door. "Alexander?" She could hear the shock in her voice as the door closed behind her.

He looked up from the papers he was reading through, recognition crossing his face before it was replaced with a plastic smile.

Mortification flooded over her. "Oh. I should probably use an official title, huh? Like Prince Alexander or sir or Duke whatever-it-is."

The polite smile stayed in place. "Julia, right?"

"Right." Did he only remember her name because she'd introduced herself to Christopher last week?

The car shifted into gear and pulled away from her rental. "Are you enjoying your visit to Ravenzario?"

"Except for the part where my son and I were detained by police when we arrived, it's been wonderful." She twisted the hem of her shirt between her fingers.

"Your son?" His brows pulled together. "I don't think I knew you had a son. But you were both detained? Did they say why?"

Julia shrugged. "Not really. They asked us some questions and then let us go. Even gave us some money and a hotel room as compensation for our trouble."

"That's good." He shifted in his seat and she could see him better. "I know we saw each other at the hospital last week, but can you help me remember where I knew you from before that? I'm afraid, I don't quite..."

"Of course." She smiled. Evidently, she hadn't made nearly the impression on him that he made on her. "We did a project together in Professor Putane's Political Science class. He usually taught grad school and hated being with us undergrads. Then, after a frat party one time, you took me back to my place." Three weeks later, she'd discovered she was pregnant. "The apartments on ElmBrook Road in Serenity Landing."

She could nearly see the wheels turning in his head. Then it clicked for him, and he snapped his fingers. "Right! There was that picture of us in the student newspaper that time. Studying on the quad, wasn't it?"

"Sounds right." Julia didn't tell him she'd scrapbooked the picture, long before she knew anything else about it. Besides the gigantic crush, how many other times would she be in the school paper?

The limo pulled into a parking lot on the side of the road. "I do hope I'm not keeping you from anything important?"

"Not particularly. I have a meeting, but figured I was going to be nearly an hour early as it was." He smiled at her. "So where's your son?"

"The children's program at the hotel." She felt the need to explain. "Last fall, when we were planning our Spring Break trip, your wedding was all over the news, and he decided he'd rather come here instead of going to Disney World."

Alexander raised a brow. "We won over Disney?"

She quirked a half smile his direction. "I told him we'd gone to college together. He started researching Ravenzario for a school project. The rest, as they say, is history. I did *not* expect to run into you while we were here, though if there was some sort of public event we could get to, I told him we'd try."

Alexander chuckled. "I can do better than that. Tell you what. Will you be here Friday night?"

"We leave for Rome Saturday morning and fly out Sunday, but we're planning to stay in Acron."

"Why don't you come to a dinner we're having. It'll be a few hundred people and I can't promise I'll have time to do more than say 'hi', but I'll make sure to at least talk to him for a minute and take a picture with him."

Julia gave him the most genuine smile she'd experienced in a while. "That would be *amazing!*"

He chuckled. "For old times' sake. I may even be able to arrange it for you to stay on the property. I'm not sure yet. A lot of people from the banquet will be there from out of town, and

Queen Christiana may have already promised the cottage to someone else. I bet your son would love it, though. How old is he?"

"Seven."

"Oh yeah." He leaned over and whispered, "It has a secret doorway and everything."

Julia laughed. "He'd love that, but it's not necessary. We have the reservations in Acron so we can be on the ferry. It leaves Saturday night, and we didn't get to do the things we'd planned because of being detained. We looked at staying in Pagosa but no ferries cross to the other island that will get us there in time."

He peered out the window, though she couldn't see what he was looking at. "If you decide to come, I'll make sure you can get to the ferry before it leaves Acron. It's a once in a lifetime opportunity for your son." Alexander looked at her again. "What's his name?"

Julia looked at her hands. "Alex. His name is Alex."

lexander felt sucker punched. "Alex?" This woman couldn't have named her kid...No. Certainly not. He remembered her after she told him about the project, but he'd never known her *well*. "Good name." What else was there to say?

"After my grandfather. He practically raised me."

Relief washed over him. "Still a great name." He glanced at his watch. "I wonder what's taking them so long."

"There was no jack in the car, but I'd guess they have one."

"You'd think one of these cars would."

She shifted in her seat. "You know, if you have somewhere to be, they can leave me here and take you on." Julia pointed to the store across the street. "I can wait there."

Alexander shook his head. "It's only about a ten minute drive from here, and I have about half an hour before I need to arrive."

At that moment, activity increased. He turned to see the little car pulling into the lot. "Guess they got it fixed."

Relief was evident on her face. "Good."

Opening the door himself, he climbed out of the backseat. Turning he held out a hand to help her. Polite, nothing else.

At his motion, Justin emerged from the car behind them. "Give Justin your information and itinerary so he can contact you if necessary and make the arrangements for Friday."

She reached up and gave him a quick hug. This one didn't catch him off-guard like the one in the hospital had. He gave her a slight squeeze and stepped away.

"Thank you again." Julia walked toward Justin and stopped to talk to him while Alexander took his seat in the car.

The manila folder didn't help him find any more answers than it had the first sixteen times he'd looked through it. His uncle-in-law had disappeared after being released. No interviews. No anything. He'd lost his tail after three hours and had not shown up on anyone's radar since.

Alexander put his foot down about Christiana. Tony agreed. She wasn't leaving the palace. Period.

Christiana chafed under the restrictions. She understood them, even agreed with them, but being confined to the apartment except when surrounded by heavy security, made her cranky. When she had not felt well enough to be out and about, it had been much easier to abide by the rules, but she felt better. Much better. Almost good even.

At least she was not confined to bed.

One of the other bedrooms had quickly been converted into a make-shift office and that was where she currently sat, trying to finalize the seating chart for the banquet in two days. It made her head hurt. A notification popped up on the computer in front of her. Two more. A woman and her son. Friends of Alexander's who he just found out were in town.

"Where on earth will we put them?" Christiana rubbed her temples as Diana leaned over the diagram of the banquet room.

"How old is the son?"

"I have no idea, but if this is a college friend, no more than ten or so?"

"Why don't we put them with David and Annie?" Diana moved a few tags around. "It'll split their family off from Poppo, but you wanted him at your table anyway, right?"

Christiana nodded. "That will fill out the head table while giving a reason to split their family. There will only be the three children there, correct?"

"Five. Lily and Elana and their mothers are at the table, too. Both of their fathers are unable to attend. This is actually a perfect solution."

The headache continued to build behind her eyes. "Then we are done?"

"Unless someone cancels or something else comes up, yes."

"Thank you, God." The plans were coming together very nicely. The menu had been finalized the week before. The seating chart was now taken care of. "Is there anything else? Music is set, correct?"

"Yes, ma'am. I confirmed with the quartet's manager this morning, and he sent over the playlist. There's nothing objectionable on it. Exactly what you requested."

"Thank you, Diana."

"The Baicampo property has been sealed off since Sunday night, after we found out about the pardon." The decision had been made Monday night to move the venue from the palace to the ballroom at Alexander's property. Easier to seal off and fewer people in and out of the palace was a good thing. The only thing scheduled was a wedding the next day. Christiana had called the bride herself and asked if she would put off the decorating until the next morning. Palace staff would assist in any way possible. The bride and groom had both been happy to help out, especially when she asked if their entire wedding party would like to attend the banquet.

"Good. Tony is aware of the additional guests?"

"I would presume so, but I will call him and make sure."

Christiana glanced at the clock. No wonder her headache did not seem to be abating. "I believe it is time for me to call it a day and get some dinner."

"I believe that is a wonderful plan, ma'am." Diana smiled at her. "We accomplished everything we needed to."

"Good." Christiana stood, the heels of her hands digging into her back as she stretched backward. Stiff would lead to sore if she was not careful. A two-man security team waited outside every door, following her to each new room, even the bathroom. She went to her room and changed out of the business suit she wore to work most days, though her commute could be measured in steps rather than miles. She rubbed lotion over her rapidly expanding belly and was rewarded by a fluttering. Not the first time she felt it, it still brought tears to her eyes. Her child. Hers and Alexander's child moved within her. Would he like to feel the movement when the baby's strength grew enough?

The door behind her opened, and Christiana squealed reaching for her robe. Clutching it to her chest, she looked to the door.

Alexander stood there, his eyes round before he looked to the ceiling. "I'm sorry, Christiana. Diana said you'd just come in here. I didn't think there had been time..." He shook his head. "Sorry."

There should not be anything for him to be sorry for. When would they reach the point in their marriage where seeing one another in a state of undress would not be apology worthy? "I will be right back." She backed into the bathroom, shut the door far enough behind her he could not see and slipped the robe on, tying it as she emerged back into the bedroom. "What can I do for you, Alexander?"

She noticed his eyes trained on her midsection, on the semi-noticeable baby bump.

"I wanted to let you know I invited an old friend to the banquet."

"I saw the notice, and we have them seated with David, Annie, Elana, and Lily. We moved Poppo and Nanny to sit at the head table."

He nodded. "That's perfect. I also checked with Tony. The north cottage isn't being used, and I arranged for them to stay there." He rubbed the back of his neck with one hand. "Turns out her son is fascinated by, well, me. She and I went to college together. I haven't seen her in years, but he wanted to visit the country where 'mommy's friend is the prince.'" Alexander crossed his arms. "He'll get a kick out of that secret bookcase panel."

Christiana nodded. "Yes, he will." She had loved it whenever she stayed there as a child. In fact, it had been her primary residence when in Ravenzario. Never in the palace proper. She had always thought that unusual...

"Is that all right with you?"

She looked back up at him. "I have no problems with it. No one else will be using it." There was another secret entry. This one a passage she did not believe anyone knew about. She discovered it late one night when she visited before starting high school in Montevaro's elite Montevarian Preporatory Academy with Addie.

"Paul said dinner is ready when we are." He turned to leave. She wanted to call him back, to ask about his day, but something held her back. If he wanted to spend more time with her, he would. Her head told her maybe he waited for her to make some sort of move. Her heart was afraid he would not respond the way she dreamed.

"I will be there momentarily."

Alexander paused before leaving, but continued without looking back at her or speaking. She dressed quickly in a pair of maternity yoga pants and a soft t-shirt she generally only wore when she would see no one.

Time for the most uncomfortable part of her day.

Dinner with her husband.

Alexander hated the awkwardness between himself and Christiana. Walking in on her clothed in so little didn't help any. His first good look at her belly in quite some time. She had definitely started showing. He longed to rest his hand there, to try to feel movement, to talk to his unborn child. Hadn't he seen a study that said a baby would know not only his mother's voice but his father's at birth?

He sat at the head of the table, something she insisted on when they ate alone, since he was the head of their little family and all. When at a public function, she took it as the monarch.

She came in a moment later, looking utterly adorable and relaxed in a way he'd never seen. Hair in a sloppy ponytail, a soft pink t-shirt that he bet felt as soft as it looked, comfortable pants and... He snickered a bit. Socks. Had he ever seen her leave her bedroom without shoes?

Just once, maybe after the baby was born, he wanted to take her sock-footed and go to the ball room and slide around like little kids. The floor in there would be perfect, and he'd bet she never had.

She sat next to him. The meal was brought in. Normally, he tried to make small talk with whatever staff came in, but he found himself in no mood for that tonight. After a few bites, Christiana broke the silence.

"How was your day?" She took a small bite.

"Fine. Meetings went well."

"Anything new on, you know."

There was the biggest source of his frustration. "Not yet."

"Queen Adeline and King Antonio both called earlier and offered the services of their intelligence arms. My uncle visited both countries a number of times in the last decade. Perhaps there is something there."

"Tony talked to them, Italy, France, and Spain back when it all went down. No one had anything of any consequence at that point."

"Maybe something has turned up since then, and no one put it together."

"Perhaps." He didn't hold out much hope, but he'd let her hang on to it.

"What is your schedule for the rest of the week?"

"I'll be in the palace until at least Monday. Nothing outside planned." For a reason. And even Monday he wouldn't go out of town. Not until this thing was sorted out.

Something in his gut told him there would be a shoe falling, and soon. What exactly it would be, he had no idea, but something.

The rest of dinner was quiet. Christiana went to her office to a little more work. Alexander thought about going to Baicampo to go over everything again, but Christopher was already at the property helping oversee security and other arrangements for Friday night. It left the other bedroom empty for Alexander, and he fell asleep wanting something he couldn't have.

His wife in his arms.

He woke up wishing the same thing, yet before he could blink, Friday night arrived. He stood with Christiana in the ante room waiting for the announcement of their arrival.

She turned to him. "Your tie is crooked." He looked down at her as she reached up to tweak it. "Better."

Before she could move away, he caught her around the waist and pulled her close to him. "You look beautiful tonight, Tia." Her hands clutched at his shoulders, and her eyes fluttered closed at the nickname. His head bent. *Kiss her.* When was the last time he'd really kissed his wife?

The softest touch before parting. He felt her breath on his face. He'd have to move only a fraction of an inch to kiss her more fully. As he gathered his courage, a throat cleared behind him.

"Everyone is seated, ma'am."

That was all it took. Christiana moved back out of his arms. She moved the mirror to check her hair it seemed.

"Justin?" Alexander spoke quietly hoping she wouldn't hear.

"Yes, sir?"

"Never interrupt me when I'm about to kiss my wife."

Did he think she could not hear him? Christiana presumed that to be the case, though she did not understand why he had barely kissed her, soft as the brush of butterfly wings. Had he planned to kiss her again before Justin interrupted? She could see Justin's smirk in the mirror. What about it was funny?

She fiddled with one of the curls of hair on the side of her face before turning. "I am ready." Holding her skirt up, she moved to Alexander's side and slid her hand into his offered elbow.

Her entire being buzzed with his nearness. She could hear the announcement, the scraping of the chairs as the door opened. Together, they walked in, straight to the dance floor.

How had she forgotten they would dance the first dance then eat?

Propriety dictated the distance between them as they waltzed around the floor, but it also demanded she lock her eyes with his part of the time. It was not the first time she danced with him, but once again he amazed her with the ease he led her. Though the dance did not take particularly long, she was still out of breath when they came to a stop in the precise middle of the floor. How did he do that? Did he practice without her?

Alexander stepped back from her and bowed deeply at the waist. She inclined her head his direction. When he held his hand out, she took it, quite properly holding their hands at shoulder height for the walk to the head table. He stood to the side as she moved to the dais.

"Ladies and gentlemen, thank you for your attendance and your gracious acceptance of the venue change. I am indebted to you for your understanding of so many things. Not just a trip across the water in dress-up clothes." A laugh. "But of my disappearance several months ago on one of the best days of my life. You cannot begin to understand my gratitude for what you did for me that night. Coming together to give me memories of my parents, little brother, and our nanny." She had to hold the tears in. "You brought them to life for me in a way no one else ever has. And it truly was a complete surprise."

She looked over at Alexander who smiled his support. "Since that time a number of revelations have come to light about my relationship with Prince Alexander. Some questioned the rationale of marrying a man I did not love in the conventional romantic sense. In my wildest dreams, I could have not imagined a man who would understand from an offhanded comment, how much that night would mean to me." In more ways than one. Especially in the conception of his child she now carried, but they did not need to know that. "You know that I have been bedridden much of the last couple months, but during those times, I often had one of the scrapbooks with me."

"I learned about my mother's childhood, my father's courtship of her, his determination to win the heart and the hand of the green-eyed beauty from Vashta. I saw pictures of myself as a child 'working the ropes.' Pictures from your point-of-view, taken by those of you who came to wish us well on so many occasions. From the deepest parts of my being, I thank you for your continued support. I could not ask for more."

She stepped back and smiled, turning to accept Alexander's escort to her seat. Before she could take a single step, the applause began. The chairs scraped again, and the crowd rose to their feet, almost as one.

"Long live Queen Christiana!" someone shouted.

"Long live Queen Christiana!" others shouted back. Several times.

She took Alexander's offered elbow, her fingers clenching the inside of the arm of his coat. She held her other fingers to her lips and kissed them, waving to one side then repeating the action to the other. How had she become so blessed?

"They love you, Christiana." She had not noticed Alexander bending his head, but his words, warm on her ear, did not startle her. Their truth did. Yes, this was a friendly crowd, such as it were, but the outpouring from all of her people overwhelmed her.

She blew one more kiss to the crowd as the applause began to die down. Alexander held her chair as she slid into it. Poppo sat on her other side and squeezed her hand as her husband took his seat.

Poppo leaned toward her. "You've done well, sweet girl. Your parents would be very proud of you."

The preacher who had performed their wedding came forward and asked them to bow their heads. As he thanked God for the meal, Christiana thanked God for the people He sent into her life to offset those who would do her harm.

Peace settled over her. It would be a good night.

Julia talked with the woman sitting next to her. She'd been asked to dance a couple of times, but declined. Alex tried to dance with Annie, and he was doing his best to dance with Lily, but really they were just jumping around. The little girl was having the time of her life.

"May I have this dance?"

She startled a bit, but looked up to see Alexander bowing toward her. "Of course."

He held out his hand, and she took it as he turned to the other woman. With a wink, he asked her to save him one for later. She laughed and agreed. Alexander led her to the dance floor, though his attention seemed to be elsewhere. Looking for his wife, perhaps? Seeing the way they looked at each other during the first dance of the evening, anyone would know they adored each other.

His attention still hadn't returned to her when they started dancing. Lines creased his forehead. Worry?

"Is everything okay, Alexander?"

He looked back at her and twirled her around. She could see the queen dancing with his twin brother. The only way she could tell the difference between the two was the red sash distinguishing Alexander as the prince consort.

"I've got a lot on my mind, that's all."

Right. The uncle's release.

"Have you enjoyed your trip to Ravenzario? Flat tire aside?" He grinned.

She smiled back. "It's been wonderful. Your tips helped a lot." And using his name had opened a few doors, but he didn't need to know that. She hadn't insinuated anything, just mentioned that the duke had been the one to recommend a place. "Tonight is spectacular. Thank you for inviting us and making arrangements for the dress and tux for Alex."

"My assistant can work wonders. So, what was your favorite part?"

This. Right now. Dancing with a handsome man. If only he adored her the way her high school crush had adored Alex Slate. There was no point even day dreaming about such a thing, though. Maybe Chris Slate... "I couldn't pick," she finally said. "But Alex is convinced tonight will be the best part. Staying on palace grounds." And she didn't mention the stress caused when she'd heard her apartment had been broken into, even if her mom couldn't figure out what might be missing. At least she wouldn't have to replace anything on her non-existent income.

"What is it?"

She shook herself. "What?"

"Something's wrong."

"Oh." She might as well tell him. "I lost my job last week. The trip was already mostly paid for or non-refundable, so we came anyway, but it's been hanging over my head."

"Why'd you lose it? Downsized?"

Julia closed her eyes and hoped he wouldn't think she blamed him. "No. I went to see my boss's brother at the hospital the day I saw you. Because of the extra traffic and news crews and everything, I was late to work. That wouldn't have been a big deal, except for the presentation I was supposed to set up for. My boss had to do it, and everything was running behind, and he fired me." She shrugged. "I'm hoping when I get back, that he won't be as mad, and he'll rehire me. Overall, he really likes me." Maybe too much. "This was just a really bad time to forget." Especially given what she now suspected. Her eyes filled with liquid, but she forced it back.

"What else is going on? There's something else, isn't there?"

"My apartment was broken into yesterday, though I don't think anything's missing, and..." She looked around to make sure no one else was nearby. "I think I'm pregnant."

Dancing with so many women he didn't know could be tedious. At least this time no one tried to slip their number in his coat pocket. After nearly an hour of non-stop movement, he knew the first break would come soon. Justin motioned to him as the dance ended. He bowed to Julia, who'd just dropped a bombshell, and walked to the edge of the floor before anyone else could claim him. He didn't particularly like to leave her alone, but to dance with anyone but Christiana more than once was to invite gossip he couldn't afford.

His eyes found his wife on the dance floor. Her soft green dress stood out for its simplicity, and he admired it as she twirled in the arms of Minority Leader Michaels. The man had done everything in his power this week to help find her uncle after his release.

It was the biggest cloud over his evening.

Justin whispered something about the trip back to the palace, and Alexander nodded absent-mindedly. Julia and Alex would join him, Christiana, and Christopher for the trip to the mainland. Justin motioned to a young woman looking nervous. The bride getting married tomorrow. Right.

He asked her to dance, and she accepted. Once on the dance floor, she seemed ill at ease.

"Relax, Ginger. I don't bite."

She laughed. "I know, but you're not the same man who gave us the tour last year."

"Sure I am." He glanced down. "I just get to wear this silly blue sash thing now. Is everything ready?"

"It was very kind of the queen to offer all the assistance we needed to get ready for tomorrow. She could have just used her monarch's privilege to rearrange stuff."

"She's not like that."

"I had a chance to talk with her for a few minutes earlier. It's easy to see why you love her."

He didn't answer so she continued.

"I know the story and all. Let's face it. Most girls around here are royal watchers. We all dream of marrying Prince Charming and being swept off our feet to become a princess. What's more important, though, is that the right Prince Charming comes along, with or without the tiara waiting. I found mine in Jonny. The queen found hers in you. You're her Prince Charming and her white knight all wrapped up in one package. She loves you, and you love her. Anyone here tonight could tell you that." He twirled her again trying to get her to stop. "And the way you glance at her baby bump? The way her hand is on it when she doesn't realize it? You're both beyond blessed, and you both know it, even if you won't quite confess such to each other or to the public just yet."

The song came to an end and the first break of the night began. He bowed to Ginger, who just smiled at him, and went to find his wife. She walked out of the ballroom back into the ante room they'd stood in earlier. He followed her to find her sprawled on the comfortable chair placed there for just such a reason.

"Are you all right?" he asked, kneeling next to her.

"My feet hurt, but I will be fine. I just needed a minute away to collapse a bit. I cannot exactly look like this in front of everyone."

He reached for her hand and squeezed lightly. "You're doing fabulously. Everyone I've talked with loves you. They're so excited for the baby."

She smiled weakly. "I am, too."

"I know. I know you're ready to be done with being sick and everything. When we get home, I'll give you the best foot rub you've ever had and tuck you in."

"That sounds heavenly." She sat up and held out her hands.

He stood and took them, pulling her up. "You ready?"

"As I ever will be."

Tucking her hand into his elbow, they walked back into the ballroom. This time there was no announcement, and really, no one noticed. Together, they made their way to several tables, talking with those sitting there.

When the music started again, they separated, each ending up with a different dance partner. The next two hours went by quickly and, before he knew it, the dancing ended, and it was time to head back to the palace.

The call had come too early for a Saturday morning, but it was one she would not turn down. "Prince William." She nodded at his image on the screen. "How are things in Mevendia?"

"Very well, Your Majesty. My father was quite pleased with the deal your husband negotiated. Believed it to be quite fair."

"My husband is a shrewd businessman, but one who believes in finding a win-win situation for everyone."

"Well, he did in this situation." She could see him shifting in his chair.

"So what can I do for you today?"

"We have been following the developments in Ravenzario this week, cousin." The man was an exceptionally distant cousin of hers. The royal families of the three countries she spent time in growing up - her own, Mevendia, and Montevaro - were all descended from the same family, over a thousand years earlier. "Mevendia wishes to offer her support in whatever way we can."

"I heard your father had been in contact with my security people. There has been some troubling news in my country this week." She sighed. "I am not certain what, if anything, you can do to help, though, William."

"Perhaps nothing, but knowing you have others on your side can often be an emotional boost if nothing else."

"Thank you."

He leaned forward on his desk. She had been in his office

before and could visualize the dark wood she could not see. "Today's news is the most concerning for you, though, is it not?"

Christiana rested her arms on her own desk in her make-shift office. "Pardon?"

"Today's news."

She shook her head. "I have heard no news today. Nothing of great import since my uncle's release on Tuesday."

William winced. "I am sorry, Christiana. I thought surely someone would have told you by now."

Diana buzzed from the other room, but Christiana ignored her. "What news?"

He sighed. "Prince Alexander's affair."

A very unladylike snort of laughter came from Christiana. "My husband? An affair? I hardly think so."

Right?

What about the woman he hugged at the hospital? Had she not been a bit dissatisfied with his explanation?

"The pictures are in the papers this morning, Christiana. Not just the tabloids either. They were together a couple of days ago."

She shook her head. "Impossible. He has not left the palace since the release." One hand covered her belly. "Alexander is quite protective."

"Was he really there all day Wednesday?"

Christiana reached for her tablet and searched the schedule, groaning when she saw the entry. "He did have a meeting." She scrolled through the travel time notes. "And he was gone a good deal longer than needed."

"Look it up. Or better yet, ask him about it. If he has nothing to hide, he will tell you the whole story."

She gave the best smile she could. "I will. Thank you for your support, William. Even though we are only three hundred and second cousins, your support means the world to me."

He chuckled at the old joke about their relationship. "You are still among my favorite royal cousins, Christiana. You and Addie.

Next winter, after the baby comes, we should all get together for a ski trip here in Mevendia. It will be just like old times." Nestled between Montevaro and Switzerland, Mevendia had the best skiing of the three countries, though all had their share of mountainous terrain. The three cousins were close enough in age that they had spent a fair bit of time together. She would need their support to get through whatever came her way. The airtight mutual defense compact had survived over a thousand years and would not crumble on her watch.

And she learned every day that she might not need defense from just foreign armies.

William's voice brought her back to the conversation. "If our intelligence agencies can help in any way, be sure to have your people call. Our men have instructions to help in whatever way they can."

Christiana tapped a pen against the desk, knowing it would drive him crazy but it helped her think. "I will have Tony call later today, but the only thing I know of would be to trace any of my uncle's movements or contacts in Mevendia and see if any of them are untoward or perhaps part of Mevendia's seedy underbelly."

William chuckled. "Mevendia does not have much of a seedy underbelly, Christiana."

"Neither does Ravenzario, yet my fiancé purchased drugs to kill me with from some of them."

"Touché. I will talk to my father and the heads of security and intelligence and see what we might have."

She hesitated before broaching the next subject. "I spoke with Yvette the other day. The wedding plans seem to be coming along."

William sighed. "I still don't understand why she has to go through with all of it. I'm sorry, Christiana, but your brother is dead. The wedding is only going to be interesting because of its train wreck properties. My sister is going to be left at the altar by a man who's been dead nearly two decades. You couldn't talk my father into letting it go?"

"No. I tried." She had tried very hard. "Antonio insisted the wedding plans go on."

"Even though the groom was buried when he was just a couple years old?"

William's words caught her off-guard. Did he not know the bodies had never been found? Of course, the outcome had been no different than if they had. She had wondered though...did Antonio know something no one else did? Did he believe there was a different reason the bodies had never been found?

Surely not. No one would have kept this from her for so long. "I do not know why the insistence, but please make sure Yvette knows she can call me if she needs anything."

"I believe she and Lizbeth have things mostly under control, but I will let her know."

They exchanged a few more pleasantries before Christiana severed the connection. Taking a deep breath, she went to the Ravenzario Chronicle's home page. The headline blared at her.

Prince Alexander Cavorts with Mistress, Invites Son to Banquet

Feeling sucker punched, she quickly scanned the article. The woman lived in Serenity Landing. Had a son named Alex. Were invited to last night's banquet and stayed on the property. Nothing new there. Christiana had met the woman and her son. She had not realized Julia was her husband's alleged paramour.

She went back to the top of the page and clicked on the slideshow of related photos. The first picture was a black and white photo of a much younger Alexander sitting on the grass next to a young lady. Books were spread around them, but they both laughed. She could see the twinkle in his eyes. The one she thought he reserved for her in their private moments.

The caption said it had been taken on the quad of his college campus. She did the math off of the date. He would have been barely twenty-one. The next photo was one of Julia with her newborn son, on the day of his birth. How had they obtained such a photo without the other woman's help? The date caught her attention and caused her to do another bit of math. Just over nine months after the first photo. She clicked again. The photo through the hospital doors. Julia and her son in Ravenzario the weekend before. The next photo gut-punched her. Alexander told her he had run into an old friend and invited them to the banquet. He had not told her about the hour spent together in the back of his limo or the intimate-looking hug when she emerged.

Five more photos. Could she make it through them? Alexander and Julia dancing the night before. Not too close. Talking and congenial but nothing too out of the ordinary. The next was Alexander down on one knee talking to a seated Alex after dinner. The little boy looked awed. And the resemblance...there certainly was one. Not as much the dishwater brown hair, but the dusky hazel eyes and deep dimples. Nothing definitive, but enough to make tabloids pick up the story. But enough for mainstream news outlets? The last picture told her why they had. Alexander standing at the door of the cottage. A long lens must have been used, but it showed him talking to Julia. How did they get so close?

His tuxedo jacket hung over one arm. His shirt was untucked and his suspenders and tails hung down. Julia looked to be dressed down. Certainly not in the gown she wore to the banquet. Two hours after the banquet ended, he told her he was headed to the security office. Christiana closed her eyes and clicked the next button.

Alexander leaned toward the other woman. Were they about to kiss? She clicked the screen. The last picture. None of him kissing her goodnight. She breathed a prayer of thanks for small favors.

The intercom buzzed again. This time, Christiana reached a shaky hand toward it. "Yes, Diana?"

"Ma'am, there's something I need to show you." Her discomfort came through loud and clear.

"I have already seen it."

33

Alexander paced his office. "Where do they get these things?" Justin and Tony both typed furiously on their computers trying to find answers.

"Is she still on the property?" Tony asked.

"As far as I know." He pulled up another article on his tablet and read basically the same information. "Nothing has *ever* happened with Julia. Ever."

"I know, sir." Tony's distracted answer kept Alexander from commenting further.

He went to the palace's official Facebook page and started scrolling through the comments. Most of them were fairly scathing. Calling him names. Berating him for even thinking about cheating on his wife. A few cautioned patience because they'd seen him with Christiana before and didn't believe a word of it. Most were supportive of Christiana at the very minimum. That was good. She needed the support. Better they think him a cad than turn on her for "poor judgment" or whatever she feared they would think.

Justin stepped out to his office and took a call. When he

returned, his grim face told Alexander what he needed to know. Not good news.

"She's suing for back child support."

"What?" Alexander exploded. "How? I *never* slept with her. I never even *kissed* her. I *cannot* be his father! A DNA test will show that in no time."

"Then we'll insist on having one done." Justin sat back in his seat. "Your lawyer will be here in a few minutes. He's coming through security now."

Charlyn walked in with a notepad in her hand. "We need to try to spin this."

"There's nothing to spin!" Alexander insisted. "He's not my kid. He's a nice kid, but not mine."

"And we need to get your side of the story out there."

"She's here on palace grounds. Get her in here so we can talk to her, convince her to tell the truth." Visions of Tom Cruise and Jack Nicholson danced in his head.

"No. That would just make things worse." A man walked in, his suit nearly as nice as Alexander's. "I'm Ben Tyler, attorney for the royal family. We'll get a court order for the DNA test and go from there." Ben looked him dead in the eye. "I know what you've said, but, sir, if there is *anything* I need to know, now is the time to tell me."

"No. I never slept with her." Alexander ran his hand through his hair. "I know it's hard to believe, in this day and age, not to mention the whole *2 Cool 4 School* thing, but I was a virgin when I married the queen. Neither one of us have ever been with anyone else."

"So where did these pictures come from?"

He sank into one of the chairs. "The pictures are real. We had a couple classes together in college. I remember the photographer telling us jokes to get us to laugh for the newspaper photo. I took her home, once, a long time ago, after a party where she had too much to drink. I ran into her at the hospital. She had a flat tire the other day, and she sat in the limo with me for a while so it could get changed. Her son is fascinated with 'mom's friend, the prince' so I asked if they'd like to come last night and stay in the north cottage. I would have done that for just about anyone I know."

"What about being detained by the cops and the money you supposedly gave her?"

Alexander just shook his head. "I have no idea about any of that. She told me she'd been detained, and they put her up in a nice hotel and gave her some cash for her inconvenience. She never gave any indication that she thought it came from me."

"What about money to tide her over until she gets a job?"

"What?" It was too much, all too fast. "How do they know about that?"

"So it's true?"

"She lost her job last week, in part because of the traffic around the hospital while we were there. I told her to contact one of the charities I work with back in Serenity Landing, and that I'd make sure they didn't get turned out on the street or lose their car."

Ben took out a legal pad. "Walk me through the whole thing. From the time you met her until today. Anything you can think of that has anything to do with Julia or Alex."

Alexander let out a breath and started from the beginning.

"Mom?"

Julia looked up from her tablet. "Yeah?" Alex laid on the couch and stared at the ceiling.

"When are we leaving?"

"The prince said he'd send someone over to get us and take us to the ferry when the time comes. They must be running late." She went back to her book. "Why don't you write a thank you note or draw a picture?"

Alex got his coloring book and crayons out. It would keep him occupied for a little while.

"Did you find the bookcase?" Alexander had stopped by the night before to make sure they were settled in, and he'd told her the secret to finding the hidden room. Alex had already been asleep, but she'd given him hints all morning.

"No!" Alex shot up and took his stuff with him and ran off to find the bookcase. "I'll work in there!"

Julia smiled. According to Alexander, Christiana had spent a fair amount of time in this cottage. The queen's stamp was everywhere. The abundance of unicorns, most tasteful, had to have come from the monarch herself. Decidedly feminine in nature, the rest of the decor spoke of an earlier elegance. The furnishings in the living room alone would cost Julia about five years' salary. When she had a job.

Alexander's recommendation to call the Helping Hands organization in Serenity Landing surprised her. She'd never looked for handouts, not even as a single mom trying to finish her degree. But now she had to look out for what was best for Alex and, she was more convinced than ever, the new baby. She'd taken a test before leaving Serenity Landing and it was negative, but she feared it had been too early.

"I found it, Mom!" Alex's exuberant cry made her smile.

She wanted to get online and catch up with the news back home, but apparently the very nice quarters didn't come with Wi-Fi and the data service signal on her tablet was too weak to load anything. Instead, she curled up in a window seat overlooking the Mediterranean Sea and read the book she'd been working on for several days.

An hour later, with the book nearly finished, the hero and heroine were having their biggest fight yet, a knock at the door surprised her

Julia set the tablet down and went to the door. "Your Majesty?" Was she supposed to curtsy? She did, just a bit, just in case. "To what do we owe this honor?"

The queen didn't look very welcoming. In fact, she looked downright mad. "I just have one question."

What could Julia know the queen would want to? "Anything."

"Are you pregnant with my husband's child?"

The woman's face blanched. An admission? Or shock?

She moved to the side and motioned Christiana in. Nice of her since it was Christiana's property.

"I don't know where you heard that..." Julia started.

Christiana waved her hand. "Where I heard it does not matter." She shut the door behind her. "Is it true?"

"That I'm pregnant or that I'm pregnant with the duke's child?" The cautious words unsettled Christiana.

"Either."

Julia sank into one of the chairs. "I think I'm pregnant, but if so, there is no chance the baby's father is the duke."

"Is he the father of your son?"

The other woman's brows pulled together. "No. I've never slept with your husband, ma'am. Not in college and certainly not in the last few weeks. I might have slept with a few boyfriends, but never a married man."

Christiana pulled out the paper copy of the day's newspaper. "Then how do you explain this?"

Julia took it from her and skimmed through it. "I can't. All I can say is that some of it is true. Alexander and I had a few classes together in college. I did see him in Springfield last week, and he did offer to make sure Alex, the baby, and I would be okay since I lost my job, but through a charity in Serenity Landing, not personally."

"What about the money?"

Christiana watched as she pulled an envelope out of her purse. "There's only two hundred dollars missing from there. I was told the money came from the police to make up for inconveniencing us last weekend. Honest."

To her surprise, Christiana found herself inclined to believe her. "So who told the papers this? Where did the pictures come from?"

"What pictures?"

Christiana knew there was no Wi-Fi in the cottage. "A picture of the two of you from college. Another of your son when he was born. He shares a name with my husband. Pictures from last night and the limo the other day."

"I had a flat tire. I had no idea Alexander would come by, much less that his security team would change it for me. We talked. I had to remind him how he knew me. That's it."

A text message came in on her phone. Despite the ability to get a phone call, texts still went through. Christiana looked at it. SHE'S SUING FOR SUPPORT. THERE'S NO TRUTH TO ANY OF IT. CALLING A PRESS CONFERENCE IN TWENTY MINUTES. WILL YOU BE THERE?

Alexander needed her support. If she believed the stories were not true, he deserved it. But she had to ask. "If Alexander is not the father of your son, why are you suing him for back support?" Her phone buzzed again.

WHERE ARE YOU? YOU DIDN'T TAKE YOUR GUARDS.

"I'm not. I know who Alex's father is, and I'm lucky if I get a couple hundred bucks a year from him."

"Will you say that at the press conference?"

"Of course." Julia grabbed her purse. "When and where?"

Christiana tapped a text back to Alexander. SEE YOU IN TEN.

"Alex! We have to go!" Julia slid her feet into a pair of tennis shoes. "He's named for my grandfather."

Christiana nodded. "I understand."

Alex ran out of the back room. "Can we see the palace?"

"I will show you some of it."

"No. You won't."

Christiana froze at the familiar voice. She closed her eyes, breathed a prayer, and turned, hoping against hope she was wrong.

She was not.

There, gun in hand, stood her uncle.

34

Alexander took a deep breath and waited. He paced and waited. He stopped himself from running his hand through his hair and waited. He glared at Christopher and waited. "Do you know where she is?" he finally asked Tony. Again.

"No, sir. She left the residence without telling anyone where she was going."

"She's not in the garden?"

"No, sir."

"Do we have her statement?" He could hear the reporters getting restless. If they waited too much longer, they'd just be mad. And that wouldn't be good for getting them on their side. He knew some of the major news organizations in the States had stationed reporters in the area after the wedding. This would be all over the news back home.

Charlyn held up the folder. "Right here."

He took it from her and before they could stop him, walked into the press room. The buzz picked up before quieting down as he took his place behind the bank of microphones. "Ladies and gentlemen, I will read a statement from my wife, make a statement of my own, and perhaps take a question or two." He cleared his throat and opened the folders. "My wife, Her Majesty Queen Christiana, regrets her inability to be here, but as you all know, this pregnancy has been quite difficult on her, though she has been doing much better lately. The stress of today has precluded her from being here for the moment. She says, 'I stand by my husband. He has never given me any reason to doubt his fidelity, and I do not doubt it now. The allegations brought against him are false, and I look forward to his full vindication.'"

Alexander took a deep breath and flipped the page. "My sentiments echo those of my wife. I have not in the recent or distant past had any sort of relationship with Ms. Quisenberry, other than that of classmates and acquaintances in college. I am not the father of her son, nor am I the father of her child if she is indeed pregnant. I do not know why these accusations have been made, but I guarantee they are false. I look forward to clearing my name. We are requesting DNA testing as soon as possible." Did he want to do this? He knew he had no choice. To refuse to answer questions would implicate him in the press and in the court of public opinion. "I will take a few questions."

The cacophony of voices shouting at him overwhelmed him until he pointed at Matt Markinson. The man had proven to be a friendly, completely honest journalist. He wouldn't sugar coat, but he wouldn't blow up a scandal where there was none.

"If there is no relationship between you and this woman, how do you explain the photo from Wednesday? What about their stay on palace grounds last night?"

Alexander launched into an explanation about the flat tire. "It was never my decision to stop. Honestly, I didn't even see her vehicle until after the motorcade halted. I was working in the back of my car and am glad my men are looking out for others besides myself. Ms. Quisenberry and I talked for about an hour. I didn't remember her at first, but once she reminded me of the project we worked on together my junior year of college, we reminisced, and she caught me up on some mutual friends.

"As for their accommodations last night, I would have offered them to any number of old friends and not her specifically. As for the photo in the papers this morning, I have no idea who took it, but that is under investigation. I took my wife back to our apartments, went to consult with the head of security about some other matters, and decided to check in on them. At no time was I ever alone with her." The photo didn't show his security officer less than four feet away. "I was inside the cottage for about five minutes to show her how to find a room hidden behind a bookcase so her son could find it this morning."

He called on a woman from a local television station. "For the moment, let's consider what you're saying to be true..."

"It is," Alexander interrupted.

She gave a half-eye roll his way. Not the first time she'd heard that from a guy caught cheating on his wife, he supposed. Though in his case it really was true. "Let's say what you're saying is true. What motivation does this woman have for making the accusations? A comparison of blood types *could* prove your case very quickly or a DNA test in just a bit more time. So why would she make false claims?"

"I honestly have no idea. I am hoping we can sit down, probably with our lawyers, and figure this out. The *only* reason I've come up with is some sort of blackmail or wanting money, but though I didn't know her well, that doesn't strike me as the kind of thing she'd do."

He started to call on another reporter, but the back door banged open.

There, chased by guards, stood Alex. Covered in blood. Panting. Terrified.

Alexander shook himself out of his shock and bolted toward the boy. "What is it?"

He tried to catch his breath. "Mom. Shot. Queen."

Tony leaned over. "Your mom shot the queen?"

Alex shook his head, his hand pressed into his side.

"The queen shot your mom?"

Another shake. "Man. Shot mom. Chased queen."

Alexander turned to see Tony's eyes go as wide as his own. He grabbed Tony's walkie talkie, knowing the man could get another one and took off, sprinting toward the cottage. He heard Tony trying to get more information out of the kid. There wasn't time.

He pounded through hallways and bolted out a side door, wishing the whole time for his sneakers instead of dress shoes. The door to the cottage stood open, and he slowed as he neared it. His fingers itched to pull his pocket pistol out, but he waited. A cry sounded, but it wasn't Christiana.

Entering carefully, he saw Julia lying on the ground, covered in blood and crying out. He hurried to her side and spoke into the walkie. "Julia down in the cottage." Setting it on the ground, he reached for her head. "Are you okay?"

"I think so." She grimaced and whimpered. "It hurts, but most of the blood is from where I cut my head." He moved her hand away from her arm. "He just grazed me with the bullet."

The angry red wound didn't look life threatening and while the gash in her forehead would need stitches it wasn't either. "Where'd they go?"

She shook her head. "I'm not sure. Christiana did some stuff to that wall," She nodded toward the large stone fireplace. "It opened up."

"What did she do?"

Julia told him as best she could remember. Pushing a stone here, shifting the thing that holds the poker there, pulling down on the sconce on the side. With a groan, the wall began to move. As it opened, Alexander snatched the walkie talkie. "Tell them I've turned my sound down but will report in when I can. Tell them how to open it but to stay back."

She nodded and laid her head back on the floor.

Taking a deep breath and praying hard, Alexander walked into the dark.

Seventeen steps until it veers right.

All the hours Christiana spent exploring as a teen on school breaks and later as essentially a queen-in-exile in her own backyard were paying off. For fun, she would see how far she could get without turning on her flashlight. The one she left in the nook she now clutched in her hand, but she refused to turn it on.

Why, oh why, had she slipped out without her security guards? Yes, they were smothering. They had good reason to be. The man chasing her could not have asked to find her in a better, more vulnerable, position.

Except he had not known about this tunnel.

Nine steps to three stairs down.

She could hear him behind her. Yelling for her. Her head start was not nearly enough, but she knew of no way to make the wall close faster than it did. And she knew he did not know about this tunnel nor where it led. If she could make it to the end...was there time? Should she hide in the alcove and pray he did not find her?

How much further to the hidden door?

Twenty-three steps to the three stairs up, sloping but straight for another fifteen then hard left.

She moved as quickly as she could, but his voice came ever closer. At step twelve, she slowed, not wanting to run into the wall.

"Why couldn't you just go along with it? Let me convince everyone you were crazy. Take over the throne. Run things the way I saw fit." His voice echoed through the tunnel. "Your grandfather took my inheritance! I deserve this!"

What was he talking about?

Just a bit further.

A few more feet, and she would reach the end. In her head, Christiana walked through the steps to open the other wall. She would not have much time. It closed less slowly than the other door but not quickly enough given the footsteps nearing her. He did not have to catch up to her before she reached it. She only needed to be slowed down long enough for him to grab her ankle as she climbed out.

She pressed one indentation on the wall, followed by another, then a third. With a groan, it started to move.

"After everything I did to insinuate myself into your family. After all my hard work, you had to mess everything up. You and that meddling husband of yours. He's next, you know."

Alexander could take care of himself. She knew that. The second the door opened enough for her to squeeze through, Christiana did.

Now the hard part.

She put her foot on one of the slight footholds and reached up. From the outside, it appeared to be a basement window well at the end of an alley, covered over with stone many years earlier.

Could she still hoist herself up?

"I see you!"

She had no choice. Crying to God for strength, she straightened her arms and pulled herself to street level.

Now to get away. He lunged for her but she swung her legs up in time and stood so she could run down the alley as fast as she dared. If she could make it to the square, she would be safe.

She turned the corner and skidded to a stop.

When had the black metal gate been put in?

And how would she get over it?

Alexander walked as quickly as he could until the wall swung shut behind him. He could hear Henry's voice up ahead but couldn't make out the words. Deciding he was far enough back, he pulled his phone out of his pocket and turned on the flashlight. It allowed him to move much more quickly, though he still tried not to make any noise.

Did Christiana have a light? Henry couldn't have her yet, or he wouldn't be yelling, his words reverberating back to Alexander. The voice grew louder, the words more distinct. Something about her grandfather stealing his birthright?

A groaning sound slid through the tunnel. Another door? Around the sharp right turn ahead, he could see light. A little cry from Christiana spurred him forward.

He rounded the corner to see her foot disappear over a wall. Her uncle scrambled after her. Alexander picked up his pace. He'd never figure out how to open that door again. Before he could slide through the opening, the other man was gone. Alexander made it just as the door slid shut.

Back in the open, he pulled the walkie out. Over the top of the wall, he saw her uncle disappear around a corner. Hoisting himself up easily, he put the walkie to his mouth, turning the sound up just enough to hear.

"Tony?"

"Where are you?"

"The tunnel comes out near the square." He thought that was where they were. Rounding the corner he saw his suspicion was correct. The black metal gate hung open, leading into the plaza. "Christiana made it out and was ahead of him." Tony started barking orders even before he severed the connection.

Alexander stopped and scanned the area. There.

In the middle of the pedestrian plaza.

He stood, looking around much as Alexander did, a gun hanging at his side.

Too many people around to risk a shoot-out.

No one seemed to have noticed anything out of the ordinary. Just Saturday morning shoppers going about their business.

Alexander stuck to the sidewalk near the buildings, trying to stay in the shadows, hoping Henry would overlook a man in his search for the queen. As his back turned toward Alexander, it was time.

He moved quickly through the crowds, weaving between families and packs of friends, praying that no one would recognize him for a few more minutes.

Twenty feet.

Fifteen.

Ten feet.

The other man's rotation would turn toward Alexander in just a few seconds.

Time.

He ran the last seven or eight feet and put his shoulder square into Henry's back, dropping him to the brick street below. Alexander rose up to his knees, sitting on the other man's back and trying to get Henry's hands under control. Instead, he found himself lying on his back.

With a roar, he twisted away from the fist headed for his face. Alexander turned and rolled, using his legs to take Henry with him. When he managed to get on top, he used his fists to pummel the other man.

One part of his mind noticed the crowd starting to gather. Some yelled for a fight. Others moved to pull him off. Realizing Henry's motion had ceased, he backed off. He turned to one of the men holding him. "Do you recognize me?"

Realization crossed the man's face. "Sir..."

"No time to explain." He shrugged the man's hands off. "This man is a danger to the queen. He's trying to kill her. Detain him until the palace guards arrive." Sirens in the distance said it would be soon.

The man nodded and moved to stand guard over the fallen

villain. Alexander turned. Rotating, focusing on the shops. She would have ducked into one. Which one? Not the one closest to the entrance. Too obvious.

Another rotation.

She would have gone further away. A place she could hide. Maybe someone she trusted. But who?

The queen's father did most of his shopping there. As a child, the queen loved to hide among the tie-racks.

Martin's words echoed in his head. Where was the shop?

There.

Alexander ran across the uneven bricks to the store. He yanked on the door handle, but it was locked. He pounded. "Let me in! I need to find her!"

An eyeball appeared from behind the shade. "Who?"

"My wife. She's safe. I have to find her."

The man nodded. The door opened just a smidge, but Alexander pushed his way in. "Where is she?"

"In the back."

He turned and slid past racks of suits, tables of shirts, and broke through the swinging door in the back of the room. "Christiana? Honey? It's me. Alexander. He's down. They're holding him until the guards get here."

A sniffle caught his attention, and he turned to see her shoes peeking out from under a table. He lifted the tablecloth and smiled at her. It took everything in him to do so. She was disheveled, covered in blood, and scared.

And not nearly ready to come out.

So he went in after her.

Huddled and hunched, he sat next to her and pulled her into his arms. "It's okay. It's over. Are you hurt?"

She shook her head against him. "It is Julia's blood. Does Tony have him yet?"

"Not yet. We fought in the plaza. Some men were watching

him while I came to find you. Tony and his troops are on their way."

She huddled into him, her slender fingers gripping his shirt. "It's not over until he's in handcuffs and back on Pirate's Island." If possible, she folded herself into a smaller ball. "Is Julia all right?"

Alexander kissed the side of her head. "I think so. Her head was bleeding pretty badly but the gunshot just grazed her."

"Good. And Alex?"

"He ran into the press conference covered in blood. Got everyone's attention."

Her grip on his shirt started to relax. He could feel the stress leaving her body.

A voice crackled over the radio. "Alexander? Check in."

He depressed the button. "We're in the suit shop."

A crash.

A scream.

And their safe hiding spot was history.

35

Alexander found her. Henry could, too.

He had.

Christiana clutched at her husband, trying to absorb his strength. He moved until his mouth was next to her ear as crashing sounds continued elsewhere in the store. "Lay down, flat against the wall."

Somehow, she did not know how, but they both did. She lay with her back to the wall, stretched out flat under the long work table. Alexander blocked her view with his body, shielding her and the baby. She felt more than saw him pull something out of his pocket.

"Do you know how to use this?" He slid his pocket pistol into her hand.

"Yes." She did not want to. She did not know if she would actually be able to pull the trigger, but she knew how.

"If I have to leave you here to get to him, stay put. Be ready. If anyone but me or Tony lifts that table cloth, shoot him. Do you understand that? Anyone. He may still have others on the inside."

"I understand."

The crashing sounds grew closer. The cold metal chilled her to the bone. She kept her three fingers and thumb wrapped around the grip and her pointer finger safely along the barrel. He maneuvered until he lay on his back, his head facing out where he could see, she imagined.

But then he whipped it around. His fingers found her face and threaded through her disheveled hair. His lips on hers. Hard. Fierce. Desperate. And gone.

"I love you, Christiana. No matter what happens in the next few minutes, I want you to know how much I love you and the baby." Another brush of the lips and he whispered, fiercely. "Stay. Here."

"I love you, too."

But he'd already rolled away, leaving her alone.

Unprotected.

She brought her hands together in front of her chest, praying she would never need to decide to pull the trigger.

Grunts.

Shouts.

Sounds of body blows.

Crashes.

Flashes of movement under the small opening above the floor.

A gunshot.

Another crash.

Silence.

"Christiana?"

She nearly wept at the sound of Alexander's voice.

"It's me, sweetheart. I'm going to lift the tablecloth."

Christiana kept her finger off the trigger and pointed the barrel down toward her feet.

Pounding feet came into the room. Voices she recognized.

Blinding light.

A face she loved.

"It's over. Are you okay?" Alexander reached down to take the pistol from her. He slid it back into his pocket holster and put the whole thing back in his pocket before coming back to help her.

She nodded and let him help her slide out from under the table.

"Don't look," he whispered.

"What happened?"

He wrapped an arm around her waist and tucked her close to him. They walked into the front of the store, now swarming with police and security. "We fought. He won't bother you anymore." His hold on her tightened, and she started to feel safe.

Not bother her anymore? What did that mean? "Is he...?" She could not finish.

"No. I don't think so. Just unconscious." He stumbled and pulled her with him.

One of the security guards was at his side supporting him as Christopher pushed his way through. Her brother-in-law looked them both up and down then took a step forward.

Just in time to catch Alexander as he collapsed.

Christopher lowered him to the ground.

Christiana saw the blood.

And screamed.

Alexander felt weighed down. Beeping came from somewhere off to the right. His mouth felt like it was filled with cotton balls.

Gentle fingers brushed against his forehead.

He tried to blink, but the light was too much.

"Alexander?"

Her soft voice called to him. His mouth opened, but no sound came out.

"Here."

A straw between his lips. A small sip. "What happened?" He tried to blink his eyes open, but the light still hurt. "Too bright."

He heard her move and a second later, the light dimmed outside his eyelids.

"Better?" She sat back down at his side.

Alexander blinked his eyes open. "Yes." He turned his head to see Christiana's tear-streaked face. He reached for her with his hand, the one unencumbered by the IV. "What is it?"

"How do you feel?"

He bit back a groan. "Like I was in a bar fight."

That got a smile. "How many bar fights have you been in, Xander?"

A chuckle escaped before he could stop it, but it quickly turned to whimpers. "Ow. Don't make me laugh."

"How many?"

"None, but it's what I imagine a bar fight would feel like after it ended." He traced her cheek with his finger. "Where's your uncle?"

"Pirate's Island Medical Center. He is being charged with treason this time, and there is no way he will win."

"Good." He tried, unsuccessfully to sit up a bit straighter. "What about Julia?"

"She and Alex are in the west wing of the palace. The doctor did not want her flying for a few days, and the cottage is part of the investigation."

"We're going to have to have a talk about that cottage and the secret passage no one else knew about."

"I know."

She held out the straw for him, and he took another sip. "How long have I been here?"

"Yesterday. The medicine knocked you out."

"You're okay?"

"I am."

He reached over and rested his hand on her belly. "And the baby?"

She covered his hand with both of hers. "Dr. McCall said the baby is fine."

Alexander wanted to say something else, but before he could the door opened. That was when he really looked around. "Where am I?"

The white-coated man answered. "Hospital section of the palace. We even do surgery and deliver babies here when needed. We didn't feel your injuries were severe enough to warrant the hospital when we've got all this at our disposal." He picked up a binder from the foot of the bed. "How're you feeling?"

"Like I got run over by a truck." He shifted again.

"I thought it was like getting in a bar fight."

Alexander looked up to see Christiana smiling at him. "I'm guessing they feel about the same."

Christiana moved back as the doctor started doing doctor-y stuff, like looking at his eyes. "You're looking much better. I think I'll release you out of here tomorrow morning. I do want to keep an eye on you one more night."

He glanced at Christiana leaning against the wall, biting her lip. She'd already spent one night alone. "Come on, doc. I won't leave the palace. You can even have the nurse come check on me every hour, but I'd kind of like to sleep in my own bed." He noticed her face fall, just a bit, and he doubted anyone else would have noticed.

The doctor chuckled. "You mean with your wife?"

Alexander grinned back. "You know it." Christiana straightened.

"Very well." He gave them both his stern doctor look. "Nothing but sleeping. You need *rest*."

"Yes, sir." Like he would have the energy for anything else.

"All right. I'll get some paperwork together. You don't need discharged like a hospital, but I do have some instructions for you to take care of that bullet wound."

Alexander's head snapped around. "Bullet wound?"

"You didn't notice pain in your thigh?"

Now that he mentioned it... "I hurt all over, but yeah."

"A fairly simple through and through of the soft tissue in your right thigh. No bone or blood vessel or nerve damage so we cleaned it out, stitched it up, and have you on antibiotics."

"Crutches?"

"You'll need to stay off it for a while. We'll talk more about it later."

Christiana spoke. "So he will be confined to bed for a few days?" Was there a bit of sadistic glee hidden in her voice?

"Maybe not to bed, but he definitely won't be up and around much. Gunshot wounds take time to heal." He made another note in the binder and turned to the queen. "Would you be so kind as to either retrieve or have someone retrieve some clothes for your husband? Perhaps loose shorts and a t-shirt." She nodded and walked away. "I'll send someone in to help you get dressed and ready to move. I know a lot of men would rather not need their wives to help them in this state. Later, perhaps your valet can. Particularly with your wife's pregnancy, it's probably best if she doesn't help lift you."

Alexander nodded. "Good plan. She loves the idea of me being confined to bed for a few days, you know. After how long she had to stay there, she just might be a bit too happy about it."

The doctor started to say something else, but before he could Christopher walked in. The doctor took his leave and promised to return shortly.

The look on Christopher's face caused Alexander's light-hearted comment to die on his lips. "What is it?"

Julia looked over at Alex, sleeping peacefully on the exceptionally large bed in the beautifully appointed bedroom suite. She clicked on the television that hung from the other wall. As expected, the news program led with the exciting afternoon.

"Gunshots sounded in Pagosa Plaza yesterday as Henry Eit chased after Queen Christiana in an apparent assassination attempt. Details are sketchy, but he seems to have used a secret entrance to get onto palace grounds while the queen used another secret tunnel to escape into the Plaza."

The picture changed to a still shot of Alexander fighting Henry Eit. *With the Duke of Testudines not far behind, the queen escaped to safety in a shop owned by a long-time family friend. After believing he subdued Henry Eit, the prince followed her only to be shot in the ensuing scuffle after Eit gave chase.*

Julia winced as the picture changed to one of a very disheveled Queen Christiana walking next to the gurney. She clutched Prince Alexander's hand as he was loaded into an ambulance.

The duke is recovering in the medical portion of the palace. The queen, the duke, and their unborn child are all expected to be just fine. Henry Eit was released earlier this week on a Good Friday Pardon because he was not convicted of treason before. It seems likely he will not escape that conviction this time.

Tears filled her eyes as a picture of her son appeared, covered in her blood, with Prince Alexander kneeling next to him.

The country became aware of the situation when Alex, son of the woman believed to claim to have more than one of Prince Alexander's children, ran into a press conference covered in his mother's blood. Both Alex and Julia Quisenberry are believed to be fine. She denies making the paternity claims or filing for back child support.

Of course she denied it. She didn't do it. Julia clicked it off. No need to watch more. The mere sight of her son, covered in her blood, broke her heart. They should have been somewhere over the Atlantic by this point. Queen Christiana told her she would personally make sure they arrived home safely as soon as reasonably possible. Most likely she'd pay to change their airline tickets. It was the most Julia would ask for. Maybe the queen would upgrade their ferry tickets to a cabin...

The pounding in her head prevented any further thought, and she decided the pillow was calling her name, even though it was only early evening. Sliding in next to Alex she reached over and brushed his hair off his forehead. In the morning, she'd have to tell him again just how proud she was of him.

Christiana paced around the living area of their apartment. After some clothes had been gathered for Alexander, she remained behind, pulling back the covers on his side of the bed. One of the maids offered to help her, but she insisted on doing it herself. She should be the one to take care of her husband with his injuries. Not the injuries themselves, but making him comfortable.

But once she had the room ready, all she had was time to wait for him to arrive. Had he meant what he said under that table? Or was it just the trauma? Her eyes darted to the room where he had stayed so many nights since they returned from their honeymoon. In reality, he had likely slept in there more than he had slept with her.

Would he be comfortable sharing a bed with her again? His words to the doctor about wanting to be home with his wife certainly indicated he expected to. Plus the giant TV screen with all of its accoutrements was in that room, and surely he would enjoy some American baseball on it.

At the sound of commotion in the hall, she stopped her pacing and turned to face the door. Christopher walked in and held the door open. Alexander's foot entered first followed by the rest of him in a wheelchair pushed by Martin. Her husband's smile seemed weak as Martin pushed the chair toward the bedroom.

"I turned down the covers and lowered the TV screen." She thought Martin would know where to go, but she did not want Christopher to know how often Alexander had been sleeping in the other room.

"Yes, ma'am." Martin did not change his direction at all, so perhaps he was already headed for the correct room.

Christiana twisted her hands together, but hung back. Christopher and Martin helped Alexander put his arms around their shoulders. They lifted him out of the wheelchair, but Christopher nearly tripped over it. Christiana rushed over and pulled it out of the way as they turned so he could sit on the edge of the bed. Martin helped with his leg as he swiveled.

Alexander's lips were pressed into a tight line, turning white from the strain.

"Are you sure you are okay to be here?" she asked. "Should you be back at the hospital?" Or in the hospital rooms of the palace at least.

"No." The word seemed forced out of his lips. "I'd rather not be in a hospital room of any kind." Martin situated some pillows on the bed then lifted Alexander's leg onto them. Her husband relaxed against the pillows propped behind him as it finally settled.

Martin took hold of the wheelchair. "I'll be back in a few minutes, sir. If you need anything, page me, and I'll send someone if I'm not back yet."

Alexander nodded. "Thanks, but I think I just want to sleep. Thank your brother for me, would you? He kept the queen safe."

"I will, sir."

He looked at Christiana and knew she was coming up with a way to thank the shopkeeper as well. His eyes began to flutter closed as Martin left.

"Do you want me to stay here tonight?" Christopher crossed his arms and moved his legs shoulder-width apart. He looked as intimidating as Alexander could.

Her husband didn't even open his eyes. "No. You're welcome to, if you want, but don't feel you have to. There's plenty of help around if I need it."

"Yeah. But how many of them want to help you get to the bathroom?" She saw him roll his eyes. "As your twin brother, I figure that's my responsibility."

Christiana wanted to contradict him. To inform him that, as Alexander's wife, it was her responsibility, but two things stopped her. Her fear that she would not be strong enough to help him as he needed and her fear that he would not want her to.

"No. Martin or someone else can help if I need them." He seemed to sink even further into the bed. "I'm fine but stay if you want."

Christopher rested a hand on his brother's shoulder. "I may, but I'll probably go over to Biacampo for the night." He turned and smiled at her. "Keep him in line, would you?"

"I will try," Christiana told him with a smile of her own. "But I doubt he will want to rest for as long as the doctor would like."

"Probably not." Christopher nodded. "No matter where I stay tonight, I'll be back tomorrow to check on him."

Christiana went to follow him out of the room. "I appreciate that."

"Christiana?"

She turned at the sound of Alexander's voice. "Yes?"

She could barely hear his reply and wondered if the nearly broken sound was only her imagination. "Would you stay?"

Christiana hesitated, torn between her desire to do so and propriety's dictates. "Let me see your brother out," she finally answered. "I will be back momentarily."

A hand on her shoulder drew her attention. "I can show myself out." Christopher gave her a quick peck on the cheek. "Take care of my brother. And my sister-in-law." Who? "And my niece or nephew." Right. Herself.

She smiled. "I will. Thank you for your support, Christopher."

He squeezed her shoulder again. "Anytime."

Christiana took a deep breath and turned back into the bedroom. She wanted to help. But would he let her? And would she know how?

Alexander winced as he shifted a bit on the bed, trying to find a more comfortable position.

"What can I do to help?" Christiana's soft voice carried over to him.

He patted her side of the bed. "Just come sit with me?" More than anything, he needed her close, needed to know she was okay.

The other side of the bed dipped, and he felt her roll toward him. "I want to hold you," he whispered. "But I don't think I can."

More movement. A small hand slipping into his, the delicate fingers sliding between his own. Her other arm hugged his as she rested her head on his shoulder, stretching her body along his. Her leg hooked over his good one, and he winced. Good was a relative term, but he didn't want her to move it.

"Is this all right?"

"Perfect." Not perfect. But as close to perfect as it was going to get the day after getting shot. He twisted his head to brush a kiss against her forehead. "How are you?"

His cheek rested against her hair as she spoke. "I am fine. A little shaken up still, but otherwise fine. So is the baby. Dr. McCall did a scan yesterday just to make sure, and she said everything looked good."

"Good."

"Christopher looked quite serious when he came in. What did he say?"

"He was mad at me for getting shot. We scared him, too, you know." As much as Alexander didn't want to ask, he had to know. "Has Tony figured out how Henry got onto palace grounds?"

"Another passageway that comes from the beach and exits near the cottage. He lucked into me being there. He planned to go to another tunnel no one knew about that would bring him in here." She shuddered against him. "It has now been alarmed. No one else can get in here, but Tony pointed out that this is why we had guards at all times. Even in here." His thumb rubbed against her hand. "They found his lair, I guess you would call it. A room in that passageway that held all of his paperwork they never found. He lived in this apartment, you know. Moving in here was supposed to be a way to exorcise him from my life. Knowing how easily he could get in makes me feel much less secure, despite his imprisonment and the alarms."

"I'll keep you safe." If only he could wrap his arms around her, pull her close, and make her feel safe.

"You will never believe what they found." Her voice sounded small, scared.

"What's that?" He tried to hold her hand a little tighter.

A long pause. "He is not really my uncle."

Alexander blinked his eyes open. "What?"

"Since we discovered his duplicity, I wondered how my mother could be related to such an awful man. But she was not. He claimed to be her half-brother, from a fling my grandfather had before he married my grandmother. I knew that much, but he was not really her half-brother after all. The claims were made while she and my father barely knew each other. At least that was the public story. They were quite serious, but the press did not know this until several months later."

Another silence. "So he managed to infiltrate your family?"

She nodded against him. "He forged documents and knew things about my grandfather and this girlfriend. He convinced everyone he was this long lost son."

"Do they know why?"

"My great-grandfather." She sighed and snuggled closer. "King Richard IV of Ravenzario. He, apparently, took some land from this man's family as payment for back taxes and penalties for a fraud scheme they had run. His family blamed the royal family for their ruin. Somehow he discovered the courtship was serious and decided the way to get back at the royal family was by becoming a member of the royal in-laws. The paperwork seems to indicate he did not know anything about the Commonwealth agreement or the marriage contract. Eventually, he chose a man to get close to me, his nephew. His nephew would kill me and become king. Since my uncle was never convicted of treason, the new king could then pardon him on Easter."

"What if they had convicted him of treason?"

"The new king would have used his special monarch's exemption, a once in a lifetime chance, to pardon a traitor."

Alexander kissed her head again. "It almost worked, but I am so very glad it didn't."

Hot liquid landed on his bare shoulder. Tears. "But it did. He had my parents' car tampered with."

It took several seconds for that to sink in. "He killed your parents? Your brother and the nanny?"

Her fresh grief tore at his heart. "I was supposed to be with them. He planned to take out all four of us, but a cold kept me at home." Her voice caught. "He planned to kill me at least three times. He killed my brother."

"Sit up."

He could feel her withdraw, physically and emotionally, just like she had that day in the reception room. This time he wouldn't let her go. He winced as his arm reached for her, wrapping around her and pulling her back close to him. Her arm snuck across his abdomen, holding him as he held her.

"I have no one left."

He closed his eyes at her agonized whisper.

"At least he was family, you know? And now I am alone."

"Tia, sweetheart, I can't move the way I need to, so can you sit up and look at me?"

She sniffled but did as he asked. He reached out and rubbed his thumb across her cheek, burying his fingers in her silky hair. "You are *not* alone anymore, sweetheart." Her blue eyes shimmered with unshed tears. "I know I can't replace what you lost, that my parents and brother can't replace yours, but you are *not* alone. You have me, my family." The pad of his thumb brushed against the tears. "Our baby. You're not alone, love. Never again will you be alone."

His hand curved behind her neck to gently pull her close, absorbing her sobs in his chest, crying a tear or two of his own for her loss.

"How can God be in all of this, Alexander? I always believed God has a hand in everything. My parents were at church every week. While I lived in Montevaro, King Jedidiah made sure I was at church every Sunday and passed his beliefs on to me. My non-uncle managed to keep me from going here, but after he was arrested, I went whenever I could. But how could God be in the murder of my parents? Of my brother? Of the attempts on my life?"

His hand rubbed up and down her back. "I don't know what the plan is. God's ways are above ours. We may never understand, but there is some good. At least I think it's good."

"What good?"

A deep breath steadied his nerves. "Us. If your parents had lived, if there hadn't been a threat on your life and an arrest, there is no way we would have gotten married. I'm not glad they died, but I'm glad you're in my life. I'm so very glad *you* are my wife, and that has nothing to do with who your parents are or your address. It's because I love you." His first time to tell her that outside of the life threatening situation the day before. "I love you. I love our baby. And I'm glad I get to spend my life with you, loving you."

His words reached into the furthest parts of Christiana's broken heart and began to bind them back together. She knew only time, and God, would truly be able to do so, but knowing this incredible man loved her would go a long way toward helping that process. She leaned over, kissed him softly, again and again and again, before lying back down at his side.

"I love you, too, Alexander. I don't know when, or how, but I do."

His arm tightened around her shoulders.

"I am so very glad you are in my life."

They lay there together, holding each other until she dozed off. When she awoke dusk had fallen outside the window. Alexander's even breathing told her he slept still. Likely the medicine helped him sleep. She knew he needed it, so she slid out the other side of the bed, stretching her back and reaching for the ceiling. Her eyes landed on the panel where she was told the passage came out. Two new small black boxes were mounted on the wall. An alarm that would go off if the passageway was opened. Tony promised a more discrete alarm would be put in place soon.

She closed the door behind her, wincing at the click.

"Did you have a nice nap?" Diana looked up from the desk that still resided in the living area.

"Yes." She sat in one of the chairs. "Alexander is still sleeping. I expect he will for some time."

"The doctor said the medicine would knock him out." Diana glanced at the clock. "The nurse will be by in a few minutes to check on him."

A quick knock followed by the door opening had Christiana turn around. For once she did not stand but rather just nodded as Tony walked in.

"Do you have an update?" she asked.

Tony handed over a manila folder as he sat across from her. "We've been using the documents found in the tunnel to round up anyone else that might still be loyal to him. So far we've found a couple that don't really surprise me given some of the other stuff that's gone on the last few days. The police captain that detained Ms. Quisenberry and her son is one of them. But overall, just like we thought, many of them were fired and/or prosecuted almost two years ago." He hesitated before going on. "The scariest one, though, is the member of the duke's expanded security detail. He was part of the plan, along with the captain, to set up the flat tire and subsequent rescue."

Christiana felt the blood leave her face.

"He was never alone with your husband."

The relief began to set in. "Good." She flipped through the papers, not stopping to look too thoroughly. "And what of Ms. Quisenberry and her son?"

"The recognition ceremony for Ms. Quisenberry and Mr. Giuseppe will be held before the Quisenberrys leave." He looked over at her. "Martin and Franco have another brother who is mayor of Whisper Cove. You've met him a couple of times."

She nodded. "Of course." She did remember the man, though not well.

"Do you know when the Quisenberrys will be leaving?"

Christiana shook her head. "No. I am hoping she will accept a ride either on the royal jet or on the Bayfield plane with Christopher when he returned home. She has had a rough few days, and I would like to see her return in comfort."

Tony nodded. "I'll talk to Christopher and see how long he's planning to stay." He made a notation. "I think that would be best anyway. In fact, I'd like to post a guard with her for a few weeks after she returns home, just to make sure there's no fall out. She's had some threats, likely from those who either haven't followed up to see she really had nothing to do with all of this or who don't believe it."

"Please make sure she is taken care of. I do not want anything to happen to her." Their moments of stand-off with her uncle had bonded them. In fact, she needed to see Julia before long, even before the ceremony and thank her. "How is Alex?" She nodded at Diana who picked up her pen. "I would like to make sure they both get counseling when they return home. It is likely Alex will be traumatized. They both will. Will you see that they do and that the bills are sent here?"

Diana made a note on the pad in front of her. "Yes, ma'am. That's a great idea. Why don't I contact the duke's mother? She likely knows a good counselor. Then we can give Ms. Quisenberry at least one option from the get-go."

"Very good." Christiana closed her eyes. There was something else she needed to speak with Tony about, but it was not coming to her.

"The other end of the passage leading to the square has been covered over." That was it. As much as she had loved being able to escape the confines of the cottage, it was best that it be sealed now that its existence was known. "Cameras and alarms are going in tomorrow. A guard remains posted until then."

"What about the other end of the passage that comes to this apartment?"

"A guard is stationed outside. We are still combing through the room. I can't help but feel we're still missing some documents or other evidence there. A secret safe or something, perhaps. As you know, the end in your bedroom has been alarmed. In about two weeks, the alarms will be replaced with new ones created to look like the molding near the ceiling and baseboards. They won't be noticeable unless you look closely."

Diana jumped in. "We know how you feel about preserving as much of the history of the palace as possible, ma'am. I know it's not the same, but I think it's a good compromise."

Christiana agreed and said so. "Do we know of any other tunnels or secret rooms?"

"There are floor plans that we've discovered. I haven't had a chance to pour over them yet, but I would hope there are some notations on there. Since we know where a couple of the entrances and exits are now, maybe that will help us find the locations for the others."

Before anything else could be said, a knock came at the door. Diana answered and let the nurse in. After speaking to her, Diana led her to the bedroom so she could look in on Alexander.

"Do you have any plans for the next few days, ma'am?"

Christiana turned her attention back to Tony.

"For leaving the palace that is?"

She shook her head. "I would like to, sometime very soon. I think I need to, but nothing specific."

"I will get with Charlyn and start making some preliminary plans for later in the week. Especially with the prince laid up and your pregnancy, I think that will be fine." He made a few notations on his tablet and stood. "If you need anything, you know how to find us." Tony bowed slightly and left.

The nurse exited the bedroom with Diana right behind her.

"How is he?" Christiana asked, worst case scenarios playing out in her mind.

The nurse dropped into a quick curtsy. "He's doing fine, Your Majesty." The nurse checked the binder in her hand. "His vitals are right where I expected them to be, and he's fallen back asleep already. He will likely sleep a lot as the meds make him tired."

"They have a place for you to stay for the next few days?" Christiana looked at Diana to confirm.

"Yes, ma'am. The room is lovely. Thank you for making the arrangements."

Christiana waved a dismissive hand. "It is the least we can do if you are going to be here twenty-four hours a day. I would imagine we will not need you most of the time, but we are glad you will be available if we do." She stood to shake the woman's hand. "Please, if some emergency comes up, there will be no need to stand on any formality or deference. And if the duke is not following orders, you have my permission to make him."

The corner of the nurse's mouth twitched. "Yes, ma'am."

Diana showed her out while Christiana decided it was time for a long bath and bed. Being chased through the streets and shot at left her sore. Standing vigil over her unconscious husband left her exhausted. She thanked Diana and shut the door behind her. Hearing Alexander breathe comforted her in a way little else could, and she decided to forgo the bath. She changed into her pajamas and lay next to him, her head on his pillow as she drifted to sleep.

Julia fidgeted and tugged on the hem of her shirt. In minutes, she would be escorted into the presence of the queen. The reception room, she'd been told. Not the throne room. Thank goodness. This whole thing was intimidating enough. At least the last time, she'd had no warning the queen was coming. No time to be nervous.

"She's not an ogre, you know."

Julia looked up to see Alexander standing there, arms crossed in front of him and a stern look on his face. Except...

"Christopher?" It couldn't be Alexander, not with an uninjured leg.

He nodded and pushed off the wall, unfolding his arms to hold out a hand. "Julia, right?"

She shook it and nodded. Something about him made her insides constrict. Not necessarily in a bad way, but nonetheless. Were his eyes the same color as Alexander's? She seemed to remember them being hazel years earlier, but here, now, Christopher's were more of a dark brown.

"Any idea why the queen summoned both of us?" he asked.

She shook her head. "I didn't know she did. I just know I was asked to come." A shrug. "And when you're staying at the palace, and the queen requests your presence, you go. Unless you're puking. Then it's probably better not to."

He chuckled, but didn't smile. "Probably."

Had she done something to offend the duke's brother? Though he shook her hand, there seemed to be something off about her interaction with him. Before she could ask him about it, the door opened, and a man in a butler's tuxedo ushered them into the room.

The queen sat, looking rather regal, in a chair opposite the door. Julia glanced up at Christopher but he wasn't looking at her. They followed the butler, until they were about six feet in front of the queen. Unsure of what else to do, Julia did her best to curtsy as the butler announced, "Ms. Julia Quisenberry and Mr. Christopher Bayfield."

Christopher didn't wait for anything else. He crossed the remaining few feet and bent to give the queen a kiss on the cheek. "How're you feeling?"

The queen smiled up at him. "Well rested for the first time in ages, thank you."

"And my brother?"

"Snores like a bear, but I would imagine you know that even better than I."

He laughed. A full laugh this time, rather than the half chuckle she'd gotten. "Yes, he does."

The queen turned to Julia. "And you, Ms. Quisenberry? Are your accommodations acceptable?"

She had to clear her throat. "They're lovely, ma'am. We appreciate your generosity."

The queen shifted slightly, a subtle movement that served to put Julia a bit more at ease, as she motioned to the small couch across from her. "Please, have a seat." Julia sat, completely aware of how close Christopher's arm was to hers. "And your son? How is he doing?"

"He's had nightmares the last couple of nights, unfortunately, but during the day, he's fine. He loves exploring the parts of the palace he has access to."

"Thank you for respecting the boundaries in place."

"Of course." Did people really try to sneak through areas deemed off-limits when there was so much fabulousness to explore in the areas that weren't?

The queen changed the subject. "Now, there is the matter of returning to the States."

Right. Here it came. *Thank you for taking a bullet for me, sort of, and helping me escape, but here's your return ticket in steerage on a slow boat home. You don't mind taking Titanic II, do you?*

The queen's voice cut through her thoughts. "Christopher, you are returning to Serenity Landing tomorrow, correct?"

"Yes." Was that wariness in his voice? Why?

"Your brother and I were hoping Ms. Quisenberry and her son could accompany you on the Bayfield Enterprises plane. We're happy to send Royal Air One, but it seems ridiculous to send both of them when it is not necessary."

Christopher shifted next to her. "Of course. I'd be happy to escort them back to the States."

Wait. Were they going home in a *private jet?* Julia tried to assimilate the words.

The queen was speaking to her again. "I trust that is acceptable? We will see that your hired car is returned and any fees covered."

Julia struggled to find her voice. "Thank you. That would be wonderful. I appreciate it." She turned to Christopher, who seemed to be about two degrees shy of glaring at her. "If it's not too much trouble, that is."

Queen Christiana laughed. "You are not too much trouble. Christopher will be going to the same place you are. And I have no doubt he is currently the only passenger expected on board." She arched a regal brow at her brother-in-law. "You do not have any other traveling companions, do you?"

Like a woman? That seemed to be the implication in the queen's voice, though Julia hadn't heard about the royal brother-in-law cavorting with any particular females. And since she had nothing else to do, she'd spent plenty of time trawling the royal/celebrity stalker sites.

"No, I don't. Ms. Quisenberry and her son are more than welcome to join me, though I can't promise to be the best travel companion. I'll be working most of the trip."

Julia spoke up. "Then we'll do our best not to bother you." She'd have to talk to Alex about it and make sure he understood.

Something unidentified crossed the queen's face as she smiled. "Very well. That is taken care of. Ms. Quisenberry, Christopher, perhaps it would be best if you would exchange phone numbers so you can work out the arrangements." She looked at Christopher. "Please tell Justin when you know for certain what time you will be leaving, and he will make transportation arrangements."

Christopher nodded and stood. "You got it. Anything else?"

Something was getting his goat.

Queen Christiana just smiled sweetly and shook her head. "No. That is all. Thank you both for coming."

And that was her cue. Julia stood. "Thank you again, ma'am."

The queen waved her hand again. "None of this ma'am stuff. Please, call me Christiana."

Julia felt her eyebrows shoot up. "Um, sure. Thank you again, Christiana. We appreciate your hospitality."

The door opened behind them.

Christopher had started to leave, but a glare from the queen stopped him. "Before you go, there is something I would like to give you."

About ten people flooded into the room, including some guy snapping pictures. Great. The butler stood between Julia and the queen. Christiana stood and smiled at her. "For service above and beyond the call of duty in service to the crown, it is my honor..." The butler held out a velvet box, about three inches by five and snapped it open. "...to bestow upon Franco Giuseppe of Whisper Cove and owner of Pagosa Plaza Men's Apparel and Ms. Julia Quisenberry of Serenity Landing, Missouri, the United States, the Order of the Chelonii." The queen took the ribbon and medal out of the box. "This is the oldest honor in the Commonwealth and only given to a select few. I have not yet had the privilege of giving any of these, but no matter how many there are, these two will likely remain the most important. Without your assistance, I would likely not be here today. You helped save my life and the life of my unborn child. For this you have my eternal gratitude."

Julia blinked several times as the queen approached her then fastened the ribbon around her neck.

Stepping back, she spoke again. "On behalf of my people, my husband, and myself, I thank you."

A few more blinks and another cleared throat later, Julia

managed to speak. "I'd say I'm happy to, which I am, and anytime, but I'd really prefer never to do any of that again."

Those assembled laughed and the queen smiled. "I understand. I would prefer it never be needed either. Alexander wishes he could be here, but unfortunately, he is still not up and around."

Julia nodded. "I completely understand. Please give him my best, and let him know I'm praying for a speedy recovery."

"Of course." She turned and did the same with the other man standing there. "Mr. Giuseppe, you opened your store to me while locking the world out and were wounded yourself in my defense. You have my eternal gratitude."

Julia saw the man blinking back tears of his own. "It was an honor, Your Majesty. A twisted ankle is nothing in defense of my queen." Julia knew Mr. Giuseppe was playing down his injury. He wore a medical boot on one foot and had used a crutch on his way in.

The ceremony seemed to come quickly to an end, though the queen promised a banquet in their honor would be held in a couple of months.

Christiana rubbed her stomach as those around them began to disperse. "Now, if you will excuse me, I think I will go check on my husband and rest for a bit myself."

A minute later, she was left alone in the room with Christopher. Julia looked up at him to say thank you, but his face had taken on a hard look.

He leaned closer, his tone harsh. "I don't know what game you're playing, but trust me, it won't work."

Before she could recover from the shock, close her mouth, and issue a retort, he was gone.

lexander shifted against the pillows propping him up as the door to the bedroom opened. Tony walked in, a completely serious look on his face. "What is it?"

"I have to go," the head of security answered as he closed the door behind him. "Soon."

"I know. What are you going to tell Christiana?"

"That I haven't used any vacation since her parents died, and it's finally time for me to take a few weeks."

"I'll do whatever I can to help from here. Are you telling anyone else? Antonio?"

Tony shook his head. "No. The fewer who know the better. I won't leave the country for a couple weeks, but I'll start my vacation time sooner than that. I need to do some research that I can't really do while working."

"Okay. Keep me in the loop?"

"Of course."

The door opened again. A slow smile crossed Alexander's face as Christiana walked in this time. Though he'd slept much of the last twenty-four hours, he had a very definite memory of her lying next to him and telling him she loved him.

And kissing him. He definitely remembered her kissing him.

"I'm glad you're feeling better, sir." Tony nodded his head their general direction and left.

"Where have you been?" Alexander asked as she sat gingerly on the edge of the bed.

"Bestowing the Order of the Chelonii to Ms. Quisenberry and Mr. Giuseppe." He took her hand. "She and Alex will be flying back to Serenity Landing with your brother when he leaves tomorrow."

Alexander raised a brow at her. "Are you sure that's a good idea? He knows she had nothing to do with your uncle, but I get the sense he's still not crazy about her." If he had the chance while he was coherent enough, Alexander would try to get it out of his brother.

She leaned over and kissed him. "Of course. He is flying home anyway, and I refuse to let her fly coach." His wife shuddered. "Not after what she did for us and causing her to be delayed. It is ridiculous for us to send both planes at essentially the same time."

"I don't have a problem with it. In fact, I agree with you, but I'm not sure he does."

Another kiss. "Do we have to talk about him?"

Alexander shook his head. "No. In fact, I'd rather talk about something else."

"Such as?"

Another slow grin. "What we talked about last night." He chuckled at her look. "About how I love you, and you love me, and then we could smooch some more."

She ducked her head as a pretty pink color climbed up her cheeks. "I seem to remember that conversation."

He reached out to touch her face with his fingertips, before wrapping a hand around the back of her neck and tugging her toward him. "I love you, Queen Christiana Elizabeth Marissa Abigail the First."

"Oh, please." Her breath brushed his lips just before hers did. Slow, soft, sweet. Not enough but it would have to be.

For now.

A few minutes later, she sat curled up in his arms again. "There's something I've been meaning to ask you."

She moved to look at him. "What's that?"

"Did you ever have a coronation? You were so young. I would have thought there would be one when you came of age, but with everything the way it was..."

Her eyes widened. "You have not seen the pictures?"

He shook his head. "No."

She picked up the remote and lowered the screen.

"So you did have one?"

There was no answer as she picked up the keyboard and typed her password in. A few clicks and she turned to him. "There was a coronation." Another click and a picture appeared on the screen. "At the funeral."

Alexander pushed himself into a seated position, his eyes narrowing as he ignored the pain shooting through his leg. "At their funeral?"

The long shot had to have been taken from somewhere high in the ceiling of the cathedral. On the stage were four caskets - two with large flower arrangements on top, one small casket with a medium sized arrangement, and one full size with a smaller one. Slightly in front, and right in the center stood a little girl. Even from the great distance, he could tell. There appeared to be a crown on her head and the robe trailed behind her all the way to the other end of the caskets. "Seriously?"

Her defensive tone caught him off-guard. "I had no choice in the matter, Alexander."

"I know. I just can't believe he did that." Another click. This shot was straight up the aisle and much closer. His wife, as a little girl, stood there, a large crown on her head, the robes enveloping her. He could see bits of casket on either side, but what drew his attention were the wide, scared eyes and the tear-stained cheeks.

And the teddy bear peeking from between the center of the robes.

His heart broke, ached, for the little girl who'd lost everyone in the world who cared about her. He reached for her grown-up self, pulled her close and held her tight. "I'm sorry, sweetheart. I can't imagine anyone thinking this was a good idea and letting him do it."

"Some of the papers Tony and his men found included early drafts of a document that indicated this was my parents' wishes. That the coronation of my brother or myself be held quickly should anything happen to my father."

"And people bought that?"

"I do not know, but they did it."

He lay back down, pulling her with him. "I'm so sorry," he whispered into her hair. They lay there for some time before something clicked. "Why haven't I seen pictures before?"

"When he was arrested, I mentioned something in passing to Diana about how much they bothered me. There were not many around, but there were some. There usually are coronation pictures around, you know. Or portraits before cameras, of course. I did not realize for some time that they had all been removed."

"Would you like a real coronation? You couldn't have known what you were saying when it came to taking the oath."

She shrugged. "I do not know. It seems to be an extravagant expense."

He let it drop, but would put Justin on finding out how much it would cost and whether the people would approve. Even something simple, something to help overwrite the awful memory that currently accompanied her coronation.

For the time being, he was content. She turned, her blue eyes still filled with tears. "I thought about what you said and you are right. Without everything else, we would not be here. You. Me. Our baby." She kissed him again. "I love you, Alexander, and I thank God for you."

"I love you," he whispered, his heart overflowing. He kissed her, again and again.

God had given him the perfect woman. His wife. His friend. His lover. The mother of his child.

He had won her heart, and he couldn't be happier.

LETTER TO READERS

Dear Reader,

Thank you for joining Queen Christiana and Prince Alexander in *Winning the Queen's Heart*! I appreciate you and hope you enjoyed it! This is the second book in the Brides of Belles Montagnes series! Two more stories of the royal families of Mevendia and Ravenzario will be told this fall and winter. And, yes, Jonathan's story is coming, too! After the acknowledgments, you will find a preview of *Protecting the Prince*, a novella which will be FREE for a limited time to all newsletter subscribers! You'll also find chapter 1 of *Finding Mr. Write*, book 1 in the CANDID Romance series which is FREE on all retailers! Many of you have likely already read *Good Enough for a Princess*, but if not, it too is FREE on all retailers!

I see a meme floating around Facebook from time to time that tells readers what they can do to help their favorite authors. Buying their next book or giving a copy away is kind of a no-brainer, but the biggest thing you can do is write a review. If you enjoyed *Winning the Queen's Heart* would you consider doing just that?

I would LOVE to hear from you! My email address is books@candidpublications.com. To stay up-to-date on releases, you can sign up for my newsletter (there's fun stuff - like the novella about Nicklaus and his nanny and what happened to them after the car accident!

You'll also get notices of sales, including special preorder pricing! And I won't spam!) or there's always "What's in the Works" or "What I'm Working On Now" on my website :). You can find my website and blog at www.carolmoncado.com. I blog most Sundays and about once more each month at www.InspyRomance.com. And, of course, there's Facebook and my Facebook profile, Author Carol Moncado. If you recently liked my Facebook *page* (Carol Moncado Books)...I hope you'll "follow" the profile as well. Facebook recently changed the rules again which means very few people (often 1-5% of "likes") will see anything I post there. Following the profile will show you my book updates, updates about books from authors I love, funny cat (or dog or dinosaur!) memes, inspirational quotes, and all sorts of fun stuff!! I hope to see you there soon!

Thanks again!

ACKNOWLEDGMENTS

They say writing is a solitary endeavor and it absolutely can be. Sitting in front of the computer for hours on end, talking to imaginary people.

And having them talk back ;).

But the reality is no one walks alone. Since I began this writing journey nearly six years ago, I can't begin to name all of those who've helped me along the way. My husband, Matt, who has always, *always* believed in me. All of the rest of my family and in-loves who never once looked at me like I was nuts for wanting to be a writer. Jan Christiansen (my "other mother") has always believed in me and Stacy Christiansen Spangler who has been my dearest friend for longer than I can remember.

For *Winning the Queen's Heart* specifically - I can't begin to count the number of text messages Emily N. and Ginger V. put up with trying to sort things out. Ginger Solomon, author of *One Choice*, has been invaluable with her proofreading services.

And Jerenda F. - thank you for letting me borrow your Poppo and Nanny. I appreciate you!

Then there's my writer friends. My NovelSista, Jessica Keller

Koschnitzky, sister of my hear. She is part of my BritCrit gals. Joanna Politano (who has talked me down off more virtual ledges than anyone), Jen Cvelvar (the best case of misidentification *ever*), Kristy Cambron (who is more beautiful inside and out than any one person should be allowed to be), and Stacey Zink (who never, ever fails to have a fabulous encouraging word) are BritCritters, too. We do a lot more living than we do critting, and I wouldn't have it any other way. All five of them are beyond gifted as writers, and I thank God they're in my life. There's my MozArks ACFW peeps who laugh with me, critique, and encourage to no end. And Melanie Dickerson. What would I do without you?

Then there's the InspyRomance crew, the CIA, my Spicy peeps (you know who you are!), and all of the others who've helped me along on this journey.

I've said it before, but I could go on for days about beloved mentors like Janice Thompson who has poured her time and energy into this newbie, going above and beyond for me. People like one of my spiciest friends, Pepper Basham, who inspires me daily, or Julie Lessman, who has prayed me to this point. People like Jeane Wynn (*the* top publicist in the business) and Kathleen Y'Barbo (one of the top authors) who take me along on late night Wal-Mart runs and kidnap me to Chili's so I'm writing on a full stomach. All of these and so many more are not only mentors, but *friends* - I am beyond blessed! And, of course, there's Tamela Hancock Murray, agent extraordinaire, who believed in me enough to want to be my agent and encourages me always.

I said I could go on for days, and I could keep going. On and on. I know I've forgotten many people and I hate that. But you, dear reader, would quickly get bored.

So THANK YOU to all of those who have helped me along the way. I couldn't have done this without you and you have my eternal gratitude. To the HUNDREDS of you (I'm gobsmacked!) who pre-ordered and encouraged me without knowing it as that little number continued to climb, you have my eternal gratitude. I hope you stick around for the next one!

And, of course, last but never, *ever*, least, to Jesus Christ, without whom none of this would be possible - or worth it.

Protecting the Prince

Tony Browning stepped off the plane in Athmetica, the capital city of the Sovereign Commonwealth of Athmetis. The unseasonable weather caused heat to roil off the tarmac in visible waves and threatened to give Tony heat stroke. The suit he wore was suitable for the current weather in Ravenzario but much too warm for Athmetis. Why hadn't he thought to check the temperature?

For this trip, he was on his own. No chauffeur would meet him at the airport. No car would whisk him away to his destination. In fact, no one official knew he was here. He'd used his position as Queen Christiana's head of security to gain diplomatic status in the island nation, but only because it afforded him less hassle. If, as he suspected, he ended up in the United States, he'd travel even more conventionally.

Once through the airport, skipping baggage claim, he hailed a taxi and took it to the hotel, in a village a few kilometers away, where he'd stay for the next couple of days.

If he couldn't find any sign of the young prince and his nanny here, he'd move on to the next location on his list.

"Sir?"

Tony blinked as the driver got his attention. "Yes?"

"We've arrived."

He shook himself out of his stupor. "My apologies." Tony started to open the door, but paused. "Are you familiar with this area?"

"Of course!" His chest puffed up, as though offended Tony would ask such a thing. "I rode my bike around the entire village as a child. You want to go somewhere, I know the best way to get there."

"You grew up here?" Could this be the stroke of luck he needed?

"Two streets over. My Yaya worked at this very hotel."

"What's your name?"

"Rex Cromer, sir."

"Rex, can I hire you for the next couple of days?" Confusion filled the other man's face. "I need a guide who knows this area well. You would need to be on call twenty-four hours a day, but you will be well-compensated." Tony named a figure he knew would entice the other man.

"What's the catch?" Rex's eyes narrowed.

"No catch. I'm doing research into some people I believe came here in late 1999 or very early 2000. I need to find them. They may or may not still be in the area, but if at all possible, I need to know where they went."

Could Rex's eyes narrow any further? "Why? Are you a hit man?"

Tony laughed. "Quite the opposite. They ran from a family member who was quite dangerous. He has finally been put in prison for life. It is safe for them to come home, but no one knows exactly where they are anymore. I know where their first destination, here in Athmetis was supposed to be, but beyond that, we don't know." Time to lay most of the cards on the table. "To be honest I'm not even completely sure what names they used, just that they didn't use their real names."

He could see Rex turn the proposal over in his head. "Very

well. You were to have been my last fare for the day, and I have two days off. You should talk to my Yaya. She's known everyone in this area for the last sixty years or longer."

Within ten minutes, Tony had been ushered into Yaya's home. After exchanging pleasantries, he got down to business, pulling photos out of his pocket. "Do you remember seeing either of these people around the turn of the century?"`

Yaya took the photos and examined them carefully with the help of a magnifying glass. "So young," she murmured as she held the photo of Prince Nicklaus. "So sad."

"So sad?" Tony's heart constricted. Had something happened to the prince and his caretaker in the intervening years? They hadn't even considered that possibility.

"So sad his parents died so young." She looked up and stared Tony in the eyes. "His sister and he were the only remaining members of their immediate family, no?"

She knew? How?

Yaya must have seen the questions in his eyes. "Rex, please get our guest something to drink."

"Of course, Yaya." His gaze shifted between Tony and his grandmother, but he left.

"Who are you?" she demanded as soon as Rex was out of earshot. "Why do you want to know about these two people?"

Tony pulled out his credentials. "I am the head of Queen Christiana of Ravenzario's security detail, ma'am."

She took them and examined them closely. Satisfied, she returned them. "Very well. You may call me Yaya."

He bowed his head slightly in acknowledgment.

"Do you believe in fate?" she asked.

Tony shook his head. "No, ma'am. But I do believe in divine guidance. I believe the Lord leads us places we need to be, when we need to be there."

"It is why your queen is still alive."

"Correct. She was sick when the car..."

Yaya waved a hand. "No. I read the papers, young man. I saw the stories about Henry Eit." She spit into the planter next to her chair. "No good, that man. I know this for many years. But, if the papers are to be believed, the only reason you were finally able to arrest him was because Duke Alexander overheard something he should not have, correct?"

"Yes, ma'am."

"Then you understand when I tell you I believe God brought you to the right taxi driver today."

Tony blinked slowly. "What do you mean?"

"Come. I show you." Yaya slowly stood. Tony reached for her to give her a hand, but she waved him off.

He followed her to the courtyard and toward a decorative door, covered with hanging plants. One of Yaya's wrinkled hands reached through the greenery and did something Tony couldn't see. The door swung open revealing a small room behind it. He looked at Yaya. "What is this?"

"This is the place Michaela and Nicklaus stayed when they fled Ravenzario."

Michelle Metcalf set her suitcase down next to her bed. It was good to be home.

"Michelle?" Nicholas's voice carried up the stairs. "Where do you want the rest of this stuff?"

"I don't care," she called back. "We'll deal with it later."

There was a thump followed by quick steps up the staircase. Nicholas rounded the corner into her room. "You glad to be back, Mom?"

He'd been in her care for twenty years and had called her mom most of that time, but it never failed to both make her uneasy and fill her with love. It was good that he called her by name, too. It reminded her he wasn't really her son.

"The cruise was wonderful." She smiled as he flopped onto her bed. "Thank you for the gift."

"I'm just bummed we had to wait so long to take it. It was supposed to be a way to get out of the Midwest during the winter, not when it's almost summer."

Michelle shook her head and gave him a mock glare. "You had classes, exams, and none of the cruises we wanted to take coincided with your spring break. Waiting until the semester ended was perfect."

"I still can't believe you wouldn't let me get international texting on my phone while we were gone. I only sent Tessa three messages the whole time."

Nicholas had saved for two years to buy them the cruise, but household expenses, including cell phones, were paid by Michelle's job. The account filled with funds from King Richard prior to his death hadn't been touched in many years. Not since they'd fled Athmetis weeks after the assassination. The money had been used to purchase plane tickets to the United States. Some of it she later used to purchase their first home. King Richard's connections, including a couple of men whose names she still didn't know, had helped her secure what she needed but once the plane landed in the U.S., they had been on their own.

Deciding a single woman with a young son and no visible means of income would be suspicious, Michelle took the first job she could find. The daycare provided her with a place for Nicholas to be with her at all times, but still be around other children. For months he didn't even sleep in his own room for Michelle's peace of mind and because of the nightmares that continued to plague him. Her own sleep had often been less than restful with fears for Nicholas's safety always in the forefront of her mind. When she did doze off, she'd been hounded by dreams of her own.

The icy water. The king yelling at her to take Nicklaus and go. The fear of being found too soon. The fear of drowning. Of freezing as she tried to carry the terrified three-year-old to the safe house only she and the king knew about. The small, secret rooms in Ravenzario. The trail left to Athmetis. The short stay underground. Virtually no time outside of that little room for over a month. It had, quite literally, nearly driven her insane.

Michelle shook her head to clear it of the distant memories. Why were they suddenly in the forefront of her mind? "What?" she asked, dimly aware Nicholas had asked a question.

"I asked if you heard about the guy who used to live down in the Springfield, Missouri area?" He was used to her wool gathering, but he still seemed annoyed.

She hoisted the suitcase and set it on the bed next to him. "No, I don't believe I did."

"I heard some people talking about some rumors on the ship the day we boarded, but I forgot all about it until a minute ago." He tapped on his phone. "Yep. There's this guy from near Springfield who married some queen in Europe."

A feeling of dread filled Michelle's stomach. She'd carefully followed the goings on in Ravenzario and knew of the coincidence. What were the odds sweet Christiana would have married a man who lived less than four hours from her brother? She'd watched the wedding, even more astounded at the man chosen to walk the queen down the aisle. Michelle picked up one of the few remaining clean shirts and turned to put in her drawer. "I heard something about the wedding. Last fall, wasn't it?"

"Yeah. You watched part of it, didn't you?" He went on before she could answer. "But apparently, he got shot just a little over a week ago."

She couldn't turn around. He'd see it written all over her face. "What?"

"Uh..." He must be reading an article. "So this Alexander guy married the queen last fall. I guess her uncle was a bad dude who'd been arrested, but he was given some kind of Easter pardon."

A pardon? How had she missed that? She'd read about his arrest when it happened two years earlier and waited impatiently for someone to contact her, to tell her it was safe to finally return to her homeland, but no one ever did.

"He somehow got onto the palace grounds and tried to kill the queen. I guess she managed to get away."

Michelle silently cheered her former charge. She always had been an ingenious little girl. The pictures from after the accident nearly broke Michelle's heart.

"But Alexander - he's a duke now, I guess - was fighting this uncle and got shot in the leg. He's going to be okay and this time, the uncle was charged with treason."

Could it really be safe? He'd gone after Christiana again. She knew that, after nearly two decades running the country, he had to have far-reaching tentacles. The stories a few months earlier about Christiana's first fiancé proved that. The acquisition of an Easter pardon did so again. No. Until someone came to tell her it was safe, she wouldn't tell Nicholas the truth, and they wouldn't return. Until they *had* to.

"Mom?"

Nicholas caught her attention again and she turned. "What is it?"

Before she realized what was happening, he'd rolled off the bed and stood in front of her. "What's wrong, Mom?"

"What do you mean?"

He gently wiped the tears off one of her cheeks. "You're crying."

She managed to give him a small smile. "I suppose I am."

"Why?"

"I didn't want to tell you before the cruise, but I learned some-thing recently." She hadn't known before the cruise, but she didn't want to tell him exactly when she'd received the information.

"We've been safe here a long time, but it's time to start thinking about moving."

Nicholas crossed his arms in front of his chest. "What brought that up?"

"That comment you made about the pardon. I received word that one of the men who would like to harm us was pardoned not too long ago. I'd hoped to wait until I had more information to tell you, but that mention of it must have triggered something in me." She hated lying to him, but she couldn't tell him the whole truth. Not yet. She prayed he wouldn't pick up on her duplicity.

"So we're moving again?" He'd hate it, but he'd already resigned himself to the idea.

"I don't know yet." She reached for a Kleenex. "Let me do some research, and I'll let you know soon." The research would be more about where to go than if they would move. By the end of the month, they'd be settled somewhere new.

Available Now!

Tony Browning has worked for the Ravenzarian royal family since he was fifteen. The day after he took over as head of security, the king's sabotaged vehicle went over a guard rail, killing all inside. Or so everyone has always believed. Tony has discovered the prince, now grown, and his nanny may have survived. He uses decades old data to try and track them down - and make up for the tragedy that has haunted him all these years..

Michaela Engel has spent eighteen years keeping Prince Nicklaus's identity secret - and keeping him safe from the threats that haunt their every step. It's nearly time to tell her charge who he really is and return him to their homeland.

Before they can leave, Michaela and Nicklaus find themselves on the run once again. This time they find a new friend, one with a background in security, who's willing to help them stay safe. Michaela finds herself falling for Anthony, but can she trust him with her heart when they're done Protecting the Prince?

GRACE TO SAVE PREVIEW

SEPTEMBER 11, 2001

A ringing jolted Travis Harders from a deep sleep. He cursed as the phone knocked to the floor with a clatter. "This better be good," he snapped when he got the handset in place.

A glance at the clock nearly made him groan.

4:07.

"You'll be hearing from the police soon."

He rubbed the sleep out of his eyes with the heel of one hand and tried to process the statement. The words didn't really register as the guy, whoever he was, kept talking until Travis interrupted. "What? Who is this?"

"Mark's dad." Right. Travis's best friend. "You remember us? The ones who treated you like family? Let you live with us?"

Travis's stomach sank. Mark's family had practically adopted him when he moved from southwest Missouri to the Big Apple. They had filled the gap in his life left by parents who disapproved of Travis's choice to move to New York. Mark's parents let him spend holidays and birthdays with them, with Travis making only the obligatory phone calls back home.

But none of that explained why Mark's dad would be calling the police.

"Who is it?" a sleepy Jennifer asked.

Travis covered the mouthpiece and whispered to his girl-friend, "No one." His feet hit the cool floor, and he headed for the other room. At least he had a place to escape to. Being an out-of-work-actor-turned-barista didn't pay much, but he'd lucked into a fabulous apartment. Closing the French door behind him, he tried to focus on the voice yelling from the other end of the line.

But he only caught "my daughter" and "spring break" and "drugged."

If possible, Travis's stomach clenched further as that night flooded back to him. Memories of bringing her back to this very apartment when she was in no condition to go home without risking the wrath of her parents. But after what happened between them...it was only right for him to be on the receiving end of her dad's anger. "I don't know what she told you sir, but..."

"I know all I need to know," he bellowed.

Even though he was in the other room, Travis lowered the volume on the handset. "I take full responsibility for..."

"You're right, you do!" He let loose a string of obscenities. "You'll spend years in prison! Drugging a girl! Sleeping with her!"

"What?" His whole world spun. Travis regretted every minute of that night after they got back to the apartment, but he hadn't drugged her. He didn't even know where to get those kinds of drugs. They weren't in love, never had been, but to place the blame solely on him? The next morning, they'd talked about it enough to know she hadn't blamed him.

What changed? Feeling sucker punched, Travis hung up on the man. What he said didn't matter. Travis would find out when he was on trial for something he didn't do. On autopilot, he dressed for his five a.m. shift. Coffees of the World wasn't the best job, but it had flexible hours and had led to finding this sublet. There was no shortage of interesting characters to populate his imagination. Like the skinny brunette with the shoulder length bob who worked for Morgan Stanley and always ordered a short nonfat mocha, decaf, no foam, no sugar, no whip. She could be the heroine in one of his screenplays even if he never knew her name.

He kissed Jennifer's hair and told her he'd call after work. Five flights of stairs later, the sounds of the city waking up greeted him as he walked toward the train that would take him to the Trade Center. Standing at the top of the subway steps, he changed his mind. Travis headed for his car parked a couple streets over and called in.

Two hours later, he stopped in McLean for gas about seven thirty, filling up the tank of his Toyota Corolla hatchback. Three hours after that, he could still drive for a while longer before he'd need to stop again. He contemplated leaving the state, but decided not to, instead turning northward before leaving Allegany County.

He'd gone through more emotions than he knew he had, none of them good. Anger. Fear. Frustration. Blame. Worry. Intimidation. In western New York, things were more peaceful than they ever were in downtown Manhattan, but his insides were in utter turmoil at the thought of an arrest and trial.

His favorite heavy metal CD blared from the speakers. During the lull between songs, Travis could hear his cell phone vibrating on the passenger seat where he'd tossed it. After an hour and a half of the stupid thing ringing nearly nonstop, he finally snatched it up.

"What?" Travis growled.

"Are you okay?" Though he only talked to her twice a year, there was no mistaking his mother's voice.

Or the panic in it.

The tremor set him on edge. "Yeah. Why?"

"Thank you, Jesus," she whispered, though Travis couldn't figure out what she was thanking Him for. "Where are you? You got out okay? Were you working? There was no answer at your apartment."

Why was Mom calling just to ask if he was okay? Why was she frantic? "I'm in western New York State. Out for a drive. Get out of where?" Could Mark's dad have called already?

"You don't know?" Frenzy changed to disbelief.

"Know what?" Travis held the phone against his shoulder as he downshifted into a turn.

He could hear the tears over the static-filled line. "Two planes, Trav. They hit the Towers. Both of the buildings are on fire."

His heart thudded to a stop. "What?" Hadn't a bomber hit the Empire State Building in WWII? But two planes? On a brilliantly clear day? No weather in sight. "How bad is it?" he croaked.

"They're saying it's a terror attack. The Pentagon is on fire. There's another plane out there somewhere. Big jets, Travis. I saw the second one hit. The explosion. Papers flying everywhere. The people..." Her voice broke. "You really weren't there?" she confirmed.

"No, Mom. I'm not anywhere near there." But he needed to find a place to stop. A television. He had to see for himself. Tens of thousands of people would be dead and dying. Did he know any of them?

"There are people jumping, falling, out of the upper stories. I can't imagine." He could almost see her pacing around the kitchen alternately running her hands through her hair and wringing them together. "They're jumping from a hundred stories up. What could be so bad to make that the better option?" Her voice caught. "I don't know how I can watch this, Trav, but I can't turn away. All I can do is pray."

Pray. Right. A face flashed before Travis. The uptight former-football-player-turned-businessman from the 102nd floor of the

North Tower with his caramel macchiato and corny joke of the day. Was he one of those jumping?

She gasped then whispered. "Dear God, no. No!" Her scream made him move the phone even as his stomach sank.

He pulled into a café parking lot near Danville. "What?"

"The tower. It's gone. Just gone. The south one, I think." Her voice trailed off in prayer.

The shock he'd felt after the phone call from Mark's dad paled compared to what he felt now. "Mom, I gotta go." Jen. His friends. His coworkers. He needed to make calls of his own. Find out if they were okay. And Mark. His best friend had been a firefighter for a year. He'd be down there. Inside one of the Towers. Travis hadn't talked to him since that night, the March before, but part of him, the part that still believed there was a God in heaven, whispered a prayer that Mark was somewhere safe as faces of customers and friends flashed through Travis's mind.

The blonde. The cute, petite one who ordered a crunchy, cinnamon pastry and half caf, double tall, easy hazelnut, non-fat, no foam with whip extra hot latte on Tuesdays. She flirted shamelessly, though he knew she was recently and happily engaged to some guy in Tower Seven. Her family lived near his in Serenity Landing, Missouri, and she worked at the Marriot World Trade Center in the shadow of the Towers. Could it have survived the collapse? Was Joanna now buried underneath the rubble?

"Be safe, Travis. Do you have somewhere you can go? They're evacuating Manhattan."

"I'll be okay." He hesitated. "I love you, Mom. You, Dad, Jay. I love all of you. I'll call when I can, but I have to try to find out about my friends, about my girlfriend. I'll talk to you soon."

His mom's "I love you," came through the line as he clicked his phone off.

He started his first call as he walked into the café. Call after call failed as he stood with others, watching the screen in horror as the second tower crashed down. His problems. Mark's dad.

Mark's sister. All of it fled as the enormity of what was happening sunk in.

The whole world had changed.

December 18, 2001
"It's a girl."

Abi Connealy collapsed back onto the bed, tears streaming down her cheeks as a newborn squawk filled the delivery room.

A girl.

A million thoughts flew through her mind, few of them happy, as a nurse laid the baby on her chest. So small. So scrunched up and red. Dark hair. Abi couldn't see her eyes as she wrapped her arms around the tiny bundle. "Hi, baby," she whispered. "I'm so glad you're here."

"How are you?"

Abi looked up at Brenda Wardman. Her brother's girlfriend had been a rock the last few months. She didn't need to clarify, because Abi knew what she meant. "I don't know." The voice mail she'd left her parents on the way to the hospital remained unanswered unless Brenda knew something she didn't.

Her fingers brushed over the cheek of the tiny girl. "She's perfect, Bren." Another tear fell, this one landing on her new daughter's face as Abi closed her eyes.

The nurse took the baby to the warmer and did whatever it was nurses did, but Abi didn't see any of it. Her eyes remained closed, and she clasped Brenda's hand as more hot tears streaked into her ears. Just under twenty-four hours of labor meant she didn't have the energy to wipe them away. She knew she didn't have the will to do so even if she could have.

"Do you know what you're going to do?"

Abi wanted to yell at her friend for bringing up the most difficult decision of her life just moments after the birth of her daughter. But since Abi hadn't made up her mind beforehand, Brenda needed to know to help make the arrangements.

Except Abi didn't know.

Not for sure. She knew what the smart decision was, though her head and her heart didn't agree. But she had to put her baby first. "I'll have them call."

"It's going to be fine," Brenda tried to reassure her, but Abi heard the doubt in her friend's voice.

Right.

Fine.

Once the social worker arrived, she'd never be fine again.

Somehow, Abi managed to doze for several hours during the afternoon, but after listening to the message from her parents, the one that told her all she needed to know without really saying anything, her eyes refused to close. Instead, she stared at the bracelet encircling her wrist, rotating it around time and time again.

A knock sounded half a second before the door pushed open. "Hi, there, Abi. Someone's looking for her mama." The nurse compared the baby's bracelet to Abi's before lifting the blanketed bundle out of the clear bassinet. "The card says you're giving her formula?"

There was no judgment in the woman's voice, but Abi felt her own condemnation eating away at her. All she could do was nod.

After a few minutes of helping them get situated, the nurse started to leave, but stopped before walking out the door. "The emotions are normal, honey. They get everyone at one point or another."

Abi nodded but didn't take her eyes off the little cheeks sucking in and out. She memorized the sounds, the smells, the essence of the tiny bundle in her arms. Or tried to. Even as she did, she knew it would never work. In the morning, a social worker would come and Abi would sign the papers put in front of her.

And she'd never see her daughter again.

But when the social worker sat in the chair by the window, asking the questions, one tripped Abi up.

"Do you know who her father is?"

The night was burned in Abi's memory banks. Part of it anyway. When she hesitated too long, the worker prompted her again. Abi nodded. "Yes. I know who the father is."

"Then we'll need his signature, too."

"He doesn't know," she whispered. "I haven't talked to him since. I was going to, but then 9/11..." Her voice trailed off.

"Was he in the Towers?" the social worker asked as gently as she could.

Abi shook her head. "I don't he was. I mean, I know he wasn't one of the three thousand, but I don't know if he was there or not." She'd called his apartment from a pay phone a few weeks later. When he answered, she hung up.

"If you know who he is, we have to have him sign away his parental rights, sweetie."

Something she hadn't considered when she made this plan.

The nurse walked in, once again pushing the bassinet. Her face fell when she saw the social worker. "I'm sorry. I didn't realize you were..."

With a swipe of the overused Kleenex, Abi wiped her face. "I wasn't sure, but now I can't anyway."

The social worker left a couple of fliers and walked out with a sympathetic smile. The nurse awkwardly helped Abi get situated to feed her daughter one more time.

"Do you have a name you like?" The woman sat on the edge of the bed holding Abi's empty water bottle.

"Cassandra."

"That's beautiful."

"It was my grandmother's name. She died this past summer."

The grandmother who would have adored meeting her great-granddaughter, who would have taken Abi and the baby in when she needed somewhere to turn. Had given Abi hope she'd do just that before succumbing to a sudden, massive stroke.

Abi didn't have anyone else like that in her life. Brenda would if she could, but there was no way. Abi had no other family. No one else in her life who would support her no matter what.

Darkness descended, but Abi refused to send little Cassie back to the nursery. She didn't know what she planned to do about adoption, but she wouldn't give up another minute with her baby.

Yet another round of tears leaked down her face as Abi cuddled the tiny bundle against her chest. With all but one light turned out, the desperate whisper ripped from her throat. "God? Are you there?" She'd never prayed before, but this seemed like the time to start if there ever was one. "I don't know what to do."

Baby Cassandra yawned and blinked her eyes open, staring up at her mother. The light caught them just right and struck Abi with the bright blue.

Then it hit her.

The one place she could take her daughter where she'd be safe. And loved.

December 23, 2001

Two days before Christmas, Abi sat in a coffee shop on Long Island and waited. Calling him had taken every ounce of courage she had. Leaving the voicemail took more.

Sitting there, Abi didn't know if she could go through with it. The stroller with her little girl sat to her right. On the other side of it, Brenda sat with her back to the door. Diners nearby sipped on gourmet coffee, but Abi focused on the stationary in front of her. She arrived early so she could write the note, but the paper remained nearly blank.

When she'd arrived at her parents' Long Island home after leaving the hospital, a note reiterated her father's threat. Since then, Abi had planned what to say, but realized she'd never make it through even the shortest speech. She'd planned the words to write, but now the time had come to put pen to paper, and she only managed his name. A glance at her watch told her she didn't have much time. If she didn't write it now, she'd have to make the speech. No way could she do that.

She picked up the Mont Blanc knock-off she'd received for graduation from her grandmother and scribbled a few lines. Her heart squeezed as she reread the note. She couldn't be a student and a mom. But *this*? Abi had her suitcase packed. She wouldn't return to her parents' home but would crash at Brenda's for a few days while her friend went out of town. Brenda knew most of what happened, but not everything. Abi's fingers furrowed through her hair, and she turned to stare out the window. There he stood. His six-foot frame seemed shorter with his shoulders slumped and hands shoved deep in the pockets of his coat. He looked at his watch and trudged across the street.

The bell over the door jangled. Abi crossed through the unfinished sentence, scribbled a last sentiment and her name, and shoved the note in her purse as he sat down across from her.

"Hi." At the sound of his voice, the knots in her gut tightened.

Abi looked up, knowing he'd see the remnants of her tears. She twisted the napkin in her hands and tried not the think about the weight she'd gained. And if he'd notice.

"Thanks for coming. I wanted to try to explain, but..." Abi shrugged. "After 9/11, after Mark..." The thoughts of her brother nearly overwhelmed her already overwrought emotions. "Daddy isn't going to pursue anything. I tried to tell him you weren't guilty, but he didn't believe me at first. He found your name in my journal on 9/11-before it was '9/11.' I'd left it lying out by accident." This time the shrug was a mere halfhearted lift of one shoulder.

"Mark?" he interrupted. "I read the list of firefighters a bunch of times to make sure he wasn't there."

"He wasn't on the lists. He was killed at a fire on 9/11. Not at the Trade Center. Another fire where they didn't have enough manpower because of everything else. They think he died right around the time the first tower fell."

Were those tears in his eyes? He and Mark hadn't spoken in months. "I'm so sorry."

Cassandra let out a cry. The disguised Brenda made a shushing sound, but Abi didn't look. She couldn't. It was too much. She had to get out. "Can you excuse me for a minute?"

She didn't wait for a reply but motioned toward the back, leaving before he had a chance to stop her. Brenda went out the front door. Abi dug the paper out and waved the barista over. "Can you give this to that guy?"

The woman nodded. Abi fled to the other side of the street and collapsed in Brenda's arms.

Travis read the note three times before it began to sink in.
Dear Travis,

She had to have written it earlier. There hadn't been time since she excused herself.

I hate doing this to you, especially like this. I tried to handle it on my own. I thought I could, but this semester was so hard. Even more than just everything on 9/11 and Mark. I can't do it. I can't be a college student and a mom.

It took several minutes for that to really register.

A mom?

He read on, his disbelief growing with each word.

The baby in the stroller is yours. From that night. I hate that I haven't told you sooner, but I didn't know how. I couldn't tell my parents what happened, not all of it. They would blame you, and it wasn't your fault. I know this is the coward's way out, but I can't tell you to your face. Everything you need for a couple of days is in the diaper bag and the duffel on the bottom of the stroller. So is her birth certificate.

Her name is Cassandra. She's only a few days old. Please take good care of her for me. I won't be home for a while so you can't reach me. My parents left for vacation out of the country, so they wouldn't be here when she was born.

I wish things had worked out the way we planned. The way we talked about all those times. I wish

Whatever she wished, she didn't finish the thought before scribbling through it. About like their relationship had been. A wish that was never finished. He went back to the letter.

Tell Cassandra I love her.

I'm sorry.

Abi

He read it two more times, starting to come to grips with what it meant.

And then the baby began to fuss.

Taking a deep, steadying breath to fortify himself, he turned to the blanket tented over the handle of the car seat. Lifting up one corner, he saw pink. Fuzzy bunnies on the toes of a sleeper. A tiny foot kicking those bunnies in the air. He looked further and saw the bluest eyes he'd ever seen staring back at him, almost as though she knew who he was.

Her father.

Her daddy.

The one responsible for her from here on out.

And in that moment, he fell helplessly in love.

December 25, 2001

Christmas night, the little gray Toyota turned off I-44, south towards Serenity Landing, as the wailing in the backseat reached a new level.

"I'm sorry, Cassandra. We're almost there. I'll get you something to eat in a ten minutes, I promise." Jennifer kicked him out the moment he tried to explain his arrival at the apartment with a baby. Instead, he'd boxed up all his worldly belongings along with the things Abi had left for the baby and packed it in his car. They headed for the only place he knew he could get the help he needed until he had a better handle on things.

Over twelve hundred miles. Stopping every two or three hours to feed his daughter or change her diaper. Sometimes more often than that. Always taking much longer than it should. Failing to take into account how many things would be closed on Christmas Day, he ran out of the bottled water when he needed to make one more meal for his daughter. He pressed the pedal a little closer to the floor in an effort to reach Serenity Landing a little faster.

The newborn squalling had quieted a bit when Travis finally pulled to a stop in front of the house where he'd grown up. In the front window, a Christmas tree stood, multi-colored lights twinkling. In the window next to it, he could see Mom and Dad sitting at the dining room table, though he knew they wouldn't be able to see him. His brother walked in with a platter, piled high with a turkey way too big for the three of them. They'd be eating leftovers for a month.

Another squeak came from the back. "Okay, baby. We're here."

Somehow, Travis managed to get the diaper bag and the baby seat out of the car and headed toward the door, snow crunching under his boots with each step. The smell of oak burning in the fireplace both comforted him and heightened his anxiety. What if they turned him away? Then what?

Should he knock?

He hadn't been home in two and a half years. Did he just walk in?

Even with his hands full, Travis managed to press the doorbell. He took a deep breath and blew it out slowly, finishing as the door opened.

Mom stood there, her jaw hanging down for a second before her hands covered her mouth. "Travis!"

He tried to smile but failed miserably. "Hi, Mom." In the space of a heartbeat, he saw what he needed to in her eyes. Forgiveness. Acceptance. Love. Grace. With a prayer tossed heavenward, he tried again to smile, this time successfully. "There's someone I want you to meet."

Available Now!

Travis Harders has been a single dad since the day he learned he had a daughter with his only one-night stand. Fifteen years later, he and Cassie are getting along just fine and he's even fallen in love. The last thing he expects to find on his doorstep one Tuesday morning is Cassie's mom - the one person he thought he'd never see again - and she's asking the impossible.

Circumstances, including her firefighter brother's death on 9/11, forced Abi Connealy into a decision she's spent years regretting and her daughter grew up without her. But now, a family crisis compels her to do the one thing she swore she never would: find the daughter she'd abandoned just a few days after birth.

Shocked when Travis doesn't send her packing, Abi prays to a God she doesn't believe in that her relationship with her daughter will be restored. Travis plans to propose to his girlfriend, but their relationship hits the rocks as he and Abi both struggle with the long-dormant feelings that never had the chance to develop.

When Cassie demonstrates incredible grace toward the grandfather who refuses to acknowledge her existence, Abi begins to learn the love of a Savior - a Savior who has more than enough Grace to Save.

ABOUT THE AUTHOR

When she's not writing about her imaginary friends, USA Today Bestselling Author Carol Moncado prefers binge watching pretty much anything to working out. She believes peanut butter M&Ms are the perfect food and Dr. Pepper should come in an IV. When not hanging out with her hubby, four kids, and two dogs who weigh less than most hard cover books, she's probably reading in her Southwest Missouri home.

Summers find her at the local aquatic center with her four fish, er, kids. Fall finds her doing the band mom thing. Winters find her snuggled into a blanket in front of a fire with the dogs. Spring finds her sneezing and recovering from the rest of the year.

She used to teach American Government at a community college, but her indie career, with over twenty titles released, has allowed her to write full time. She's a founding member and former President of MozArks ACFW, blogger at InspyRomance, and is represented by Tamela Hancock Murray of the Steve Laube Agency.

www.carolmoncado.com
books@candidpublications.com

OTHER BOOKS BY CAROL MONCADO

The CANDID Romance Series

Finding Mr. Write
Finally Mr. Write
Falling for Mr. Write

The Monarchies of Belles Montagnes Series
(Previously titled The Montevaro Monarchy
and The Brides of Belles Montagnes series)

Good Enough for a Princess
Along Came a Prince
More than a Princess
Hand-Me-Down Princess
Winning the Queen's Heart
Protecting the Prince (Novella)
Prince from her Past

Serenity Landing Second Chances

Discovering Home
Glimpsing Hope
Reclaiming Hearts

Crowns & Courtships

Heart of a Prince
The Inadvertent Princess
A Royally Beautiful Mess

Crowns & Courtships Novellas

Dare You
A Kaerasti for Clari

Serenity Landing Tuesdays of Grace
9/11 Tribute Series

Grace to Save

Serenity Landing Lifeguards
Summer Novellas

The Lifeguard, the New Guy, & Frozen Custard
(previously titled: The Lifeguards, the Swim Team, & Frozen Custard)
The Lifeguard, the Abandoned Heiress, & Frozen Custard

Serenity Landing Teachers
Christmas Novellas

Gifts of Love
Manuscripts & Mistletoe
Premieres & Paparazzi

Mallard Lake Township

Ballots, Bargains, & the Bakery (novella)

Timeline/Order for Crowns & Courtships and Novellas
1. *A Kaerasti for Clari*
2. *Dare You*
(the first two can be read in either order, but technically this is the timeline)
3. *Heart of a Prince*
4. *The Inadvertent Princess*
5. *A Royally Beautiful Mess*

Made in the USA
Las Vegas, NV
05 March 2022

45101343R00208